LONG
ROAD HOME

ALSO BY RONALD B. TAYLOR

Nonfiction

Sweatshops in the Sun
Chavez and the Farm Workers
The Kid Business

LONG ROAD HOME

RONALD B. TAYLOR

HENRY HOLT AND COMPANY
NEW YORK

Published by Henry Holt and Company, Inc.,
115 West 18th Street, New York, New York 10011.
Distributed in Canada by Fitzhenry & Whiteside Limited,
195 Allstate Parkway, Markham, Ontario L3R 4T8.

Library of Congress Cataloging-in-Publication Data
Taylor, Ronald B.
Long road home.
I. Title.
PS3570.A9526L65   1989   813′.54   88-13039
ISBN 0-8050-0633-8

Henry Holt books are available at special discounts
for bulk purchases for sales promotions, premiums,
fund-raising, or educational use. Special editions
or book excerpts can also be created to specification.

For details, contact:

Special Sales Director
Henry Holt and Company, Inc.
115 West 18th Street
New York, New York 10011

First Edition

Designer: Katy Riegel
Printed in the United States of America
1 3 5 7 9 10 8 6 4 2

TO DOROTHY,
who gave me the time to write.

The people in flight streamed out on 66, sometimes a single car, sometimes a little caravan. All day they rolled slowly along the road, and at night they stopped near water. In the day ancient leaky radiators sent up columns of steam, loose connecting rods hammered and pounded. . . .

Listen to the motor. . . . Listen to the pounding old jalopy . . . That rattle—that's tappets. Don't hurt a bit. Tappets can rattle till Jesus comes again without no harm. But that thudding . . . Maybe a bearing's startin' to go. . . .

'F we can on'y get to California . . .

Two hundred and fifty thousand people over the road. Fifty thousand old cars—wounded, steaming. Wrecks along the road, abandoned. Well, what happened to them? What happened to the folks in that car?

John Steinbeck,
The Grapes of Wrath

LONG
ROAD HOME

1

The service station was one of those lonely, run-down places along the highway, a sun-blistered garage and cafe with two gas pumps out front under a wooden canopy. Used wheels and tires were hung along the outside walls, for sale. Inside, the garage was dark and oily, the workbench cluttered with tools and car parts; there was a long pit in the center of the concrete floor with steps leading down into it so the mechanic could work underneath a car, if he had one to repair. When there was no business, he sat in the shade under the canopy, leaning his chair back against the wall. To pass the time he whittled and listened to the country music playing on the nickel juke box inside the cafe where his wife was baking pies or stirring leftovers into the soup pot. Sometimes the grumbling sounds of a passing truck caught his attention and he would look up as the vehicle rolled on by, then stare out across the highway and the railroad tracks into the sweltering emptiness of the land. Out here the valley was a level plain so wide he could barely make out the rise of the Coast Range in the distance. Beyond those low brown mountains were cooling coastal fogs and crashing surf; they had vacationed there by the sea once, the mechanic and his wife, and he would think about that for a while, then return to his whittling, the sharp point of his jackknife curling tiny slivers off a block of soft pine.

It wasn't much past ten yet but already the day was hot. The mercury in the big thermometer hanging on a post by the gas pumps was up near a hundred and out on the highway heat waves shimmered over the blacktop. In the distance, a train whistled: the northbound *San Joaquin Daylight*, right on time. As the locomotive thundered past, black smoke belching from its stack, the mechanic waved to the engineer.

The train's red lights disappeared in the summer haze, but the mechanic continued to stare up the empty tracks that paralleled the highway, slicing razor-straight for hundreds of miles through the flat, fertile land. At first he didn't notice the overheated sedan boiling slowly along the highway toward him; it was a battered '32 Ford sedan towing a heavily loaded two-wheel trailer. What attracted his attention, finally, was the steam blowing out of the radiator and swirling around the hood. A second jalopy chugged along right behind the sedan, a spindly '29 Model A pickup with a big load tarped and roped down tight. The first driver spotted the service station and stuck his arm out, signaling to stop.

As the vehicles slowed and turned in, the mechanic counted six people crowded in the sedan and two more in the pickup; from the worn, dusty look of their outfit, they were a hard-traveling bunch, down on their luck. With a snap, the mechanic folded the blade of his jackknife and got up; the vehicles stopped on either side of the gas pumps, the sedan under the canopy, the Model A out in the sun.

Doors flew open and people began piling out, all but the young, freckle-faced kid with the big ears who was driving the sedan. He kept the engine going and yelled, "Susie! Hose 'er down!"

One of the two redheaded girls grabbed the coiled water hose hanging on the corner post by the gas pump and, twisting the faucet on, she squirted water through the grill, cooling the radiator, then, with practiced skill, knocked the radiator cap loose and jumped back as a fountain of steam whooshed out. When the geyser died, she yelled to the driver, "Okay, Jake, keep 'er runnin'," and matter-of-factly began filling the radiator.

The older redheaded girl, taller and thinner than the first, had ahold of a small, moon-faced boy who was about to pee his pants. "Mister, where's the necessary?"

"Out back, yonder." The mechanic motioned with his thumb.

"Much obliged." She started for the outhouse. "Hold on, Benjy! We're 'most there."

Radiator filled, the young driver revved the clattering engine a few more times, then let it idle down. By the sound of it, the mechanic guessed the rods were loose and the water pump likely was shot. They needed more than water, but, by the looks of them, they probably didn't have any money. "Folks need some gas?"

The question was addressed to the man of the outfit, a wiry fellow in his late thirties who was wearing faded overalls and scruffy boots, run over at the heels. He pushed back a big, sweat-stained cowboy hat and looked over at his wife. "Bessie?"

The mechanic watched as the woman unknotted an old sock and counted out some coins. Finally, she nodded. "A dollar's worth."

"Regular?"

"Yes, sir."

She was a small, handsome woman, dressed in old work pants and a sweat-stained cotton shirt. Her hair, soft and yellow as corn silk, was pulled back tight in a bun and she wore no makeup. Her eyes were startling blue, set wide apart under a strong brow, and she had a square, determined jaw, solid as an anvil. Hard times, sandstorms and drought had left their record etched deeply in lines and wrinkles on her face, long days in the sun had tanned her skin; the soft, flat sounds of Oklahoma were in her voice.

"Ma!" The tall, thin driver of the Model A called to the woman, "I need gas too." He was in his twenties and had her dusty-blond good looks.

"Just a minute." The woman counted a dollar out to the mechanic and then slipped between the pumps. Steering her oldest son back behind the Model A, out of earshot, she asked, "Cain't ya make do till we fin' work? We ain' got but thirty-three cents lef'."

"No way, Ma. She's dang near dry now. Maybe that feller'll take somethin' in trade. Got that extry wheel an' tire from when we fixed the sedan after the wreck."

The mechanic was carefully watching the big glass reservoir atop the pump and stopped the gasoline flow into the sedan's tank as the amber level neared the six-gallon mark; gently he squeezed the nozzle once, then again, measuring out exactly a dollar's worth. Although he couldn't hear what the woman was saying to her son, he watched them as he hung the nozzle up and began cranking the long handle on the gas pump back and forth, refilling the glass reservoir. He was taking the measure of these fruit tramps. Not that he disliked them, they were probably good people, and besides he'd picked fruit himself when he and his missus had first landed in the valley. But that was back in '28, before so many had started coming out; now here it was 1937 and there were thousands on the road, thick as locusts and more of them coming out every day. People hereabouts called them Okies, but they weren't just from Oklahoma, hell, they came from all over the South and, for the most part, they were just folks down on their luck. Still, it paid to keep a watch on them because when a man's family is hungry, there's no telling what he might try.

That freckled-faced young buck driving the sedan, the one they called Jake, he wasn't old enough to have a driver's license yet, couldn't be more than thirteen or fourteen and he was so skinny his hand-me-down overalls flapped around him. That kid was a spitting image of his father, same big ears, rusty-brown hair and sharp, bony features, same falcon-yellow eyes and hooked nose. The boy hadn't started shaving yet and he was bareheaded, with an open, friendly look to him. The man, on the other hand, had a thick mustache and wore that big cowboy hat; he wasn't tall, maybe five-eight or -nine, all gristle and bone and he walked with a kind of lurch that favored his left hip. He didn't look old so much as worn down and there was something about him that let you know he was about as friendly as a tangle of rusty barbed wire.

Susie, the girl who had filled the radiator, now she was going to be a real looker; already more woman than child, she had her mother's face and bright blue eyes and her hair was like red-gold when it caught the sunlight. Both of the girls wore faded old work dresses and the older one was plain, thin and flat chested. The little fella, the one the older girl had taken to the outhouse, he was odd, somehow.

At first the mechanic hadn't paid much attention to the third girl, the dark-haired one, because she stayed in the pickup, then he noticed she was nursing a baby. After that he kept glancing back that way and every once in a while he'd catch a glimpse of her tit and that young 'un nuzzling and sucking away. She was pretty, the dark-haired girl, not more than twenty and it was plain that she wasn't no kin, her skin dark as it was, like maybe she had some Indian blood in her. Wasn't hard to guess that she was the older boy's woman.

By the time the mechanic had finished refilling the glass reservoir he'd seen enough to know that he was going to get paid in kind. Long ago he had fixed a price on such transactions; for a usable tire and wheel he pumped ten gallons in the Model A's tank. The woman thanked him, "Much obliged, mister," then they all climbed back into the two vehicles and the family pulled out, the car and trailer in the lead, the Model A chugging right along behind.

2

Their name was Robertson, Ertie and Bessie Robertson, and they were from Nolan County, Texas, west of Abilene. Until that spring they'd been renting a nice little place out on Bitter Creek, forty acres of pasture and hay land. Ertie had made his living around livestock, buying and selling horses and mules. He had a good pulling team of Morgans that he hired out and he was a bucking horse rider, in the rodeos. Those who knew him said he was a hell of a hand with stock and they were quick to add that his wife Bessie's quilts nearly always too a prize at the county fair. They had five children, she and Ertie; there was James Earl, then Mary Ellen, Jake, Susie, and little Benjy, who was slow in the head. Benjy'd come along later, after times had started getting hard, and from the first Bessie had noticed the boy was different. When he was just three, she took him to camp meeting for a praying, hoping for a miracle that didn't happen. Afterward, the preacher told her that, judging from times and all, it was clear that God was angry and distributing sorrows all around, like He did sometimes. The preacher was right about one thing, times were sure enough hard.

The Robertson place was about twelve miles out of Sweetwater, by good road, located right along the creek. It had some rich bottomland and there was plenty of water for irrigating the hay and grain, before that part of the country dried up. Along about 1935 dust storms commenced blowing up out of the high plains, great big ones that blasted the corn and sanded up the fields so bad nothing could grow; then everything went to hell. Lots of folks just packed up and left, took to the road. The Robertsons hung on longer than most, but finally they had to call it quits too. They left out of Nolan County early in the spring of '37, heading for California and a fresh start.

April sixth. That was the day they'd headed west, a Tuesday. Jake remembered it was bright and sunny, not a breath of wind blowing. They'd packed the trailer and James Earl's pickup the night before and started at sunup, locked the doors and drove away. When they stopped at the gate, Jake looked back just once, then they hit out for the highway. They'd come a long ways since then, made it to California without a hitch and started looking for work. Jake drove most of the time, and sitting there, hands on the steering wheel, he thought a lot about that day they'd left Bitter Creek, ran it over in his mind, time and again. It was a sad day, sure enough, but kind of exciting too, and those first weeks hadn't been too bad, they'd camped out along the roads and chopped some cotton in Arizona, tied carrots in Brawley, then came on north into the fruit and got their first look at the San Joaquin Valley. Lord, it was big. Coming down out of the Tehachapi Mountains and seeing it for the first time was breathtaking; the land as level as a table for as far as you could see, and green. They just knew there was work down there getting all those crops in; had to be.

But hard times were following them. Jake was certain of it. They'd driven down into the valley in early May and here it was August and they were less than a dollar away from dead broke, still tramping up and down the state, working where they could find it, but never for long because there were so many folks doing the same thing, seemed like hundreds of them crowding into every orchard, grabbing at the plums and peaches, picking the apple trees clean so fast there wasn't hardly a day's work for nobody. One thing certain, Jake was learning that California was a whole lot bigger than it looked in the geography books. Christ, it took days to drive from one end to the other, and, as things were turning out, this wasn't the land of milk and honey, not by a long shot.

Weary now, Jake brushed a hand through his unruly rusty-brown hair, pushing it back off his bony forehead, then glanced into the rearview mirror, checking to make sure the trailer tarp was still lashed down tight and that James Earl's little pickup was still there following along. Since early that morning they'd been scouting the back roads, searching for signs that the late peach harvest had started. Once, just before they'd stopped for gas, they spotted some tall ladders and stacks of lug boxes set out among the trees. Workers were camped nearby, lots of them, so they stopped and asked a crew boss if he was hiring.

"Sure. Pitch your tents right over yonder by the canal, soon's the peaches come ripe, we'll put you on."

"How long'll that be?"

"Three, maybe four days, hot as it is."

They couldn't wait. It was either find work or go hungry. They thanked the man and drove on until the gas gauges were near empty and steam was hissing out of the sedan's radiator. At the gas station the mechanic told them he'd heard just that morning that they were picking at the El Adobe Ranch, down in Jefferson County.

"How far's that, mister?"

"Maybe an hour's drive, no more'n that."

So they headed south. By noon the temperature was over a hundred and inside the car it felt like hell's own oven, even with the windows open. Sweaty and limp-tired, Jake drove steadily, peering through the bug-spattered windshield at the silvery mirages in the distance, one after another, each one distorting the tall power poles, turning them into wiggly, disconnected lines; blurry images of oncoming cars and trucks rose up out of the quicksilver lakes, suddenly breaking free and whizzing by.

Bessie was dozing in the backseat, a wisp of yellow hair fallen across her forehead. Now and then Jake caught a glimpse of her in the mirror and thought how pretty she looked when her face relaxed and the worries were gone. He remembered how hopeful she'd been when they'd started off for California. She had been so certain they'd quickly find work and a place to settle down. That hadn't happened, but she never gave up hope and whenever Pa'd get mad about something that happened to them out here on the road, she'd just get that look in her eyes and say something like "Settle down now, folks's born to trouble, tha's what it says in the Book. We ain' so special we gonna miss out on it."

Jake shifted his weight in the seat, leaning forward to let the hot wind blowing through the windows cool his sweaty back. Absorbed in thought, he paid little attention to the panorama whizzing by, barns and farmhouses tucked deep in under clumps of shade trees, sun-baked fields and vine rows neatly patterned, divided into rectangles and squares, forties, eighties and hundred sixties, each acreage watered by irrigation canals. Here and there big electric pumps lifted white gushing water from deep out of the earth, spilling wet coolness into the ditches. Every five or ten miles along the highway there were small towns, one looking much like the other: tree-lined streets, a tall water tower, brick store buildings downtown, with law offices signed in gold in the second-story windows, a bank on the corner with cement pillars made to look like marble, then, on the outskirts, the motor-car garages, warehouses and service stations and out on the highway beyond, the stands that looked like giant oranges, with pretty girls inside squeezing fresh juice. The sight made him thirsty, but they never stopped, just kept going on down the long, long highway.

Up ahead, Jake spotted a row of signs, burnt-orange in color, five of them set one after another like a row of crosses and, as he passed the first, he started reading them aloud:

WITHIN THIS VALE

OF TOIL AND SIN

YOUR HEAD GROWS BALD

BUT NOT YOUR CHIN

Susie and Mary Ellen chimed in on the last sign, yelling:

BURMA SHAVE!

Ertie had been dozing up front, beside Jake. He pushed back his hat and glanced over at his son just as Jake rubbed a hand over his chin. Ertie chuckled. "Need my razor?"

"Naw," Jake grinned self-consciously.

Ertie pulled out a near-empty sack of Bull Durham and started rolling a smoke. "I'll strop it up nice an' sharp for ya."

In the backseat Susie wiggled crankily. "Dammit, Mary Ellen! Move over!"

"You girls stop fightin'," Bessie ordered.

"But Ma, she's pushin' an' crowdin'!"

"Girl, don' you back-talk me, an' I don' want to hear ya swearin', neither. You still ain' too big to whup."

"Hung-ree," Benjy whimpered. He'd been resting his head in Mary Ellen's lap and now he struggled to sit up.

"Hand me the water jug." Bessie leaned forward, reaching as Ertie handed the burlap-covered gallon bottle back to her. She took the cap off and tilted the jug up to Benjy's mouth, helping him take a few warm swallows.

Jake fought to stay alert. Driving was one of his chores, that and helping James Earl keep the vehicles in good repair. In the case of the sedan, that was proving to be a real challenge, even for a pair of handy shade-tree mechanics. On the way out to California the speedometer had turned a hundred thousand miles; the car was hard to start in the mornings and here lately, it had started shuddering at unexpected times, one minute they'd be rolling along down the highway as nice as you please, the next minute the front wheels started to wobble, sending violent jerks up the steering column. All Jake could do was hang on and slow down. Once the speed dropped below forty-five miles an hour the shimmy faded away, but by then the sudden vibration had startled everyone.

His mother would ask anxiously, "Ever'thang okay?"

And he would answer, "Yeah, Ma. But we gotta get 'er fixed 'fore a dang wheel flies off. King pins is shot."

"Just slow down, we ain' in that big a hurry. Just slow down an' we'll make do."

That exasperated Jake. Bessie didn't drive, nor did she understand a thing about cars, so that was always her answer. Make do. And Ertie was no help, since he'd never bothered to learn anything about cars and wasn't much of a driver either. Oh, he could get all four wheels pointed in the same direction, but riding with Ertie Robertson could sometimes be downright terrifying. From a dead stop he would rev the engine then suddenly pop the clutch and the car would lurch forward in big jumps, heading off toward one side of the road or the other, with Ertie fighting the steering wheel and grinding through the gears, swearing and hollering like he would with a team of runaway mules. Once lined out, he herded the car along pretty well, but if something off the road caught his attention, he might turn to look at whatever it was and let the car go its own way.

Once, a telephone pole hit the car. Well, that was the way Ertie told it, anyway. Jake had been asleep at the time and all he knew was that the car slammed to a stop and the pole was mashed up against the fender and radiator. No one was hurt, but they'd banged up the front end pretty bad. When the dust settled, Ertie climbed out and looked at the telephone pole, and gave the pole a kick. "Durn thang's set too close to the road." He grinned, sheepishly, and slapped the rumpled fender. "Hell, that ain't so bad, we can pry it back and you fellas can straighten up that wheel in no time, cain'cha?"

They'd done the best they could, but the wheels still didn't run true. Jake was finding out that the sedan was a sight harder to work on than the Model A. Now there was a good kind of car, the Model A, damn thing never quit. James Earl had bought it wrecked and rebuilt it just before he and Billie Jo had decided to get married. Well, to tell the truth, there hadn't been much choice about a wedding, since she was already four months along. Anyway, he'd bought it while he had that job at the gypsum plant in Sweetwater and things weren't looking so bad. That was before he got laid off, of course. Then, just before they headed for California, James Earl had built a frame over the pickup bed, out of two-by-fours, with a ridgepole and everything. When they stopped for the night, it took only a jiffy to rig a tent over the pickup bed so that James Earl and Billie Jo and the baby had a room to themselves.

Billie Jo was a pretty girl, with long black hair and eyes like a cat, but what Jake liked the most were her tits, he peeked at them whenever he got a chance. When she was nursing Li'l Beth he could get plenty of good looks and he reckoned she had the best-looking tits in the world, better than Susie's and poor Mary Ellen, hers looked like fried eggs, sunny-side up. She'd never get a man.

They were in southern Fresno County now. Bessie leaned forward. "Jake, where was it that feller back there said we's to turn off?"

"First country road after we cross the Kings River. Don't worry, Ma, I'm watchin'."

They crossed the river and turned west, like the mechanic had said. From there it was twenty miles to El Adobe, maybe a bit more. A half hour later Jake could see orchards and, far to the south, meandering lines of oaks and cottonwoods that marked the course of the Palo Rojo River. The big ranch was supposed to be four miles this side of the Palo Rojo, on Road 17. In a few minutes he could make out a sprawling fortress of white buildings shaded by spreading sycamores and eucalyptus trees and tall rows of royal palms. "There's El Adobe, up ahead." On the west side of the road were vast green fields of cotton, alfalfa and vineyards, and across the road, to the east, were hundreds of acres planted to trees, peaches, plums, nectarines. As he drove closer to the ranch, he could see heavily laden orchards with stacks of lug boxes filled with golden fruit and people on tall ladders picking high in the trees, lots of them.

"Ma!" Susie was hanging out the window. "There must be a thousand people here! Look at 'em!"

Jake slowed and pulled across the road, stopping near a wall of lug boxes stacked five feet high, full of peaches. Workers were bringing lugs out of the orchard, carrying the forty-pound boxes to a checker near the stack. The checker, clipboard in hand, looked the fruit over, checked it off and tallied the count. Sticking his head out the window, Jake yelled over, "You fellers hirin'?"

The checker nodded and pointed toward the ranch headquarters. "Go on up to the office, they'll put you on a crew."

"Thanks." Jake shifted into first gear and drove on. Up ahead they could see the store and office buildings and across the way there was a bright orange windsock and a landing strip. "Hey, look, they got their own airport!"

The runway paralleled the road and, down at the far end, a gleaming silver monoplane taxied out, ready for takeoff, the spin of its prop gleaming in the midday sun. The pilot in the enclosed cabin wore sunglasses and had a cigar clamped tight in his jaws. They could hear the plane's powerful engine as it revved up; the ship spun half around, kicking up clouds of dust as the pilot lined up with the runway and gunned to full throttle. Jake watched as the nose lifted and the plane was airborne, wheels retracting into the wings.

"Hey, watch out!" Ertie yelled.

The car had drifted off the road. Startled, Jake pulled the sedan back onto the blacktop, mumbling, "Sorry."

Just past the airport, he pulled up in front of the El Adobe Store and Post Office. James Earl parked beside him and they all piled out, stretching and looking around. Tall sycamores and elms shaded the store building, a long, low structure with a covered front porch down its full length. Out in front, two gasoline pumps stood erect on a concrete island, sunlight sparkling through the amber fuel in the cylindrical glass reservoirs.

The store and post office were on the left, the offices over on the right, across a wide dirt lane that appeared to be the main access to the farm. Truckloads of peaches rumbled in off the county road, drivers downshifting through the gears as they headed into the lane and headed back to the packing shed, on the left, behind the store. The shed was enormous, an open-sided building at least two hundred yards long with truck-high loading docks all along the side. As the trucks backed up to the dock, gangs of sweating workers unloaded the boxes onto hand trucks and trundled the fruit into the sorting lines where hundreds of women hand-sorted, graded and packed the fruit in fancy boxes with brightly colored labels. El Adobe even had its own railroad spur and a big ice-house. The whole place was full of sound, horns honking, men shouting, machinery snarling and clanking. The dusty air reeked of pungent, rotting fruit.

Across from the packing sheds were the barnlike shops, dark inside, except for the occasional blinding flash of an arc welder. Behind the shops were the equipment yards, and out back, beyond the shops and packing shed, past the icehouse, there was a huge labor camp, a collection of shanty cabins that looked like nothing more than wooden boxes set back-to-back along rutted, trash-littered streets. Behind the cabins were tents, lots of them, and beyond the tents a canal bank and the orchards.

"Pa." Jake turned to his father. "Wan' me to go see if they're hirin'?"

"I better go with ya." Ertie limped along beside his son.

Up on the office building veranda a screen door banged and a big man in a white shirt and neatly pressed slacks stood there in the shade, arms folded. "Howdy. Hunting for work?"

"Yes, sir." Jake smiled up at the man.

"You folks ever pick peaches before?"

"Yep." Ertie didn't smile.

"Can you climb a ladder with that gimpy leg?"

"It ain' no bother." Ertie tugged his hat down a little and stood there, tense.

"What happened, fall out of a tree?"

When Ertie didn't answer right off, Jake glanced at his father and could see the tiniest movement of his jaw muscles, the first sign of anger, and he started to say something to the man. "Pa, he . . ."

Ertie put his hand on his son's arm, silencing him. "Horse fell on me few years back. Cain't run no foot races, but I get around right smart."

"Well, fine. What's your name?"

"Robertson."

"Tell ya what, Robertson, I'm going to put you all on Jethro Hammer's crew. Big fella, can't miss him. We're picking fresh, paying a nickel a box. Housing's free, but the cabins are full. I'll call down to the camp boss and tell him to sign you up and show you where to pitch your tent. You can start first thing in the morning."

Bessie had come up as they were talking. "Mister, can we go to work now?"

The man looked at his wristwatch. "Past noon. By the time you signed for your buckets and got out there you wouldn't hardly have time to work out the deposit."

"Deposit?" Bessie was standing beside Ertie now.

"On the picking buckets."

"Mister, we got our own buckets." Ertie's voice was edgy.

"We issue picking buckets and there's a twenty-five-cent deposit on each one. This is a big operation and we do things one way. Without a deposit, folks forget who owns the buckets. We'll deduct the deposit from your pay and you get this deposit back when you finish up. Now you go on back and get your camp set up. You'll get in a good day tomorrow."

"If'n it's all the same, we'll work some this afternoon," Bessie persisted.

"Suit yourself," the man shrugged. "I'll tell the camp boss to send you on out."

The camp, all but deserted now, was a miserable-looking place. Too many people had been crowded into it, there were tents pitched in the narrow spaces between cabins, shanty lean-tos had been tacked up against cabin walls to make more room and there was debris everywhere. Road-weary cars and trucks were parked helter-skelter about the camp, here and there they saw decrepit old outhouses, but nowhere was there any sign of a water supply, no pipes, no faucets or storage tanks.

"Looks like we gotta use canal water." Bessie looked disdainfully about the camp, wrinkling her nose at the disorder and rotting odors.

Jake stopped the car. Up ahead there was a bridge over the canal and beyond were the orchards. He got out and went back to talk with James Earl. "See any sign of a camp boss?"

"There was an office sign, back at the shed." James Earl nodded back the way they'd come. "I'll go ask."

He was back in a short time, carrying a stack of picking buckets. "We're all signed up, said for us to find an empty spot back over yonder and park, pitch camp there when we come in this evenin', said they was workin' just over that bridge and down about a half mile."

By late afternoon Ertie was working on his nineteenth box, standing high atop his ladder, picking steadily. From his perch he could see Jake in the next tree and catch a glimpse now and then of James Earl, back in the tree beyond; Bessie and the girls were across the next row and Benjy was curled up in the dirt, playing with a wooden block under a tree near where Li'l Beth was cradled in a picking box. They were both out of the blazing sun that burned down on the orchard, but even in the shade the heat was stifling, the air close and sweaty, full of the smells of plowed earth and rotting fruit. The infant fussed crankily, then cried out. Billie Jo came down out of the tree and picked the child up, checking her diapers. The orchard was filled with noise; workers calling to one another, trucks growling slowly along dirt lanes, brakes squealing as muscled young men tossed off empty lugs and loaded full boxes for the packing house. Somewhere not far away, another picker whistled a jaunty little tune and Ertie mentally hummed along:

> Seven-cent cotton and forty-cent meat,
> How in the world can a poor man eat?
> Flour up high and cotton down low,
> How in the world can we raise the dough?

Clothes worn out, shoes run down,
Old slouch hat with a hole in the crown;
Back nearly broke and fingers all sore,
Cotton gone down to rise no more . . .

Suddenly the air was filled with the roar of a low-flying airplane. The silver monoplane flashed over the treetops, its gear down, reaching for the landing.

"Pa!" Jake twisted around on his ladder, watching the plane disappear. "Ain' she a purty sight?"

Ertie grinned and waved, yelling, "Damn fool! Near took me off the ladder!"

Jake laughed.

Shifting his weight to ease the pain in his left hip, Ertie resumed picking, the words of the song still running through his mind:

Mules in the barn, no crops laid by,
Corn crib empty and the cow's gone dry.

A sharp branch snagged and ripped through the sleeve of his shirt, scratching the soft underside of his forearm.

"Goddammit!" He pulled back, watching the droplets of blood bead up under the torn cloth. The wound was slight, nothing more than a stinging scratch, but it made him angry. His gnarled fingers fumbled instinctively in the bib pocket of his faded overalls for his tobacco, pulling out a limp Bull Durham sack. He gave the near-empty pouch a disappointing shake. Hungry and tired, he wanted a smoke, but decided to wait until quitting time. Putting the tobacco away, he pulled out his pocketwatch, a handsome silver timepiece like the railroad men carried, but fancier, decorated with scrolls and intricate patterns fashioned like vines and grapes. There was an inscription on the cover:

ERTIE ROBERTSON
CHAMPION BRONC RIDER
SALINA, KANSAS 1934

He pushed the stem and the cover popped open: twelve to four. Inset in the watch cover was a tiny enamel miniature of him making a winning ride on a bucking horse. Ertie stared at the picture, remembering that bronc they called the Strawberry Roan, mean son of a bitch in the chutes and when the gate opened that old stud reared out and bucked high, duckin' back every jump, felt like he was going right out from under you. Hell of a horse. And the artist had captured an amazing amount of detail, Ertie's big, black hat, the yellow chaps with red diamonds on the batwings, he could even make out the buck rein. Seventy dollars. Ertie pulled a peach off and took a bite, wiping the drips off his chin with a sleeve. That's what he'd won, seventy dollars and it sure beat shoveling dirt for two dollars a day on the WPA, or picking fruit. He threw the half-eaten peach away, climbed down the ladder and emptied his bucket.

Sitting on the bottom rung of the ladder, he took out his little tally book and began calculating the day's take: there were twenty boxes to the dollar, so he'd made ninety-five cents, less the quarter deposit. For a whole afternoon's work. Shit. A trickle of sweat rolled down his bony forehead and into the corner of his eye, stinging. He brushed at it with his upper arm, ducking his head down to the sleeve, then went back up the ladder, determined to fill another lug. Only after he'd done so did he quit. Standing between the rows he yelled up at Bessie, "Hey, woman!"

Partially hidden in the foliage, she pushed a limb aside and squinted down. "Yeah?"

"Ya close t' finished on that box?"

"Couple more buckets. The girls has got another'n near full."

"I'm goin' up 'n cash out. Y'all finish up an' come on in." Just as he bent to pick up the lug he heard a scream.

"Paa!" Susie was running toward him, but looking back in fear. "Paaa!"

Jake was after her, an angry scowl across his freckled face. He hurled a peach and missed, grabbed up another and splattered it between her shoulder blades.

"Oww! Goddammit, that hurt!"

"Stop it!" Bessie came quickly down out of the tree.

Susie was behind her father now, dodging around him as Jake circled, his fists doubled.

Ertie put his hand out. "Whoa up, thar!"

"But Pa, she stuck an' ol' rotten peach down my back. It stinks like cold shit." Jake's shirttail was out and one strap of his baggy overalls had fallen off his shoulder.

Bessie stormed over. "Quit it, you two! You'll get us fired." She aimed a swat at Jake's rump, but he jumped out of the way and retreated. "You're both gonna get them foul mouths of yorn washed out with lye soap when we get back to camp."

Susie clung to her father.

"Ah, woman, leave 'em be. They was only havin' some fun." Ertie gave Susie an affectionate shove. "Go an' help your ma fill up them last boxes." He bent down and lifted the heavy lug, caught his balance and headed for the check stand down at the end of the row.

The checker, a dark-skinned fellow they called Dago, was dressed in a khaki work shirt and pants and had a ponderous belly that sagged over his belt. Wearily, Ertie set the box down and leaned against the wall of stacked lugs. He wiped the sweat and dirt from his face with a red bandanna, then rolled his last cigarette, flicked a cracked thumbnail over a match head and, cupping his hands around the flare, lit up, careful not to singe his mustache.

Throughout the orchard, other workers were finishing up, carrying the last lugs to the checkers. Drawing in a lungful of smoke, Ertie watched as a pickup came speeding down the lane and skidded to a stop near the check stand. The driver got out, slammed the door and stood there, fists jammed into his hips, looking around in an impatient way that made it obvious he owned the place. The farmer was a short, square-set man, built low to the ground like a bulldog. He wore rough work clothes, tan pants stuffed into the tops of scruffy boots, a matching tan shirt, pockets crammed with notebooks, pencils and extra cigars. A snap-brim felt hat was pushed back on his balding head, revealing the mashed-in face of a club fighter; he puffed on the stub of a cigar that was clamped between his teeth. Sunlight glinted off wire-rimmed aviator's glasses, smoked dark to shield his eyes.

The big crew boss, Jethro Hammer, came striding out of the trees, nodding, friendly-like. "Hi thar, Mr. Wardlow." Hammer was a huge man, standing well over six feet, and he had a round, friendly face turned red by the sun. The sounds of East Texas were in his voice and, dressed like he was in overalls and a floppy hat, it wasn't hard to guess that he'd probably come out to California just like they all had. The crews liked him, said he was a fair man.

Titus Wardlow grunted something in return, then nodded his head, signaling for the crew boss to step around back of the pickup for a talk; the sounds of the harvest covered whatever it was they were saying. Just then James Earl and Jake walked out of the trees, carrying two more lugs. They set them down with a thud and Ertie asked, "Where's yor ma, 'n the girls?"

"Comin' 'long." Jake flopped down in the shade of the boxes, exhausted. Barefoot, he liked to wiggle his toes in the soft hot earth.

Ertie took a last drag on his cigarette and crushed out the coal with his thumb and fingers, pulled out his tally book and pencil stub and marked down the three lugs. "How many more they got?"

"Couple." James Earl brushed a wisp of blond hair from his eyes. "Come on, let's go back an' help Ma." He nudged Jake's foot.

"Ah, shit." Jake struggled to his feet and followed his older brother.

Ertie licked the tip of his pencil and labored over the figures. Finally satisfied with the tally, he called to the checker, "Hey Dago, mark us down for five more, an' cash us out."

Two other workers came up, calling, "Seventy-two. Two lugs an' we're callin' it a day."

Dago looked over the fruit and nodded. "Two more for seventy-two." He penciled an entry on his tally sheet, made out a pay slip and handed it to them, then turned back to Ertie. "You fellas checkin' out?"

"Yep."

"Wha'cher ID number?"

"Hundred twenny-six. Got five more."

"You an' the boys only brought in three."

"Rest of them comin' right along." Ertie nodded toward the trees.

James Earl and Jake were carrying two more lugs, walking beside their mother who had the empty buckets. Mary Ellen and Susie were behind them, one on either side of Benjy, playfully lifting and swinging the boy between them as they walked along. Through the orchard shadows a shaft of sunlight flashed on Susie's red-gold hair, highlighting it. Billie Jo, carrying Li'l Beth in her arms, walked along behind the girls, her long black hair hiding her sweet, sulky face and pale blue eyes.

Dago penciled numbers on the tally sheet. "That's five dollars and twenty cents, less the dollar seventy-five for the buckets. Total's three forty-five."

Startled, Ertie protested. "Hey, wait, we got a hundred twelve boxes. Way I figger it that comes to five sixty, less the deduct for the buckets. You owe us three eighty-five, mister."

"Nope, ya got a hundred four picked." He jabbed a pencil on the tally sheet and his voice was belligerent. Just then an old woman struggled up with a box. "Hold on a min' while I check 'er off."

Ertie was quickly angry. "Listen, mister, you better count again. We got three eighty-five a-comin'."

Bessie, sensing the confrontation as she walked up, tried to intervene. "Ertie . . ."

Dago tallied the woman's lug, then turned back to Ertie, not trying to hide his hostility. "The count's a hundred four."

Ertie held out his little tally book, shaking it. "Look here . . ."

James Earl and Jake had stacked the lugs and were near their father, tense. Over beyond the stacks of boxes Jake saw Jethro Hammer and another fellow standing by a ranch pickup, and the other guy looked like the pilot of the plane. Hammer and the pilot stopped talking and were looking this way, at Ertie and Dago.

Bessie grabbed Ertie's arm and tried to pull him aside, hissing, "Let it be!"

Ertie jerked his arm loose, but she persisted, speaking softly but emphatically. "Ertie Robertson, listen to me a minute!" She tugged him over under a tree and the rest of the family followed. "We gotta work, and I say—"

"Woman, he's cheatin' us."

"Ertie, the crew boss's right over there, an' that fella with him looks like the farmer." She glanced nervously around.

"Jeesus Christ, Ma," Jake interrupted, trying to get in between his parents. "We was cheated . . ."

"Boy, hush your mouth. We got us a job of work, so jus' hush up." Then turning to her husband, her voice softening, she pleaded, "Ertie, please! It's only forty cents."

Ertie stood there, not moving, uncertain. Finally, he shrugged in disgust, and limped back to the checker. "Okay, gimme the slip."

"One hundred four boxes." Dago filled in the blanks on the pay chit, tore it off the book and handed it to Ertie.

Jake couldn't believe it. His father had backed down.

"Come on," Bessie sighed, holding out her arms and shooing her family ahead of her, heading them back to camp. "We're goin' to have meat tonight."

But Jake hung back, still eyeing Dago angrily as Wardlow came up to the checker. "What the hell was that all about?"

Jake stepped back close to a tree, staying out of sight, but he was close enough to hear Dago answer. "Goddamn Okie tried to run up his count."

"Fire him." Wardlow took the cigar out of his mouth and spit.

Jethro Hammer interceded, "Titus, they're good pickers. Come in 'bout noon, but they made over two tons between 'em. Might jus' been a mistake."

Dago scowled at Hammer's intrusion, but said nothing.

Wardlow looked at the clipboard, then handed it back. "Okay, but keep an eye on 'im. I don't want no goddamn troublemakers around here."

As Wardlow got into the pickup and drove off, Hammer grabbed the checker's shirt front in a great wad and slammed him up against the boxes. "Listen you dago prick, I ever catch you cheatin' workers again, I'll break you in two. Hear me?"

"I didn't cheat them, they—"

"I ain' caught you yet, but that fella did and you're lucky he didn't cut you up or bust your head open. I woulda."

Jake wanted to cheer and, at the same time, he felt disgusted because his father hadn't lit into that dago bastard. Feeling let down, Jake jammed his hands deep in his overalls pockets and followed his parents back toward camp. Up ahead, Susie was waiting for him. "Le's go swimmin' in the canal."

"Naw, I don' wanna." Jake pulled away as she reached for his hand.

Surprised, Susie asked, "What's matter?"

Jake shook his head, not saying anything.

"Come on." Susie tugged at him. "Swimmin'll feel good, git the itchy fuzz off."

Damn, that sounded good. Jake perked up, his anger fading. "Race ya to camp."

It was nearly a half mile to the canal. Breathless by the time they reached the bridge and pounded across, they ran to the trailer, dug out their cutoff jeans and changed in the car. When the rest of the family finally came up to the bridge, Susie was standing up on the railing, dripping wet in her cutoffs and an old undershirt that clung to her rounding young breasts. Two teenage boys were at the rail, gawking up at her nipples.

Indifferent to their stares, she yelled, "Ma! Pa! Watch!" and jumped, screaming and laughing as she splashed into the water near where Jake was dog-paddling toward the bank. The boys jumped in after her.

"Jake! Susie!" Bessie called. "You two git out of there now, we got to get camp set up."

With practiced efficiency the whole family pitched camp; the men put up the two wall tents facing each other, leaving enough space in between to rig the canvas rain fly over what they called the "kitchen." Once the tents were up and the fly rigged, James Earl moved the Model A in close to the tents, parking it so that the vehicle formed the third wall of the kitchen area. The girls started carrying in the mattresses, bedding, boxes of clothing and utensils. Billie Jo unloaded the pickup and James Earl rigged their tent over the truckbed. She made up their bed in the back and Li'l Beth's bed on the front seat.

Once the chores were well started, Bessie went down the street to inspect the outhouse and it wasn't long before she came storming back up the street, a determined look on her face.

"Ma, where'd ya want the filter set up?" Jake asked as she came into the kitchen. The filter was a relatively simple contraption, a twenty-gallon oil drum cut in half, the halves stacked like big cups, one on top of the other; holes had been punched in the top half and charcoal was added to filter the water as it trickled through into the bottom half. James Earl had welded a spigot on the bottom half, and they bragged that theirs was the only camp with its own tap water.

But Bessie wasn't thinking about the filter right now. "Never mind that, James Earl can set it up." She found the broom and was looking for scrub brushes. "You get a couple of buckets of water and come with me, we gotta clean up that crapper."

"Ma," Jake protested. "That ain' our job!"

"Don' argue, young man, get some water." Bessie had the brushes and lye soap.

"Why do we gotta do it?"

"Boy, you git a move on, we ain' gonna use that crapper, filthy as it is."

Jake shook his head in disgust, but did as he was told. It was the same everywhere they went, the outhouses were never clean enough; two-holers and four-holers, they broomed them out, sloshed sudsy water over the seats and scrubbed them down, hard, with lye soap. This one was a combination his-and-hers, two holes, set back-to-back with a one-inch plank wall between them. As they worked, the crews were coming in from the orchards and some of the workers stopped and stared. Bessie just ignored the looks, but Jake felt humiliated.

"Hey, lady!" one man shouted. "Ain' the outhouse good 'nuff for ya?"

Jake grabbed up a bucket of dirty water but before he could throw it, Bessie intervened sharply: "Put that down!" Seething, Jake obeyed and went back to scrubbing.

By the time they got back, camp was almost all set up, the two big sawhorses were in place under the kitchen fly and Ertie and Mary Ellen were laying the planks across them, forming the dining table. While Mary Ellen spread the oilcloth table cover, Ertie glanced around, then pulled up an empty nail keg that served as a stool and sat down with a sigh, reaching for a smoke. But he was out of tobacco. "Any coffee left?"

Bessie shook her head. "Used up the last this mornin'."

Benjy fussed hungrily, tugging at Mary Ellen's skirt until she picked him up. "Ma, we gotta get something for supper."

Bessie looked over at Ertie. "Why don' we let the girls run to the store an' cash out? They can get the groceries."

Ertie nodded and pulled out their pay slip, handing it to Mary Ellen. "Bring me back some tobacco."

"You girls get us two pounds of hamburg, some flour, lard and coffee, small as they got." Bessie rummaged through the boxes that doubled as cupboards. "Need a can of milk too. An' Mary Ellen, make sure ya don' buy more'n we need for night an' the mornin', prices bound to be high at that company store. Get a little bit of sugar too, while yor at it." She straightened up, putting her hands on her tired back, stretching. "After we get a full day's work, we'll go in town for groceries. Woman in the next row said wasn't but maybe twenty miles into Jeff City. Got a big

Safeway store there. You girls go on now, take Benjy too."

James Earl had the filter set up and was filling the upper tank, carrying water from the canal, two buckets at a time. Billie Jo was in the pickup nursing Li'l Beth. Bessie sent Jake out to scout up some firewood while she puttered around the kitchen, setting things right, lighting the little two-burner kerosene camp stove, putting water on. Wasn't much else to do until the girls got back.

Jake came running into camp. "Ma, cain' find no wood nowheres. Feller down the street said most folks that needs wood for cookin' has to go clean to the river, said there's lots of dead and downed stuff, but it's near three miles away."

Bessie shook her head in resignation. "Okay, we'll get by usin' the stove." Wearily, she sat down across the table from Ertie, who had his little tally book out, thumbing the pages. She reached a hand out to his and smiled a brave smile. "It coulda been a mistake."

"Wasn' no mistake." Still angry, he wanted a smoke and a drink.

"Ertie, honey, forget it, ain' worth the fuss." When Ertie didn't say anything, she went on. "Honey, thar's lots a work here, when the peaches is picked, there'll be the grapes an' then the cotton. Feel the Lord's lookin' down on us this time. Gotta chance ta make us some money, get a little bit ahead, maybe."

Across the way three men were hunkered down beside an old Dodge truck, talking and passing a whiskey bottle back and forth. Ertie'd seen them come in from work as he was putting up the fly and roping it down tight. Two of the fellows were young, maybe in their late teens or early twenties. The third was older, a stout little man with a round face, wrinkled as a prune. He was bald, except for a white fringe of frizzy hair that stood out like he'd stuck his finger in an electric socket and got a shock. That and his glasses gave him kind of a comical look, the lenses being near as thick as the end of soda-pop bottles. There didn't look to be a woman about the camp, cluttered up as it was. The prune-faced man, as though sensing Ertie's stare, glanced across the street and waved, friendly-like, shouting, "Hydee, neighbor! Come on over an' have a sip."

Grinning, Ertie got up and limped across the street. "Don' mind if I do."

"Name's Jackson, Will Henry Jackson." The man got up, a smile adding more wrinkles to his face as he shook Ertie's hand. "And these're my boys, Harlan an' Buford."

The boys were short like their father, and sturdy. Their hair was black and they were both darkly tanned.

"Here." Will Henry offered Ertie a drink.

"Obliged." Ertie took a gulp and shuddered. "Tha's good likker." He took another swallow and held the bottle out to Harlan. "Weather hot 'nuff fer y'all lately?"

"An' then some. 'Spect we coulda fried an egg on Pa's bald head, thar." Buford chuckled.

"It sure brought the peaches on fast." Will Henry's prune face wrinkled tight in a sour little frown. "Lots of fruit comin' ripe, but they got the picking price down so low the three of us didn't make but six dollars, and we went at 'er at first light."

"Like that ever'where." Ertie nodded, welcoming the whiskey's fiery glow.

"You all been in the peaches before?"

"Yep. Tried most everything along the way."

Will Henry took a big swallow of whiskey and handed the bottle to Ertie. "Where y'all from?"

"Sweetwater, Texas."

"We're from Oklahoma, Washita County. Had an eighty on shares out west of Cordell a ways, growin' cotton 'n some corn."

"My Bessie's from Binger." Ertie took a sip and passed it on.

Will Henry was happily surprised. "Lordy, Lord, ain' this a small ol' world. What's her family name?"

"Larson, her ol' man's a blacksmith there in Binger."

"Can' say as I know 'im, but I reckon we know the town well 'nuff, don' we boys? My, my, don' the Lord work in strange ways, you campin' right 'cross from us, 'n all."

"When'd y'all come out to Californee?" Harlan asked.

"This past spring."

"We been out here since 'thirty-five. We're union men." Harlan said it with pride. "You fellas in the union?"

"No." Ertie frowned and shook his head. "Why?"

"Jus' wonderin'."

Ertie held the bottle up to see how much was left and, sad to see so little remained, he took a small swallow and handed it back.

Buford asked, "Y'all farmin' in Sweetwater?"

Ertie picked up a sliver of a stick and scratched circles in the dirt. "Grew some feed, but mostly I was breaking horses and mules, doin' a little teamin'."

Will Henry finished off the bottle and chucked it toward a rubbish heap back of the car. It fell short, spinning in the dust. "We had a good team of mules back home," he said. "Big and strong. Clydesdale blood in 'em, I reckon. Biggest mules ya ever saw, and smart as a whip, the both of them. Crackerjacks when it come to plowin'."

Now they were on a subject Ertie liked to talk about. "Mules're smarter'n horses, lots of ways, but they can be ornery as hell. Always favored horses, myself, I had this pair of Morgans, sunlight sorrels they was, with white blazes and stockings, pretty team and hell for stout, could outpull anything in the county."

"What happened to 'em?"

"Had to sell 'em." Ertie jabbed the stick hard into the ground, breaking it in half.

No one spoke for a few minutes, then Will Henry's look turned sour again. "We had hell too, back home. Good crop an' bad, seemed like we always owed more than we got back. Finally went busted. After we'd settled up with the furnishin' man didn't have but twenty-six dollars and some change. Been takin' her the hard way ever since."

"Didn't have much more'n that when we come out." Ertie shifted uncomfortably, feeling a little drunk and vaguely angry. It was the kind of anger that near drove him crazy lately because it had no shape or focus, it was just there and seemed like there wasn't anything he could do about it. "Time's tough, ain' no two ways around that. Sometimes makes a fella so mad he wants to haul off an' hit somebody."

"You folks in Nipomo last year? For the peas?"

Ertie shook his head. "We come out this spring."

"Oh, yeah, ya tol' me that." Will Henry nodded, embarrassed by the slip. "Well, it was Nipomo that got us started thinkin' 'bout the union. It's over on the coast a ways, an' we was there for the peas, a year ago spring. Mister, it was bad, let me tell ya. Them was starvin' times. Musta been six hundred famblies in that camp and ever' one of 'em goin' hungry. Been rainin' for weeks an' no work 'cause the fields was so muddy ya couldn't get into 'em an' nobody had a cryin' dime to buy groceries, folks was flat starved out, but when we asked for help, county relief workers turned us away, said we hadn't lived in the county for a year so we wasn't qualified for no handouts. There was babies sick, but weren't no doctor'd come out, so they died, just like my Sary died. Sary was my wife, lay in that tent a-burnin' up with fever . . ." Will Henry stopped talking and just squatted there, eyes watery and dull, like he'd gone into a trance of some kind.

Buford watched his father anxiously for a moment, then put a hand on his shoulder. "Pa?"

Will Henry looked up, puzzled for an instant, then he took off his glasses, rubbed his face with one hand and got back his self-control. Glasses back on, he looked square at Ertie, the thick lenses magnifying hatred in his eyes. "Mister, what happened up there ain' right. No sir. What's happenin' everywhere ain' right. Good Book says 'Thou shalt not oppress thy hired man,' that's in Deuteronomy an' in Jeremiah an' Malachi it says God's gonna punish them bastards for 'pressin' us."

Surprised by the sudden tirade, Ertie stood up. "You a preacher or somethin'?"

"We ain' preachers." Will Henry stood up too. "Me 'n my boys here's just workers, like you. Us workin' people, we don' have to take it. No sir! God's a-goin' to help us make a union so we can fight back. He's gonna help us punish them greedy bastards." Will Henry had taken out his wallet as he talked and he showed Ertie a dog-eared union card. "There's my bona fides, mister."

UNITED CANNERY, AGRICULTURE, PACKING AND ALLIED WORKERS OF AMERICA was spelled out across the top of the card and below it was the imprint of the CIO. "We call it U-Ca-Pa-Wa for short, kind of like an Indian name. Me 'n the boys joined up later that summer, over in Salinas. Figgered it was time to pitch in with the rest of the fellas an' fight for an honest day's pay. Had us a strike there, in the vegetables."

"Didja win?"

"No." Will Henry shook his head sadly. "Could've, though, if ever'body'd walked out them fields. Figgered we hadn't done 'nuff organizin' ahead of time. CIO's got some guys helpin' us now, teachin' us how to get organized. It's gonna take time, but by God, we'll win the next one, believe you me."

"Maybe so." Ertie backed away. "But we ain' waitin' 'round for no damn union. I figger a man can do better on his own."

"Pickin' fruit?"

"Hell, no." Ertie was exasperated. "These farmers's never goin' to change, no matter what. Soon's we can we're gonna catch on somewhere's else, meantime, boss don't treat us right, fuck 'im. We just go on down the road. Don't take crap from nobody."

"But that don' change nothin'."

"Hell it don'. Lets 'em know they cain' treat us like niggers."

Just then Susie came running up. "Pa! Pa, here's yor Bull Durham." She handed him a sack. "An' here's the change from the groceries." She dropped several brass coins in his hand.

Amazed, Ertie stared at the coins. They were crudely minted slugs, about the size of a quarter; each slug had the words EL ADOBE stamped on one side and the denomination on the other— a dollar, half dollar, and two ten-cent pieces. "What's this?"

"Ain' it funny?" Susie giggled. "They make their own money here. Spend it in the store."

"Jeesus H. Christ!" Ertie exploded.

Susie stepped back, frightened and puzzled. "What's wrong, Pa?"

Ignoring her question, Ertie turned to Will Henry. "You get paid in brass money too?"

"Shor, only time they pay ya cash money is when yor ready to leave. Tha's one of the thangs we're gonna change, union's gonna demand we get paid ever' day in cash money."

"When's that?"

"Gotta get organized first. That's what I wanted to talk to ya 'bout. Meetin' tonight, down at the union fellers' camp, along the river."

"Shit!" Ertie couldn't believe this. "Hell, I ain' takin' no brass money and I damn sure ain' waitin' for you all to git yorselves organized, neither." Ertie stormed off, heading toward the store and headquarters.

Jake saw his father limping furiously out of camp and up the lane. "Pa! Wait up, Pa! Where ya goin'?"

"To get paid in real money."

There was still a line of workers at the pay window as Ertie went up the stairs and stood on the porch. Most were men, young and old, tired and dirty. Some were talking, others waited quietly, heads down. Others, women mostly, were going in and out of the store, and every time the door opened, a bell tinkled. Impatiently, Ertie got in line and made himself a cigarette, gave the end a twist, then felt around in his pockets for a match. When he couldn't find one, he turned to the man behind him, a scarecrow, tall and thin, wearing a frayed straw hat. "Got a light, partner?"

"Sho." The scarecrow rummaged around in his baggy overalls and came up with a kitchen match.

"Thanks." Ertie lit his cigarette, then pulled the coins out and looked at them again, still not quite believing they'd worked all day for some brass slugs. Maybe the girls got flimflammed. He asked the scarecrow, "Ever'body get paid in brass money?"

"First day?" The scarecrow chuckled and the *yuk-yuk-yuk* sounds sent little jerks and shudders through his skeletal frame.

"Hell, I ain' jokin'." Ertie's voice was edged with anger.

"No offense, mister." The scarecrow was contrite and wanting to be friendly. "Bothered me some too, at first, but hell, there ain't much a feller can do about it. That's the way they do here."

"Hell, they cheat ya on your count an' pay ya off in brass." Ertie was disgusted. "Got us workin' for nothin'. That's rawhide slavery, it surely is!"

The scarecrow looked nervously around. "Friend, I wouldn't make a fuss about it, that won' do nothin' but git ya fired."

"What the hell happens if ya ask for cash money?"

The scarecrow shrugged. "We don't make trouble. Fella's gotta work when he can. Winters here is mighty long."

"Ain' that long. There's always work if ya want it bad 'nuff." Looking through the window bars Ertie could see a skinny little fellow in a green eyeshade who was reading off numbers to a bigger man in a white shirt who double-checked the numbers. Then Green Eyeshade counted out the brass coins. It was efficient, and fast. No one protested.

The man in front of him turned away from the window recounting the coins in his hand and the clerk in the green eyeshade called out, "Next."

Ertie stepped up and pushed his brass coins through the window. "I want cash money for these, mister."

"What?"

"That ain' cash money." Ertie pointed to the brass coins. "Mister, I worked damn hard today, and so'd my family. If's all the same, I'll take my pay in cash money."

"Only time we pay cash is when you leave. Those coins are good as gold in these parts, spend 'em anywhere."

"Mister, that may look like gold to you, but it's brass to me. Now I ain' lookin' for no trouble, but I'm a 'merican and by Gawd when I work I git paid in 'merican money."

"I just tol' you it'll spend anywhere. Next."

There were grumbles up and down the pay line, but Ertie ignored them. "Mister, you give me some real 'merican money an' you do it right now."

"You sayin' Titus Wardlow ain't good for it."

"I ain' sayin' nothin' but that I don't want no brass money, goddammit." Ertie rattled the bars.

Somebody in line behind him yelled, "Hey! What's holdin' thangs up up thar!"

"Get that troublemaker out of there!" someone else demanded.

"Move out'n the way!"

Ertie whirled on the workers behind him. "Fuck you! What kinda men are you, takin' their goddamn brass money. I get paid in 'merican, by Gawd."

The clerk slammed the pay window closed and there was the sound of a wooden bar falling into place. Across the dirt lane an office door banged and Titus Wardlow, followed by the big ranch manager and a shotgun-toting bruiser, came storming across the lane and up the steps, two at a time. "What the hell's going on here?"

"Mister, all I—" Ertie began to explain, but Wardlow brushed him aside and stood there in the midst of the workers, fists clenched, glaring. The guard, shotgun at the ready, had taken up a position not ten feet away. Ross, the ranch manager, went inside, then came back out with the clerk in the green eyeshade, who pointed to Ertie. "Mr. Wardlow, that Okie there was making trouble."

"What happened?"

"He wouldn't take his pay, said he wanted real money."

"Pay him off!" Wardlow turned and squared off on Ertie. "You're fired!" That's all he said, just "You're fired!" and wheeled away and was down the steps, yelling back, "Run his ass out of here."

The guard started for Ertie, but Ross waved him back. Wardlow's instructions were explicit: Any sign of trouble was to be put down quickly, decisively. No agitator was to be given a chance to make a scene that might stir up further trouble. The ranch manager barked, "Pay him off!"

Storming mad, Ertie asked, "You gonna cheat us out of the bucket deposits too?"

"You'll get your deposit when we get the buckets. Now get your ass off this ranch." Ross turned to the man with the shotgun. "Shorty, make sure he's out before dark."

Even at sunset, the valley was still oven-hot. Long blue shadows fell across the highway as Jake drove east toward Highway 99. In the passenger seat beside him Ertie was re-counting the three dollars and forty-five cents in greenbacks and silver. Satisfied, he put the money in the sock and handed it back to Bessie.

"Pa." Susie leaned forward, the hot wind blowing in her hair. "What'd ya done if he hadn't paid us off in 'merican money?"

Jake chimed in, "Wouldja've got out the ol' forty-four–forty pistol an' stuck it under his nose?"

Ertie smiled at the idea, showing his crooked yellow teeth. The nickel-plated Remington .44-40 pistol was wrapped in a scrap of old blanket in a box in the trailer. He seldom took it out, but it was there.

"Wouldja done it, Pa?" Susie joined in.

"Don' know. Maybe." Ertie reached back and playfully tousled Susie's hair, then, pulling a strand gently, he said, "Sunlight sorrel, that's what it looks like. Purtiest hair I ever did see."

"You two!" Bessie slumped angrily back in the corner.

"But Ma." Susie turned to her mother. "They was cheatin' . . ."

"Girl, it was a job."

3

The sleek, low-wing monoplane sped across a cloudless summer sky, heading north-by-northwest from Bakersfield up the valley; a polished aluminum speedster that had the look of a pursuit ship. Titus Wardlow was at the controls, chewing thoughtfully on the stump of a cold cigar as he fiddled with the throttle, coaxing a little more performance out of the powerful engine. Air speed: coming up on two hundred fifteen miles an hour. Grunting in satisfaction, he glanced at his heading—322 degrees—then checked the manifold pressure, fuel gauges and engine temperature readings, and settled back in the comfortable tan leather seat. Scanning the sky for traffic, alert, yet relaxed, he enjoyed the feel of power and control that flying gave him, especially in this ship, a Spartan Exec with a four-hundred-horsepower radial Wasp Junior and fully retractable landing gear.

Ed Kleindecker, sitting tall and thin in the seat next to Wardlow, glanced at the airspeed. "This baby really moves!"

"Yeah," Wardlow grunted, his bulldog features scowling happily.

"How much you have to give for it?"

"None of your fucking business," Wardlow snapped. His voice was harsh, his words clipped. Every trace of Georgia was gone, put behind him long ago.

Kleindecker laughed. He was younger, a soft-spoken farmer with open, handsome features. "Goddammit, Titus, you're so tight you squeak. How come you'd put out so much on a plane like this. It must've cost you thirty grand."

Harold Barkham was riding in the backseat, reading the *Los Angeles Times*. Because of the engine's roar, he couldn't hear very well, but talk of money interested him. Leaning forward, he shouted, "What cost thirty grand?"

"This airplane! It must have set Titus back thirty grand!"

"Twenty-three seven fifty," Barkham yelled back, his gold teeth flashing through a mischievous grin. He was a dark, pudgy man with squirrel-puffed cheeks and graying hair.

"You son of a bitch!" Wardlow half turned, looking back at the older farmer in the rear seat, angry not so much because Barkham knew how much the plane had cost him—there was little that Harold Barkham didn't know about Jefferson County business since he and his brother owned the bank—but because Barkham had blurted out the figure, and with such obvious delight.

When old Tom Barkham died, he'd left the family businesses to his three sons, Tom Junior, Harold, and the youngest boy, the one they called Rooster. Rooster Barkham had gone his own way, taking his share and moving back over to Hyattville, where the Barkhams were from, while young Tom and Harold stuck together, Harold working the farm and Tom taking over as president and chief operating officer of the Jefferson City Bank. While Tom actually ran the bank, Harold was on the board of directors and made it a point to keep track of what was going on financially around the county; he knew who was behind in his loan payments and when a foreclosure was coming up, things like that.

Wardlow didn't like being kidded about the Spartan and he resented Harold's snooping, but there wasn't much he could do about it, at least not for a while yet. The Jeff City Bank had been financing Wardlow ever since he'd quit old man Kleindecker and gone off on his own, back in the twenties, when Ed Kleindecker here was still a kid in school. In those days young Tom Barkham was just taking ahold of the bank and was proving to be as good a financial advisor as his father, who had helped Wardlow buy his first piece of ground. From the beginning the Barkhams had backed him, stuck by him in the good years and the bad, and he appreciated that; without their help he couldn't have built El Adobe, but times were changing and the Jeff City bank was small, too small for what he had in mind.

Rolling the cold cigar stub from one side of his mouth to the other, Wardlow scanned the instruments again, adjusting his course for the ranch, then focused his thoughts on the mortgages, recalculating how much of his paper the Barkhams held; there was the open ground where he grew cotton and alfalfa, the vineyards and orchard lands, plus what he owed on the airplane; rounded off, that totaled nearly a half million dollars, not counting this year's operating loans, but those short-term debts weren't anything to worry about, not when he was coming in with nearly two bales of cotton to the acre this season. That was really going to put him over the top, if everything went smoothly, give him enough to step over into that railroad land and develop it.

The play on the railroad land was a big gamble, the biggest he'd ever taken, and he'd be making it in another man's game, which was always dangerous. But when Grady Armor had approached him with the proposal it all sounded good. Grady owned Armor Cotton Oil and was aggressively expanding, building more gins, financing more big operators through his connections with America First National Bank. The deal hinged on Wardlow picking up the leases on the railroad land as they expired, putting together a single operation that would tie up fifteen sections out in the Devil's Den country, south of the lake bottoms. It was all dryland farming now, planted to barley and wheat or used for sheep graze. Farmers down there had been renting that arid land from the railroad for years, dirt cheap, and wouldn't give up those leases easily, so he had to move quietly. Grady had assured him the railroad's land agent was all lined up for the deal and would offer them options to buy, conditioned on their proposal to develop the land. It was rough, arid country, criss-crossed by dry gullies. The deal they were cooking up called for him to level at least a third of the land on the ranch and to put in irrigation wells and canals, all within the first three years. It would be expensive, but with irrigation and the new fertilizers he was trying, he'd make that damn land bloom.

Wardlow looked out the plane's left window, searching the dry brown horizon to see if he could pick out the Devil's Den through the haze. In the distance he could make out Kettleman City and Blackwell's Corner and the railroad land was just beyond, lost in the shimmering haze. Wardlow knew he was crowding his luck, but it was exhilarating. He liked the tight feeling of apprehension, the expectant, fearful joy of the big gamble. If everything went right, it wouldn't be too many more years before his operations would be as big as anybody's, including those guys down in the lake bottom. Renting the railroad land was just the first step.

Flying at fifty-five hundred feet, Wardlow scanned the skies. To the east, off his right wing, the Sierra Nevadas flanked the valley, a range of peaks reaching nearly three miles into the sky; ahead the wide valley stretched into the distant haze so far there seemed no end to the neatly patterned fields and orchards; to the west were the rounded, brown hills of the Coast Range; below, and off to the right, he could see Highway 99 and the Southern Pacific main line cutting up through the valley, linking the towns one to another.

"Kidding aside, Titus. What'll it do?"

Wardlow glanced at Kleindecker. "What?"

"What'll the Spartan do?"

"Two thirty-five."

The young farmer whistled in appreciation.

"Clip the wings, add some power and she'll do two-fifty."

Kleindecker looked at him skeptically.

"Look what Hughes did with his Northrup Gamma, put in that new engine, was only a hundred horses more, but it gave him another fifteen miles an hour." Wardlow looked across the cockpit and winked. "And a new world speed record, L.A. to New York in seven hours, twenty-eight minutes."

Kleindecker grinned. Wardlow liked to talk about flying, it was one of the few times he seemed to relax. Where a few other ranchers had small planes, J-Cubs or Taylorcrafts to fly around their places, mostly, Wardlow went in for speed and he liked to go to the races. "Who'll win the Bendix this year?"

"Frank Fuller." Wardlow stretched, then took ahold of the controls again. "He'll average better than two-fifty all the way to Cleveland in that Seversky."

"Hear there's a couple of women entered in the National Air Races this year."

"Yeah. Jackie Cochran's racing cross-country and Roxanne Darling's entered in the Thompson Trophy Race. First woman ever to try to qualify for a big-time closed-course race. She's going up against Roscoe Turner and those guys."

Barkham was leaning forward again. "Bart Darling's wife?"

"Yeah. She's a hell of a flyer."

"Damn good looker, too, from what I've seen of her in the papers. Ever get into her pants?" Barkham grinned.

Wardlow didn't say anything, but anger reddened up the back of his neck. Barkham was just trying to be funny, knowing damn well that Titus was married to Kleindecker's cousin Barbara. Barbara Wardlow was a Braddock, from the Braddock Land and Cattle Company and she and Ed Kleindecker were like brother and sister. A man should never kid around about something like that, not in front of Ed.

"Harold, read your goddamn newspaper." Kleindecker was disgusted by the man's inept sense of humor. He turned to Wardlow. "You going to the nationals?"

"Thinking about it," Wardlow nodded. Yeah, he'd been thinking about it a lot since meeting Roxanne Darling at the Cal Pacific races in Oakland earlier in the year. He'd just landed and had been sitting there in the cockpit writing up the log when Roxie had climbed on the wing, that boyish grin on her face, and said, "Hi! What'll she do?"

It was the Spartan that had attracted her and he'd taken her for a hop, letting her take the controls, amazed at the way she handled the ship. She was aggressive, he sensed that from the start, and he knew from talk around the hangars that she was married to a rich oilman in Bakersfield, a wildcatter who spent much of his time on drilling rigs around the world. Bart Darling had bought her the Red Ryder Special, hired Tom Axelrod to rebuild it and gave her a blank check to go racing. Unlike Cochran and two or three other women who competed for the long-distance records, Roxanne flew head-to-head against men in the more dangerous, closed-course pylon racing, like the Thompson in Cleveland.

Wardlow adjusted the fuel mixture, then let his thoughts drift back to Roxie. She was a damn good pilot, but an awful cook; the sight of her short blond hair and fresh good looks, gray eyes snapping bright and that impish grin teasing her mouth, was exciting; the smell and the feel of her athletic young body pleased him. It was Roxie who'd talked about flying the Spartan in the Bendix and it was Roxie who talked about going to bed. She was fast and she liked sex. The first time she had taken off her bra he had been astounded how full and round her breasts were, those beautiful tits and that wondrous tight cunt, not like Barbara, loose and indifferent, lying there without enthusiasm, pretending, if she thought about sex at all. Roxanne was a natural blonde, she had a small waist and a marvelously round ass and when those long, shapely legs opened up to him he was lost in the joy of fucking someone who loved fucking.

Uncomfortably he shifted around in the Spartan's seat, thinking about last night, after the association meeting. When the meeting in the Basque Hotel's big, sparsely furnished dining room finally broke up he'd slipped away from the rest of the farmers and driven out to her house on the bluffs overlooking the Kern River. They had made love and afterward she suggested they go racing, together; when he wasn't farming, they could fly the Spartan in long-distance air races, why, with a bigger engine and the right mechanic, they could enter it in the '38 Bendix. They'd have a whole year to get ready and, with luck, they'd finish in the top five. She made it sound so damned exciting he impulsively agreed, without thinking of the consequences. Now he was having second thoughts. Winning, or getting forced down somewhere, would mean publicity and there was no way he could afford to get tangled up in an affair, not while he was putting the Devil's Den deal together. No, he would fly the race alone, from L.A. to Cleveland, and be there to watch her fly in the Thompson; they'd be together at the nationals, that was enough for now.

Wardlow scanned the sky for traffic, wishing now that he was alone up here. Flying was something very private, an experience that really couldn't be shared with anyone, except Roxie. When he was tense or angry flying was his escape, rolling a wing over, swooping down and back up through a loop, marveling at how like a fighter the Spartan performed. For a few minutes he could live for the thrill of high-performance flight, the demand for total concentration. He had bought the Spartan simply because he wanted the airplane. It had been a compulsive act that he didn't totally understand, trading in his little StaggerWing Beechcraft on this bigger, faster ship, but he was pleased with himself for doing it.

Flying the Spartan was different from piloting Sopwith Camels in the war. Those old kites had been fun, true. They were fantastically light and responsive to the controls, but their little Le Rhone rotary engines were just fascinating toys compared to the big Wasp Junior in this baby. Even so, the memories of the Camel's open cockpit and the blue smoke blowing off that little spinning engine were so sharp he could still smell the castor oil. It was crazy, but true, he could still smell castor oil, and sometimes the nightmare would recur: machine gun bullets stitching tattered holes across the wings and engine cowl, the plane spinning out of control, the torque slamming him against the side of the cockpit as he fought for control, blinded by fire and smoke, the earth spinning crazily toward him.

He awoke in a French hospital. Clint Braddock was standing beside his bed, a worried smile on his thin, handsome face, Clint, dead now eight years, killed in a plane crash in 1929 as he took off from the land company's strip. Clint Braddock had been Wardlow's squadron leader and his friend, the ace who had tucked the fledgling under his wing and taught him how to fight in the air. And it had been Clint who sat with Lieutenant Titus Wardlow as he drank glasses of cognac one after another and talked about his grandfather, Major Titus Wardlow, who served under General George E. Pickett and who died at Gettysburg, on Cemetery Ridge. As a boy, young Lieutenant Wardlow had read the citation and seen the hero's medal; on July 3, 1863, Major Titus Wardlow led his men in the charge up Cemetery Ridge to the copse of trees where the Yankees lay behind the barricades, their deadly musket fire ripping and riddling through Pickett's brigade, turning the proud gray ranks into tattered, bloody heaps of dying men. Major Wardlow fell on the Yankee barricades and died there, shot full of holes. Young Lieutenant Wardlow, his mind fogged by alcohol, told Clint Braddock how his father, Walter Joseph Wardlow, became keeper of that legendary act of heroism and of the memories and customs of a Georgia before the war. Walter Joseph Wardlow, who was called W. J., not only rebuilt Merrimack, the Wardlow cotton plantation, he used it as the foundation upon which he built a business empire that included ginning, shipping and railroad interests. W. J. had ties to financial houses and markets in Atlanta and New Orleans and faraway London. It had taken twenty years of hard, ruthless effort, and after success was assured, he married and carried on the family line, fathering six children. Lieutenant Titus Wardlow was the sixth child and the third son of W. J. Wardlow.

Young Titus Wardlow had learned very early that he was in competition with his brothers in everything that he did. Their father not only encouraged that, he insisted on it. Titus could still remember his father's scorn as W. J. stood in the gin yard, shouting at his youngest son, "You're not tough enough! Not man enough! You quit!"

He'd been ten, going on eleven, and as he stood there in front of his father, shirt torn, nose bleeding and one eye swollen shut, he wanted to scream back at this man who hated him so much, but he dared not. Young Titus had been fighting with his older brother, Walter, Jr., who was fourteen and who stood there beside their father, defiant and dirty, his clothes also showing signs of the scuffle. There was a smirk on Walter's face as W. J. raged at young Titus, "You are a disgrace to the Wardlow name. You gave up! Don't snivel excuses to me, boy, you gave up! No Wardlow quits! Ever!"

It made no difference how the fight had started, nor did their father seem to realize that his oldest son was a coward and a bully. Life was a contest, and victory, not technique, was the valued goal. It was a lesson the young Titus Wardlow never forgot. Over and over again he had tried to prove himself as a fighter and then as a pilot, but W. J. didn't seem to notice; it was as if he'd written off his youngest son.

The war ended for Lieutenant Titus Wardlow there in that French hospital, ended before he could become an ace. His score was two aircraft shot down, three balloons destroyed, not nearly enough to return home a hero. From the very beginning, Titus had been determined to win his father's approval. Braddock had seen that in the aggressive way Titus flew into combat, never thinking about himself, only his goal, to become an ace. But Braddock also sensed that W. J. Wardlow would never accept his youngest son, no matter how hard Titus tried. Once, when they had been drinking in a cabaret, Clint Braddock suggested to Titus that California was a place where a restless young fellow could get a start ranching. After the crash, Braddock repeated his suggestion, trying to convince his young friend that raising cattle and farming in the San Joaquin Valley made more sense than trying to go back home to Georgia and the Wardlow plantation. But Titus wouldn't listen. He was a flier and he had a plan, a dream really, but a big one. Fast freight and passengers, that was what the airplane was destined for, and a smart guy who could fly would be in on the start of it. Newer, bigger planes were being built all the time and, with the right kind of financing, there was money to be made. As sharp as W. J. was, he'd see the opportunities, once Titus spelled it out for him.

Sitting at the Spartan's controls, feeling its speed and power, Wardlow thought about those early dreams and how far the aircraft industry had come since the last war. Look what Donald Douglas had done; that new twin-engine DC-3 of his was carrying twenty-one passengers at 195 miles an hour, flying coast-to-coast. And Pan Am's big four-engine clippers were flying the Pacific.

"Hey, Titus! Ed! Listen to this." Harold Barkham was leaning forward again, yelling over the engine noise as he held up a section of the folded newspaper, "They've got a story in the *Times* here about the goddamn Okies! Look at that headline."

SQUATTER ARMY WAGES GRIM BATTLE FOR LIFE
Hunger and Disease Stalk
50,000 Transients in San Joaquin Valley

Barkham pushed the paper between the front seats so they could see it. "Can you believe that! Here, listen, I'll read some of it! Starts off from Bakersfield: 'A battle for life, for food and a place to live is being waged here by thousands of dust bowl refugees who have been driven to California by debt and drought! Human squalor awaits the visitor looking beyond the roadside today in the San Joaquin Valley! Within an hour, the skeptic must admit he has seen disaster, privation, filth and threats of epidemic! The families follow the crops seasonally, picking fruit and chopping cotton, but their pay is low and they work at most only half the days of the year! The worst time for these impoverished people is when the cotton picking ends in November! After that there is little or no work until March, little or no money, little food ...' "

"Shit!" Wardlow glanced furiously back at Barkham. "Fucking reporters, all they want to do is sell newspapers."

Barkham scooted even further forward, and was leaning between the front seats now. "Wait, you haven't seen anything! Look at these pictures!"

Kleindecker took the paper and there, spread across the entire page, were a dozen stark photographs showing the shanty camps along the canal banks and under the bridges.

"That's just what I mean." Wardlow stabbed the paper with a finger. "They pick out a few of the worst goddamn squatter camps and make it look like it's the farmers' fault. Shit, Doc Pebble's right, those fuckin' Okies don't know how to live any better."

"Hell, Titus, it isn't just the squatter camps, some of the farm labor camps are pretty raunchy too, you got to admit that." Kleindecker was concerned.

"What're you getting at?" Wardlow demanded.

"Wouldn't cost much to fix up the camps, might save trouble in the long run." Kleindecker shifted his weight in the seat, turning toward Wardlow, shouting over the engine noise. "And yesterday, at the meeting, we could have set the cotton picking price higher. We can afford to pay a bit more."

"Ed, goddammit, we set the wages at ninety cents a hundred and that's what we'll all pay," Wardlow snapped. "You some kind of fucking do-gooder?"

"Jeesus Christ, don't get mad at me."

"Well, shit, your dad would never have talked like that."

"Dammit, Titus, this is 1937. I don't think it's necessary to drop the wages, we'd still come out all right at a dollar. All this will do is stir up union trouble again."

"Well let 'em start something, we'll just stomp the hell out of them, like we did last time." Wardlow was disgusted with the way the talk was going. "What the fuck would your old man have said if he heard you talking like that?"

"You know what he'd've said, you learned it all from him."

"You bet I did."

Although Wardlow liked the young farmer, he didn't understand him. He was so different from old man Kleindecker, and different even from his brother Bob. Going off to college had changed Ed. He was bright and his numbers were always good, he knew to the penny how much he had in a crop, but so did a lot of other growers. The problem was that Ed was still soft. He had a lot to learn, a whole damn lot.

Off the left wing Wardlow could see the city of Corcoran and, out beyond, the dry Tulare Lake bottom where immense farms sprawled across the flat sink. The sight of those vast plowed and planted fields extending mile after square mile behind a protective network of earthen levees always stirred him; they truly were factories in the fields. A grower didn't just stand around out there sucking on a straw and whistling Dixie. Fuck Old MacDonald, this was farming the way it ought to be done. Big!

Tulare Lake was one of those peculiarities of the San Joaquin Valley that he simply accepted, a marvel that outsiders always had difficulty understanding. The lake basin was perhaps thirty miles long, north-to-south, and nearly twenty wide, six hundred square miles of low-lying bottomland that once had been flooded by a shallow lake and overgrown tule marshes. Tulare Lake, in its natural form, was fed by six rivers—the Kings, Palo Rojo, Kaweah, Tule, White and Kern—and had no outlet to the ocean because the floor of the San Joaquin Valley was not really flat at all, rather it was like two shallow saucers set side by side, one north, the other south. The gentle lift of the land between the two saucers was imperceptible to the naked eye, but it was there, just southwest of Fresno, a sandy hogback that formed a natural dam across the valley; the rivers cascading out of snowy Sierra into the northern saucer merged into the San Joaquin and Sacramento rivers and flowed out through a delta into San Francisco Bay, but south of Fresno the gradient sloped into the southern basin and the six rivers emptied into the vast tule swamp the Spaniards called Los Tulares. Running in spring flood each year, these rivers spilled millions of acre feet of water into this shallow sink that had no outlet to the ocean, forming the great inland sea called Tulare Lake.

Periodically this shallow lakebed dried up in drought years and in wet years it spread over wide areas. It was never very deep, and its swampy shores were rich in vegetation. Sedges and tules grew thick beyond imagination. In the dry 1870s farmers discovered the rich lakebottom soils grew bountiful crops of grain, and to protect these lands from the spreading lake in wet years they began building levee systems to contain the lake's fluctuations. River inflows were diverted into irrigation canals and large blocks of land were planted to grain and alfalfa. At first the farmers worked around the edges of the lake, but as their experience and skills increased, they built larger levees, moving farther out into the lake bottom until finally all of it was being farmed except for the very bottom, where twenty-foot-high levees created a large, rectangular storage reservoir. Here man had tamed the swamp, turning it into one of the richest farming areas in the world; man against nature, fighting back the waters and reaping the harvest, if he was strong enough, had guts enough.

Just looking down on the lake bottoms was a pleasure. Sunlight glinted silver off the impounded lake and warmed the great squares of land that were precisely laid out in three- and four-thousand-acre parcels. These were called "checks." Some of the checks were green with cotton and alfalfa, others were yellow-brown. The wheat and barley harvests were over and the land was being plowed down, readied for another irrigation and planting.

"Ed?" Wardlow tapped the young farmer on the shoulder and pointed. "See that big levee that runs clear across the lake bottom? When I first came here, before I went to work for your dad up on the Palo Rojo, I helped build that, working on a Fresno scrapper that was pulled by a six-mule hitch. The next winter was a big snow year up in the Sierra and that spring floods gave us hell. There was no place to put the water and the lake was filing up faster than we could harvest the barley. You should've seen it, thousands of men on the levees fighting the water while we ran the harvest crews. When a levee broke the checks were so big the water spread slowly and we had ten, maybe fifteen hours before we got flooded out, so we stayed in the checks, harvesting as much as we could until we had to get out, then we hauled ass, harvesters, mules, the works. We didn't have tractors then and everything was pulled by mules, we hauled the combines up over the levees and down into the next check, harvesting the crop before that levee broke and the water got to us. Those were the days when men were tough and they gambled big."

Kleindecker nodded, not really listening to Wardlow, who was so much like his own father. He'd heard these stories before, many times.

Down on the South-Central Levee Wardlow watched a motor grader working the dirt being hauled in by a circling fleet of trucks, thinking: These young guys don't know what it was like, they were born onto the land after we made it. And he fondly remembered those early days on the Fresno scrapper, hanging onto the long trip bar with both hands, using all of his body weight to counterbalance the scoop as the team of mules lunged ahead in the harness. He thought of Indian Frank who had taught him to work the scrapper and handle the mules, Indian Frank Gomez, who was a full-blood Tachi and knew the lake bottom better than any man alive. His tribal name was Ta-weese-sa-paga, which meant "black fish that swims fast." He was a small, reedy man with ebony dark skin. But for his dark looks, he might have been a white man; certainly he walked and talked like one and there was never a better hand with stock.

It was from Frank that Titus Wardlow had learned about Tulare Lake before the first farmers settled along the rivers and began diverting the water for irrigation, before the big levees were built out in the bottom that kept the lake waters back. Before the levees, this inland sea had sustained an incredible abundance of life; the waters were rich in fish, the tule swamps and grassy prairies alive with birds, bear, deer, elk and antelope; each winter millions of waterfowl blackened the skies over the lake and nested in the reeds. The Tachi wove large tule reed rafts and lived part of the year on the water, fishing and hunting the ducks and geese.

To the Spanish living in the coastal missions, Los Tulares, like all of the San Joaquin Valley, was an untamed wilderness of useless swamps and vast, arid deserts. In winter dense tule fogs chilled the entire valley, holding all life in a dank, dripping mist, the summer sun baked the land and the Indian tribes clung to the shores of the lake and the banks of the rivers or retreated into the shady canyons of the coastal hills to the west. White explorers crossing through the valley trapped beaver and traded with the bands of Yokut Indians and left measles and the smallpox behind; the diseases swept through the Indian villages like wild prairie fires, wiping out whole clans. Those few Indians who survived were either killed by settlers or rounded up and confined to reservations, once gold was discovered at Sutter's Mill.

During the gold rush the burgeoning populations in the cities and mining camps needed food. Farmers took up land in the San Joaquin Valley, grazing livestock, plowing and planting crops, and when the golden spike was driven at Promontory Point, Utah, creating the transcontinental railroad, they had Eastern markets for Western farm produce. The government subsidized track construction by granting the railroads great blocks of land and the Southern Pacific line was pushed south from Sacramento into the San Joaquin Valley; farmers began icing down carloads of potatoes, lettuce, carrots, peaches and plums and a hundred other fresh crops, shipping them not only to San Francisco and Los Angeles, but east to Chicago and New York, at handsome profits. The railroad brought thousands of new settlers to the valley.

Wardlow had been something of a latecomer to the valley. When the war ended, he had gone home to Georgia, full of his plans about flying. But Clint Braddock had been right, there was no place for Titus there. Walter, his oldest brother, had taken over the plantation; his father, W. J., was running the rest of the businesses and still very much in charge. Oh, there was a job for Titus, if he wanted one, but W. J. quickly let his son know that he would have to prove himself. Titus tried to spell out his ideas about starting an aviation company, but that only angered W. J. To the older Wardlow airplanes were "flying contraptions," nothing more than "useless toys." He demanded that his son forget such "nonsense," but Titus persisted, stubbornly arguing that he wanted to start his own business. That led to the final blowup. Infuriated by the realization that his son would not bend to his will, W. J. slapped Titus hard across the face, yelling, "Get out! I'll have nothing more to do with you!"

Titus Wardlow had then tossed his lot in with another young flier. They bought a rakish old biwing, wood-and-wire Jenny and based it at a small flying field outside of Atlanta, giving flying lessons and offering chartered flights. When their business failed, the restless young aviators took off barnstorming across the country, putting on acrobatic air shows at county fairs and giving people rides. For a while they traveled with a wing walker, a wild young woman named Rita who had been with a circus and loved danger and daredevils, but there was never enough money to eat and buy gasoline to get to the next town. Somewhere in Nebraska, broke and discouraged, Wardlow remembered Clint Braddock's descriptions of the San Joaquin Valley and decided he'd had enough flying. Signing over his interest in the Jenny, he headed for California and found work in the Tulare Lake bottoms where he stayed for nearly a year, saving enough to buy a Model T Ford and have some money in his pocket when he looked up his old squadron leader. That spring, after the barley harvests were over, he drove north, following the Kings River upstream to where the Palo Rojo emptied into it, and asked directions to the Braddock Land and Cattle Company headquarters.

In that part of the country, it was called simply "the Land Company" and, with its distinctive Wine Cup brand, was a throwback to Mexican California, a sprawling grassland empire that extended from the confluence of the Kings and Palo Rojo rivers west up into the wrinkled coastal hills. The Braddocks had been hacendados before the gold rush. Don Louis Braddock, a sea captain from Boston, had established a trading store in Monterey in the 1830s and had been granted a quarter million acres of land by the Mexican government. He had built his hacienda on the banks of the Kings River, just north of the Palo Rojo, and founded a great ranch that produced beef and hides and blooded horses. Long after Don Louis's death, the ranch produced a new kind of wealth: oil.

Clint Braddock had been glad to see Wardlow, and he offered the young flier work. Wardlow turned him down, accepting only a few weeks lodging and introductions to neighboring ranchers and farmers. While there, he met Barbara Braddock. She was Clint's youngest sister, a strong-willed, vivacious girl in her teens. She was attracted to the restless Wardlow, liked the way he seemed to be looking for something, measuring the land and the opportunity.

Among the farmers Clint Braddock had introduced him to was Ezra Kleindecker, an irascible, tough old German who had no interest in cattle or dry-land grain farming. Kleindecker had been one of the first to divert the river into networks of canals to irrigate his land and, from the outset, he saw that the westside soils could grow vegetables, fruit and cotton. Wardlow was attracted to the cranky, restless energy of the man and his angry, thick-headed determination to change the land, to make it more productive. Kleindecker hired Wardlow and put him to work on a construction gang and the young flier once again found himself hanging on to a Fresno scrapper, digging yet another canal. When that job was finished Kleindecker kept him on, pushing harvest crews; that next spring the farmer leased Wardlow a few hundred acres, on shares. They got along, the German immigrant and the young flier who had never become an ace. They experimented with vines and trees—the older man already skillful in the arts of grafting and cultivating fruit, the younger learning those skills. Wardlow seldom acknowledged many of his feelings, but he recognized that he missed that cantankerous old man, missed the newness and excitement of it all as they changed those sprawling, empty lands, turning them into orderly, productive acres.

Chewing on the cigar, Wardlow checked the instruments and realized something was wrong. He looked again, senses alert: engine temperatures, fuel, air speed and manifold pressure, all okay. Heading? Shit! He was off course. Angrily he rocked the wings over in a tight bank, quickly correcting the error, and leveled back out.

Alarmed, Harold Barkham leaned forward, shouting, "What's wrong?"

"Nothing!" Wardlow barked.

"Relax, Harold. Titus just got to daydreaming and drifted off course." Ed Kleindecker was grinning and looking out to his right. "Hey, there's Jeff City."

"Where?" Barkham couldn't spot the town.

"Off about one o'clock." Kleindecker pointed. "See the water tower up above the trees?"

Jefferson City. It was a comfortable little town on the banks of the Rio del Palo Rojo. The river rose in the snowy crags of the Sierra Nevada, high up in the McCleod National Forest, amid the groves of redwoods that gave the river its name. Tumbling out of the mountains, it flowed westerly through the heart of the country, dividing the land north from south. Almost seventy years earlier railroad construction gangs had pitched camp on the north bank and bridged the river; in those days there was nothing at the crossing but oaks and cottonwoods surrounded by open prairie. After the tracks were laid and a parallel bridge was built for horse and wagon traffic, the town was platted and named, not for Thomas Jefferson, as outsiders later assumed, but for Jefferson Davis. The town grew up on the south bank of the river and became the center of commerce and finally the county seat. It was a pretty town with wide, tree-lined streets and a stately courthouse built of native Sierra granite.

"Dead ahead's the ranch." Wardlow pushed the plane's nose over gently, eased off on the throttle and began his descent. "Be there in ten minutes."

El Adobe was impressive from the air and the sight of its neat, white buildings, orderly fields and orchards always thrilled Wardlow. What really set the place apart was the landing strip and hangar, with the bright orange windsock high above its curved roof. While Wardlow lived in town, in a big yellow house that Barbara had built, he kept the plane out here at the ranch and had a comfortable bachelor apartment built onto the back of the hangar. It was his hideaway, a refuge. During harvests, when the pace at the ranch was hectic and he was spending long hours on the phones, selling and shipping fruit to the East, it was easier to fall into bed out here. The wife of one of his foremen, Juanita Orosco, kept the place clean, cooked for him, and looked after him like he was one of her own boys, scolding him when he didn't eat or take enough time off to be with his family.

Wardlow buzzed the ranch headquarters, banked sharply and circled back around, starting his final descent, dropping the flaps, letting the landing gear down, airspeed dropping below eighty, then seventy miles an hour. For an instant, as he looked down on all that he had created, he wondered what W. J. would say if he were still alive and could see El Adobe. It wasn't as big as Merrimack, but it was a damn good start.

The Spartan whispered in low over the orchards, as Wardlow pulled off the power, letting the ship settle into a perfect three-point landing.

4

Late in September the Robertsons pulled into one of those knocked-together squatter camps that sprang up in out-of-the-way places all over the valley. This one was located in a remote scatter of trees and willows that grew along the meandering course of a creek in the south part of Jefferson County. From a distance, motorists coming down the county road could look across the cotton fields and see the woods, leaves beginning to turn yellow now, and notice the blue smoke from the campfires; but for the most part, the tents and shanties were out of sight. There was water and plenty of wood for the makeshift stoves and open cook fires; by common agreement everyone went upstream to draw their water from the weir at the ditch turnout and did their washing down below the bridge. Most families had a tent of some sort and they fashioned additional shelter out of scrap lumber, corrugated iron, old Coca-Cola signs, whatever was available down at the county dump.

In the chill evenings, after work, there was the smell of woodsmoke and frying meat drifting through the cottonwood trees and sometimes the sounds of a fiddle or banjo could be heard. Folks visited back and forth and the talk was mostly about where there was work and where there wasn't and about the coming winter, when there'd be no work at all. At the time they all had jobs in the vineyards, up north a ways, but that harvest was coming to an end, the grapes had all been cut and spread to dry and now the raisins were being turned, then rolled and boxed and hauled to the sheds.

Each morning the school bus came down the county road and stopped to pick up some of the smaller children from the camp. Older youngsters like Jake and Susie worked in the vines alongside their parents and when all the raisins were in, they went on to the cotton in early October. They were workers now, but the sight of the school bus each morning tugged at Jake, made him feel uneasy because it meant that school had started back home too and he had expected that somehow when that happened they would be back in Nolan County, picking up their lives; it had been a fantasy, of course, but the whole damn summer had been unreal, unlike anything that had ever happened to him, and he wanted it to end. Back in April, when they'd started out for California, his parents had talked about a fresh start and it had sounded like they were headed somewhere, had a destination of some sort in mind and he'd expected that sooner or later they would arrive at a stopping point, but here it was October and school had started and they were still camped out on the road.

Not that he minded working in the cotton. Of all the crops they'd harvested since leaving Nolan County, he figured cotton was the best. Of course, that was partly because they'd picked cotton in Texas, after times got hard, so they knew the work already, and partly because farmers out here were paying ninety cents a hundredweight, which was a way better than wages paid in most other crops.

In the cotton the Robertsons stuck close together, each taking a row and working alone but keeping an eye out for one another and for Benjy and Li'l Beth, who was crawling around now and getting into everything. When it was his turn to care for Li'l Beth, Jake would spread an empty cotton sack out in the row a short ways up ahead and let her play there while he picked along, bent double over the rows, hands moving quickly, pulling and wadding the fiber, stuffing it into the long sack slung over his shoulder. When he'd worked his way up beside her, Jake would shrug out of his sack and drop down beside the baby, pretending to wrestle with her or tickling her to get a smile and gurgle. Sometimes when he held her up, she'd grab his ear or pull at his hair and laugh when he'd try to pull away. Watching out for her slowed his picking down some, but he didn't mind because he was a fast picker.

Cotton was a good crop, although the first few days of picking were painful because the rasp-sharp edges of the bolls scraped and nicked his fingers raw; his hands soon toughened and his muscles hardened to the heavy pull of the long sack so that by the end of the first week he was making three-fifty a day, more than anyone in the family, even James Earl.

The first big winter storm struck in mid-October. A cold wind gusted suddenly across the field and Jake looked up, surprised to see dark sullen clouds scudding in so low. Thunder cracked in the distance and there was the smell of rain in the air. He straightened up, glancing around the field; other workers were looking about apprehensively too. Rain meant no work until the cotton dried again. Lightning flashed and the wind swirled dirt and debris in the air as the first heavy drops of rain began falling, a few at first, then more and more until a torrential downpour deluged the fields. Thunder crashed and rumbled, like heavy barrels rolling across a wooden bridge.

At the first thunderclap Jake heard Li'l Beth's startled cry and, shrugging the sack off, he ran barefoot to where she had been sleeping, snuggled down on top of a partially filled cotton sack. James Earl was there ahead of him, just as a blast of wind and rain blew her ragged blanket away. James Earl scooped up his daughter and ran for the car. Jake grabbed her blanket and ran after them through the pelting rain. The storm sent everyone scurrying for shelter and, since they'd all come out to work that morning in the sedan to save gas, the Robertson crowded into the vehicle, dripping wet. Handing Li'l Beth to Billie Jo, James Earl shouted to Jake, "Come on, we gotta dump them sacks." The three of them, Ertie, James Earl and Jake, carried the heavy sacks to the high-sided cotton trailer, climbed up the ladder and shook them out, then helped the crew boss tarp the trailers down tight.

On the way back to camp, the downpour was so heavy the windshield wipers couldn't keep up with the deluge and the roads were sheeted with water. Jake parked in close to camp and they all scrambled into the tents to change clothes, all but Bessie who got the kerosene camp stove going under a pot of beans first. Wind whipped the tents and tore at the kitchen fly, making it pop and snap against the guy ropes. Rain beat down on the canvas and cascaded off the edges, but the kitchen area underneath it was relatively dry. Billie Jo had Li'l Beth wrapped snugly in a dry blanket and, as Susie came out of the tent, she handed the baby to her. "Here, take 'er whilst I help Ma git us somethin' to eat."

Although she was warm and dry, Li'l Beth was still fussy. Susie sat down on an overturned nail keg and folded the baby in close, nuzzling her, "Get-cha, get-cha, get-cha." The child quieted, then giggled as Susie nuzzled her again, her chubby cheeks and somber little eyes breaking into a happy face. Jake stood beside them, looking down at his niece; she was a wonder to him, just nine months old, healthy and fat, her first teeth in and giving Billie Jo's tits hell.

Billie Jo gave the pot a last stir as Bessie came back out of the tent, drying her hair. "It's 'bout ready, Ma."

"Fine." Bessie hung the towel on a nail and bent down to get some bowls and spoons out of the box under the stove.

Billie Jo gathered up Li'l Beth. "Gotta feed 'er now." Sheltering the baby from the blowing rain, she climbed up into the back of the pickup and closed the flap.

"Girl, come eat first, that baby can wait." Bessie spooned out steaming bowls full of beans.

"Go 'head, Ma, she's hungry."

Bessie set the bowls around the table, admonishing them all to "hurry up an' eat 'fore it gits cold." There was cornbread and scalding cups of coffee to go with the meal. Bessie sighed as she sat down at the head of the table. "Wisht them beans had some ham hocks in 'em, family needs meat when the weather turns bad."

They ate quickly, then holed up in the tents to wait out the storm. The wall tents were small and crowded. In the kitchen tent, where Ertie and Bessie slept, there was the double bed and so many boxes of camp gear and supplies there was little room left to move about. The other tent, also nine by twelve, was divided in half by a blanket hanging from a ridgepole; the girls slept on one side, Jake and Benjy on the other. To keep the mattress and covers up off the dirt Jake had spread their bed out on a platform of overturned lug boxes; the bedding was dry, so far, but the threadbare scrap of rug beside their bed was squishy-wet and water was dripping through a leak in one corner of the tent, where the canvas roof had been ripped and sewn back together. Jake put a bucket under the leak and now he lay on the bed listening to the pelting rain and watching the water dribbling through the canvas patch and dripping into the bucket. Benjy was curled up asleep beside him. On the other side of the blanket, he could hear his sisters paging through an old magazine.

"Mary Ellen, what's that word mean?"

"*Cosmopolitan?* That's the name of the magazine."

"I know that! But what does it mean? Why they call that girl in the picture the Cosmopolitan Lady?"

" 'Cause she's pretty. Says right here she's a glamour girl."

"But what's *cosmopolitan* mean?" Susie sounded impatient.

"Means pretty an' from the city. Gotta be rich to be cosmopolitan. See here, says her name's Olive Cawley an' she graduated from a fancy school for girls and she's a model. Poses for pictures an' thangs. Says here she's packin' to go on a trip 'round the world."

Another violent gust of wind shook the tent.

"Look, she's got three, four, five, six pairs of shoes that she's packin' for her trip."

"An' each pair's got a place in that 'ere cupboardlike thang." Susie was awed.

"That's a suitcase."

"Just for shoes?"

"That's the way glamour girls do."

Restlessly, Jake rolled over on his back and stared at the patterns of pale light and shadow on the canvas and wondered where they were really headed. Where would they wind up? Pa said their luck had to change, soon. He turned again on his side, troubled, yet bored. Remembering the old copy of *Life* that he'd saved, he reached under the mattress and pulled it out, staring at the cover. The magazine was one of several he'd found in an outhouse, left there for wiping, he guessed. The cover had caught his attention. On it was a young aviator sitting in the open cockpit of a biwinged airplane looking directly at Jake. The pilot wore a soft leather helmet and was staring intently through his goggles, calmly, almost without expression. Under the photo was a tiny caption: BOYS WITH WINGS. Inside there were action photos of army pilots training at Randolph Field, down in Texas; one spectacular picture showed six Stearman trainers flying in formation, one stepped above the other. There were crash shots, lots of them, one of them of a broken-winged ship snagged in a tree top, just hanging there. Caption said the pilot had walked away, unhurt.

Jake had been up in an airplane once. Both he and Susie had gone flying in a Gypsy Moth piloted by a barnstormer who had landed at the rodeo in Big Springs. The flier charged five dollars, but when he had found out Ertie was a bucking horse rider, he let both Jake and Susie ride for the price of one. Putting on goggles just like the fliers in the *Life* pictures wore, they were strapped in the open cockpit side by side, and the noise of the engine made them deaf. Jake felt the plane lumber along over the rough pasture and then lift into the air, so smooth, and the land fell away; down below people and cars around the rodeo grounds shrunk to Lilliputian size, like in *Gulliver's Travels*. Even the carnival Ferris wheel and loop-the-loop ride looked tiny. Slipstream winds buffeted them as the plane banked and turned, swooped down low and rode up high again. Excited, Jake laughed and yelled as the pilot looped up and over and the world spun around them like crazy. Then it was over, they bounced to earth again and Susie staggered out of the plane, sick-looking, and flopped down on the grass. Jake wanted more.

Although he had never flown since, Jake daydreamed about flight and air races and his heroes Roscoe Turner and Wiley Post, the Texan who was the first ever to solo around the world in a single-engine plane, a Lockheed Vega called the *Winnie Mae*. Jake had put up pictures on his walls of the *Winnie Mae* and Wiley Post in flight togs, a patch over the eye he lost in an oilfield accident, and he remembered how sad he was at the news that Wiley Post had died in a crash, way up in Alaska. That had been in 1935, the same year that Ertie'd been hurt so bad. Later Jake had built a model of the *Winnie Mae* out of balsa and tissue paper. It was powered by a rubber band, but the wings were warped and the model flipped over and crashed.

On the other side of the tent, Mary Ellen's voice was excited. "Lookee thar! Ain' she pretty? An' look at her weddin' dress. Oh, I hope I can have a weddin' dress half that pretty."

Jake grinned mischievously. "Mary Ellen, you ain' never gonna need no weddin' dress, flat-chested as you are."

"Jake Robertson, you shut your filthy mouth."

"Don' pay no nevermind to him," Susie said comfortingly. Then, surprised, she exclaimed, "Gawd, Mary Ellen, lookee thar. Says we can win five thousand dollars."

"Where? Le'me see!"

"In this contest. All we gotta do is finish this here sentence: 'I advise a bride to use Ivory Flakes because . . .' We can do that easy. Jake'll help us. Won'cha, Jake?"

"Shoot, nobody ever wins them things," Jake snorted.

Susie ignored her brother. "Let's do it, Mary Ellen, you're smart, an' we can make it up. If we win, I'm gonna buy me some of them pretty dresses and be a Cosmopolitan Lady. What'll you do, Mary Ellen?"

"Help us get a place to settle, then I'd use the rest to go to college."

"College?" Susie was surprised Mary Ellen was still thinking about that.

"Sure. Be a teacher. Mrs. Carstead, back in high school, she said I'd be a good teacher."

"Oh, Mary Ellen!" Susie sounded impatient now.

"Well, she did!"

"You been sayin' that ever since we left out for California."

Benjy whimpered in his sleep.

"Shut up," Jake hushed at his sisters. "You'll wake Benjy."

"You're makin' more noise than we are," Mary Ellen hissed back.

The storm let up and rain pattered softly on the canvas. Outside the tent Jake could hear his mother and father talking. She was discouraged and Ertie was a little drunk, judging from the belligerent edge in his voice.

Bessie was saying, "Sometimes I wonder how we're goin' to git through the winter."

"We'll get by." Ertie wasn't at all reassuring.

"We gotta get us a place of our own, get settled down somewheres, can't go on livin' out here on the creek banks."

"Woman, what d'ya want from me?" Ertie sounded angry.

"Wasn't blamin' nobody." She was defensive now.

"Hell, a man cain't hardly feed his own family, an' yor talkin' 'bout gettin' a place to settle down?"

"Ertie, ya wan' some coffee?"

"No! I wan' another drink."

Jake heard the crash of glass and guessed his father had finished off the bottle and thrown it away. Lately, it seemed like he was always mad at something.

Bessie was quiet now.

After a bit she tried to change the subject. "Ertie, seein' that school bus stoppin' out yonder every mornin' got me to thinkin' maybe we oughta get the kids back in school."

Jake heard his father get quickly up and his mother anxiously ask, "Ertie? Where ya goin'?"

Worried, Jake pulled on his shoes, rolled off the bed and stepped out of the tent. He saw his father limping off up the creek bank, ignoring the misting rain.

"Ma? Wha's wrong?"

Bessie looked at her son, then reached her arms around him, folding him to her. "Yor pa's mad, but it ain' really at me, or you, none of us. He's hurtin', Jake, hurtin' bad. Ain' nothin' like this ever happened to us before. Oh, we've seen hard times, but we've always pulled through . . ." Her voice trailed off.

The rain had stopped and James Earl was out of the Model A, gathering up dry kindling to build a fire. Bessie patted Jake's shoulder. "Now help yor brother get a fire goin'."

Jake looked at his mother. "Ma, did ya mean it? 'Bout us goin' to school?"

Bessie smiled. "I wisht ya could, I truly do."

"But, Ma, we cain' do it, we gotta work."

"I know it." She sighed and went to the stove. "Maybe when the cotton's done you an' Susie can go back. Wan' some coffee?"

After the first storms passed, there were a couple of days of sunshine and the Robertsons got back into the fields; then the cold, wet tule fogs settled into the valley. They awoke one gray morning and there was no dawn, no sun at all the whole day long, just a wet, dense blanket of smothering fog. They'd never seen anything like it, the whole world had vanished and they were alone in the damp, gray darkness. The familiar cottonwood trees around their camp now were only ghostly skeletons and beyond the bare branches there was nothing; just the dripping, silent emptiness.

Folks in nearby camps had told them about the tule fog, they pronounced it "too-lee" and said the fog would hang around for days, sometimes weeks without ever the sun coming out, said the fog was early this year, which meant they were likely in for a long, hard winter and no, there was no point in moving on because it was foggy like this everywhere in the valley; there was no escape. From Bakersfield clean to Sacramento, some four hundred miles or more, the dank mist rose up out of the tule swamps and the farm fields, chilling a body to the bone, so thick and dripping wet it turned everything soggy, including the cotton. Picking stopped and wouldn't start up again until the lint dried enough to be ginned, that's the way it was and would be through the rest of the harvest.

And their neighbors were right, there was no break in the gloomy fog for a week. They couldn't work and their food supplies were dwindling, day after day they kept a fire going close in next to the kitchen fly and huddled around its warmth or holed up in their tents, under the covers, hungry and depressed. Gradually the weather began to change; the fog lifted a little and by noon a weak silver sun shivered across the sky and was gone by early afternoon, disappearing into the gray half-light. It was three days more before they got back into the fields, and then for only a half day at a time because the cotton was never dry enough to pick before noon. There were so many pickers scrabbling for work, the Robertsons drove to the fields early each morning, hoping to get a head start on the rest; even so, by the time they arrived there already were dozens of jalopies parked all along both sides of the road and swarms of people were waiting for the row boss to say the field was dry enough to start picking. Building little warming fires, they waited hours to get into the fields and then the jobs never lasted long and they were back out on the road hunting for other fields, driving the back roads looking for those cardboard signs nailed to the telephone poles: PICKERS WANTED, with an arrow pointing the way.

Times were getting downright hard. They had some flour, lard and a few potatoes and were eating only two meals a day, fried dough and coffee mostly. Billie Jo was having trouble nursing Li'l Beth. The infant suckled hungrily, but quickly grew cranky and fussed much of the night. She seemed never to get enough nourishment and what she did get ran right through her, squirting out in watery brown dribbles. Alarmed, Bessie decided that Billie Jo's milk had somehow gone bad. They switched Li'l Beth to a formula of canned milk and Karo syrup and that seemed to help for a while, but none of them were eating enough to stay healthy. Benjy and Jake both had snuffling colds and Li'l Beth developed a rasping cough.

By late November several of the families camped along the

creek packed up and pulled out, headed south, they said, for work in the winter vegetables in the Imperial Valley. When would work start down there? Would be late December, maybe January, but the sun was shining down there and at least it was warm. Ertie and Bessie talked about moving too, but the choice was hard, they had less than twenty dollars in the sock. That was maybe enough to buy gas and food while they looked for work around here, finding a job now and then, or it was enough to get them to Imperial, but there'd be no work there for a month or more. How would they get along? They decided it was best to stick it out here, they were bound to find something sooner or later and, sure enough, both Ertie and James Earl did catch on to a ditchdigging job. The farmer only needed two men, and he was paying twenty cents an hour, promising a week's work, maybe more. That first evening they came home with three dollars and twenty cents and Bessie beamed. "Praise the Lord. Ertie, ya know what tomarra is? Thanksgivin'."

Buoyed by the job and a turn for the better in weather, their spirits were up, all but Jake, who was disappointed because there were only two jobs. Then he hit upon an idea, "Pa, whyn't ya lemme go huntin', maybe I can shoot us some rabbit meat for Thanksgivin' supper."

Ertie had been hoarding the last of the .22 shells, but Jake was darn near as good a shot as he was, so he agreed. "Boy, just don' be wastin' no shells, now."

"Won', Pa."

Jake was awake before dawn the next morning. It was still dark in the tent and Benjy was snuggling close next to him, trying to get away from his own, soggy side of the mattress. Smelling the warm urine, Jake swore quietly. Benjy'd wet the bed again. Feeling for his overalls and shoes, Jake rolled out of bed and quickly shivered into his clothes, pulling on the red and black mackinaw he'd ordered out of the Stockman-Farmer catalogue two summers ago. Once a proud wool coat, it was ill-fitting now, frayed and worn thin at the elbows. No matter how he tugged at the sleeves, his wrists still stuck out a country mile. Outside the sky was black and cold, but in the east he could see the first soft gray light of dawn behind the jagged peaks. He slipped into the kitchen tent, found the box he was looking for and rummaged around until he felt the small, heavy carton of .22 shells. He gave it a little shake.

The box was half empty, maybe twenty rounds left. He stuffed the box in his coat pocket and, reaching under his parents' bed, he pulled out a bundle and unwrapped the rifle, levered the chamber open and checked with his fingers to make sure it was clear.

Bessie stirred and rolled over. "You be careful, now."

"Yes'm."

His father lay dead as a log, snoring.

Jake slipped back out into the cold morning air, shivering. Away from camp he loaded the rifle, eased the hammer back down and set the safety. Veering away from the creek and out into the fields, he followed a gully that looked like an old creek bottom, dry and sandy, with lots of brushy cover. The rifle was cradled in the crook of his arm, ready, the coming day smelled clean and fresh; in the new light sparrows and blackbirds flitted about and it was easy to remember similar mornings along Bitter Creek, hearing the call of the white-wing dove, seeing the clumsy flight of the wild turkeys escaping into the bramble of mesquite and sumac and thorny live oak. The sounds, the smells and memories were so strong he almost expected to see Red, his hound, running in and out of the brush, nose down, tail wagging eagerly.

But Red wasn't there.

Jake sank down in the dirt and huddled there in the warmth of his old red and black mackinaw, wanting his dog. But he wasn't ever going to see Red again. They had left the dog in Sweetwater, down at the feed store with Mr. Perkins. Ollie Perkins owned the feed store and the forty acres out on Bitter Creek where they lived, and he was their landlord, although they'd never paid any cash rent. Mr. Perkins had made a deal with them, they raised enough hay and grain on the place to pay the rent and sometimes Ertie and Mr. Perkins went together buying and selling horses and mules. On Saturdays Jake and Susie rode into town with Ertie when he went for supplies and afterward they almost always stopped by the feed store. Mr. Perkins and Ertie were friends, as well as partners, and you could count on them sitting around talking and sipping whiskey for a good while. And, on the way back out to the ranch, Ertie sometimes let them each take a turn steering the car home.

Home. Jake missed the big old house with its wide porches, missed the musty odor of the sitting room, dark and cool in the summer when the shades were drawn and warmed in the winter by the great stone fireplace, but most of all he missed the big kitchen and the warming smells of his mother's cooking. Of an evening, after supper, they'd sit around the table, reading or studying by lanternlight or listening to the radio that sat at the end of the counter by the sink and was hooked up to big Delco batteries in the cupboard below. He missed the *Lone Ranger*, music as sharp as a bugle call, the announcer's voice drumming: "From out of the west come the thundering hoofbeats of the great horse, Silver: The Lone Ranger Rides Again!"

Homesick and forlorn, Jake sat there on the bank, remembering how he and Susie and his best friend Bobby smoked real Camel cigarettes, up in the treehouse. Bobby, who lived a mile down the road, was older and knew more and had done more things, like talking Annie Wells into taking off all her clothes. Jeesus! She'd done it, too! Down at the swimming hole. Annie had come skipping along the creek and seen their clothes hanging on a bush. They didn't know how long she had crouched down there, watching them, but when they spotted her, she'd teased them about being all naked. Jake had been mortified, but Bobby had stood right there, naked as a jaybird, and talked her out of her clothes, saying skinny-dipping was the greatest fun ever. She'd shucked the dress quick enough and, flat-chested, her tiny nipples standing out like beads, started wading into the water, but Bobby told her no, she had to take her drawers off too. At first she wouldn't, but Bobby said skinny-dipping wasn't skinny-dipping 'less you were all naked, and so she had slipped right out of her bloomers and into the water, so quick Jake didn't get much of a look. Later, as they lay warming on a rock, she let them look at hers and she looked at theirs and touched them, laughing at how their cocks grew so hard, but she wouldn't let them touch her, no matter what.

"Aw, Annie, that ain' fair, ya got to touch mine."

"No sir, Jake Robertson, my ma said never let no boys touch me there 'cause I might get a baby."

Later, after she'd grabbed her clothes and had run off, Bobby taught him how good it felt to jack off, not just playing with it like he'd been doing, but really stroking it, faster and faster until POW! like magic, his cock went off. That night at home he'd done it again, and again, and was amazed at the wonderful results. The memories gave Jake an erection and, unbuttoning his fly, he played with himself briefly, then felt exposed and foolish; out in the open like that somebody might see him.

Looking nervously around, he quickly rebuttoned his fly, got back up and started hunting again. The sun wasn't quite up yet, but it was growing light fast as he stalked quietly along, his thoughts still lingering on his memories. A big jackrabbit broke from cover, raced down the bank and across the sandy wash. Surprised, Jake snapped off a shot and missed. The rabbit zigzagged out of sight and Jake swore, "Damn." That would have been a dead rabbit if Ertie'd been shooting. Jake sat back down, thinking now of his father and the hunting trips they'd taken before the horse fell on Ertie.

Jake missed those trips and he missed going to the rodeos and watching his father ride. Those were good times, but they had ended forever in that one awful wreck two years ago. The memory of it was still sharply etched in his brain, like a nightmare: a bucking horse twisting high in the air, hooves kicking viciously out, Ertie firmly in the saddle, grinning, riding wildly, spurring, pulling hard on the buck rein for balance as the crowd cheered; the big sorrel horse high in the air, falling, head and shoulders down into the dirt, rolling, kicking hindquarters coming up and over in a somersault, crushing Ertie underneath. The crowd, stunned into silence, watched as Ertie struggled to get free, but his leg was pinned under the downed horse. Cowboys ran to help him, one grabbing the horse's head while another, an Indian named Smokey Day, pulled out his pocket knife and cut the cinches, then grabbed Ertie's shoulders and pulled him free of the wreck as the horse scrambled to its feet.

The spill crushed Ertie's pelvis and snapped his left leg just below the hip, putting him in the hospital. The accident had a devastating impact on the family's finances, but even with Ertie laid up, they might have made it okay if it hadn't been for the weather. Seemed like it wasn't ever going to rain again, crops dried up and then those blue northers roared in off the high plains, howling winds ripping down through the Cap Rock country, kicking dirt and sand into roiling black clouds so big and thick they turned the noon sky dark as black night. They were in church when the first of those double-big sandstorms hit, filling the air with grit. By the time the preacher started his sermon the sky was black and the high winds blasted the church building, sending shudders through the timbers and rattling the windows. The electric lights dimmed, flared, then winked out and the church was dark. People murmured apprehensively. The preacher fell silent. Out back somewhere there were the sounds of a door banging, then a brutal gust rocked the building hard and the stained glass window behind the altar shattered. Clouds of sand and dust swirled through the church.

"Kneel!" the preacher screamed and sank to his knees. "Kneel before God's wrath. Oh Lord! Forgive us our sins!"

The church doors flew open and the wind shrieked through the hall, people screamed and were up, fleeing. Bessie grabbed at her family, herding them out, and Jake felt a million gritty needles pricking his face as they fled to the car, but James Earl couldn't get it started. Frantic, they scrambled up into the back of a neighbor's truck and rode there, huddled in their coats, hardly able to breathe.

After the storm the lower hayfield looked like a desert, sand was piled against the barn and the outbuildings. They all pitched in to help Bessie in the garden, uncovering the rows of vegetables and watering the surviving plants. They salvaged what they could, and hung on week by week. Drought withered the crops and dried up the creek. There was still water enough in the well to keep the garden green, they had a few chickens and the cow was fresh, so Bessie and the girls sold eggs, cream and butter in town.

Ertie, all the while, was laid up in the hospital, wired and strapped so he couldn't move. There was no insurance, but they had eighteen head of horses and mules on the ranch, not counting Ertie's good saddle horse, Dynamite, or the team of Morgans that he called Baldy and Sox. Those three were not for sale, but the rest had to go, two or three at a time, to pay the hospital and doctor bills and buy what supplies they needed. That fall, for the first time, they all went into the cottonfields to work for wages, all except Ertie, who was still in the hospital. Late in the winter they brought him home lying on a makeshift bed in the back of the neighbor's truck and helped him into a bed Bessie had moved into the front room. When the weather was warm enough, she fixed up a chair and padded bench out on the porch next to the rock chimney so he could hobble out on crutches, prop his leg up and sit in the winter sun, smoking and nursing a whiskey bottle, watching the buyers look over the horses and mules out in the pasture.

Nineteen thirty-six was a hard year, all around. James Earl dropped out of high school and found work down at the gypsum mine near Sweetwater, and he was bringing home cash wages, twenty dollars a week. For a while there it looked like they might make it, then the cow died calving. Jake had never seen his mother so utterly dejected, standing there in the barn all bloody, her sleeves rolled up, a knife still in her hand and the cow and partially born calf lying there in the straw. After the cow died, it seemed like everything else went to hell. First James Earl got laid off, then came the real bad news, on a Sunday afternoon in the early spring of '37.

That Sunday, Ollie Perkins drove out to see them. By this time Ertie was up and around, although he limped and always would. At the sound of Perkins's truck Jake came running out, barefoot, with Red barking excitedly around him. Jake could see Perkins sitting behind the wheel, looking angry, yet sad, as Ertie hobbled out to greet him.

"Get out and come set." Ertie opened the truck door.

Perkins climbed out and walked along beside Ertie, making small talk that Jake couldn't hear much of, but he could tell something wasn't right.

"Ertie." Perkins sat down in a chair on the porch next to his friend. "I got bad news."

Jake sat on the edge of the porch, rubbing Red's ears, listening.

Ertie had propped his bad leg up and was building a cigarette. "You sound like the world's come to an end."

"Damn near has!"

Ertie stopped and looked at Perkins. "What d'ya mean?"

"I don' own this place no more." Perkins's voice was choked up. He cleared his throat. "Ya gotta git off. I don' own it no more."

"What?"

Behind them the screen door creaked open and Bessie came out, wiping her hands on her apron.

"Said ya gotta git off. I don' own the place no more."

"Oh Lord!" Bessie whispered.

"When?" Ertie was puzzled.

"Soon as ya can. They won' give ya more'n a couple weeks, at most."

"They?"

"Amarillo Land and Cattle Company."

"Who's that?"

"Hell, Ertie, I don' know. When the bank went under, they got my mortgages. Bought 'em up I guess. I don' know who they are."

"Goddammit, Ollie, the bank went broke back in nineteen thirty. That's seven years ago. How come ya never said nothin' till now?"

"Didn't seem that important, then." Perkins shrugged apologetically. "Was the same mortgages, I was makin' the payments an' had the equity in my place in town. That's the only thang pullin' me through now, an' I don' know how long that'll last. Hell, Ertie, half the damn farmers in the county owe me for seed and fertilizer, I'm carryin' them on the books but they can't pay me what they owe . . ." His voice trailed off.

That was how they lost their place, suddenly, and with no place to turn. Dammit, he had to get some meat, not sit around here fussing. Checking the rifle's safety, he was up and moving again, serious now, not wanting to return empty-handed. There was a chill morning breeze fresh in his freckled face and within a very few minutes he spotted a wiggle in a clump of brush, maybe twenty yards away. He tensed and brought the rifle up slowly, cocking the hammer, sighting down on a fat cottontail that hopped a few steps, then stopped, nose twitching the wind. Jake squeezed the trigger gently: CRACK.

The rabbit jerked up, kicked and flopped over dead. Excited now, Jake pressed the hunt and within the next half hour bagged another cottontail and a big jack. Satisfied, he started back for camp, walking along an old farm road that followed the creek. Another jackrabbit jumped and ran across an open field. Jake fired quickly, hitting the rabbit as it bounded high, knocking it spinning.

"Good shot, boy."

Surprised by the voice, Jake turned and saw a gaunt old man standing crookedly back in the willows, near the creek. The rheumy-eyed old-timer hadn't shaved for days and a white stubble covered his cadaverous cheeks. His tattered overalls were streaked with soot and dirt, a raggedy shirt covered his bony shoulders and stringy arms. Behind him was a lonely camp in the brush and there beside the camp was an ancient Model T Ford truck with a crude wooden house built over the bed. The truck's hood was off, and there on the ground beside it were greasy black engine parts neatly laid out on a piece of cardboard.

Jake waved and yelled, "Howdy," then ran over and picked up the rabbit. Blood oozed from a tiny hole behind the right ear. Laying the rifle aside, Jake dug out his pocketknife and quickly skinned the carcass, fastened it to the thong and hefted the four skinned rabbits, carrying them out away from him so the dripping blood wouldn't get on his overalls. As he walked back, past the old man's camp, he nodded politely.

"Fine-lookin' mess a rabbit meat ya got thar, boy." The scraggle-toothed old man looked hungrily at the kill. He was seated now on a broken kitchen chair beside a tiny fire, tin coffee cup in hand. There was no sign of food anywhere about the camp, only the coffeepot sitting in the coals. "Wan' a cup a coffee, son?"

Jake shook his head, then impulsively walked over and, untying the thong, laid a rabbit on a box by the fire. "Here, mister, we got more'n we can eat, an' the meat'll just spoil."

Before the old man could say anything, Jake turned and ran home. The sun was fully up now as he came running into camp holding the rabbits up. "Ma! Lookee!"

"Oh, Lord, ain' that grand."

Rabbit stew filled their plates that Thanksgiving supper and the money Ertie and James Earl were earning meant they could buy some more Karo and canned milk for the baby and another sack of flour. Bessie told them to bow their heads while James Earl asked a blessing. That night they went to bed certain things would improve, but they didn't. Ertie and James Earl finished the job the next day and were paid off, then the weather turned bad again. Fog, thicker than before, settled into the valley. Scouting for work each day, they drove along at five or ten miles an hour, windshield wipers banging, straining to see a few feet ahead so they wouldn't run off the road. Even with their headlights on, traffic coming the other way wasn't visible until it was right in front of them and twice they were almost hit by farm trucks. Every time they spotted a mailbox beside the road, they turned in and went up to the farmhouse, asking for work, but no one was hiring, not in this weather. When the weather cleared a little, they hunted rabbits until they ran out of shells for the rifle.

It wasn't long before they were down to one meal a day, the flour was gone and all they had left were a few potatoes. Billie

Jo's own milk had dried up and they were low on both canned milk and the Karo. When the last of that was gone, she stirred sugar in warm water and tried to get her daughter to take that, but the little girl had a barking cough and her nose was so clogged she could hardly suck on the nipple.

Ertie had seen her use the last of the syrup and milk, so he knew they were out, but watching Billie Jo try to feed the baby sugar water frustrated him. "What's that?"

Tears came to Billie Jo's eyes. "Tha's all we got left." Clutching Li'l Beth to her, she fled to the Model A, angrily closing the back flap behind her.

"Ertie, you ought'n said nothin' to her. She's doin' the best she can."

They were all at the supper table. Ertie cupped his hands around a coffee mug for warmth and took a swallow. It tasted awful; the coffee was weak and they were out of canned milk. What little sugar was left was being saved for the baby. Ertie looked at his wife, but said nothing. He wanted whiskey and a smoke, but he didn't have any tobacco or a bottle.

Jake sat diagonally across from his father, spooning up the last of his watery potato soup, uncomfortable because he could sense another fight was coming.

Bessie got up and went to the stove and came back with the coffeepot. As she sat back down, she said, "Ertie, we gotta find work."

"Woman, there ain' no jobs out there, nowhere!"

"But we gotta get somethin' to eat."

Ertie slammed his cup down. "What the hell ya want me to do, beg?"

There was a hushed silence. Everyone looked at Ertie and no one moved. Then James Earl got up, went to the pickup and climbed in the back, not saying anything. The girls edged away from the table and took Benjy to the tent with them, but Jake stayed.

Ertie looked hard at his wife, his jaw muscles working, and when he spoke, it was almost a whisper. "Woman, I'll go to hell before I'll beg."

His father was cornered, Jake sensed that, but didn't know what to do.

Bessie squared away on Ertie. "Nobody's talkin' 'bout beggin', but it's a plain fact, we ain' got no food left."

Ertie sat stark still for maybe thirty seconds, not looking at either his wife or his son, then he exploded. Suddenly jerking to his feet, he scooped up the plank tabletop and thrust it away from him. Jake tumbled out of the way as the coffeepot, soup bowls and spoons spilled all over the ground. Ertie kicked at a sawhorse and pain shot through his leg. Stunned by the hurt, he limped furiously away from camp.

Jake started to follow his father, but Bessie grabbed her son. "Let 'im be."

"But Ma!"

"Boy! I said let 'im be!"

A fast-moving storm thundered in just after dawn and by midmorning the fields were soaked again. Ertie walked through the heavy rain toward a farmhouse, downcast, rivulets of water pouring off the curled brim of his hat. Behind him, James Earl and Jake followed along, bareheaded, each clutching a ragged blanket, trying to shelter themselves from the rain. Ertie went around the house to the back door, climbed the steps and knocked. Inside he could hear heavy footfalls.

The door opened and a man stood there, peering out through the screen door. "Yes?"

"Mister, ya got any work? Cows to milk, stalls to dung out? We can chop weeds and the boys there"—Ertie nodded toward James Earl and Jake huddled under their blankets, trying to keep warm—"they're right smart mechanics, can repair tractors, tune yor pickup."

The farmer pushed the screen door partway open and stood just in out of the rain, looking at them. "Sorry, I've got no work for you boys." He sounded apologetic.

"Mister," James Earl tried to explain. "We gotta find us jobs some'eres 'cause we're plumb out of groceries and I got a baby that's sick."

Ertie stood there awkwardly, not saying anything.

Jake sensed his father's torment. "Come on, Pa, le's get out of here."

"Wait a minute," the farmer called. "I'll get the missus to fix up some food . . ."

Ertie had started to follow Jake, but the farmer's words stopped him and he bristled, "Mister, we don' want no handouts!"

But the farmer, smiling benevolently now, wasn't listening, just kept on talking. " . . . food for you and the baby, help out until you find work. Babies have to eat."

Ertie shook his head angrily and turned away with Jake.

But James Earl couldn't let Li'l Beth go hungry. He stayed and accepted the offer. "Thank ya, mister, we shorely can use something for my little girl."

"Good. Wait right there." The farmer went back inside, shutting the door. The door opened in a few minutes and the farmer shouldered the screen door half open, handing out a bulging sack. "Missus said to tell you that she put something in for everybody, including the little one."

As James Earl took the sack, Ertie and Jake were walking away, but then Ertie turned impulsively and came limping rapidly back toward the farmer, a determined look on his bony face as he unfastened the leather thong tethering his watch to the bib pocket of his overalls. "Here!" The silver watch swung from the thong as Ertie thrust it up to the farmer. "I ain' givin' this to ya, mister. Only havin' ya hold it till we pay off them eats. If ya got work when the rain lets up, we're camped a mile an' a half back across that field, in that grove a trees yonder. If ya don', well then, when we find work, we'll come back and pay ya what we owe."

"Keep your watch, we're glad to help out." The farmer started to go back inside, then paused. "You're camped in those cottonwoods down next to Outside Creek?"

"Yes sir, if that's what ya call it. Right yonder, there." James Earl pointed.

"You folks all ought to move out of there, that creek's apt to flood before long. Rain like this melts the snow up in the mountains, brings those creeks up."

"Thanks again, mister." James Earl hefted the sack up on his shoulder. "An' may the Lord bless ya."

Ertie snorted his disgust, turned away and stormed out the driveway, ashamed and angry. Jake hurried along beside his father, followed by James Earl. They walked along the road for a ways then cut across the muddy fields, traveling in silence until they were more than halfway back to camp.

"Pa?" Jake pulled the wet blanket close around him, trying to find some warmth. He was worried about the farmer's flood warning. "Pa? Ya think we oughta move out?"

Ertie didn't respond.

"We ain' got but a couple gallons of gasoline left in the sedan."

"An' the truck ain' got none at all." James Earl shifted the heavy sack of food to his other shoulder. "We siphoned 'er dry."

Ertie limped on across the field, not saying anything. When they were within site of camp, he stopped short, then turned and headed off at an angle, away from camp.

"Pa, where ya goin'?" Jake's voice was anxious.

"You fellers go on, I'll be 'long directly." Ertie's anger had dissolved into sad emptiness. Wet and cold, his belly grumbling with hunger, he walked toward the swollen creek, feeling helpless. He, Ertie Robertson, couldn't even feed his own family, no matter how hard he tried. God, he wanted a drink, wanted to get drunk.

The sack of food contained a bag of beans, some cornmeal, a slab of bacon, a pound can of coffee, a carton of Quaker oats, several cans of condensed milk and some Karo syrup. That evening the rain let up and they got a roaring campfire going. Bessie cooked up a good, solid supper that filled them up, all but Ertie. He'd come back into camp as they sat down and he'd taken the plate that Bessie dished up, but he couldn't swallow much of it and that evening he sat hunched by the fire, staring into the flames, not saying anything.

After supper Jake and James Earl set up some stick markers on the creekbank to measure how much the water was rising; by morning the sticks were gone, washed away in the muddy torrent that was running bank-full. Hastily, they broke camp and packed up the trailer, leaving the Model A behind. James Earl didn't want to go off without the pickup, but with no gas in the tank and precious little in the sedan, there was no choice. Crowded in the sedan, they headed east for the foothills, where the land was higher. Jake drove, zigzagging south and east into Tulare County, crossing roiling creeks and angry rivers choked with debris that jammed up against bridges. Roads were flooding now and they drove hub-deep through low spots. The low-rising flats and rounding foothills south of Exeter were carpeted by orange groves, dense rows of round, green trees so closely planted they were like giant hedgerows, taller than any house or barn. The highway cut a narrow swath down through the groves, an asphalt lane walled by the high green hedges. Here and there a side lane or cross road opened up and sometimes they saw a farmhouse back in the grove.

Passing by a gas station, Jake glanced at the fuel gauge. Empty. They were in trouble, but there ought to be a place to camp soon, and maybe they'd find work picking oranges. Picking started after Christmas, or so he'd heard. Up ahead through the rain Jake saw barricades across the highway and a police car, lights flashing. A highway patrolman wearing a yellow slicker got out and held up his arm.

Jake let the sedan roll to a stop and cranked down the window, rain splashing in his face. "What's wrong?"

"Bridge's out!"

"We go 'round, 'nother way?"

The cop shook his head. "Nope. Where ya headed?"

"Gotta find a dry place to camp."

The cop laughed. "Kid, there aren't any dry places. Whole damn county's flooded out."

Jake didn't know whether to be mad or not.

"Hey, I didn't mean anything." The cop's voice softened. "Listen, go back about a mile, where that gas station is on the corner, turn east there and go on up over Rocky Hill. There's a county park up that way, some other Okies are camped up there. Leastways you'll be up on high ground."

"Thanks, mister." Jake rolled the window up and made a U-turn, the heavily loaded little trailer splashing right along behind.

He found the turn easy enough and, seeing the station again, Jake looked down at the fuel gauge. "Pa, maybe we ought see if they'd let us trade somethin' for gas."

Ertie shook his head. "Jus' keep goin'."

Jake turned east. The road lifted up through the groves flanking the rounded hill, but there was no sign of a park, only the citrus groves and the hilltop above them. Then, just as he steered through a shallow S-curve, the gas pump sucked the last of the fuel from the tank and the car's engine sputtered and died. Jake managed to coast off on the edge of the road and park in a lane between the orange trees.

They were stranded.

While the women huddled in the car, Ertie and the boys pitched a tent. They all crowded inside, huddling up on the old iron bed or sitting on the saw horses and boxes to keep up out of the mud and water. Bessie fired up the kerosene stove and, with Mary Ellen's help, fried up some cornmeal mush and made coffee. Billie Jo tried to feed Li'l Beth but she had a fever and wouldn't take the bottle. That night Jake, Susie and Mary Ellen took Benjy and curled up in the car, the rest of them huddled in the tent, Bessie and Billie Jo taking turns holding Li'l Beth and sponging off her hot little head. The fever was high now and the baby's cough was a sharp, rasping sound. They had to get her to a doctor, but they were out of gas and didn't know where to turn. The only thing they could do was send somebody back to the service station to get help. It couldn't be more than three or four miles.

The storm blew itself out during the night and, at first light, Ertie set out walking with James Earl. Jake insisted on going along, although he had a runny nose and his cough was worse. Even hurrying as fast as they could, it took nearly thirty minutes to get to the intersection; at that early hour the station was closed and there was no one around. Inside they could see the telephone on the counter, but the doors were locked.

"We could break a winda," James Earl suggested.

"Hey," Jake pointed. "Here comes somebody."

A little Ford coupe wheeled in off the highway, skidding to a stop. A burly, dark-haired youngster in greasy coveralls jumped out. "What the hell you Okies doin'?"

James Earl had taken a step toward the car, but stopped. "We got a sick child, need to call a doctor, get some help."

The young fellow was maybe twenty or twenty-five, bull-necked and darkly handsome, but mean-looking. "Don' gimme that crap, you were trying to break in. Got a mind to call the cops."

Ertie's fists were doubled and he started for the young man, who retreated to the car and pulled out a heavy tire iron. "Get the hell out of here, you dirty bastards."

James Earl grabbed his father's arm. "Pa, come on, we gotta git help!"

Realizing his son was right, Ertie backed off and they left, half walking, half running. Cars and trucks whizzed past them, the drivers ignoring their distress signals. Finally, at the next intersection, they decided to split up, doubling their chances of finding a farmhouse. James Earl headed west, Ertie and Jake north. As much as his hip was paining him, Ertie set a fast pace and they were both panting for air when Jake spotted smoke rising from the chimney of a two-story house atop a low hill, far back in a grove. The sight quickened them and they hurried up the lane, Jake trotting to keep up with his father's lurching gait. Up by the house several dogs barked and two of them, big, shaggy German shepherds, charged down the drive, fangs bared.

Jake froze, then retreated, but his father charged on, yelling at the dogs, "Haaaagh!" A guttural roar, more animal than human, "Haaagh!"

Surprised, the dogs skidded to a stop, barking furiously.

Ertie let out another roar and lunged at the dogs. "Haaaaagh! Git! You sons-a-bitches!"

Intimidated, the dogs circled, hackles raised, snarling viciously, yet wary of this man-creature who was ready to attack them.

A farmer came out on the porch, shotgun cradled on one arm. He yelled at the dogs, "Bo! Dan! Get back here."

The dogs instantly obeyed, grudgingly going up the steps to the farmer, looking back, still bristling.

"Much obliged, mister." Ertie was panting for breath. "We need some help, bad."

"It's a wonder those dogs didn't tear into you." The man stood there belligerently. "What d'ya want?"

"Can ya call a doctor? We got a li'l girl that's awful bad sick"— Ertie bent down, hands on his knees, trying to catch his breath— "an' we ain' got no gas to go for help, ner medicine for 'er."

"Where's she?"

"Near five miles back over yonder. Had to camp over thar, in a grove yest'day, when we run out of gas. Mister, please help us."

"How do I know you're not trying to pull something? Doctor's in town. Why don't you go there?"

Jake bristled. "Mister, he done tol' ya, the car's outa gas!"

Ertie put a hand on Jake, silencing him. "Mister, help us get her to a hospital, or leastways call us a doctor."

"Wait here." The man turned and went inside. The dogs stayed on the porch, on guard. In a few minutes the farmer came out, still holding the shotgun. "I called the sheriff an' they said they'd send a county nurse out to check on the baby."

"Say how long it'd take?"

"Soon as they can." The man waved the shotgun. "Go on, get on out of here!"

They turned and left, Ertie limping steadily along beside his son. By the time they got back to camp there was a battered and rusty '29 Buick touring car parked near the tent. It had California plates and there was a big man in overalls standing beside it. He looked to be in his sixties, with an open, friendly face. Bessie and Billie Jo came out of the tent with Li'l Beth bundled up and started getting into the backseat of the old touring car.

"Ma!" Jake yelled, running ahead.

Bessie looked up and relief flooded her face. "Oh, there ya are. Mr. and Mrs. Mimms here's helpin' us. They says ain' no doctors'll come out here so Mr. Mimms's goin' ta drive us to the county hospital, says tha's the onlyest place to take 'er. Mrs. Mimms, she's gonna stay an' help Mary Ellen look after Benjy, fix you all some supper."

Bessie climbed in the back with Billie Jo and the infant. James Earl got up front with Mr. Mimms and they drove off. That was around noon. While they were gone, Ertie and Jake rigged up the rain fly and Mrs. Mimms helped them try to make some order out of the hasty camp, all the while chatting with them, telling them she and her husband lived just to the west a ways, in a labor camp, had a cabin there. They were orange pickers, came out from Arkansas nearly six years ago, but they still remembered how hard it was that first year, so they were glad to help out when James Earl came around.

It was sometime after ten that night when the Mimmses' Buick pulled in off the road, engine clattering loudly. Jake was in the tent when he heard the car drive up and a door bang. He ran out. In the pale moonlight he could see Mr. Mimms standing, holding the car door open. Bessie and Billie Jo were still huddled together in the dark backseat, crying. On the other side, James Earl sat halfway out of the car, hunched over, hands on his head, not moving. No one said anything, but even in the dark, Jake sensed something was awful wrong and he suddenly felt dreadful. Slowly his mother pulled herself out of the car, then turned and helped Billie

Jo out, but neither was carrying Li'l Beth. Jake looked frantically in the backseat, then beside James Earl, but the baby wasn't there!

When no one else said anything, Mr. Mimms explained to Ertie, speaking softly, "She's dead. Doctor said it was diphtheria."

Bessie, tears streaming down her face, looked up to her husband. "She couldn't breathe. Doctors even cut a tiny hole in her throat to let air in, but they said it was too late. If only—" and the words had stopped. Susie and Mary Ellen were there, clutching their mother and each other, crying.

Stunned, Jake stood still for an instant, then turned and ran off into the orange grove, fleeing the awful truth. He ran, twisting and darting through the trees, ran until he was exhausted, then collapsed against the tin side of a pump shed, sobbing.

An hour later, Bessie found him huddled there in the dark, shivering cold. She'd brought his mackinaw and, wrapping it around him, she pulled him to his feet. "Boy, come on back to camp."

Jake looked at his mother. "Ma?" He was clinging to her now, sobbing. "Why, Ma? Why'd God let her die?"

"Honey, I don' know why God took our li'l girl." Bessie pulled him close.

"Ma, they killed 'er, them damn people let 'er die." Jake pushed away, raging. "God damn them!"

"Stop it! Right now! I won' have you blaspheming." She wouldn't let him go. "Boy, listen to me!" She shook him gently, firmly. "We can't ever let them git us down. No matter what they do, we gotta be strong, gotta keep goin'! Hear me? If we're ever gonna get out of this, we gotta get us a place of our own, outa the wet, have a dry roof over us and wood floors and a good stove to keep us warm."

The county buried Li'l Beth in a weedy corner of potter's field and the welfare gave them a tank of gas to get out of the county. Before they headed south, James Earl carved Li'l Beth's name on a wooden cross and, as the family watched tearfully, he and Billie Jo placed it on their daughter's grave.

5

Up before dawn, Titus Wardlow drove rapidly out Dairy Avenue in the early morning light, only half listening to the chatter on the pickup's radio: "Good morning people! Welcome to another hot summer day in the San Joaquin Valley. It's five-thirty on this Tuesday, August sixteenth, nineteen hundred and thirty-eight and this is KMJ radio, five-eighty on your dial . . ."

Wardlow's thoughts were on the harvest, and the weather. It had turned so hot the damn peaches were going soft before his crews could get 'em picked.

". . . Yesterday's record high was a whopping hundred eleven and right now it's a warming ninety-two degrees in beautiful downtown Fresno . . ."

From Jeff City to El Adobe, it was twenty-one miles, forty-two round trip, and he made the drive from town to the ranch and back a couple of times a day. In the summer his routine seldom varied: on the ranch early, checking the crops and laying out the day's work, then a couple of hours on the phone haggling with Eastern fruit brokers over the day's prices. Every day there were problems, a broken conveyor line, a compressor motor on the fritz, and there was always business to tend to in town.

Arriving at the ranch, Wardlow sped past the store and packing shed, kicking up a roostertail of dust. Back in the labor camp, gangs of workers were climbing up into the crew trucks. Wardlow stopped near the trucks and climbed out, slamming the pickup door. As usual, he was dressed in suntans and his felt hat, his shirt pockets stuffed with notes and cigars. Scowling, he strode directly over to where his three field foremen were standing. "Yesterday the graders in the shed were throwing out too goddamn much bruised fruit. Your checkers are standing around out there with their thumbs up their asses, letting that shit get by." Wardlow stared hard at them. "Tell those bastards that if any picker brings in any bruised fruit in the lug, any at all, they're to throw it all out."

Rogers, the lead foreman, looked skeptical. "Without paying them for it?"

"You're goddamn right!" Wardlow stabbed a finger toward them. "That way they won't be so quick to bruise the fruit."

That was a harsh order. They were already pushing the crews hard, setting higher picking quotas and firing the older, slower workers. Jethro Hammer, the big Okie, protested. "Mr. Wardlow, them pickers cain' he'p but git a bad peach or two in a box, fast as we're pushin' 'em."

"This isn't a goddamn debate," Wardlow growled. "Check the fucking fruit, or I'll get somebody who can!"

Back in the office, it was nearly nine by the time he got off the phone. The markets had gone soft, like the fruit, but he sold the day's pack. Rocking back in his chair, Wardlow studied the production charts on the wall, calculating how much more fruit he could afford to pick; if the price didn't drop any further, he'd be okay for a while yet. That decided, he pulled out the Devil's Den file and leafed through it. He needed cash up front, and fast. To raise it he'd have to mortgage the house and the airplane, borrow what he could on life insurance. Titus reached for the phone and called his wife. "Barbara?"

"Yes." Her voice was cool and precise.

"Don't forget, we're meeting Tom Barkham at the bank at ten." He had to have her signature on the loan papers.

"I'll be there."

He hung up, wondering how his wife was taking this. The big house in town had been her idea. Before they were married, he'd lived in a rundown place that came with his first land. In those days he ate with the crews in the mess hall and spent most of the day working beside his men, driving them hard. It wasn't terribly important to him where he slept, but Barbara refused to live in the old house. She had grown up in the Braddock hacienda—a century-old adobe, long and low with wide, cool verandas, land-scaped courtyards, and patios shaded by aristocratic oaks—and she'd gone to the University of Southern California. She was a Kappa Alpha Theta, not a peasant's wife, and she wanted a big, showy place in town, on the golf course. Wardlow had told her a big house was out of the question and, after the wedding, they'd moved into a small house he had rented on South I Street. They lived there for six years, there they had two children, a boy they named George and a girl, Carolyn, who had long, dark hair and looked like her beautiful mother. Barbara cooked and kept house, not because she wanted to but because Titus told her there was no money for cooks or housekeepers while he was building El Adobe.

Wardlow sat at his desk, remembering the arguments they'd had. She didn't know anything about business, didn't want to, but social status was important to her. She was attracted to him be-cause he was aggressive and ambitious, she'd made that clear enough, and he'd been flattered. He was attracted by her beauty, tall and regal, and he wasn't unaware of her desire to reign over Jefferson County's social scene. She was a Braddock, after all; like her mother, she wanted position and power and was used to get-ting what she wanted. When he told her they couldn't afford to hire help, she quietly stormed back, "That's not true, we don't have to live this way. I've got money and land." The land in ques-tion was hers, an oak-shaded acre on the fourteenth fairway that her father had given her while he was still alive, but her inheri-tance from the ranch was tied up in litigation. When Titus pointed this out, she just stamped her feet, angry and beautiful. "But I'll get the money, our lawyers said so. After all it was my father who held the land company together all those years. Uncle Homer has no legitimate claim to the ranch."

"Don't bet on it. That old son of a bitch's no one to fuck with." She'd been furious with him, but rather than arguing the matter further, she coldly asked him not to be so vulgar and left the room.

Vulgar or not, his assessment of her Uncle Homer had proven accurate. Homer Braddock was a conniving, pernicious old pirate who lived on San Francisco's Nob Hill. After her father's death, Clint had blocked Homer's attempt to take over the land com-pany. When Clint died in the airplane crash, Homer Braddock had again laid claim to the company and, after a legal fight that lasted three years, a settlement was reached. The ranch was sold to Coco Oil in 1933. Barbara's share of the settlement came to just under one hundred thousand dollars. That was little enough, but with the loss of Braddock Land and Cattle, the family also lost its position and power. Barbara was stung by the loss and she was determined to reestablish her social status, this time as mistress of El Adobe. To do that she needed a base of power, a grand home on Border Links Drive.

El Adobe was a growing, prospering farm and Wardlow's reputation as a comer was firmly established; even so, he was reluctant to divert money from the ranch. Barbara was charming, and persistent. Finally he had agreed to let her build them a new home, with her money; all he asked was that it be larger and more elegant than Merrimack. She happily agreed. A house to rival a Southern plantation manor would do nicely in Jeff City. She hired an architect and sent him to Georgia to develop the plans. Then she built a two-story mansion with graceful columns and upstairs galleries opening off the bedrooms and sitting rooms. The house, painted pale yellow and trimmed in white, was set back on a broad lawn with a sweeping driveway that curved through a carriage-way and back to a three-car garage. In the back there were more expanses of lawn, a swimming pool and a large cabana for Barbara's summer parties. Ironically, the richly furnished, elegantly decorated house was proving to be a crucial asset, the linchpin of his effort to put the Devil's Den deal together. Since they owned the house debt-free, he was putting it up as collateral—that, the airplane and his life insurance. With what the bank would loan, he could put the deal together. Winning the Bendix would add another $17,000 to the pot. That would put him in good shape. Wardlow pulled a cigar out, unwrapped it and bit off the end. Lighting up, he puffed blue clouds and leaned back in the chair, thinking about land levelers and well-drilling rigs.

The phone rang. He grabbed the receiver. "Yeah?"

"Wardlow?" It was Axelrod, calling from Bakersfield. "The Spartan's ready."

"It's about time." Wardlow tried to sound impatient, but he couldn't hide his pleasure. Axelrod was Roxie's crew chief and she'd talked the cantankerous mechanic into putting the bigger engine in the Spartan. A paunchy little man with a wild shock of gray hair and a day's growth of beard, Axelrod was an irascible genius who never stayed long on any airfield, but was seldom out of work because of his skills with racing machines. Arthritis had so crippled him he moved awkwardly around the hangar, crabbing along, swearing at anything and anyone that got in his way. Somewhere in his crooked past, he had met a stranded wing walker who had lost her nerve; they married, had two sons, Skip and Jimbo, and lived like gypsies in an old trailer house pulled behind a truck loaded with his tools. Axelrod got along with almost no one, but he had taken a liking to Roxie. Because of her he had agreed to work on the Spartan. Wardlow, anxious to test the new engine, said, "I'll be down Saturday."

"Whenever your nibs is ready," Axelrod grouched. "Hold on a minute, Roxie wants to talk to you."

"Hi! Am I going to see you Saturday?"

"Sure, if you want to." Wardlow was surprised. They hadn't been together for weeks now, not since he told her he was flying the Bendix without her. At first she hadn't understood and he'd tried to explain why he was flying alone. "Goddammit, Roxie, I can't afford any complications!"

"What complications?" she had snapped back.

"You and me. People'd ask questions." Hell, if they won their pictures would be all over the papers and it would be those bastards at America First National who'd be asking the questions. Any complication, any at all, they might back out, and he wouldn't risk that, not for some cunt. Not even her. He had tried to distract her. "What about the Thompson?"

"What about it?"

"The qualifying heats are on Saturday, the same day as the Bendix. You can't fly both."

"They let Roscoe Turner fly both races, don't they?"

That was true enough. The Thompson race wasn't until Monday, so they let Turner fly his qualifying laps early Sunday morning, but that was beside the point. He was a man, the nation's top racer. "Look, you were only going along for the ride, anyway."

"Like hell! I was going to fly copilot, help you win it."

"Roxie, goddammit, I—"

"Fuck you, hot shot! I can fly circles around you." She had flipped a finger in his face and walked away.

That was six weeks ago and he hadn't seen her since. Now she was on the phone, sounding happy and excited. "Titus, I'm entered in the Bendix."

"What?"

"I'm going to beat your ass, you bastard." She said it happily, defiantly.

"In what?"

"The Red Ryder."

"You're nuts," he barked. The Ryder was a powerful little ship, barely eighteen feet, wingtip to wingtip, built for high-speed closed-course races around pylons, not for long distances. "Hell, it hasn't got the range."

"Hey listen, hot shot," she laughed, "Ax's adding a thirty-five-gallon tank behind the cockpit. That'll give me range enough to make it with only one refueling stop."

"But that'll make the ship tail-heavy."

"Ax's got that all figured out."

Wardlow couldn't believe it. Not only was she the first woman to enter the Thompson, now she was racing the Ryder cross-country. "Put Axelrod back on."

"Sure," she laughed again. "See you Saturday."

Axelrod came on the phone. "Yeah?"

"Goddammit, Ax, that ship'll never get off the ground."

"Hey, son of a bitch, don't yell at me. I had her talked out of flying the Bendix, then you came along."

"What d'ya mean?"

"Shit, you don't think it's your ugly fucking kisser she's after, do you?" Axelrod snorted what amounted to a laugh, then added, "She was badgering the hell out of me to let her fly the Ryder in both races, but I told her it wouldn't work, had her convinced she would be crazy to fly the Ryder to Cleveland and she'd given up the idea. Then you come along and offered to let her race with you. That's all she wanted, lover boy, just a chance to fly against Turner across the country and then beat him in the Thompson too."

"Offered! Christ, it was her idea, not mine!" Wardlow was angry now, remembering how Roxie had climbed up on the Spartan's wing and talked her way into flying with him. He yelled back at Ax, "She'll never get that tail-heavy little son of a bitch off the ground!"

"Like hell, we've rigged up adjustable horizontal stabilizers that'll lift her tail up a lot quicker."

"She can change the angle of the Ryder's stabilizers?" It was a revolutionary idea.

"Yeah. She'll crank them into tail-up trim for takeoff, then level 'em in flight."

"Will it work?"

"Ought to."

Ought to? Wardlow hung up, the words turning over in his mind. Ought to! Well hell, that was their problem. He put his old felt hat on, tugged it down and went out again, headed for town, mulling over the conversation as he drove. She'd wanted the Spartan, that's why she'd come on to him, yet she was asking to see him again. Somewhere in the back of his mind a warning bell sounded; he, Titus Wardlow, was going soft on a fucking cunt. A jackrabbit darted frantically in front of the truck and Wardlow braked instinctively, his thoughts jolted back to the road. He stuck a fresh cigar in his mouth and lit it, puffing hard, determined to get his mind off that cunt and keep it on business.

Barbara Wardlow stood before the mirror in the front entryway, tucking a dark curl in place under her chic new straw hat. It was a skimmer, cocked at a perky angle and banded with a red ribbon tied in a big bow. The ribbon matched her summer dress, a simple but expensive frock that swirled coolly about her as she turned, checking the seams of her stockings. Barbara played tennis and swam almost every day, keeping her full-breasted figure in admirable shape. She smoothed the dress over her hips, then, satisfied, she opened the front door and stepped out into the heat.

Carlos had brought the car around and was standing by the door, waiting to help her.

"Thank you, Carlos." She gracefully slipped behind the wheel and switched the ignition on as the gardener closed the door of the new yellow Buick convertible. With its top down, she drove out of the driveway, enjoying the car, even in this heat. The convertible was hers, big enough to be impressive, yet sporty. Unlike Titus's pickup, which was always muddy and cluttered, the Buick was waxed and it sparkled. Out of the driveway, Barbara turned right, circling around Border Links to Main Street. It was a bit

longer drive this way, but she enjoyed the sight of the big homes
and the neat golf links and stately oaks. And she wanted time to
think.

Signing the loan papers worried her. The house was her base
of power, her fortress. Titus had assured her the risks were small,
but she didn't believe that, not for a minute. Titus Wardlow didn't
take small risks. He was a hard, blunt man, quick to decision, with
no time for social graces. Although he wasn't handsome, she had
been attracted to him because he was an ambitious, even ruthless
man who was quickly acquiring wealth and power, and that excited her; he took what he wanted and he had wanted her. Oh,
maybe not at first, but he hadn't been hard to seduce. He took
her, quickly, violently, and at first that had been flattering, even
exciting. He approached courtship and marriage like everything
else he did, in a hurry. At first he had been attentive enough and
had even put up with her efforts to smooth off some of his rough
edges. She laughed, remembering the first time she'd gotten him
into a tuxedo. It had been their first Las Hadas Madrinas Guild
dance, the annual Christmas Ball. The guild supported the Children's Wing at St. Gertrude's Hospital in Fresno, and the dance,
held in the Hotel Californian's Grand Ballroom, was the biggest
social event of the year in the valley. Everyone was to be there
and it had never occurred to her that Titus wouldn't enjoy the
function as much as she did. Reluctantly, he'd worn the tux, and,
for a man who was so aggressive and self-confident in everything
else, he was surprisingly uncomfortable in the formal surround-
ings of the dinner dance. Before dinner, he'd consumed a half
dozen whiskeys and then, after they'd eaten and danced twice, he
went off in the corner with several other growers, to talk politics
and farming. There he was relaxed, his tie undone, Scotch in hand,
cigar in his mouth.

After their marriage he had less and less time for her and, in
the years that followed, for the children. That wasn't too surprising—her own father had been much like that. She enjoyed raising
children, making sure they got the proper education and social
contacts. Carolyn was turning into a beauty and already she was
the most popular girl in her class. Besides the children, church,
and the house, there was Las Hadas Madrinas. Barbara enjoyed
the guild work. It was an important charity, and, through the
social contacts in the guild, she was also helping to build El

Adobe and the Wardlow influence. Theirs was new money, she was well aware of that, but with her background and upbringing as a Braddock, she could overcome that drawback.

Barbara pulled up to the stop sign and turned east on Main, thinking about the guild's May Festival that had been held in Jeff City, in the Wardlow cabana, a gathering of wealthy and powerful people from as far away as Bakersfield and Madera. The affair attracted the valley's congressmen and state representatives from Sacramento. Even the governor and his wife had put in an appearance this past spring, and, through her sorority contacts at USC, she had managed to have a sprinkling of movie people from Hollywood to brighten up the affair. She had worked hard to create an environment that helped build El Adobe and now Titus was risking it all. That frightened her. But if he won the gamble, they would be on top. That thought was thrilling. She pushed her fears aside; Titus Wardlow was a winner, that's why she had picked him.

Main Street was a broad east-west thoroughfare that cut through the town. Barbara drove quickly along the tree-shaded street past rows of small, neat homes and well-tended yards. Up ahead, the clock in the tower of the graceful old granite courthouse showed it was nine twenty. Good. She had a couple of errands to run before meeting Titus at the bank. Past the courthouse, she stopped for the red light at Highway 99, waited for a big Rio truck to growl through the intersection, then stepped on the gas, crossing the highway, bouncing over the railroad tracks into the center of town.

A few early shoppers were bustling along the sidewalks. Up the street, Barbara saw Hirum Swinson out in front of his hardware store briskly cranking down the canvas awning that shaded the storefront and sidewalk. She pulled to the curb and parked.

"Morning, Barbara." The shopkeeper, a stocky little man with a cheerful face, came over to the car. "Going to be a hot one today."

"Morning, Hirum." She let him open the door for her. "I'd like to look at one of those new Wedgwood stoves."

"Deluxe model?" He led the way into the cavernous building. It was surprisingly cool inside. Their footsteps clattered along the hardwood floors as they passed between the display racks, heading for the refrigerators, washing machines and stoves. Hirum stopped before a gleaming new Wedgwood, praising its features. Barbara already had her mind made up, but she let him go on, enjoying the sales talk. Finally, she asked, "How much is it?"

"They're marked down to one twenty-seven."

She gave the stove a slow walkaround. "I'll give you one twenty, installed." Barbara enjoyed bargaining.

The shopkeeper shook his head reprovingly, then grinned. "Okay, but only if it's cash."

They struck a deal and Barbara left, feeling a bit victorious.

The clock in the courthouse tower had just tolled ten as she walked into the bank. There were a couple of early customers at the tellers' cages and in back, through the glass door, she could see Titus standing in his rough work clothes talking with Tom Barkham. The banker, standing a head taller than her husband, was wearing a dark blue suit and neat little bow tie.

Barkham saw her and came quickly to the glass door. "Come in, Barbara. Come in."

Barkham escorted her into his office. "We've got the papers all ready."

Titus stood a little to the side, watching as Barkham laid the papers out, explaining each one, pointing to where she should sign. The whole transaction took no more than fifteen minutes. After-ward they chatted for a moment with Barkham and then left to-gether. Outside, Titus walked his wife to her car, nodding yes when she asked if he'd be home for dinner.

Titus still had to pick up some parts for one of the trucks, but he hadn't had his morning coffee yet, so he drove on down to the Dixie Cup Cafe on the east end of Main and parked next to several other mud-spattered pickups. Inside, a couple of tractor salesmen were sitting at the counter and a half dozen farmers were hunched around a big corner table, up near the front window, clutching coffee mugs in their callused hands and talking.

"Mornin', Titus." Several voices greeted him as he came in the door. The farmers scooted around to make room for him and he dragged up another chair.

Wardlow laid his cigar in an ashtray as the waitress brought his steaming mug of coffee and poured refills all around. Old and young, they were a rough-hewn bunch with dirt and axle-grease stains on their gnarled hands, men used to hard work outdoors.

Red Barnes, a handsome fellow with carrot-gold hair, resumed the conversation. "You guys should have seen that Burl Mulkey ride in the Salinas rodeo, spurred that bronc till the fur flew."

"How'd you do, Red?"

"Roped my second calf in thirteen flat, won a third."

"Hey, Titus, your two kids swimming in the valley finals this weekend?" Angelo Monopoli asked.

Damn! He'd forgotten the swim meet. Georgie was entered in the twenty-five free and Carolyn, who was the better swimmer, was in the backstroke and the medley relay. "Yeah, they're swimming."

"You going to be there?"

"I've got to go to Bakersfield to test-fly the Spartan."

"You really going to race that airplane?"

"You bet." He took a sip of coffee, his thoughts on the Spartan. Well, he could watch the kids swim in the preliminary heats Saturday and drive down to Bakersfield that night. Carolyn might qualify and that'd make Barbara happy, but there was no way Georgie would place, that boy couldn't do anything right.

"Ain't it dangerous?"

Wardlow chuckled. "Darren, the Bendix isn't like racing those little planes around the pylons. This is cross-country, like flying from here to L.A. only I'll have a clock on me, like Red there roping calves."

"What's the top prize?" George Yates asked.

"Seventeen grand."

Yates, who was young and impressionable, whistled his appreciation. A quiet boy who had been called home from college when his father died suddenly, he was the youngest farmer at the table.

"Hey, Titus, how's your cotton looking?" Huck Hagopian, a dark little man with deepset, worried eyes, wanted to talk farming, not airplanes.

"Two bales." Wardlow said it confidently. Where others grew maybe a bale and a half an acre, he could make two. That was his edge. He asked Hagopian, "You make out on your plums?"

"Did okay. It's the raisins that've got me worried."

"Me too." Monopoli nodded in agreement. "There's still a thirty-five-thousand-ton carry-over from last year and that damn Henry Wallace sits back there in Washington telling us the ag department will give us seven fifty a ton. Hell, he can shove 'em up his ass for that price."

Wardlow's face wrinkled in a grin. "Angelo, aren't you the big Democrat who voted for Roosevelt, told us how much he was going to help the farmers."

"Titus, it's not funny, goddammit." Monopoli lit a cigarette and shook the match out.

"Hell, Angelo," Red Barnes cut in, "if you want to hear about government fuckups, listen to this. I figure it costs me nearly ten cents a pound to grow and pick my cotton but Roosevelt's set the loan price at eight cents. Then the fucking politicians and those goddamned unions want us to pay our help more."

"Way I hear it, the CIO's in on it this time," Hagopian said.

"He's right." Wardlow nodded. "From what we hear, the CIO's really pushing Olson for governor. As long as we're talking about this, I'd better let you know the association's called a meeting next week. Tuesday night. And I want every damned farmer in the county there, at the Eagles Hall."

"What's up?"

"Association's sending down a labor lawyer from San Francisco and he'll have a couple of growers from Salinas with him." Wardlow was the president of the Jefferson County Associated Farmers and spoke for all of them at the state meetings. He was also responsible for the association's antiunion efforts here in the county. "They're going to talk about how they whipped that lettuce strike last year, give us some ideas in case there's trouble here. The unions and that Upton Sinclair crowd of Communists are really pushing the liberal Democrats in this election and if they win we'll all be in trouble."

"Titus, you figure Olson'll win the primary?"

The question was on all of their minds. Before Wardlow could answer Barnes pointed out the window. "Hey, speaking of Democrats, look who's over there in front of the dime store."

Across the street Congressman Alf Young was shaking hands and passing out campaign cards. Standing well over six feet, he was a coarse, awkward man in a wilted Palm Beach suit and a Panama hat, a rawboned country mule in city-slicker harness who had served two terms on the county board of supervisors before going off to Washington.

They turned and watched Young.

"Hear he's running scared."

"Yeah, and for good reason. Primary's only a couple of weeks off."

When the congressman had shaken all of the hands he could find in front of Woolworth's, he crossed the street, heading for the cafe.

"Christ, here he comes."

Young barged through the door, all smiles and noise, his loud voice braying, "Hey there boys! Good to see you!" He came directly over to their table. "Scoot over and make room for a tired politician. I haven't even had my morning coffee yet."

Red Barnes gave a big wink behind Young's back and asked, "Alf, is it true you're supporting Olson for governor?"

The congressman's long, bony face contorted in pain. "Hell no! Not by a long ways." Alf Young loved the sound of his own voice and he wasn't shy. "Boys, there's no way I'd turn my party over to that half-assed socialist and his gang of pinkos. I'm a good Democrat, have been all my life. I admit, our party's slipped a long ways, but you listen to me! We've got some good ol' boys running in the primaries that can defeat him and that Commie crowd."

"Alf, is it true Olson would free Tom Mooney?"

"That's what he's promising." Young sat down next to Wardlow. "Says his first act as governor will be to give Mooney a full pardon."

George Yates was looking from one speaker to the next, puzzled.

Monopoli hunched forward importantly. "You hear that Mooney's even campaigning for Olson? Right from his cell in San Quentin? Mailing out flyers saying 'Free Tom Mooney, Vote for Olson.'"

"Damn! That ain't right!" Tiny slammed his fist down on the table, rattling cups and sending spoons flying.

Everyone was talking at once now.

"Proves one thing, though, Olson's got the Communists working for him."

"Hell, yes, he's even got Harry Bridges on his side."

"Who's Tom Mooney?" Yates asked. The question stopped the conversation. The young farmer, puzzled and embarrassed, asked again, "Who's Tom Mooney?"

"Hey," Alf Young laughed, "you fellows forget, young George

here wasn't even out of knee pants when Mooney was sent up for life." Young turned to Yates. "It was before the war, during a strike against the electric company. Mooney and a bunch of those union anarchists dynamited four of those big towers that carry power lines into San Francisco, then they set off a bomb during a parade down on Market Street."

"Killed ten people," Hagopian butted in. "Hurt a bunch more. Judge should have hung the whole bunch, but he let three of 'em off scot-free. Gave Mooney life."

"Why'd anyone want to let him out?"

"Olson's a Communist, and we can prove it," Congressman Young said, regaining control of the conversation. He lowered his voice. "He's been working with the CIO and the Workers Alliance, that's a known fact."

Young looked around knowingly. "I shouldn't be saying anything yet, but the House Un-American Activities Committee has finally got the goods on Olson and the others, they're all implicated. Martin Dies, the chairman, has a witness who saw them at party meetings."

Tiny pounded the table again, demanding, "Why the hell hasn't Dies said something?"

"He will. Soon. That's all I can say, for now. This is secret stuff, boys, so don't go saying anything. Okay?" He gave them a conspiratorial wink and rose from the table. "Well, I got to be getting down the street. Don't forget to vote on August thirty. If Olson doesn't win the primary, he can't run in November against Merrium. Boys, keep that thought in mind."

Saturday night Wardlow was late. Roxanne had already eaten, but she poured him a drink and then went off to the kitchen to fix him a sandwich. He sprawled on the sofa in front of a warming fire, his boots off, sipping the Scotch. The sofa, like the room itself, was huge, a long, curved length of cushions and pillows so soft they nearly engulfed him. High over the mantel on the stone fireplace the mounted head of a huge polar bear snarled furiously down at him. On either side of the fireplace other trophy heads were mounted on the walls. As Roxie came in with his tray, Wardlow raised his glass and saluted the bear. "He's quite a hunter, that husband of yours."

"That's my cheetah over there." She set the tray on the coffee table, irritated by his assumption that Bart was the hunter. "And see the lioness? I dropped her as she was charging Bart. She'd a had him, too. He'd just killed the big lion there and hadn't re-loaded." There was no mistaking the emphasis on her husband's mistake.

Except for the flickering firelight, the room was dark, but she could see that Wardlow was surprised. Good. He had better learn she wasn't just another trophy pussy to hang up on his wall. She sat down, looking directly at him, eyes snapping. "Anybody can shoot, all you do is aim and pull the trigger."

Wardlow took a bite of his sandwich and washed it down with Scotch.

"When are you going to Burbank?" Her voice was neutral now.

"Not until Friday." The race was on Saturday of the Labor Day weekend, but he had to be in San Francisco on Thursday to sign the railroad lease papers. "I've got some business up in the city. How about you?"

"Wednesday, I guess. Ax wants to get set up." She hadn't re-laxed at all and was sitting stiffly on the edge of the couch. "Going to see the railroad people?"

He nodded. Small talk, that's all it was, but he was too irritated to relax. Why was she so damn testy? Taking everything wrong? More small talk: "The Ryder ready?" The Ryder was ready, and he knew it. Axelrod had talked about how they'd coaxed every last bit of speed out of that little ship. Maybe they were trying too hard; hangar talk had it that she'd pushed the engine so hard that it had blown up at the air races in Miami and she'd been lucky to get down alive. He was curious. "What happened in Miami?"

"What do you mean?"

"I mean, what happened at the race in Miami?"

"I got down okay, didn't I?"

"Back off," Wardlow growled and gulped the last of his Scotch, handing the glass to her. "I just wondered what happened. That's all."

"Okay." She shrugged and took his glass, got up and went to the sideboard for a refill, explaining, "I went to full power and took Turner on the straight, smoked right by the son of a bitch, and I had the race won, only a lap to go, but the engine started missing, like it's done before when it's wide open." She handed him the drink and sat back down, intent now on the story. "But this time I said to hell with it, I had it won, so I kept the power on and went into the second turn vertical, pulling seventy-two inches of manifold pressure, really wrapping tight around the pylon. That's when it blew up. I heard a loud explosion, sounded like somebody'd dumped a bucket of bolts down the air intakes. I rolled out level but the ship was shaking and pounding so hard I could hardly control it, so I cut the switches. By that time I was right over the field and to get down I had to kick into a tight turn. I was so busy cranking down the landing gear and trying to get lined up that I forgot the flaps." She laughed. "It's funny now, but I couldn't figure out why everything was happening so damn fast, then I saw the flaps were still up. Shit. I yanked on the flaps, slipped off as much speed as I could, but I still hit the ground like a fucking rock.

"You know what had happened?" She was more interested now in the technology than the close call. "It was the magneto coils. At full power they got so hot they were shorting. One of the guys on another crew told us they'd had the same problem. So we changed the coils and Ax added more louvers to the cowl to direct air across the mags to keep them cooler. So now I ought to be able to fly flat out and, at full bore, that ship is faster than anything in the sky."

"Goddammit, Roxie, speed alone doesn't win races."

"You saying a woman can't win?" She had that look on her face again. "I can do any goddamn thing in an airplane that Roscoe Turner or any other son of a bitch can do, and that goes for you too."

"Come here!" Wardlow pulled her roughly to him, kissing her, needing to dominate her. She resisted, doubling her fists and beating against his chest, but he got an arm around her and held her.

She bit him, and as he jerked painfully away, she was yelling, "All right, you son of a bitch, you want to fuck, I'll fuck your balls off. Come on!" Roxie tore off her clothes, hurling them aside. "Come on, hot shot! Get it on!"

Furious, he had ahold of her again and they fought, wrestled and coupled, anger boiling to lust. Afterward Wardlow pulled his pants back on, covering the naked vulnerability of his limp cock, and lay sprawled there on the rug, spent. Roxie sat cross-legged in the firelight, arms on her knees, wondering who had won. She studied Wardlow. Even in the firelight his face was hard and ugly, yet powerful, like a bulldog. There was no softness in him, and she understood that, could deal with that, but what forces drove this man? "Tell me about Devil's Den."

"What?" Wardlow was surprised and suspicious.

"Your deal, tell me about it."

"Why?"

"Just say I want to know why I am a complication." She grinned that impish look of hers. "Don't those bankers fuck around too?"

"It's not just them. The whole fucking deal is put together with baling wire. I had to borrow against the house and the airplane and hock my life insurance to come up with the front money going in with America First National, but they don't know what I owe Tom Barkham."

"Who?"

"The bank in Jeff City."

"Oh. Want another drink?" She was up now, slipping back into her panties, her breasts jiggling.

"Yeah." He handed her his glass.

"You've got all your chips out on the line, then?" She got his drink, then curled up beside him.

"Yeah." He sipped the Scotch, set the glass down, and took out a cigar and lit up, puffing the rich, harsh smoke, relishing it.

So he was a gambler who wasn't afraid to take a big risk. But why? What was the reward? When she asked him, flat out, he just looked at her and puffed on the cigar for a while, grinning. She felt put off. "Titus, tell me."

"Because I've got a chance to triple my operations. I'm going to turn that desert into the most productive cotton ground in the valley. When I'm done, nobody'll be growing more cotton, not Boswells or Salyers, nobody."

"But how . . . ?"

"Look, the land ownership out there by Devil's Den is like a checkerboard, with the railroad owning the red squares. The black squares belong to whoever buys them."

"Why does the railroad own the red squares?"

"Back in the seventies the government gave the railroads every other section for twenty miles on either side of the right of way as a subsidy to get them to lay track through the valley. So now they own the red squares and lease them out, mostly for dry-land farming.

"I'm buying three black squares and leasing all the red ones around them, that's just under ten thousand acres." Wardlow reached up and took a notebook and pencil out of his shirt pocket, then sketched the plan. "There's no water out there, so first off I drill four wells on each of the three black sections, one well on each side." He penciled in the dots. "Then I level all of the land and irrigate it. I control the water because the wells are on my land and I've got options to buy the leased land at a fixed price in three years. That's the deal."

Drilling for water was a real gamble. A wildcat oil driller had told him he hit good water below the Corcoran clay, at around a thousand feet, but no one had ever gone down that far for irrigation water. He'd have to lift the water with big electric pumps and that would be expensive, but the whole deal looked good, provided he hit water.

"America First is putting up the development money and has the option to refinance the whole package when I buy the railroad land. The first years that banks are protected by my equity in El Adobe and the railroad can't lose because even if I default, I've improved the land. The only problem is raising cash up front." Wardlow grinned crookedly. "That's why I entered the Bendix, I can use that seventeen grand."

"Too bad, buster, I'm going to win it." She gave his head a friendly push. "But I'll loan you the money."

Dawn was still four hours away and the air was dark and cold. Wisps of light fog drifted across the Burbank Airport runways as a Staggerwing Beechcraft thundered into the air and a green and white Spartan taxied out to the starting line. Wardlow stood in a hangar doorway, his own Spartan gleaming silver in the dark behind him. A dozen planes that had entered the Bendix were taking off at half-hour intervals; the racer with the shortest elapsed time to Cleveland would win the trophy, and seventeen thousand dollars. Roxanne was sixth for takeoff, behind Jackie Cochran in that Seversky pursuit ship; Wardlow was ninth and wouldn't lift off until dawn. Axelrod stood beside him in the doorway and Roxie stretched out on a cot under the wing of the Red

Ryder, trying to get some rest. Bright floodlights illuminated the aprons and across the way, behind the fences, thousands of fans crowded expectantly around the terminal building, cheering as John Hinchy revved up his engine and took the starter's flag. The green and white Spartan roared down the runway and lifted into the dark sky.

Wardlow turned and began nervously pacing the hangar, chewing on his cigar. Racing the Bendix was a big gamble, maybe too big, but he needed cash. Deducting the twenty-five hundred that it had cost getting the ship ready, that would leave fourteen-five. Not bad for a day's work. Pacing, he mentally ticked off the checkpoints along the 2,042-mile course to Cleveland, planning to fly high and take advantage of thinner air and any tailwinds he might pick up. Weather might be a problem, there were reports of thunderstorms between Prescott and Wichita.

Roxie would be flying much lower, navigating by dead reckoning and visual contact with the ground. Because of the extra fuel tank, her biggest problem was weight distribution on takeoff; with all that gasoline behind her, the tail-heavy Red Ryder was a flying bomb. Twenty minutes before takeoff, Wardlow helped the ground crew push the little Ryder out to the starting line. Obviously nervous now, Roxie ignored them all as she gave the ship a last walk-around inspection. She was wearing a bulky flight suit, parachute harness, leather helmet with headphones and goggles. Axelrod helped her up into the cockpit and strapped her in. She checked the controls, waggling the ailerons, elevators and rudder, then cranked the stabilizers into full nose-down trim, hit the switches and yelled, "Contact!"

Standing close by the engine cowl, Axelrod cranked the starter and the prop turned, the Menasco engine coughed, belched smoke, then roared alive. He pulled the crank handle free and quickly ducked out of the way. As the engine warmed up, Roxie concentrated on her instruments, checking temperatures, manifold pressure, going through her preflight checks. Only once did she look out at Wardlow; their eyes met for an instant, then she turned back to her work. The starter's one-minute warning flag was up high above his head. Roxie closed the canopy, locked it and began slowly advancing power, her eyes on the starter as he raised the green flag in his right hand. Both flags were above his head now and he was up on tiptoes. She gunned the engine, going to full power just as the flags dropped. Normally the Ryder surged forward, but now it only lumbered slowly along the runway, tail dragging, the mighty Menasco engine roaring like a restrained tiger caught in an invisible web. Roxie pushed the control stick forward, hard against the firewall, and waited for the tail to lift as the plane began to pick up some speed. But the tail wasn't lifting. Damn! She scanned the instruments, frightened now; the engine gauges were normal, airspeed coming up on sixty miles an hour, but the tail was dragging. Come on, baby! Don't hesitate! Lift! Lift! The runway was bumpy and the ship lurched side-to-side, engine straining, still gaining speed but she was past the midpoint and still not airborne. Air speed: ninety miles an hour. The front wheels were bouncing now and the wings were trying to lift the ship into the air but the tail was still down.

Wardlow stood transfixed, fists clenched, jaws clamped down tight. Beside him Axelrod was shuffling his feet, rising up on his toes and yelling, "Get up! Up! Fly, goddamn you! Fly!"

The crowd behind the fence was hushed, then a woman shrieked, "She's going to crash!"

In the cramped cockpit, fear curdled in Roxie's throat and her survival instincts screamed: Abort! But it was too late. She had used up too much of the runway and could never stop in time, the Ryder would crash through the fence and explode. Teeth clenched, she hunched forward, stick still jammed against the firewall, watching the runway lights flicking by and the boundary fence rushing closer. The wings lifted, suddenly free, and the ship pitched up at an alarming rate, tail still dragging. At this angle the Ryder should have stalled and crashed back into the runway. Terror shot adrenaline through Roxie's chest and she felt like screaming. The tail broke free and the engine, roaring at full power, pulled the Red Ryder sharply into the sky, climbing steeply out of control.

"Nose down!" Wardlow yelled. "Nose down!"

The others stood watching in horror as the climbing racer disappeared in the darkness, engine roaring, only the tiny red and green navigational lights visible now.

Roxanne couldn't believe what was happening. She had absolutely no control. None! Even with the stick pushed clear forward, the ship climbed steeply, engine thundering. Frantically Roxie began cranking the landing gear up; her only hope was to eliminate the wind drag across the undercarriage before the Ryder stalled and dove into the ground. If the Menasco misfired now, she was dead. Scanning the instruments, she saw temperatures hot, revs at thirty-five hundred, manifold pressure pulling seventy-two inches: the same readings she'd gotten in Miami just before the engine blew up. She cranked harder on the gear lever and felt the wheels clunk into place under the wings. The ship picked up speed, the control surfaces began to respond and the nose started coming down, slowly rounding off into level flight. Quickly she shifted hands on the controls and cranked the stabilizers into trim. The Red Ryder was flying, still sluggish and terribly tail-heavy, but flying. Gently she banked, holding the control stick well forward, coming back around to pick up her heading for Palm Springs and Prescott. As she crossed over the airfield, she gently rocked her wings, signaling she was okay.

"Damn!" Axelrod let the word out in a whoosh, like a tire going flat.

Wardlow took off in the Spartan an hour and a half later, climbing out on a southeasterly heading to skirt the San Bernardino Mountains then turning directly into the sunrise. At twelve thousand feet he trimmed the ship up, adjusted the power settings and settled back for the long flight to Wichita and Cleveland. Passing over Arizona he discovered a tailwind was boosting him along. Approaching Albuquerque he computed his ground speed: two hundred ninety-five miles an hour. If he could keep this up, he'd make Cleveland in about eight hours, a winning time. Optimistic, he added a little power and thought some more about Devil's Den, how things were breaking his way, now. He had closed the deal for the three sections and the first of the railroad leases was signed. He was committed, his bets were placed, the wheel was spinning and he liked the action. In two years, three at the most, he would be growing more cotton than any man around.

Winds aloft had shifted dramatically and were blowing the Spartan off course. Cranking his loop antenna around, Wardlow got a fix on Amarillo and corrected his heading to compensate for the crosswinds. Ahead he could see thunderheads towering up thirty-five thousand feet and the air was getting turbulent. Soon he was flying between layers of dull gray clouds and sharp flashes of lightning sliced like hot, jagged wires across the sky. The Spartan was pitching and bucking, fighting against the winds. Rain splattered against the windscreen and updrafts sheered past downdrafts, standing the plane on its wing tips one minute, dropping the bottom out the next, knocking his instruments spinning. He powered through the storm, breaking free south somewhere north of Oklahoma City. He was off-course, behind time, and fuel was now a problem. Switching tanks frequently to keep the ship in balance, he reduced power and leaned out the fuel mix, setting his course for Wichita, where Axelrod's boys were waiting to refuel the Spartan. The air was clearing but he was bucking headwinds and the left fuel-tank gauge was pegged on empty. The engine missed a beat. He quickly switched to his right tank and the engine smoothed out, but the needle on that gauge was fluctuating erratically and he could only guess how much fuel remained in the right tank. Fifteen miles out from the airport the engine started missing again and he switched to the center tank, hoping that it still had a couple of gallons left. Again the engine smoothed out, but his stomach muscles were tight now, his eyes constantly scanning for roads and fields for emergency landing spots. Finally, he had the airport in sight and made a straight-in approach. Skip and Jimbo were there with the fuel truck waiting for him as he taxied up and cut the switches. Unlatching the door, he crawled out and stood on the wing, stretching his cramped muscles. "Storm bad here?"

"Field was shut down for nearly two hours," Jimbo yelled as he reeled out the gas hose.

Wardlow jumped down. "What time did Roxie land?"

"Haven't seen her." Skip had the nozzle in the wing tank now and his brother was cranking the pump handle on the truck. "She must've put down somewhere else, because of the storm."

"Call your dad?"

"Tried, but the fellow there at Burbank said Pop caught the first commercial flight out after you took off."

"You call Cleveland?"

"Na. Hell, Mr. Wardlow, she's okay. She put down somewhere else, that's all."

Wardlow started for the terminal buildings. "I'll be back in a minute. Don't forget to check the oil."

Using the airport manager's phone, he called Cleveland. "Hello? Hello? This is Titus Wardlow. Lemme talk to Gates or one of his people. Yeah, yeah. Wardlow. That's right."

Nervously he waited. "Hello. Hey, yeah, this is Wardlow. I'm in Wichita. You hear anything from Roxanne Darling? No. No, I told ya, I'm in Wichita. She was an hour and a half ahead of me but she never landed here."

He listened, nodded. "Yeah. Yeah. Okay. Keep checking, will ya? Okay."

Hanging up, he headed for the men's room to take a leak. Damn woman should have called somebody. He stopped by the cafe for a couple of candy bars and a Coke.

As he came out, Skip asked, "Any word from Roxie?"

"Nope." Wardlow peeled the second candy bar and washed it down with Coke. "How was the oil?"

"Took a couple of quarts. Don't worry, Mr. Wardlow, Roxie's probably halfway to Cleveland by now."

"Who's worrying?" Wardlow climbed in and took off, headed for St. Louis, determined to make up some of the time he'd lost in the storm. Thoughts of Roxie faded into the background as he worked at getting to Cleveland fast, fighting headwinds, computing fuel consumption, correcting his course. Other pilots were in the same trouble, so maybe he still had a chance. By the time he had the Cleveland airport in sight, he'd been in the air ten hours. He pushed the throttle wide open. The big engine surged and he flashed across the finish line flat out, then banked into a tight turn and circled to land, scanning the airport. Other racers were parked out on the aprons, surrounded by the large crowds, but he didn't see the Ryder anywhere. Wardlow landed and taxied up to the parking ramp, cut the switches and climbed wearily out of the ship, feeling grimy and tired.

Two race officials were by the wing as he jumped down. He lit a cigar, inhaled deeply and asked, "How'd I do?"

One of the officials glanced at his clipboard. "Ten hours, eleven minutes, five seconds. Puts you in fourth place so far."

Three thousand bucks. Well, at least that'd cover expenses. "What'd Roxanne Darling do?"

"She's not in yet. Have trouble with the storm?"

"Bounced me around some. Who's winning?"

"Cochran. Finished in eight hours, ten minutes, three seconds. Fuller was only fourteen minutes behind her."

Security guards were around the Spartan now, setting up rope barricades to keep the milling crowds back. Wardlow tied the plane down, then, tired and hungry, he headed for the operations building. They hadn't heard anything from Roxie either, but they said Axelrod was due in tomorrow morning. Wardlow caught a cab to the hotel, ready for a bath. The hot water felt good and he soaked for nearly an hour, sipping brandy and smoking a cigar. After getting dressed, he called the airport. There still was no word on Roxie. He gave them his room number and asked them to call when they heard anything, then went out to eat. When he returned to the hotel there were no messages. Exhausted, he fell into bed.

The phone rang at four A.M., startling Wardlow out of a dead sleep. It was Axelrod's wife. Roxie had crashed. In Oklahoma, near some place called Gage. Doctor said she was alive, but pretty badly busted up. Wardlow looked at his watch, then called the hospital. No, he couldn't talk to Roxanne Darling and they weren't going to give him the doctor's phone number. Who was calling? He started to give his own name, then changed his mind. "Her husband, dammit."

"Mr. Darling, your wife's been sedated and she's sleeping now."

"How bad is she hurt?"

"Her condition is satisfactory."

"What the hell does that mean?"

"You'll have to wait and talk to the doctor for any further information."

It was afternoon before he landed in Gage. At the hospital he bluffed his way past the nurses, saying he owned the Ryder and Roxanne was his pilot. The hospital was small and Roxie was a celebrity, a race pilot who had survived a terrible crash. Amid the antiseptic smells and the hushed noises, he found her wired and rigged to steel frames over her bed, one leg cast and suspended in traction. Her left shoulder and arm were in another cast and her head was bandaged, her face was badly bruised and lacerated, her nose broken.

Nurses and aides fluttered in and out of the room.

"Titus." She reached a hand out, whispering hoarsely. "I figured that was you that'd called, since Bart's in Saudi Arabia. I sent him a cable."

"Damn, you look awful."

"Fuck you." She gave his hand a squeeze, glad he was here. "Did you place?"

"Fourth." He looked at her, concerned. "What happened?"

"What's it look like? I crashed."

"Goddammit, I can see that!"

"Oh, hell, I'm sorry." She squeezed his hand again. "I ran out of fuel and tried to put down in a field in a crosswind. Landing gear collapsed or a wing hit a pole or something, I don't remember."

He looked down at her, not knowing what to say.

"Hey!" She brightened. "Who won?"

"Cochran."

"What was her time?"

"Eight hours and something. She and Fuller, in that other Seversky, got through before the storm hit, I guess."

A rotund little nurse with a hairy mole over her lip came into the room. "Time for your shot." Pointing a motherly finger at Wardlow, she asked him to leave, explaining, "This brave young lady needs some rest."

"Oh, crap." Roxanne frowned. "I'm not tired and we want to talk, so leave us alone."

The nurse sighed a look of disapproval, but it was easy to see she liked Roxie. "Only for a minute more. Doctor's orders." She went out and closed the door.

Roxie asked, "Can you stay?"

"No. Got a raisin crop coming off the vines."

"You son of a bitch." Anger flashed across her face. "Oh, that's right, you're the big farmer and you've got deals cooking."

He ignored the sharpness. "You hear from Axelrod?"

"Nurse said he'd be in sometime tonight. He wanted to know if you were here yet. Nurse said he sounded mad because you didn't wait for him in Cleveland."

"Hell, Roxie, when I heard you were down, I wasn't waiting for anyone."

Roxanne looked at him, her anger gone now, replaced by sudden tears. She reached out her hand again, trying to smile. "Damn you, this isn't working out the way I'd figured it would." Puzzled, he took her hand. She pulled him down to her. "You bastard, I'm falling in love with you."

6

The foggy, brittle-cold days of winter grudgingly gave way to spring and fleets of crawler tractors growled through the fields pulling gang plows and discs, preparing the warming earth for cotton planting. By March the seedlings sprouted and the ragged army of workers that had huddled through the long, starving winter in countless ditch-bank shanty camps welcomed the warming sun and the growing plants, for these were signs that there was work once more in the fields, hoeing the young cotton.

The Robertsons had been in the rows for a week now, using those short-handled hoes that forced workers to bend down close to the row, chopping and thinning with one hand, pulling weeds with the other. It was mindless, backbreaking work and Jake tried to ignore the drudgery by escaping in a memory, letting his mind drift. This morning, as sun warmed his back, he was remembering the day that Georgie Schumacher bragged that he was going to fuck Annie Wells. It was recess and they were off in one corner of the schoolyard, he and a half dozen of his chums, talking about pussy. Georgie was a skinny kid, kind of small and funny-looking, with freckles and buck teeth, but he had a lot of guts and they knew he'd try anything. As for Annie, she was a prick-tease in starched dresses who let boys look up her skirt, that much Jake knew. Anyway, Georgie said that Annie was begging him for it and before the day was over he was going to get her off in the bushes and give it to her good. After school they hung around the yard throwing a ball around, playing keepaway. When Annie came out, Georgie gave them a big wink and started after her, but she didn't go skipping off the schoolyard like they expected. Instead, she headed for the outhouse. Georgie didn't hesitate, he followed her, ducked right in behind her and the green door swung shut. And it stayed shut. Hardly believing what was happening, the guys hung around, only halfheartedly tossing the ball now as they waited and enviously watched the outhouse door. Suddenly, Mrs. Stockman, their big, bosomy teacher, came out of the schoolhouse and down the back steps fast, like she had to pee real bad. Keep-away forgotten, they watched as the heavyset teacher reached for the door. God! Georgie had forgotten to lock it. Mrs. Stockman pulled the door open and started to step inside, but there was Annie, her skirt up around her waist, her creamy legs spread wide, and Georgie was standing between 'em, bare-assed and humping away.

Mrs. Stockman let out a little gasp and jumped back, slamming the door. "Georgie Schumacher! You get your pants up and come out of there! Right now! Annie Wells, you too!"

There were some scrambling noises inside, then Georgie opened the door just a little way and peeked out. Mrs. Stockman yanked the door all the way back and grabbed Georgie by the ear, twisting it hard. With the other hand she clutched Annie's arm and dragged them both across the yard and into the schoolhouse. Annie and Georgie were expelled and afterward Georgie got a whipping but he said that was okay because now he was fucking Annie regularly. Jake thought about how she'd showed him her cunt, down at the swimming hole, and he tried to imagine that he and Bobby had fucked Annie too, wondering if it felt better than when they jacked off.

Sex was on his mind a lot these days and that was frustrating as hell because he had no privacy, no place where he could get off by himself. He tried not to think about girls so much, but that caused problems too because when he got to remembering other things, like building the treehouse in the big pecan down by the creek or going to rodeos with his father, sooner or later he felt homesick. Other times, he would be working along, lost in thought, and he'd suddenly get this funny feeling that he didn't know where he was or even what month or year it was and he'd have to stop and think. It was spring 1939. He knew that because he'd had two birthdays on the road, one lost in the horror of that first starving winter when Li'l Beth died, the second celebrated by a small cake his mother baked and a happy birthday card that Mary Ellen and Susie fashioned out of scrap paper. He'd turned fifteen last November and they surprised him with a present wrapped in newspaper and tied with a red ribbon. Eagerly he tore open the package and discovered an almost new denim cowboy shirt, with pearly white snap buttons.

"Pa found it in a secondhand store," Susie explained eagerly, and Mary Ellen added, "See if it fits, we had to guess about shortening the sleeves 'cause we didn't want to spoil the surprise."

Jake felt like crying, he was so happy, and, after trying the shirt on, he carefully put it away. Later his mother put her arm around him and gave him a hug. "That shirt's for school, when we find us a place to settle down."

Jake nodded, marveling at his mother's determination. She never gave up, just kept pressing on, always certain that God's will was being worked and that sooner or later things would get better if they didn't give up. Jake had serious reservations about God but when he expressed such doubts, Bessie scolded, "Boy, don' ya be blasphemin'! God loves us! He's testin' us, makin' us stronger, jus' like the steel tempered in a forge. Honey, Scriptures tells us people's born to trouble, that means we gotta go through the fire 'fore we can be strong, jus' like steel. I remember my daddy a hammering at his anvil, the sparks jus' flying as he pounded on a red-hot chunk of metal, makin' it just the way he wanted. Tha's what God's adoin', son, He's temperin' an' shapin' us an' makin' us strong, don't ya see?"

No, he didn't see that, not at all. What he did see was Li'l Beth playing happily on a blanket in between the rows or sucking on Billie Jo's tit. If Li'l Beth was still alive, she'd be running around by now, getting into mischief. But she was dead. They had buried her a year and a half ago and the rage and sorrow still smoldered deep inside him. He clung to those feelings, the anger and sadness, afraid that if he let them go she would truly be gone and the bastards who killed her would get away unpunished. Just who those sons of bitches were he wasn't quite sure. There was the service station guy, for one, and the farmer with the barking dogs for another, then there was that ugly son of a bitch at El Adobe, Wardlow, and that fat Dago fucker who'd cheated them. Looking back, that whole time seemed cruelly unreal. After burying Li'l

Beth, they had survived on one meal of fried dough and watery coffee a day, struggling to stay alive until spring work opened up. Then, tougher and more experienced, they returned to Jefferson County for the Model A. Working through the summer and fall, they learned to adjust their lives to the ebb and flow of the harvests, sometimes earning pretty good money, most times hardly enough to get by on. The way Jake figured it, they were working no more than a hundred days a year; when they did find work there were so many people in the fields the jobs never lasted long and they were back out on the road searching for another job or living in some crowded ditch-bank camp waiting for another crop to come ripe. Several times they'd lost work because the sedan or the Model A had broken down, stranding them on the side of the road until he and James Earl could make repairs.

While his mother might see God's plan in all of that, he damn sure didn't, but he wasn't about to say anything again. No sir. Last time, she'd marched him into the tent, got out the Bible and made him read how Job refused to curse God. The way Jake got the story, God put that fellow Job through all kinds of hell just to test him, see if he'd curse Him, but Job didn't get mad at God, never once called Him a son of a bitch. His mother said that was the point of the story; Job didn't lose his Faith, no matter how bad things got. That's the part Jake didn't understand. If God loved folks so damn much, why in hell did He let such awful things happen? To Job? And his family? Killing off Job's kids like that just to see if their pa'd get mad was just plain shitty, like letting Li'l Beth die. Jake decided God really was a son of a bitch, but the thought was immediately frightening. What if God was listening? Like his mother said? And he wished he had someone to talk to about these things, but Susie was no help, she was as confused as he was, and both James Earl and Mary Ellen were too much like Bessie.

Jake decided to ask his father. Ertie never had been much for churches and Bible-pounding preachers and this business of trotting out Job's problems didn't wash with him either, Jake was sure of it. Ertie Robertson wasn't about to let God or anyone else get away with treating his family badly, no sir, Ertie Robertson wouldn't be cheated or paid off in brass money and nobody could treat his family like trash. The whole family knew that and Jake, at least, was proud that his father stood up to the sons of bitches.

So, after Li'l Beth died, Jake had waited to see how his father would strike back. But nothing happened, and when Jake went to his father, asking why God had let her die, he got no answer. None at all. Ertie just stood there for a second, then he turned and limped off without a word.

Jake felt abandoned. His father had changed, was changing. Before that horse fell on him Ertie Robertson had been a happy-go-lucky cuss who laughed and joked a lot. Now it was like he was mad all the time, but he didn't say much or do much other than work hard and, whenever he could get the whiskey, drink himself numb. Jake remembered his mother's words, "Yor Pa's hurtin', honey, hurtin' bad. Ain' nothin' like this ever happened to us before."

That was true enough. Sometimes he dreamed they were all tumbling and skidding helplessly down a steep slide into some kind of dark hell and there was nothing to grab ahold of, no way to stop the terrifying drop. In the dream his father was gone; his mother was frightened, but she didn't make a sound; the girls were screaming and grabbing for Li'l Beth who was on the slide too, then suddenly Li'l Beth was gone, falling and disappearing into the black emptiness and the suddenness of it was devastating. In the dream he wondered, why wasn't his mother crying? She was sad, he knew that, but her jaw was set hard as an anvil and she kept saying: "We gotta take the bad with the good and keep right on goin'. One day, the Lord willin', things'll get better."

At that point the dream and reality merged because those words were one of his mother's sayings: "We gotta take the bad with the good and keep right on goin'. One day, the Lord willin', things'll get better." And things were getting better. Just a couple of days before, the farmers upped the cotton-chopping wages a nickel an hour, raising it from twenty cents to a quarter. Nobody knew why, although there was some talk about politics and the new governor and all. Bessie said it was God's will, He was finally answering their prayers. Jake was skeptical. Praying had never done much good before, so he figured it was just plain luck. He stood up and stretched his aching back, still wondering about the pay hike, remembering that actually it wasn't their first piece of good luck. Their fortunes had started to change back in November, just after his birthday. At the time they were picking the last of the cotton, the fog had settled in and it looked like another hard winter ahead. One evening after work Ertie and Jake walked by a couple of fellows hunkered down by a campfire. They were talking about how if a man could prune vines he'd find plenty of winter work. That stopped Ertie dead in his tracks. He asked how they knew about this pruning work and the older man shrugged and said, "Seen 'em doin' it last winter, up near Fresno, usin' them long-handled shears, but when we asked for a job the farmer he just laughed an' said he'd never seen an Okie yet that could prune a vine right, said we'd ruin his crop."

"Well, can ya prune?" Ertie asked.

"Hell, I don' know mister, never got to give 'er a try."

Right then Ertie'd got it in his head that he was going to get a pruning job. They headed up into Fresno County and camped near a little town called Del Ray. The vines had dropped their leaves and stood skeletal and black in the cold fog. Taking the boys with him, Ertie asked around for pruning work, but most of the grape growers just shook their heads no, not saying come back later or anything. Then one mean-talking farmer told them he wasn't about to hire people who'd never pruned vines before and, before they could say anything, the fellow walked off. Rude as the guy was, Jake half-expected his father to at least tell him to go to hell, but Ertie just shrugged and climbed back in the Model A and took a long swallow from the whiskey bottle he'd stashed under the seat.

James Earl had to hand-crank the Model A to get it started because they had a short and the battery was dead, either that or the starter motor was burned out.

"Pa?" Angry at the way the farmer treated them, Jake was standing by the pickup window wanting to say something about letting that son of a bitch talk to them like that.

Ertie leaned out the window. "Yeah?"

Jake hesitated, then shook his head. "Nothing." He quickly climbed into the back and sat on a spare tire.

Bending down in front of the radiator, James Earl cranked the engine over. It coughed, then chugged to life. Pulling the crank out, James Earl came around the fender and climbed behind the wheel, slamming the door. He yelled across to his father, "How'n hell's a feller like that know we ain' never pruned vines before?"

"Blamed if I know." Ertie shrugged and took another slug from the bottle.

When a stocky Japanese farmer at the next place turned them down because they weren't experienced, Ertie bristled, "Mister, what makes you think we can't prune?"

"I'm sorry," the farmer said and he looked sorry. "If you'd pruned before you'd know we don't start until after the first hard freeze, after Christmas. And you'd have your own shears."

Ertie studied the man's round, oriental face and his steel-dark eyes set in almond slits. Sensing no hostility, Ertie nodded. "Thank ya. I reckon we're kinda green. Truth is, mister, we need work an' we're willin' to tackle anything that needs doin'. Boys here are right good mechanics, if any of yor machinery needs fixin'."

The farmer's name was Kitahara and he seemed to like Ertie's frankness. "Tell you what, my tractor needs some work and there are a few other jobs around the place. Won't be much to do until we start pruning, but if that's okay, you can camp out back of the barn, there."

It frosted hard the week after Christmas. Kitahara showed them how to prune and he worked along beside them, talking openly about how his own father had come to California from Hokkaido as an immigrant worker, one of thousands imported by valley farmers forty years earlier. Kitahara's vineyards were a family operation and his two teenage sons helped out with the pruning after school, but other than that, the farmer had no other help. Even putting in short days, they finished Kitahara's vines in a couple of weeks and he sent them over to work for a neighbor. Through January and early February they found jobs enough to keep food on the table and still put a little money in the sock. It rained hard in February and March, then the sun came out and spring work opened up. By April they were in Jefferson County chopping cotton with the short-handled hoes. Jake hated the goddamn tool; his back and legs knotted with pain so he could hardly straighten up. Late in the afternoon, when they got back to camp, all he wanted to do was flop on his bed, but there were still chores to do.

They were camped down in the sandy bottoms along Old River Road, just a couple of hundred yards east of a big iron bridge that arched across Old River Slough. Lots of people were camped there, living in tents mostly, but some folks had stuck posts in the ground and added themselves a shack, using scraps of wood or corrugated iron sheeting and cardboard. The riverbed was dry, so they hauled their water from an irrigation canal a half mile further east up the road. Looking west from the shanty camp, on the other side of the bridge and through the tall sycamores they could see the backside of Hyattville, old houses and dilapidated store buildings along the river bank.

That evening after work, Bessie asked Jake to drive her to town for groceries. Rumbling across the bridge, Jake turned onto High Street, driving past the Shell gas station and a whitewashed barn that had once been a livery stable and was now a tractor dealership and blacksmith shop. Three brand-new John Deere tractors sat out in front, all pretty green and bright yellow. Up ahead, the dusty street was lined with sun-blasted storefronts and a weary old two-story brick hotel that leaned out over the cracked sidewalks. Down the street a ways, at the corner of High and Fifth, there was another two-story building, this one constructed of blue granite. It was an imposing structure built in 1882, when Hyattville was still the county seat, and was called the Barkham Building. The name and date were chiseled boldly in stone high under the cornice. At street level the building housed Barkham's Mercantile and upstairs were rows of offices, most of them empty now.

The Hyattville Market was located at the west end of town, a couple of blocks from the Barkham Building. A couple of older fellows in rough work clothes were sitting on a bench out in front of the store, idly whittling and talking as Jake pulled into the curb and parked. The men paused and watched Jake and his mother climb out of the car, doors slamming.

"Evenin', ma'am," one of the men nodded.

Recognizing a neighbor, Bessie returned the nod. "Evenin'."

The other fellow was sixty-five, maybe seventy, all skin and bones, with a wild thatch of white hair and rheumy eyes that stared out of hollowed sockets at Jake. A smile wrinkled across his gaunt face. "Hey, there, sonny! How's the hunter?"

Bessie glanced at the old man and then at Jake, who looked puzzled.

The old-timer chuckled. "Ma'am, that boy of yorn is a cracker-jack shot. I seen 'im knock a big ol' jackrabbit a spinning at near a hundred yards."

Recognizing the old man, Jake's freckled face broke into a bashful grin. "Ever git that truck of yorn back on the road?"

"You bet. She's a-sittin' right yonder." The old man pointed across the street to the ancient Model T Ford with the wood cabin built on back.

"That's swell." Jake stood there for a moment, barefoot and in his patched overalls, not knowing what else to say, then he followed his mother into the store. Inside the market was dark and cool and smelled like coffee and spices.

Picking up a basket, Bessie asked, "Who was that?"

"Don' know his name, but he was camped a ways down the bank from us that first winter. Looked plumb starved out, so I give'm one of them rabbits I shot."

Bessie gave her son an affectionate pat. "Now ya stay out of mischief while I tend to the shoppin'."

"Yes'm." Jake sidled over to the magazine rack and stood there looking at the covers of *Life* and *Saturday Evening Post* and *Liberty* and the westerns with pictures of cowboys firing pistols from the backs of bucking horses, wagon trains circled against warring Indians, rustlers stampeding cattle. He picked up *Range Wars*, flipped through the pages to the first story: "Track of the Grizzly."

There on the title page was the menacing silhouette of a bushwhacker sighting down the barrel of a Winchester rifle at a young cowboy who was just coming out of a log cabin and was headed for the horse corral. In the background there was a creek and beyond that meadows filled with grazing cattle. Jake started reading: "Lancy Boyd had brought his small herd of cows into the high country early in the spring, hoping to get on the range before the Circle Bar waddies pushed the big herds up through Gunnison Pass and turned them loose here in the meadows . . ."

The front doorbell tinkled and the rheumy-eyed old-timer came in, stood near the counter and looked around until he saw Jake reading. Nodding to himself, the old man dug into his pocket and pulled out some coins, asking the clerk, "How much for that magazine the boy's readin'?"

"Ten cents."

The old man counted out a nickel and five pennies, then went back outside, satisfied.

Oblivious to what had just happened, Jake was absorbed in *Range Wars* and the story of Lancy Boyd, last of the small ranchers still running cattle in the high country. Wade Gunnison wanted Lancy off the high range. This was public graze, but Gunnison claimed all of the high country and the valley below, claimed it by blood right because he had tamed this land, fought the Indians, buried his wife and two sons under the valley sod. Gunnison wasn't about to let anyone homestead on the land he considered Circle Bar. The Circle Bar pistoleros had driven off all of the small ranchers except Lancy, who wouldn't be pushed. He would fight and die first.

"Jake!"

Startled, Jake dropped his hand, holding the magazine down at his side. "What?"

Bessie was at the counter, unloading her basket. "Boy, put that magazine back and git on over here."

Reluctantly, Jake closed *Range Wars* and was putting it back when he overheard the clerk telling Bessie, "Oh, that's all right. Feller out there in front, he paid for the magazine, tol' me to give it to the boy, there."

Jake grinned and quickly found his place: "The bushwhacker's second shot kicked gravel and sand into Lancy's face as he jerked his pistol clear and fired instinctively, thumbing the hammer back and squeezing the trigger: BLAM! BLAM!"

"Jake Robertson!"

"Ma!" Jake looked up, distressed. "She said that feller bought it for me."

"Well bring it on then, but I need ya to fetch a sack of taters."

The clerk was a stout, jowly woman with red-painted lips, dark penciled eyebrows and a black swirl of hair piled high like a beehive. She pointed. "Taters is back through them doors there, stacked off in the far corner."

Jake stuck the magazine in his pocket and went off on the chore.

"Where y'all from?" the clerk asked in a friendly way.

"Sweetwater, Texas."

"Why, we come from the Cap Rock country, up around Lubbock." The clerk smiled. "My name's Gilda, Gilda Simmons. Where y'all staying?"

"Up the road a ways, we're camped in that ol' wash above the bridge, where folks stays."

The clerk tapped a tin of snuff on the counter, opened it and tucked a pinch in her lip. "We stayed out there when we first come. Now we got a house of our own here in town. You lookin' to buy someplace?"

"No." Bessie sighed and shook her head sadly.

"Ought to think about it." The clerk smiled. "This here's a right neighborly town. You'd like it. Used to be the county seat and was named after Jonathan Hyatt who run the ferry. Him and old Tom Barkham, the daddy to the one that has the bank over in Jeff City, they went partners and built the hotel. That was back in the sixties sometime, before the railroad come through the valley. That hotel, it was the only two-story brick buildin' in the county back in them days."

"Ferry?" Bessie looked surprised.

The clerk laughed. "Wasn't always dry like it is now. The slough used to be the main channel of the Palo Rojo River, till the big flood, back in ninety-two. River jumped its banks and cut a new course, went looping south clean down by Jeff City, leavin' Old River high and dry, except in wet years. Back in them days, Jeff City wasn't but a siding on the railroad, had a few grain elevators and a store or two, but it wasn't much, they say. Wasn't too many years after that that the board of supervisors up and moved the county seat down there. Wasn't for that, Hyattville'd be as big as Jeff City probably, but small like this makes it nice for folks like us. You'd like it here."

"We cain' afford to even think about buyin' property, hard as times is." Bessie sighed again.

As Jake came staggering back with the sack of potatoes balanced on his shoulder, Gilda Simmons was telling Bessie about a house that was for sale, one that they could probably afford. "It's a real nice place, got a good roof and the walls are sound. Ain' but a couple of miles out on Old River Road. Payments cain' be much more'n ten dollars a month."

"Sounds right nice." Bessie pulled out three one-dollar bills and a five. "How much do I owe ya?"

Gilda Simmons punched the adding machine keys, pulled the crank and the number dials whirled *click-clickety-click-click.* "That'll be four thirty-three. Why don't ya just take a look at the place, my husband'd be glad to take ya out there, show ya around."

Gilda Simmons didn't mention that the house was a worn-out

boxcar that had been fixed up or that her husband had several of these old railroad cars for sale, all of them located on a strip of alkali land that belonged to Judge Rooster Barkham. The judge was the only Barkham still living in Hyattville and he had come back, after being raised over in Jeff City. But it was here that the Barkhams got their start. Even after old Tom moved over to Jeff City, he had kept the mercantile store open and when Rooster grew up and came back from law school, he settled in Hyattville, took over the business and expanded his interests. He bought the Hyattville Market and began dabbling in real estate, farm foreclosures mostly, that and buying up vacant properties at tax sales.

Rooster Barkham was called Rooster because he looked like a banty rooster, all puffed up and strutting in his sporty jackets, bow ties and gold lodge ring with its sparkling diamond. Every four years the voters returned him to the bench of the Hyattville Justice Court, a paying job for a lawyer. Some said he got reelected because he was popular, but most likely it was because most folks owed him a debt of some kind.

Gus Simmons was Judge Barkham's land agent and general handyman; when rents or payments came due, it was Gus Simmons who came around to collect and it was said he worked on a percentage. Simmons wasn't much taller than the portly little judge, but he was a whole lot thinner, a dark, mean-looking fella, even when he smiled and showed all those scraggly yellow teeth. With times hard like they were, Simmons went around the county with Rooster Barkham's money in his jeans bidding on foreclosed properties, grabbing up abandoned cabins that could be hauled to Hyattville and put down on those empty lots that Rooster owned. Getting ahold of the railroad cars had been Simmons's idea, but it hadn't taken much to convince the judge that they'd make a good profit. Simmons had spotted a dozen of the worn-out boxcars sitting out back of the Southern Pacific yards in Fresno; the wheel trucks had been stripped out from under them and the railroad man said he'd let them go for thirty dollars each, provided Simmons hauled them off. Simmons scoffed at that price and said he'd pay twenty and the railroad could deliver them. The railroad man said he'd take twenty-four dollars, and send a crew over to help Simmons load 'em up on the dollies. Simmons agreed and said he'd take ten of the cars.

The railroad man blew up. "Goddammit, we were talking all twelve cars."

"Nope. Got no use for twelve, all I need is ten." Simmons started to walk away, then hesitated. "Seein' as them cars is just clutterin' thangs up, like they are, tell ya what; I'll move them other two off for ya, won't charge ya but ten dollars apiece to get them out of yor way."

Surprised and disgusted, the railroad man looked at Simmons in disbelief. Shaking his head, he waved at the cars. "You can have 'em all, two hundred fifty dollars, take it or leave it."

Simmons jacked the boxcars up onto wheeled dollies and towed them one at a time down the highway to Jefferson County, locating them out along Old River Road. He remodeled each boxcar, taking off the big sliding doors, adding a ten-by-twenty room on the backside. He partitioned off tiny bedrooms at either end of the car and called the space in between a "sitting room," then, to keep the sitting room from being oppressively small, Simmons left the double-wide doorway on the backside open into the add-on room. On the front side of the railroad car, he framed in an entryway and added on a porch. The whole job, including paint, cost him less than a hundred fifty dollars. He billed Rooster Barkham three hundred dollars for each house and Rooster set the selling price at six hundred.

Jake didn't know any of this, of course, but when he heard Mrs. Simmons talking about a house, he got a funny feeling. He didn't like the clerk, but he could see that his mother wanted to take a look at the place. That night she didn't say anything directly to Ertie or the girls about the house, but she did talk about what a nice place Hyattville seemed, so friendly and all, and she told them how it used to be the county seat. Ertie had lived too long with Bessie not to know she was up to something, so he was ready when she mentioned the house and suggested that it wouldn't hurt to go out and take a look at it. He said no, as a matter of course, but that was only to make it clear he wasn't about to buy a house. There was no way they could afford anything like that, not the way things were going. She tried coaxing him, saying it wouldn't hurt just to look, and finally he gave in. "Woman, if it'll make ya happy, we'll go look at the place, but don' be gittin' no ideas 'bout buyin' it."

The next Sunday they met Simmons in town and followed him out Old River Road. Right off, Jake decided he didn't like the guy—he looked about as trustworthy as a junkyard dog. When they pulled up in front of the house Jake was startled to see that it was a boxcar, one of a whole row of boxcars made over into houses.

"Oh, my." Bessie sucked in her breath.

Jake glanced in the mirror and saw her disappointment, but only for a fleeting second. Jaw firmly set, eyes bright, she grabbed the door handle. "Well, we're here, let's take a look."

Ertie was slouched down in the seat. "Shit!" He said it under his breath, but they all heard it.

"Here we are, folks." Simmons walked up, smiling through that junkyard-dog look of his. The house, pale cream in color, was the third one down from the corner. As they walked through the powdery-white alkali to the front door Jake noticed the neighbors on either side had planted sapling trees and gardens.

"This is just the place for you," Simmons said as he inserted the key in the big padlock on the front door and pushed it open. Ushering the Robertsons in, he lowered his voice, warning them, "but in all honesty, I've got to tell you that I've already showed it to another family and they liked the place a whole lot. Said they'd be back, so I don't know how long it'll be on the market."

Stepping into the front room, Jake was depressed by its tiny size, like a dollhouse. Simmons might call it snug, but hell, there was hardly room to turn around, even without furniture. Jake heard his mother suck in her breath again.

Ertie walked right straight through the house and out the back door, slamming it.

Bessie opened the two small windows on either side of the front door, hoping that would help, then set about inspecting the place, saying, "James Earl and Billie Jo could take one bedroom, the girls the other. Pa and I'll put our bed out there in one corner of the big room, the other side'll make a right nice place for the kitchen. We can put up a curtain for privacy. Jake there, an' Benjy can sleep here in the sitting room, get one of them fold-out beds."

Jake had followed his older sister into one of the bedrooms. "Damn house's no bigger'n a chicken coop."

"Hush up, Ma'll hear ya," Mary Ellen hissed.

"Shit, I don' care. Lookit, I kin nearly touch the walls." He reached his arms out.

"Can't neither. Ain't even close."

Starting at one wall, Jake stepped off the width, heel against toe. "Ain' eight feet wide."

"Better'n livin' in that tent with the blanket down the middle."

"Yeah." Jake grinned. "Least this way I won' have to smell your farts."

"Oh!" Mary Ellen stormed out of the tiny bedroom, nearly bumping into their mother. "Ma, ya gotta do somethin' 'bout that boy's dirty mouth."

Billie Jo had been talking to Bessie when Mary Ellen interrupted. She glanced irritably at her sister-in-law and continued talking. "Me an' James Earl kin sleep out in the truck an' the boys kin have the other bedroom."

Bessie ignored Mary Ellen. "Billie Jo, I won' have the two of you outside. We're a family, an' you'll sleep in the bedroom. That's all there is to it."

Restlessly Jake slid the bedroom window open and leaned out. His father was standing out back, forlornly looking around the weed-choked alkali flat. Jake got a knee up on the window sill and clambered out, dropped to the ground and went over to stand beside his father.

Ertie shook his head. "Shor ain' much, is it?"

"Ma, she ain' too happy with it neither, but I think . . ."

The back door slammed and Simmons came out, all yellow-toothed smiles. "You could put a nice garden in back here, maybe even keep a hog or two for meat. Wouldn't take much to fix up the fences, boys there can knock down the weeds in no time."

The lot was long and narrow and a path led back through the tumbleweeds and puncture vines to a sagging outhouse. Jake was an expert on outhouses. Without even looking inside, he knew it was filthy, stunk and had black widow spiders crawling around under the seat.

Ertie asked Simmons, "How'd ya figger a man'd water that garden, mister?"

"Why, look over yonder. The neighbor there's got a crackerjack garden, an' see that tank, up next to the house? Fills it once or twice a week, hauls water from Hyattville. Get it from the town well, there at the water tower, back of Barkham's. All ya need is a tank like that one over yonder and you're in business. When ya get a little ahead, you can drill a well. Good water down about sixty feet, they tell me."

"An' how much more'd that cost?" Ertie didn't like this guy or his slick sales pitch.

Bored, Jake went back into the house and poked around the bare kitchen, opening and closing the windows. Over in one corner there was a box of trash, floor sweepings mostly, a broken dinner plate and a burned-out coffeepot. Wrinkled up there on top was an envelope, with some writing on it. Jake bent over and picked it up, smoothing it out. The envelope, empty now, was addressed to somebody named Lincoln Stevens, c/o General Delivery, Hyattville, and had been postmarked February 21, 1939, in Big Stone Gap, Virginia. There were some penciled numbers scribbled on the back, with pluses and minuses, like someone had been doing some figuring and then angrily crossed it out.

"Ma, lookee here." Jake went into the front room, holding out the envelope. "Musta been the folks livin' here before."

Bessie glanced at the envelope. " 'Spect so. Where's yor Pa?"

"Wonder what happened to 'em?" Jake looked the envelope over again, then realized his mother had asked a question. "Oh, Pa's out back talkin' with that Simmons fella."

"What's he sayin'?" Bessie was anxious now.

"Simmons, he's sayin' how we'd plant a garden, put in a water system . . ."

"No, no. Mean what's yor Pa sayin'?"

"Pa, he don' much like that Simmons fella." Jake noticed he was getting taller than his mother. "Ma, I don' neither."

A worried look came over Bessie's face and she was quickly out the back door. Surprised, Jake followed her.

Simmons, hearing the door bang, turned to Bessie. "Well now, we were just talking about how you could grow much of what you'd need for your table right back here. What do you think of the place?"

She moved quickly between them. "Mr. Simmons, I thank ya for showin' it to us. We gotta think about it some more, 'cause six hundred fifty dollars is a lot of money. We gotta talk it over."

"I can see how much ya want this place." Simmons was solicitous now. "An' I know times is hard. Tell you what, you make us an offer of say, six hundred even, I think I can talk the judge into agreeing. That'd make the down payment only a hundred twenty dollars an' you'd move right in, use that extra fifty ta fix the place up." Turning to Ertie, he added, "That'd pay fer a first-class water tank."

Ertie's face hardened.

Bessie had ahold of her husband's arm, gently turning him away, while answering Simmons. "We couldn't pay more'n fifty-five down. That's all we got put by."

Jake shot a surprised look at his mother. Everyone in the family kidded her about what hard bargains she drove and here she was throwing all their cards on the table face up. Why?

"Well now," Simmons responded, "I'm sure we can work something out, if you put up some earnest money. Judge Barkham's a man who has a genu-wine interest in helping folks. He may be the justice of the peace an' brother to the Barkhams in Jeff City, but he's just plain folks around here. You ask anybody. He'll help ya, if you're willin' to help yourselves, you'll see."

"Gotta think 'bout it first." Bessie was insistent.

"Don't know how much longer this place'll be on the market, Mrs. Robertson. Like I said, there's another family that's awful interested in it too. Good deals like this don't come along very often."

Bessie could feel Ertie's muscles tense up. He'd only agreed to come look the place over, nothing more, and now she needed time to convince him that this was their only chance to settle down, but Simmons was pushing too hard. Angry and frightened, she turned on Simmons. "I tol' ya we're goin' to think on it! Leave us be!"

Surprised by the sudden flare of anger, Simmons quickly backed off. "Of course. Of course. I was jus' wanting to be helpful, I know how much ya want a nice place like this."

It wasn't a nice place. They all knew that and so did Simmons. Jake hated the man for trying to bullshit them and he thought about how his mother must feel, remembering her kitchen back in Texas, remembering how she could look out the curtained windows and see the hayfields along Bitter Creek, see the wild turkeys in the pecan trees and hear the lonesome doves' call. That was a nice place, spacious and sunny, with water piped into the sink. He missed the good smells coming from the big cook stove and was homesick as he remembered how he used to sprawl on the rug in front of the fireplace in the front room reading or just staring into the coals while heat from the stone chimney rose through the second story, warming the bedrooms upstairs. Compared to that, the railroad house wasn't nice at all. But on the way back to camp, Bessie pointed out that the railroad house did offer them shelter and some permanency. They could add on, make something of it once they'd moved in. From the way she was carrying on, Jake knew his mother meant to have that house, one way or another.

That night, after the evening dishes had all been washed and the camp cleaned up, Bessie slipped into the kitchen tent and quietly fetched the sock out of the box under the bed, unknotted it and shook the coins and bills out on the bed.

Ertie lay on the bed, his head propped up by one arm, smoking. They were alone now as he watched her count the money.

"Sixty-five dollars and sixty-three cents." She put the bills and coins back in the sock and reknotted the top. "We put all but ten of that down as earnest money, won't take us long to get the rest, working like we are."

"Whoa up thar, woman." Ertie sat up. "I ain't agreed ta nothin' but goin' out thar with ya to take a look, I ain' never said nothin' 'bout buyin' us a damned boxcar an' callin' it a house."

"But Ertie, we gotta get off the road before winter, get us someplace snug an' this'd be a start."

Ertie snorted in disgust and reached under the bed for his whiskey bottle. "Woman, I don't trust that feller." He uncorked the bottle and took a long swallow, relishing the warming glow as it spread down his gullet.

"Well." Bessie looked at her husband for a long time, trying to judge his mood, wondering how to talk without getting tangled up in a fight. "When we was lookin' at that house, I could see you'n him wasn't hittin' it off too good."

Ertie nodded. " 'Nother minute or two and I'd a tol' that jasper to go straight to hell an' take that boxcar with 'im."

"I know. An' I know it ain' much of a place neither, but the payments is only goin' to be ten or twelve dollars a month, Ertie. Don' ya see, it's our only chance." She was convinced that God was giving them this opportunity and another wasn't likely to come along. Her best chance was to try and make him see that this place would help them get their independence, give them shelter no matter what happened.

Ertie looked at his wife through the whiskey's afterglow, feeling mellow. He grinned and took a long drag on his cigarette. "Well, yor dang shor right about one thing, that ain' much of a place."

"Ertie, lookee here." She reached out, touching his hand; her voice was soft and without challenge. "I ain't goin' against whatever you think is right for us, but I gotta say what I think."

He nodded, giving her permission to go on.

"I know you don' wan' to be tied down, but don' ya see what's holdin' us down is bein' on the road, never knowin' where we're goin' or how long we'll have work. The way I see it, we ain' never gonna be free if we don't own us someplace where we can be safe. We git a place of our own, that'll be what makes us free." She paused, hesitant to bring up again what had happened to them that awful first winter, but it had to be said because it lay at the very heart of her argument. "I ain' layin' no blames, but I never wan' to see us go through what we did that winter, never again want ta see ya havin' to beg jus' to get us some food to eat."

It was out and she sat silently, watching, not knowing whether to go on or not.

Ertie sucked in another long drag on his cigarette, still not saying anything.

Bessie decided to keep talking. "We have a place, we'd truly be free, a place where we could grow food for the winters and not have to depend on nobody. When there was lots of work close by, we'd live at home and drive out, when there wasn't you an' the boys could travel to the crops. Billie Jo belongs with James Earl so she and Susie or Mary Ellen could go along to cook and keep camp and help out in the fields too. Then, in the fall, you'd be back here, and we'd all be pickin' grapes and cotton. Wintertimes you an' the boys can work for Kitahara an' his neighbors pruning. It ain' more'n a twenty mile drive to them places."

As she talked, he took another drink and listened, then asked, "What if we give 'im that fifty-five dollars an' then cain' keep makin' them payments?"

Again she looked at him for a moment before answering, realizing that she was on delicate ground now. The wrong word or thought might challenge him and he'd say no, quickly, decisively.

But she had to press on, despite the dangers. It was a risk, sure, but he'd taken risks before. "Ertie, ever' time you entered a rodeo you put up your entry fees. Sometimes you even borrowed the money to enter, remember? You was takin' a chance, wasn't ya?"

He nodded and started to say something, but she kept right on talking.

"Well, this way we'd be puttin up our money, takin' a chance." Gently, firmly she nudged him toward the idea, all the while letting him know the decision was his to make. Finally, when there wasn't anything else to say, she reached up, gently touching his face, and whispered, "Ertie, I don' want us to go on livin' like trash."

"I don' neither." The words escaped from behind that hard, masculine wall that was his defense, the wall that was battered and cracked now and no longer shielded him as it had. Instinctively, he reached out and put his arms around her, the residues of anger and suspicion draining away in a flood of longing. He pulled her to him and, for the first time in weeks, they made love. Without putting it into words, the decision was made.

The next day the whole family drove into Hyattville and found Simmons, who telephoned Rooster Barkham. "Sure, we can go right on over, the judge's expecting us and, by the way, he's agreed on the six-hundred-dollar price, with a hundred twenty down."

They parked out in front of the blue granite building and climbed out of the cars. Simmons herded them past the big display windows of Barkham's Mercantile and Jake, looking in, saw rows of new bicycles and racks of rifles and shotguns. His mother paused to look at a gleaming white washing machine with a double-roller wringer that had no crank handle and Jake guessed it must be run by electricity. Past the windows Simmons directed them up a double-wide flight of stairs. The offices of BARKHAM ENTERPRISES, INC., were at the far end of a long hallway illuminated only by the pale light of skylights in the high ceiling. Their footsteps echoed as Simmons now led the way and held the office door open for them. Inside, Jake was impressed with the luxury of the place, deep burgundy carpeting, tall windows draped in matching colors, golden overstuffed couches and chairs. On the walls were paintings of wild ducks in winter flight and startled deer in wilderness landscapes. Overhead, polished brass chandeliers provided light for the two secretaries working at their antique oak desks.

One of the secretaries looked up, told the Robertsons to take a seat and then spoke softly with Simmons, glancing at Ertie and Bessie occasionally. She nodded, got up and went into an inner office. A few minutes later Judge Rooster Barkham came bouncing out, a rotund, dapper little man in a flashy royal blue blazer with brass buttons. He had on a stiff white shirt and a bright red bow tie. When he saw the Robertsons, he stopped, reared back on his heels and smiled broadly as Simmons made the introductions. At Simmons's urging, Ertie explained how they could only afford to put fifty-five dollars down as earnest money. The judge, standing with feet wide-spread, chest puffed out, hands in the pockets of his powder-blue slacks, listened as Ertie explained they would have the remaining sixty-five dollars of the down payment at least by cotton harvest time.

"Simmons." Rooster Barkham beamed and rocked forward, then back on his heels again, his chest still puffed way out. "These folks look like honest, hard-working people to me, the kind we like to help get a start. Let's trust 'em. Shirley here can make out the papers in a jiffy and take their deposit, and we'll hold the house for them until, say October thirty-first, provided they make the payments of course.

"Remember"—he turned and spoke directly to Ertie—"you start the regular payments now, twelve dollars and sixty-eight cents a month, due the first day of the month, and on October thirty-first you will owe the final sixty-five dollars on the down payment. It would be wise if you tried to pay something on that every month too. All right?"

Ertie and Bessie both nodded. One of the secretaries pulled out standard contract and note forms, slipped carbon paper between the sheets and was quickly typing in the information and figures as the judge talked. She asked them a few questions, typed the answers, pulled the papers out of her typewriter with a snappy efficiency and put them on the desk ready for their signature.

Ertie picked up the contract and scanned the small print, his finger slowly tracing each line as he tried to get some idea of what it was he was signing. He knew his letters and numbers and could read some, but not enough to understand the legal language of the contract.

"You go ahead, read them over," Judge Barkham said, obviously a little irritated. "Take your time, it's wise to see what you're signing."

Jake could see that his father was troubling over the words so he edged in closer, looking over Ertie's shoulder. Bessie and the others crowded around, trying to see.

Ertie looked around at them, then, turning away from the judge, he whispered, "What's this here mean?"

Mary Ellen leaned over the document and read the lines that Ertie was pointing to. "Says if we're thirty days dee-linquent we for-fit all payments and interests in the property."

The judge took the contract from Ertie. "Mr. Robertson, don't you worry about that, that's just a legal formality that we lawyers put in every contract."

Ertie nodded, still suspicious, but not wanting to let on how little he understood.

"Ertie, isn't it?" The judge put a friendly hand on Ertie's bony shoulder. "You don't mind if I call you Ertie do you? Good. Well, don't you worry about all that legal mumbo-jumbo, you and your boys look like hard workers, you won't have any trouble keeping up with those payments."

Ertie had traded too many horses not to know he was getting a hard sell by a real slicker, but Bessie was right, they had to take a chance on getting someplace of their own. It was a gamble, like putting up entrance fees at a rodeo, only then he knew what he was getting into, now he didn't, and the idea of putting his family in a damn boxcar was galling.

The judge put the contract on the desk with the other loan papers, reared back once again and, in his most reassuring voice, explained that he understood how tough times were. "All I ask is that you pay something every month. Do that and things'll work out just fine." He picked up a pen, dipped it in the inkwell and handed it to Ertie. "Just sign right here and here."

Ertie hesitated and Jake heard his mother suck in her breath. Everyone was looking at Ertie and he was staring at the pen in his hand. Then, like a man condemned, he bent over the desk and slowly began to scrawl his name on the documents.

The judge watched and nodded approvingly. "Good. Good, right there on that line. That's it, now the other one. Fine. Fine."

When Ertie had signed the last paper, the judge took up the pen, dipped it in the inkwell again and, with a flourish, signed and dated each document. "Simmons here will finish up."

As the judge turned away, Bessie's enthusiasm bubbled over. She stepped right up and shook Rooster Barkham's hand, catching him by surprise. As she was pumping his hand, she told him, "We'll move right in an' start fixin' 'er up. We still got two, maybe three weeks work herebouts choppin' cotton, so we'll have some time 'fore we head out again."

"Move in?" Rooster Barkham pulled away. "Move in?"

"Yes, sir." Bessie was puzzled by his reaction.

Ignoring her, the judge turned to Simmons. "Tell them they can move in after they have made the full down payment." Then a calculating little grin tugged at the corners of his mouth. "But they can work on the place if they like, fix it up to suit themselves."

Simmons gave them the key to the padlocked front door and cautioned them not to try to live there before they completed making the down payment. Bessie was disappointed, but at least the place was partially theirs now and it was only a couple of miles from camp.

At the time they were working for a small grower out west of town a ways. Each evening after work they spent a couple of hours scrubbing floors, patching knotholes, clearing out the weeds until that cotton-chopping job was finished. Then, while the rest of the family looked for work, James Earl and Jake started building a new outhouse. The plan was for them to build a two-holer, separated back-to-back, one side for men, the other for women. The first thing they did was slosh kerosene on the old privy and burn it, then they filled the hole, using dirt from the new pit they were digging closer up by the house. While Jake finished up digging the new hole, James Earl went into town and bought some used lumber from Simmons. By nightfall they had the structure framed and were ready to put on the roof and siding.

Ertie and the rest of the family were already back in camp when James Earl turned the Model A off Old River Road and, double-clutching into first gear, bounced over the ruts and across the sandy bottom. Jake jumped out. "Ma, we got 'er all framed in, ya oughta see 'er."

James Earl sat in the pickup, gunning the engine a little and letting the clutch out, pushing it in, letting it out, moving the pickup back and forth.

Ertie limped over. "What'cha doin'?"

"She ain' shiftin' right. Seems like the throw-out bearing's gettin' ready to go out, er somethin'. I ain' sure." James Earl glanced at his father. "Find any work?"

"Na." Ertie shook his head. "But somethin'll turn up tomarra."

The next day James Earl and Jake roofed and sided the out-house, hung the two doors and rigged a stout spring on them so they would swing tight shut. They rasped and sanded the seats, rounding off the edges of the holes so there would be no splinters. With tight-mesh wire screen they covered the vent openings under the eaves, making the construction bugtight. There'd be no flies buzzing around inside this one, no black widows lurking under the seat, no siree. Job finished, they were sitting on the front porch when they saw the sedan coming along Old River Road. Ertie was at the wheel, driving in his own haphazard way.

"Here comes Pa an' them." Jake straightened up.

The old Ford sedan careened in off the road and skidded to a stop. The engine coughed, backfired and died. Doors opened and Ertie and the girls climbed out, pushing Benjy along with them, but Bessie just sat there deep in the backseat, looking forlorn. With a big sigh she wearily grabbed the front seat and pulled herself out.

James Earl walked out to the car. "What's wrong, Ma?"

"Ain' no work to be found nowhere."

"Come on, Ma." Jake was eager to show Bessie the outhouse. "Take a look at 'er. She's all done."

Bessie brightened a bit and they all followed Jake around back.

"See, Ma." One at a time, Jake opened the doors and let them slam shut. "An' see, we got the vent holes screened, so won' be no flies."

The rest of the family stood back as Bessie inspected both sides. "Go ahead, Ma, be the first to use it." Susie was excited. "Go on, that's the girls' side."

Bessie blushed and shook her head. "Ain' necessary."

"Like 'er, Ma?"

"It's grand." Bessie was smiling, but Jake could tell his mother really wasn't thinking about the crapper. It wasn't hard to guess she was worried about their first payment coming due. They could make most of the May first payment, but they were short sixteen dollars, if they were going to pay another ten each month on the down payment. The immediate problem was that most of the cottonfields had been thinned and weeded, so there wasn't much more work around here, but it was still too early to go north into the cherries. They didn't come ripe until around the second week of May. By hanging around Jefferson County they might get two or three more days' work; if they headed north, maybe they could find a job here or there along the way—and, hot as it was, the cherries might be early. On basic decisions like this, they talked over the options, listening to what everyone had to say, but it was Ertie who decided what was best. He was for packing up and leaving.

Once the decision was made, Bessie took charge, like a crew boss. While they were packing up, she hummed one of her favorite hymns. And Jake overheard her tell Mary Ellen, "God's lookin' down on us. I can jus' feel it. We're going to find us work and we're going to make them payments, ever' one. By cotton-pickin' time, we can move in, put in a winter garden, just like the man said."

With that, they headed back out on the road, the sedan and trailer with its tightly roped load taking the lead, the Model A pickup chugging right along behind.

7

Dirty and dripping sweat, Jake crawled slowly over the rock-hard clods, pulling up garlic plants, clipping off the roots and tops with those A-shaped shears that the contractor sold for half a buck. Tossing the bulbs into his hamper, he inched across the field on his hands and knees, clip-clip-toss, clip-clip-toss, all the while hoping that the cooling coastal fog would blow back in again, but the fog had long since burned off and there was no way for anyone in the garlic fields to escape the brassy sun.

Working in the garlic was the meanest fucking job in the whole damn world and it only paid a penny a hamper, three hampers to a full gunnysack. Each evening when they added up their wages, the seven of them were making three, maybe four dollars a day, hardly enough to fill their bellies and have enough saved up to get down the road. There was no way they could catch up on what they owed, no matter how hard they tried. So where was God now? Here it was damn near August and they owed near seventy dollars, counting the hospital bill and the house payments they'd missed. Worried, Jake stopped clipping and sat there trying to figure the numbers. They'd made the first house payment on May first, right on time. He smoothed a patch of dirt and scratched in $12.68. Their plan was to send another ten dollars every month to work off what they owed on the down payment; that way they wouldn't have to come up with that sixty-five all at once in October. But they just didn't have that extra ten on May first. They did find enough work to send the full twenty-two sixty-eight by

June first. Jake scratched more numbers in the dirt. Right after that, just as they were finishing up in the cherries, they ran into trouble. Benjy got awful sick with a bellyache, so bad they finally hurried him to the hospital crying in pain, but the doctor wouldn't even let them in until they put up ten dollars, cash money. Later a nurse said they'd taken out Benjy's appendix and that cost another forty-five dollars, even if they were a charity case. That put them in a real bind because the cherry harvest was over but they couldn't go find more work until Benjy was well enough to leave. Even then the nurse wouldn't release him until they paid another ten dollars and signed a debt paper promising to make payments every month.

By the time they found jobs and were picking fruit again they were so far behind they didn't have the July first payment. Bessie managed to scrape twenty dollars together by the middle of the month and they sent half to Simmons and half to the hospital. The way Jake figured it, they still owed at least forty-five bucks. They just had to hope that the judge meant it when he said he'd go along with them if they paid something every month. What was really worrisome was that the way things were going right now it didn't look like they'd have enough to make any kind of payment come the first of August, not unless their luck changed.

One evening after work a man came by camp and was telling anyone who'd listen that he and a bunch of tomato farmers had jobs for them back over in the San Joaquin Valley, said they needed lots of workers and were paying good wages, seven cents a hamper.

"Where at, mister?"

"Over in Jefferson County. Know where Colby is?"

Ertie nodded.

"Well, it's out east of there a ways, take Avenue Five east, ya'll see signs for pickers nailed up on the power poles. Just follow them."

That sounded promising, so they packed up the next morning and headed east, back over the Coast Range toward the valley. The narrow, two-lane highway snaked steeply up through the dry canyons. Jake shifted down into second gear, then first, and the overheating engine growled up through the twisting turns, radiator steaming. Topping out at Pacheco Pass, James Earl signaled and Jake pulled over; something was wrong with the pickup. While everyone else got out and stretched, James Earl and Jake huddled around the old Model A. "Clutch's clear gone." James Earl kicked at a tire. "Been havin' to rev up the engine an' jam 'er in gear ever' time I shift."

"Got no clutch at all?"

"None 'tall. Had to kill the engine in gear or we'd never get goin' again."

"How ya gonna start 'er up again?"

"Starter'll pull 'er over a few times, 'nuff to get the engine goin'." James Earl looked worried. "Worst part is, she won' stay in second comin' down. I don' wan' to take no chances, so I'm gonna taker 'er down the hill in first."

"All the way?"

"Cain' help it, grade's too steep for jus' brakes alone. Burn'm out."

It was another twenty long miles down through the canyons and out onto the plains and they took it at five miles an hour, the Model A in the lead, '32 Ford and trailer following along behind, trying to stay on the shoulder of the highway so the cars and trucks that backed up behind them could get around. Out in the flats, they crossed the valley and turned south on Highway 99, traveling now at a steady forty-five miles an hour. As dusk softened into evening and the air began to cool, Jake turned on the headlights. Traffic wasn't heavy, a few cars zipping past, an occasional truck. Just after dark the flashing headlight of a locomotive rushed toward them, and, in an instant, thundered past, orange flames flaring from the firebox, lighted windows of the passenger cars blurring by, great iron wheels clacking down the rails into silence. Suddenly the night was empty.

"Jake?" Bessie sounded tired.

"Yeah?"

"Soon as ya see a spot where we can camp, pull over. We gotta rest, fix some supper."

Up ahead Jake spotted a bridge and some trees and took his foot off the gas.

"Here'll do," his mother said wearily.

Jake flashed the lights, signaling to James Earl, and they pulled off the road. Too tired to set up tents, they built a small fire, quickly cooked and ate some supper, spread their beds on the sandy ditch-bank and fell asleep, all except Jake, who lay there looking up at the stars, listening to the night sounds, the traffic out on the highway, crickets in the weeds, the breathing and murmuring of the rest of the family. A shooting star streaked across the heavens, a marvel so sudden his eyes almost missed it, and he watched more intently, hoping to see another. Was God really up there?

The next morning they were up and packed before sunup, but the Model A's battery was too weak to start the engine in gear. James Earl got out and gave the wheel another frustrated kick. "We'll have to try a push start."

They unhooked the trailer and Jake eased the sedan in behind the pickup, nudging against the bumper. Because they had to start it in gear, James Earl wouldn't be able to stop again. That meant he and Billie Jo had to keep right on going, leaving Jake and the rest of the family behind. James Earl climbed into the pickup. "I'll go slow till ya catch up."

Sitting behind the wheel, Jake nodded and at James Earl's signal he gunned ahead, tires spinning gravel, sedan pushing hard against the Model A, moving it slowly ahead against the drag of the gears and engine, picking up speed. James Earl choked the carburetor and floored the gas pedal, waving his brother on frantically. The Model A engine chugged, backfired, and chugged to life. Jake braked and turned back for the trailer and the rest of the family as the pickup sped off.

With the Model A in the lead, they drove on south through Fresno County, crossing the Kings River into Jefferson County just after dawn. The tomato fields were nearly fifteen miles east of Colby and, as it turned out, the fellow who had recruited them was a labor contractor, not a farmer, the pay was a nickel, not seven cents, and there were hundreds of workers crowded in the vines. The Robertsons worked until midafternoon, then cashed in and asked where they could pitch their tents. The crew boss knew of a camp up the road five or six miles, on the north bank of the Kings River. Following his directions, they crossed the river and turned west along River Bend Road. Once an oak forest, this was riverbottom farming country. The meandering river formed the boundary between Fresno and Jefferson Counties, except where it looped way south for a mile or two; there both banks were in Jefferson County. The camp was supposed be there, in the loop.

"Ain' that it?" Susie leaned out of the window and pointed to a large, rambling shanty that had been roofed and sided with heavy green tarpaper. The green shanty was in a clearing along the river, out back were tool sheds and a dozen or more rusting junked cars, some of them tipped on their sides. Beyond the wrecks and kind of off to one side were forty-five or fifty tents and makeshift shelters set out under the trees.

"Gotta be it." Jake signaled to James Earl and they turned off onto a rutted dirt road. The camp was fenced off and the road crossed over a cattle guard near the green tarpaper shanty.

"Oh, my." Bessie sounded worried. "Wonder if they charge to camp here?"

"Man never said nothin' 'bout havin' to pay." Jake eased the sedan across the cattle guard and heard the Model A rattle across the grid of steel pipes behind him. James Earl pulled off to one side and killed the engine.

A giant, gray-bearded man in grease-blackened overalls leaned heavily on a pair of crutches in the shanty yard, watching them. The right pantleg of his grimy overalls had been scissored off at mid-thigh and was pinned closed to protect the stump of his missing leg. Behind him, nailed above the shanty's double-wide doorway, was a sign:

BULL'S CAMP
No Niggers Or Mexicans Allowed

Bull Skinner wore no shirt. He was a powerful man with burly shoulders and muscled arms, tanned a butternut-brown. Tattooed on the round of one shoulder there was a grinning skull with a rattlesnake slithering through the eye sockets, on the other was the Marine Corps emblem and the words DEATH BEFORE DIS-HONOR; a black panther clawed its bloody way up his right forearm and a hula girl wiggled her ass on the left.

"Howdy, folks," Bull Skinner's voice boomed, "huntin' fer a place to roost?"

Bessie scooted up close to the back window. "How much?"

"Fifty cents, ma'am. For fifty cents ya got hot showers, a washhouse, clean outhouses and there ain't no law goin' to bother ya here, if that's a worry." Bull grinned, then waved an arm. "Look around. If ya don' stay, no hard feelin's. Ya can pay in cash or kind. Need to work on the cars, I got parts and tools and ya can use the hoist, there. Charge fifty cents for that."

Jake glanced at his father, then back at his mother. "We gotta work on the pickup."

"I know," Bessie sighed. "We oughta do some laundry too, get ourselves cleaned up. But no more'n a day or two."

Ertie nodded in agreement.

"Okay, mister, we'll stay." Jake handed Bull the half dollar his mother gave him. "Where d'ya want us to camp?"

Bull gestured off to the right. " 'Bout halfway down there oughta be a couple spots in there somewhere."

James Earl was standing by the Model A. "We leave 'er parked there for a bit?"

"Shor." Bull scratched his grizzled beard. "Got problems?"

"Clutch's shot an' the transmission needs work."

"Come on around after ya get settled, see what we can do."

Jake drove back past the sheds and junked cars, took the right-hand fork in the road and drove into the camp. Tents and knocked-together shanties lined a half dozen streets that meandered through the grove of oaks. In a clearing near the center of the campground Jake could see a large open-air washhouse built on a concrete slab and sheltered by a tin roof. Under the tin canopy were rows of sinks and large drainboards and down at one end four shower stalls had been built out of rusting, corrugated panels of iron, two for ladies, two for gents. River water was piped to the washhouse and heated in an ancient boiler. Beside the boiler were stacks of firewood.

Jake pulled into an empty spot shaded by an oak. After they set up camp and retrieved James Earl's pickup, Jake and Susie ran off exploring the network of footpaths linking the campsites to the outhouses and washhouse and they wandered along by the river, chucking rocks, skipping them across the deep, green-running water.

Susie picked up a short piece of limb wood and hurled it out into the swift current, watching as it swept downstream. "This here river's mean-lookin', 'spect it'd drown ya if ya was to go swimmin'." She picked up another stick and tossed it into the water. "We better git back, Ma'll be startin' supper soon an' we still got chores to do."

"Look!" Jake was pointing across the river.

"What?"

"Sshh. Rabbit. Thar." He continued to point. "Damn, another one. Wisht I had the twenty-two." Impulsively, he took off running. "Race ya back."

"Jake, no fair! Ya got a head start." Susie was right after him.

Back in camp, James Earl was down under the Model A, inspecting the transmission. Bessie and Billie Jo were setting the kitchen straight and Mary Ellen was making biscuits. Ertie had the .22 rifle out and was sitting at the table cleaning it. The big nickel-plated revolver was lying on the table, gleaming in the afternoon sunlight.

Jake and Susie ran into camp, yelling, "Pa! Pa, we seen some jackrabbits. Big ones!"

"Whar?"

"Across the river thar a ways, can I go huntin'?" Jake, out of breath, touched the pistol's walnut grips reverently.

Susie flopped down on a box. "Biggest dang rabbits ya ever did see!"

"Hold on, you two," Bessie said. "We need some wood."

"Somebody's comin'." Mary Ellen stopped rolling dough and stared up the road.

Bull Skinner lumbered toward them on his crutches.

"Wonder what he wants?" Bessie paused.

Bull had stopped by the Model A, asking James Earl, "Need a good jack an' some blocks?"

"How much?"

"Quarter."

"Come on in an' set." Ertie waved at one of the small kegs that served as camp stools.

"Don' mind if I do." Bull put a pint jar of homemade whiskey on the table, laid his crutches aside and sat down. "Evenin', ma'am. How you all?"

"Jus' fine." Bessie nodded, then scolded Jake and Susie. "The two of ya, go git us some wood!"

Bull unscrewed the top of the pint jar and pushed it toward Ertie. "Like a taste?"

Ertie took a swallow and the fiery liquid sent a shudder through him. "Whooeee! Tha's shor got a kick to it." He took another slug and set the jar back down. "Damn, that's good."

Bull held the jar up, offering it to Bessie. "Ma'am?"

"No." Bessie shook her head disapprovingly.

Bull downed a swallow himself and pushed the jar back toward Ertie. "If yer thirsty, I sell the stuff, fifty cents a pint. That there's on the house."

Ertie saw that Bull had his eye on the big pistol. "Go ahead, take a look at 'er if ya want."

"Remington?" Bull carefully picked up the weapon.

Ertie nodded. "Forty-four–forty."

Bull eared the hammer back to half-cock and spun the cylinder. Noticing the three notches filed on the shoulder of the pistol grips, he asked, "These real?"

"Guess so, they was there when I got 'er."

"How'd you come by it?"

"Well, I was wranglin' horses for a big cow outfit out in West Texas, was younger'n Jake there at the time. Ol' Billie Blue, the cook, he had this pistol in his bedroll. Said he bought it from a U.S. marshal's widda. I give a month's pay for it and had to rustle wood for the rest of the roundup, to boot. She shoots nice, wanna giver 'er a try?"

"Why shor." Bull laid the pistol down and took a drink.

"Jus' lemme finish up here an' we'll take 'er down by the river for a little target practice."

"That cook, he ever say how that marshal got killed?"

"Shoot-out, up in the Panhandle someplace."

"Be interestin' if this old shootin' iron could talk. That'd be some story."

" 'Spect so." Ertie wiped off the rifle and laid it down, chuckling to himself.

"What's funny?"

"Jus' thinkin' 'bout them days. Was two cowboys that I was travelin' with and me nothin' but a green kid with a hand-me-down saddle and an old pair of clodhopper shoes. Damn, I'd a sold my soul for a real pair of cowboy boots. Well, Hugh and Old Ty, that was their names, Hugh Nutter and Ty Treywick, they tol' the Spanish Bit ramrod that I was a hell of a hand with a horse and if he didn't hire me they'd ride on to the next outfit. Now they was two top hands, you could see that easy enough, an' the outfit being shorthanded, the ramrod said he'd try me out wrangling horses. That's how I got my first job."

Ertie gave the rifle a final wipe, worked the lever action, cocking and uncocking it a few times, then laid the piece down and looked around, hollering, "Jake! Jake! Where'd that boy go?"

"Here he comes now." Bull took another sip of whiskey.

Jake dumped an armful of limb wood by the fire.

"Boy, run fetch me tha' box a forty-four ca'tridges, will ya? An' somethin' we kin shoot at."

"Kin I shoot 'er too? Huh, Pa?"

"Shor." Ertie, feeling a bit drunk, grabbed up the pistol and headed for the river, Bull swinging right along behind him.

Bessie hollered, "Don' you all be gone too long, supper'll be ready soon."

Down by the river the air was warm and filled with the pungent odor of moldering leaves. Birds flitted through the trees and there was no sound save the murmur of the river and the occasional, quickening *tap-tap-tap* of a woodpecker.

"Got 'em, Pa!" Jake ran up with an armload of cans and bottles. Handing the cartridge box to Ertie, he dashed on down to the sandy river's edge and set out the targets.

Ertie opened the box, counting. He had thirty-three rounds left, including those in the cylinder. Jake came running back, a happy look on his homely face. When he was out of the way, Ertie quickly raised the pistol and fired: BOOM!

A glass jar shattered and the deafening explosion rang in their ears. Gunsmoke drifted around them.

"Good shot, Pa." Jake looked eagerly at the pistol, hoping.

Ertie handed it to Bull. "Give 'er a try. Watch now, 'cause she's got a light trigger."

Bull leaned on his crutches and, clutching the pistol in both of his big hands, he cocked and fired: BOOM!

Sand kicked up beside a soup can. "Damn, that shor is a touchy trigger."

"Give 'er another try."

Bull took careful aim and fired again, nicking a can, sending it spinning sideways. "She kicks like a goddamn mule."

"No harder'n yor likker."

Bull handed the pistol to Jake and Ertie stepped in close behind his son, coaching. "Use both hands an' don' cock it till yor almost on target."

Heart pounding, Jake raised the heavy pistol and with both thumbs eared the hammer back.

"Careful," Ertie cautioned, "squeeeeze 'er off."

BOOM!

The shot went way high. Jake looked anxiously at his father. "Kin I try again? Please?" His second shot was wide, but not by much, and reluctantly he handed the pistol back to Ertie.

"How much ya want for it?" Bull wanted that pistol.

"Ain' for sale." Ertie crouched and fired, shattering another bottle.

"Give ya ten dollars cash money."

"Whoa, thar, partner, I wouldn't take five times that, even if it was for sale." Ertie ejected the spent shells and started reloading the pistol.

"You shor set store on that hawgleg, don' ya."

"Yup." Ertie was a little drunk and knew it.

"Tell ya what, le's have a little contest." Bull leaned heavily on his crutches eyeing Ertie. "Six rounds each, ten dollars cash an' a month's rent against your pistol."

Ertie grinned, and shook his head. "Na."

" 'Fraid I kin outshoot'cha?"

"Nope." The grin on Ertie's bony face widened a little and his hawk-yellow eyes hardened. "Hell, I tol' ya it's worth fifty dollars, more if times wasn't so tough."

"Awright, I'll throw in fifteen dollars cash."

"Make 'er forty, an' a gallon o' yor best."

"Pa, no!" Jake stared at his father in disbelief. "Not the Remington!"

"Twenty." Bull looked evenly at Ertie. "An' a quart."

"Make it thirty-five."

"Pa! no!"

"Twenty-five."

"Done." The deal was struck. Bull turned on his crutches. "But hol' on a min' okay? I gotta take a piss."

As the big man headed toward a clump of willows, Jake squared off in front of his father, near tears. "Pa, ya cain't. Yor drunk."

"Hush up boy, I'm goin' ta win us enough to catch up that payment we missed." Ertie spun the cylinder.

Bull came swinging back. "That pistol's good as mine!"

"You first." Ertie offered the Remington to Bull.

Bull shook his head. "Nope!" He dug out a coin and flipped it in the air. "Call it."

"Heads."

Ertie won the toss and handed the pistol over. Bull stepped up to the line they'd toed in the sand, leaned on his crutches and brought the weapon up in both hands: BOOM!

Sand exploded beside a can, knocking it over. Bull cocked and fired again, missing, but his third shot was a clean hit. He fired again and again, missing twice more. Swearing softly, he lowered the pistol, rested, then brought it up and fired again, drilling a can dead-center, driving it back, a huge jagged hole opened in the rusty metal.

Ejecting the shells, Bull roared, "Three down, le's see ya beat that."

"Three hell." Ertie was flabbergasted. "Shit, the sand knocked the first one down."

"Down's down." Bull handed the pistol over, grip first.

"Like hell." Ertie was mad and he could feel the adrenaline cutting through the dulling whiskey-fuzz. He reloaded the pistol and turned to Jake. "Throw one of them little milk cans out in the river."

"What?" Jake stared in disbelief at his father.

"Go on. I'll show the son of a bitch who kin shoot."

"Who ya callin' som'bitch?"

Ertie ignored the question. "Throw it, dammit!"

"Pa. No!"

"Throw it, goddammit!"

Angrily, Jake ran down to the river's edge, picked up a condensed milk can and hurled it out into the river, then scooted back out of the way as the can bobbed downstream.

In one sweeping motion Ertie brought the pistol up and fired: BOOM!

Water spouted just behind the can, a clean miss. Ertie couldn't believe it. The pistol sagged to his side, he took a deep breath and in the same fluid motion brought it up again, firing twice at the targets in the sand: BOOM! BOOM!

One shot kicked a can high in the air, the second missed. Slowly he cocked and fired again, shattering a bottle. His fifth shot sent another can rolling. They were tied, three and three. Ertie raised the pistol slowly, cocking the hammer. The barrel came in line, but wavered. He lowered the pistol, easing the hammer off, turned and walked back a ways, then came up to the line and quickly raised the pistol and fired: BOOM!

The shot went high. "Shit." Ertie stood there, angry and frustrated.

"Ha! Ha! Som'bitch yerself!" Bull laughed loudly. "Gotta shoot another round."

"Bullshit. One shot each, first miss loses."

Bull looked at Ertie for a second. "Awright, but you shoot first."

Still angry because Bull claimed the sand shot, Ertie reloaded, cocked and fired: BOOM!

The can spun crazily across the sand and the forty-four slug ricocheted, sounding a high whine into the distance.

Bull took the pistol, got set and raised his big, muscled arms, the pistol gripped in both hands. The death head on his shoulder grinned at Ertie. Nearby the sound of a woodpecker drilled the silence. Bull squeezed off the shot: BOOM!

The slug kicked up sand, a clean miss. Bull looked at Ertie for a second, then laughed. "You win, you som'bitch!"

"Yahooo!" Jake yelled and jumped. "Heeeyaa! We won!"

Bull handed over the pistol and twenty-five dollars. "I get to help ya drink that quart, don' I?"

"Why shor." Ertie gave the pistol and near-empty box of shells to Jake. "Put 'em away, will ya boy?"

Jake nodded, a happy smile all over his face. He shoved the box in his pocket and, clutching the pistol, took off running, dodging barefoot through the junk and weeds, yelling, "Pa won! Pa won! Now ya kin send ol' man Simmons the money on our propertee!"

"Come on, let's git that quart."

Forgetting supper, Ertie quickly agreed and limped along after Bull. The still was in one of the sheds, hidden behind piles of junked car parts, and it wasn't just a quick and dirty operation, no siree. The big copper boiler and tubing were polished and well cared for, even neat. Awed, Ertie asked, "Law don' bother ya none?"

"Naw. Windy Scott, the sheriff, he's a good ol' boy and ya might say he's got a part interest in the business." Bull handed a jug to Ertie. "You was a cowboy, no foolin'?"

"From the ground up." They flopped down on the corn sacks and Ertie pulled out his watch, fumbled it open. "Won that in Salina, Kansas."

"How'd ya come to take up the cowboy life?"

"Run off from home. That son of a bitch my ma was livin' with was all the time beatin' on me. One day I couldn't take it no more. I grabbed up a hunk of pipe and split his head open."

"Kill 'im?"

"Wisht I had. He got back up bleedin' bad an' come at me yellin' to kill me. I skinned out an' never went back. We was livin' in the oilfields, up in Oklahoma. I headed south, hitched rides and walked a lot, slept down under bridges. Ended up in Abilene, livin' in the back alleys, findin' odd jobs when I could, stealin' somethin' to eat when I couldn't. That's when them two cowpunchers picked me up like a stray pup, fed me and took me with 'em, learned me most of what I know." Ertie was quiet for a bit, then chuckled. "Them two got me my first piece of ass. We'd finished the roundup and they took me to the whorehouse, said it was time I learned to fuck. I shor took to them lessons, let me tell you. Them whores thought it was cute, learnin' me, and after my money ran out they were fuckin' me for free. Hugh and Ty they finally drug me out of there, said I'd wear my pecker out if I wasn't careful."

"How come you still ain't cowboyin'?"

Ertie's face turned sour. "Horse fell on me. Stove me up inside."

"That where the limp comes from?"

"Yup."

They were quiet for a while, sipping on the jug, passing it back and forth, then Ertie asked, "How'd ya lose yor leg?"

"Durin' the war, place called Belleau Wood. A shell hit right smack in the trench, blowed ever'body but me to hell. Tha's what they tol' me anyways, I don' 'member none of it. All I remember is wakin' up in the hospital a one-legged marine." Bull held up the jug. "Here's to the fuckin' marines."

That next afternoon Bessie had Jake drive her into the Colby post office to mail a money order and note:

Dear Mr. Simmons,

Here is $25 to make up for what we missed in July and pay on what we owe for August. We got us jobs and are making steady money. Please tell Judge Barkham we are trying hard to pay him something every month, like he said.

Sincerely,
Mrs. Ertie Robertson

It was true, they were making pretty good money in the tomatoes, but fixing the Model A cost them nearly twelve dollars. Bessie balked at the price. "James Earl, we ain't got that kind of money. We owe the hospital another twenty-five dollars and there's still forty-five due on the down payment for the house, plus we gotta make the payments."

"Ain' got no choice, Ma. It's that or junk the Model A an' all of us crowd up in the sedan."

Bessie sighed and nodded. They had to keep the pickup running.

One evening a flatbed truck with high stake sides and a canvas top pulled into Bull's Camp and parked just down the lane from the Robertsons'. The driver got out, stretched and looked around. He was a surprisingly tall, thin man, standing way over six feet. His wife was a short and heavyset woman with dark, graying hair. Crawling out of the back of the truck came a strapping teenage boy. A few minutes later a rattletrap Chevy pulled in beside the truck, the engine backfiring and dying in a puff of black smoke. A young woman climbed out of the Chevy and her husband handed out one cranky little girl then another, twins by their looks.

Bessie was standing at the kerosene stove stirring a skillet of gravy, but her attention was on the family across the way. She had seen the man before, she was certain. So tall he kind of stooped to be closer to those around him, he was homely enough to sour milk, but homely in a friendly way. His face was long and boney, cheeks sunken, eyes set deep in their sockets, and he had a big, sharp nose that was a little crooked, a bent beak that hung over a generous, smiling mouth full of yellowed teeth. He wore no hat and his gray-black hair had been cropped short and now grew shaggy-wild, standing out every which way.

The man helped his boys unload the truck, then he said something to his wife and headed for the washhouse. As he ambled past their camp in a loose-jointed, gangling walk, Bessie recognized him: Elijah Parsons!

"Mary Ellen." Bessie quickly removed her old apron and laid it aside. "Come over here and stir this for me."

Mary Ellen was by the fire, putting a pan of biscuits in the Dutch oven. She looked up. "What's wrong, Ma?"

"That's Lige Parsons goin' by."

"Who?" Mary Ellen quickly fit the heavy iron lid on the Dutch oven, scooped a shovelful of coals over it and stood up, looking around.

"Here"—Bessie handed her the spoon—"don' let it burn," and she hurried to catch the man, calling his name. "Lige?"

He stopped, turned half around. "Ma'am?"

"You're Lige Parsons?"

"Yes'm." Stooping a little, he looked at her, puzzled.

"Yor sister Midge." Bessie smiled slyly, enjoying her advantage. "How is she?"

Lige Parsons hesitated, still puzzled. "She's dead."

"Oh my." Bessie's hand flew to her mouth. "When?"

"Say, now I 'member you, yor Bessie Larson? From Binger?"

Bessie nodded, wiping at her eyes. "What happened ta Midge?"

"Died birthin' a chil'." Lige put his hand gently on Bessie's shoulder.

"When?" She whispered the question.

"Winter of 'twenty-three, she an' that drummer she married was livin' in St. Louis." Lige paused, then changed the subject. "Ya out here with yor folks? Lan's sake I ain' seen Anders Larson since I quit workin' at the blacksmith shop."

"No, him an' the boys's still back in Binger." She brushed a wisp of blond hair back from her eyes. "Anyways, I'm married, got a family of my own, now. We're camped right yonder." She motioned with her hand, then added, "I got to get supper on. Yor more than welcome to join us."

"Thank ya kindly, but I reckon R'becky'll already have the pot on. But we'd be proud to come over after, for a visit."

Bessie went back to camp happy, yet sad. Mary Ellen was curious and Bessie explained that Lige had worked for her father at the forge and that Midge Parsons had been her best friend all through school. Mary Ellen knelt by the fire and checked the biscuits, listening as her mother talked.

"She know Pa, too?"

"Shor." Bessie stirred the gravy. "We saw him at the same

time. He'd come ta Binger to ride in the Fourth of July parade and rodeo and his horse had thrown a shoe and he come by the forge to get 'im shod. Well Midge was there too and we saw right off he wasn' from 'round Caddo County. He was wearing a big black Texas hat, a fancy snap-button shirt made outa red silk, an' woolly chaps. Had on Mexican silver spurs with big rowels that jingled ever' step he took. Oh, he wasn't handsome, not in a purty way, but he was shor good-looking. Asked me to ride up behind him in the parade, but my daddy wouldn't hear of that, so Midge, she said she'd do it and she did. I was so mad at her. After the parade, we went to the rodeo, the whole town did, and I watched him ride. Oh, he was flashy, fanning that horse with his hat, but he outsmarted hisself an' that horse throwed 'im, hard. He got right up again an' waved at us, never lettin' on how bad his arm was hurtin'. Found out later it was broke.

"I wanted to see him again, so that night I snuck out to the dance, but I was late gettin' there 'cause I had to wait until my daddy went to bed 'cause he didn't believe none in dancin'. Anyways, soon as I walked into the dance I seen yor pa right off, his arm was in a cast, had it in one of them slings around his neck, an' he was dancin' with Midge. Soon as he seen me, he come right over an' asked me to dance."

"Did ya know right then you was goin' to marry him?"

"Why land sakes, no. Girl, you been readin' too many of them fancy magazine stories." Bessie wiped her hands on her apron, enjoying the moment as much as her daughter. No, she didn't know right then, but later she guessed it might happen when he told her he was looking for work and promised to settle down. They were married in November.

"Ma, what about Midge? Was ya still friends after you'n Pa was married?"

"Why shor, but we didn't see each other much after yor pa an' me'd moved out on the farm 'cause times was hard and there was just the two of us to make a crop. By then she was seein' that drummer who used to come through sellin' dry goods an' talkin' about runnin' off with him." Bessie wiped away a tear. "Girl, quit gabbin' an' set the table."

Mary Ellen looked sympathetically at her mother. "Was it a good farm?"

The question caught Bessie by surprise.

"Back in Binger?"

"Yeah."

"Good 'nuff, I s'pose. Yor pa he didn't like farmin' none too well, wanted to raise hay an' grain and pasture some stock but the landlord wanted cotton planted, so cotton it was. We figgered if we got one good crop off that land we'd make 'nuff cash money to go off on our own, buy some green colts that he could break to harness or saddle.

"My how we worked that crop, weedin' an' thinnin' and that fall we hired a couple of niggers to help with the picking, but times was hard, like I said, an' when it come time to settle up, the landlord had us owin' him. Yor pa was mad clean through, but there weren't nothin' we could do but put in 'nother crop of cotton an' try again. It was a good crop too, but come settlin'-up time, we was still owing an' yor pa, he figgered that landlord fella was cheatin' on the books."

Mary Ellen knew the story. "That why we moved to Sweetwater, wasn't it, 'cause Pa got mad?"

"Shor he was mad." Bessie was irritated by the question. "It wasn't hard to see that we wasn't never goin' out of that man's debt, not croppin' on shares that-a-way, so we moved to Texas."

"But Grandpa an' Uncle Hobart an' them stayed?"

"Was different for them." Bessie was defensive. "They got the blacksmith shop. Folks always needin' a blacksmith."

Mary Ellen hated coming to California, hated being an Okie, and she blamed her father. "But us trampin' 'round out here like trash, that's his fault. If he'd a stuck it out farmin', 'stead of goin' off rodeoin', maybe—"

"Daughter!" Bessie cut Mary Ellen off. "That's what he knowed how to do and he won 'nuff to pay off that landlord an' get us moved to Sweetwater."

"But we didn't do no better there, always scrabblin' 'round, you an' the rest of us tryin' ta make ends meet whilst he went off and got busted up like that." The words, pent up for so long, were rushing out. "If he hadn't been off rodeoin'—"

"You best keep your mouth shut 'less you know what yor talkin' about, girl. We was near broke, an' the onliest thang he knowed how to do to make us cash money was to rodeo. Ain' a finer man set on a horse, an' don' you forget it."

"But Ma, you blame 'im too." Mary Ellen retreated. "I've heard ya arguing 'bout how him all the time goin' off."

"Girl, you best hush up!"

But it was true, they had argued about his rodeoing, later, after moving to Texas. During those first years in Oklahoma, he worked hard farming but she soon saw he wasn't cut out for plowing and planting and he wouldn't be cheated; nor could Anders Larson dominate him as he did her. Looking back on it now, Bessie could see that trouble between those two had been inevitable.

Even so, she missed Binger and the visits to her mother's grave. Life had been hard after her mother's death, trying to keep house and stay in school, and she had found solace there in the quiet of the cemetery. Each Sunday in church she had listened to the wrathful words of her father's God, then retreated to the cemetery—kneeling there beside that quiet grave she could feel her mother's gentle presence, hear her nurturing voice urging her to be patient and to endure. Lovingly, she would replace the flowers in the green vase and pull the weeds, knowing that her visits made her mother happy. After she married and moved to the farm, those visits grew less frequent—and now, who took care of the grave now? A tear rolled down her cheek. Angry with herself for being so sentimental, she brushed it away. "Supper's on the table! Jake! James Earl! Come on now!"

The Parsons came over after the supper dishes had all been slicked up and, after the handshakes and howdys, they all settled around the fire talking crops and work, getting acquainted. Lige's wife R'becky was a short, heavyset woman with hefty arms and strong hands. Curly brown hair with wisps of gray ringed around her sun-browned face, she had faded blue eyes and a pushed-up little nose, dusted with freckles. There was about her a warm, motherly look and she wasn't shy about her children. The oldest, she said, was Albert, who was twenty-four and back in Arkansas; Bobby George, just a year younger, was married and off on his own, working somewhere in California or maybe Arizona. It was easy to see that not knowing just where he was made her sad. Junior Parsons, who drove the beat-up Chevy parked over by their truck, was married too. He was maybe a bit older than James Earl and, sitting there in the firelight taking a sip from the jug that Ertie had passed around, he looked a lot like his father, long and lanky. Maybelle, his wife, sat on a blanket at his feet. Not much past seventeen, she was a cherubic girl with curly brown hair and a full figure that was already dumpy. Snuggled sleepily on the blanket next to her were the two little girls, Bertie and Bobbie. Standing behind Junior, Archie Parsons was near as tall and gangling as his father, but better-looking; about Mary Ellen's age, he seemed shy, standing there just back out of the fire, not saying anything.

Lige was talking about the Ozarks and farming in a rocky patch of ground in a small valley north of the Arkansas River. By the sound of it, it was a pretty country, with forests and creeks, a country where a hunter could usually find some meat for his table, even if the soil was worn out and wouldn't grow much.

"How's come ya was to leave?" Jake asked.

Lige stared into the fire for a minute, then looked up. "Oh they was hard times an' some good times, but seems like hard times was winnin' the race. Prices wen' to hell. We was workin' hard but goin' in the hole worse an' worse, groceries gone, likker jug empty. Settin' 'round the eatin' table of a night, with nothin' but a few crumbs of cornbread and a lick of molasses an' ya look at the kids an' think, 'I kin do better than this, get a job a work some'eres.' Me an' a couple of other fellas we wen' up in the wheat harvest, clear to the Dakotas an' back, hit a purty good lick, too. Then, the next year went to Ioway to tossel corn, got there early an' found a job cuttin' cockleburs, first."

"Cockleburs? What fer?"

"By golly, I still don' know, some kinda state law, they said. Had to cut 'em down along the highways. Anyways we done that for a dollar a day, then went to tosselin' corn. After that we went on up into the wheat harvest, got on with a big crew and stayed the season, then come on back to Ioway to pick corn. I made a little money, but it was a lonesome life, so R'becky an' me decided we'd try California. That was the fall of 'thirty-two. We picked cotton that winter in Arizona an' come on into Brawley the next spring. Been out here ever since, just a poundin' up and down that highway, followin' that white line from one job to the next, but it seems like we don' never get ahead."

Junior took a drag on his cigarette, nodding. "That's 'cause we don' have us a union yet."

"Hush boy." R'becky whispered the words.

"Well, it's true."

"Boy." Lige looked at Junior. "That's 'nuff!"

"How 'bout some music?" R'becky slapped Lige on the knee.

"Yeah, Pa, fiddle us a tune," Archie said.

Lige grinned his homely grin. "Why shor. Junior, go git the fiddle and bring along yor gi-tar."

Junior quickly fetched the instruments and, after Lige pulled the fiddle from the tow sack and rosined up the bow, they tuned up, strumming, picking, bowing. Lige looked up. "What'll ya have?"

" 'Walk Along John.' "

Lige gave the strings a final adjustment and struck up the old tune and Junior backed him up. The song had a quick, lively pace and feet began tapping. Finishing the one tune, Lige went quickly to another and the music drifted out into the warm summer evening, an invitation to the people in other camps. They began coming over in twos and fours, rough-handed men in overalls and jeans, worn-out women in faded dresses, and barefoot children, all of them standing back out of the firelight until they were invited into the growing circle. A man named Grimes brought his mouth harp and an old fella with a white beard and glasses joined in with his banjo. Folks began singing and clapping:

> Get outa the way for Old Dan Tucker
> Come too late to git his supper
> Supper's done and the meat's a-fryin'
> Old Dan Tucker's a-standin' an a-cryin'

Across the fire, Jake saw a girl in a yellow dress swaying with the music, her bare feet shuffling a tiny dance step. Her hair, long and blond, was the color of pulled taffy and it swirled around her sweet, playful features. God, she was beautiful, just about the most beautiful girl he'd ever seen. Swallowing hard, he edged his way slowly around the fire, staying back out of the light, trying to keep her in sight as he edged through the crowd so he could just be close to her.

The song ended and someone called for "Seven Cent Cotton."

Lige looked at Junior, who nodded and took the lead, singing in a husky voice:

> *Seven cent cotton and forty cent meat*
> *How in the world can a poor man eat?*
> *Flour up high and cotton down low*
> *How in the world can we raise the dough?*

The song was a favorite and the people began clapping and singing along.

> *Clothes worn out, shoes run down*
> *Old slouch hat with a hole in the crown;*
> *Back nearly broke and fingers all sore,*
> *Cotton gone down to rise no more.*

Jake was only a few feet away from the blonde now and he couldn't take his eyes off her lithe body and the round, soft swell of her breasts. She was a golden angel with mischievous eyes, a pert little nose and full, pouty lips that he wanted to kiss. He stood there gawking, heart pounding. Suddenly, she turned and looked at him, smiling. He almost fainted. Heart in his throat, he blushed and tried to smile back, then bashfully looked away. When he looked back, she was gone. He glanced quickly around, less cautious now. She was standing just the other side of a mean-looking older fellow who had a rock-hard face and a black patch over one eye. She peeked around the man and their eyes met again for an instant. She turned away, singing and clapping along, pretending to ignore him.

> *Twen'y cent gasoline, thirty cent oil*
> *That's what makes the radiator boil.*
> *Engine a-missin', payments due*
> *What in the hell are you gonna do?*

When the song ended, Lige struck up a jig and somebody said they ought to find Buck Horn because that hillbilly could sure enough call the squares. A youngster volunteered to go off and fetch him, others hurried back to their camps to get lanterns and more firewood. Ertie and a couple of others took up a quick collection and headed for Bull's cabin for more whiskey. By the time they got back, with Bull swinging along right behind them, a half dozen lanterns were hanging from ropes and tree limbs, the musicians were playing and couples were dancing.

"Hi." The blonde came over and stood beside Jake. "Wha'chur name?"

"Jake Robertson, wha'churs?"

"Clara Tarpin, from Oklahoma. Where y'all from?"

"Texas." Jake wanted to touch her hair; instead he turned to watch the dancers. "Tha's my sister Mary Ellen out there"—he pointed—"the skinny one with the reddish hair. Think she's soft on that Archie Parsons."

Clara was close beside him now. "This here yor camp?"

"Yep."

"It's a nice'n." She took his hand. "Ya wanna dance?"

Surprised, he mumbled, "Na," and pulled away.

I love pie
I love puddin'
Crazy 'bout the gal
They call Sally Gooden

"Wha's matter, ya scared?"

"Na, I jus' don' wanna." He toed the ground nervously. "Do 'er jus' fine, if I wanna, but I don' wanna."

The next tune was a quadrille. "Come on." Clara pulled on him. "Ain' hard, jis listen ta him callin' an' do what ever'one else does."

Reluctantly, he let her lead him out among the dancers as the caller timed in with the music, "Swang 'er high, swang her low, don' step on that purty little toe."

Jake tried self-consciously to keep up but his feet tangled as he turned the wrong way and he stumbled. Dancers laughed good-naturedly and tried to help him but the attention was too much for him. He broke and darted away, like a frightened colt.

"Jake!" Clara ran after him.

Free of the dancers, he stopped and looked back. Clara wasn't laughing. She reached out and took his hand, pulling him close. "I'm sorry. Don' feel bad." Standing up on her toes, she quickly kissed him. Surprised, Jake awkwardly grasped Clara, kissing her back.

Two men walked out of the dark behind them and one snickered as they passed by. Jake broke off the kiss and tugged Clara's hand. "Come on."

"Whar we goin'?"

"The car." He led her around back to where the sedan was parked. They climbed in the back seat and nestled down, close now, listening to the music:

> *My house is a dugout, and covered with soil,*
> *The walls are not straight, according to Hoyle,*
> *The roof has no slope, it's perfectly plain,*
> *I always get wet, if it happens to rain*

"Hear that song?" Clara sat up excitedly. "It's about the county right next to where we lived, when I was little." She sang along:

> *Hurrah for Greer County, the land of the free,*
> *The home of the grasshopper, the bedbug and the flea*

Clara's voice was sweet and saucy and Jake listened, excited by her closeness. Trying to be casual, he put his arm around her and she leaned back again, snuggling closer.

"Where's Greer County?"

"Like the song says, it's where:

> *A rattlesnake hisses right over my head,*
> *A neat little centipede, without the least fear,*
> *Crawls over my pillow and into my ear.*"

She laughed. "Oh, Jake, it was the worst place."

"But, where's it at?"

"On the Indian lands out in Oklahoma. Us kids was jus' little shavers then an' my daddy he was workin' for the railroad."

"You was livin' with the Injuns?"

"Naw, not them dirty thangs." She sat up in surprise. "They used to come around the tie camp once in a while but Grandpa he run 'em off with that ol' shotgun of his, threatened to blow a hole clean through 'em."

"What was ya doin' there anyways?"

"Cuttin' ties. See, them Indian lands was covered with scrubby li'l post oaks an' the railroad men hired crews to cut 'em down and split ties to go under the railroad tracks."

Jake wanted another kiss but her shoulder was in the way and she was still talking, asking questions.

"How long ya been ou'chere in California?"

"Couple years." Jake scootched around, trying to get a better angle before he made a move on her lips.

"Jake, wha'chu wiggling so much for?"

"I don' know." He sagged back against the seat, embarrassed.

"Yor daddy a farmer?"

"Naw. We was in the livestock business. Had a great big ol' barn an' corrals where Pa'd break the horses and mules. He used to be a cowboy an' was a real good bronc rider."

"A cowboy?" Clara sat up again, turning toward him.

"Yeah, he rodeoed too."

She was facing him now. Seizing the opportunity, he quickly leaned in close and their heads bumped, but he found her lips and kissed her and felt her arm circle his neck as she kissed back, her tongue tickling between his lips. That was a surprise.

Clara pushed him back gently and snuggled back down in his arms again. "Yor pa doesn' look like a cowboy." There was a touch of skepticism in her voice. "How come y'all workin' the crops, if he's such a good cowboy?"

"Buckin' horse fell over on 'im and broke him up, bad. He cain' ride no more." Jake fell silent for a while, then, curious, he asked, "Was that yor pa? With the patch over his eye?"

"Yeah."

"What happened? To his eye, I mean."

"That was before I was borned. Momma said he was on a track-layin' crew, drivin' spikes, when one of 'em broke and flew up an' hit him in the face. Put his eye out an' he lost his job."

Clara had four brothers, a couple of sisters and a passel of cousins that she had to look out for because she was the oldest. They all traveled with her Grandpa Tarpin and his third wife, who was as mean as he was. Grandpa Tarpin had three sons; there was her father, whose name was Dolph, then Harmon and Ott, who each had a wife and a bunch of snotnosed kids. As Clara talked, Jake nuzzled her and looked at her breasts, wanting to touch them.

They looked so soft. Slowly, heart pounding, he moved his left hand inch by inch across his own chest toward hers, stealthy as a spider creeping up to its prey. The anticipation was unbearable. His hand pounced on her unguarded breast.

Clara jumped. "Jake, don't!"

Mortified, he pleaded. "Please!"

"How do I know you love me?"

"I love you!" His hand was back squarely on her breast.

"Jake, please don't." She pushed him away and sat up, her hand on the door latch. "I gotta go."

"Ya mad?"

"Oh, no." She kissed him quickly and was out of the car.

The work in that first tomato field lasted most of the week and then they had to find other fields that were hiring pickers, which took time. One afternoon when the Robertsons were back in camp early after an unsuccessful morning of searching for work, Ertie saw Lige sitting on an old picking box patching an inner tube and he wandered over to visit. Squatting down on his heels, he asked, "Takin' a day off?"

"Might say so. Things are slowin' down. Figger we'll finish up at Wasserman's sometime next week and it'll be time to move on down the road." Lige had a small scraper and was roughing up the rubber where he wanted the patch. "Figger maybe we'll be heading for Kakorian's."

"Kakorian's?" Ertie was surprised to hear Lige was thinking about leaving. "Where's that?"

"Out west of Jeff City maybe fifteen miles, Armenian farmer. He's got some raisin grapes and a hundred acres of cotton."

Ertie smoked for a while, watching Lige daub glue onto the tube.

"You all stayin' on here?"

"Don' know." Ertie shifted his weight to ease the pain in his hip. "Hadn't thought much about it. Still got free rent for a while yet."

"Not much work left here'bouts." Lige tested the glue with his finger to see if it had set up yet.

"That's for damn sure."

"Yor welcome to tag along with us, if ya like. Kakorian usually hires two, sometimes three families to work in the raisins and ya can stay on for the cotton. He don' crowd up the fields with workers the way many of 'em does an' he's got a nice place to camp, out by the barn."

Lige seemed so at ease with the world around him. Ertie took a drag on his cigarette. "Yor used to it, ain'cha?"

The question puzzled Lige. "What?"

"Followin' the crops." Ertie sucked in another drag. "I mean y'all seem so easygoin'."

"Why not?" Lige tested the glue again.

"Don' ya ever get mad the way farmers treat ya like dirt? Or when they cheat ya? Or pay ya off in brass money?"

"El Adobe!" Lige laughed, and shook his head. "Oughta stay away from places like that."

"Hell, if it ain' that place, it's another, don' treat ya no better'n a goddamn nigger." Ertie stood up, bristling.

"Aw, sit down. I didn' mean no offense," Lige said in a friendly way. "But ya gotta expect some trouble when you work on them big farms."

"We work where we can find it." Ertie was still testy.

"We did too, till we got thangs figgered out. Now I got two rules, I don' never work for a labor contractor an' I won' hire on no big outfits like El Adobe. Why, Lord-a-mighty no. I head for the small places, they're friendlier and they pay better."

"Yeah, I reckon that's so." Ertie hunkered down.

Lige opened the can of patching materials, took out a rubber square and cut off what he needed.

Ertie lit another cigarette. After a while he asked, "Ya ever think of goin' back?"

"Where?"

"Home, to the Ozarks."

"Wouldn't do no good, ain' nothin' back there but starvin' times." Lige inspected the patch he'd cut. "Why ya ask?"

Ertie shrugged.

Lige daubed glue on the patch and carefully stuck it to the glued spot on the tube, pressing it firmly in place.

"I was jus' wondering what'd been like if we'd stayed."

"What good's wonderin' do? Ya didn't stay."

"Shit!" Ertie shook his head and looked at Lige, who was exasperatingly even-tempered. "Don' ya ever get mad?"

"Shore. We even went out on strike once."

"Ya did?"

"Yeah." Lige grinned. "Shut the whole damn harvest down from Bakersfield clean up to Madera. Papers said there was eighteen thousand of us on strike and I guess that was pretty close to right. We had them cotton farmers backed into a pinch all right, till they come at us with guns, there in Pixley. We was havin' a meetin' outside the train depot, in the parkin' lot. Must of been five hundred of us there when them farmers drove up, a whole posse of 'em, and they jumped out and started shootin' right into the crowd. Killed two Mexican fellas, wounded a bunch more people. After the shootin' the government boys stepped in, ordered them farmers to pay six bits. Was the killin' that did it, not our strike. They made a big show of arrestin' eleven of them farmers, but jury let 'em all off."

Ertie was surprised. "You a union man?"

"Hell no." Lige was still holding the patch tight. "Thought you knowed me better'n that. Unions ain' never goin' to do us no good, we're on the move too much."

"Why'd ya strike then?"

"Ertie, ever' now an then them sons a bitches's gotta be showed we ain' gonna put up with but so much. It's like gettin' a mule's attention, ya hit him up alongside the head with a two-by-four. It wakes'm up. He's still a mule, but he pays more attention. Strike don't change nothin' much, but you do it at the right time and it damn sure catches their attention. They pay a little more money for a while, treat ya a little better till they forget what happened. Then ya gotta wake 'em up again. Secret's knowin' when the time's right, when the folks is so mad they'll just say 'Go to hell' an' have at it. 'Tween times, I jus' go 'round them labor agitators, work for the little guys. When a farmer like Kakorian gets to know ya he wants ya back ever' year and pretty soon ya got someplace to work ever'where ya go, like a route. If it's August, yor here, at Bull's and workin' for ol' John Geddes or Simon Garabedian or Marshall Wasserman over near Farmersville. When it's comin' September, it's time to head for Kakorian's." Lige inspected the patch and began putting the tube back in the tire. "Ya wanna go along with us?"

"I reckon."

Jake was in love. Each day after work he went by Clara's camp and waited for her to come out of the ragtag collection of tents and shanty lean-tos. The Tarpin camp was crowded with noisy, dirty-faced kids and cluttered with trash. Clara's father and her uncles were sullen, mean-looking men who never gave him more than a suspicious glance when he came around. Clara wanted to get away from them as much as Jake did and together they explored the nearby woods until they found an isolated spot down by the river, a little clearing where they could be alone.

Her family was working in the tomatoes too, but in different fields, and one afternoon she came rushing out. "Heard what happened?"

"Yeah, they cut the wages ever'where to three cents."

"That ain' all, there was union guys in the field an' they started yellin' strike an' jeez, Jake, ever'body got mad an' jus' up an' walked right out. Union guys tol' them crew bosses nobody'd work for less than a nickel."

Jake was surprised because nothing like that had happened in their fields, but the next morning as they drove to work, all crowded into the sedan to save gas, they ran into a police barricade and mobs of angry strikers milling around in the road, yelling and shaking their fists at a bunch of Mexicans working in the fields. Mexicans. Hundreds of them in the tomatoes. Jake pulled up to the barricade and stuck his head out the window to ask what was going on just as two deputies charged the car, one yelling and pointing. "Get your ass out of here! Ain't no Okies comin' through here!"

"But we was workin' here yesterday!"

The second deputy slammed a nightstick down hard on the fender, WHACK! "Git that jalopy turned around and out of here 'fore I throw your asses in jail!" WHACK! Another dent in the fender.

"Jake, do what he says!" Bessie pleaded. Everyone else in the car was quiet. Jake glanced at his father, who was reaching under the seat, grabbing a tire iron, hatred etched all over his face. Ertie was between his two sons and James Earl yelled at Jake, "Git out of here! Thar's too many of 'em!"

Frightened and furious, Jake spun the wheel and made a fast U-turn, tires squealing, gravel flying.

Back in camp, Jake ran over to Clara's and they went down by the river to their hiding place. Bewildered by it all, Jake shook his head. "I ain' never seen nothin' like that before, all that law an' they wouldn't let us past to work. Wouldn't even let us drive down the roads to them other fields so we hadda come back here."

"Jake?" Clara sounded frightened.

"Yeah?"

"What's gonna happen?"

"I don' know. We gotta find work 'cause we're behind on the house payments."

"Ya gonna leave outa here?"

"Don' know."

"Oh, Jake, I don' wanna lose you." She clung to him.

Jake didn't say anything, just held her close for a long time, one hand cupping a breast, rubbing it gently. Realizing that she hadn't stopped him, he started to fumble with the buttons on the front of her dress and she helped him, slipping the material down off her shoulders, exposing her breasts. Her skin was so soft-white and her nipples stood erect, like tiny bottlecaps. But just above her left breast there was an angry red scar, there in the hollow of her shoulder, and there was another on her back, above the shoulderblade. Distracted by the sight, Jake touched the scars tenderly. "What happened?"

"Pa hit me with his belt. Buckle did that."

"Why?" Protective anger flooded through him.

"Him an' Ott was drunk. Mama got after Pa 'bout somethin' an' Ott, he said somethin'. Mama called Ott a pig and Pa he started beatin' on her, so I grabbed up a chunk of firewood and hit him with it an' he come after me with his belt."

She clung to him, sobbing. She'd never before said much about her life. Now she started talking about her father, how she hated him, hated them all. "Mama's right, Ott's a pig but Grandpa's worse 'cause he was always tryin' to put his hands on me, tryin' to do dirty thangs."

Listening, Jake had never felt closer to anyone. He wanted her, wanted to protect her and he told her that if her father ever did anything like that again, he'd kill him. He swore it. "I'll kill him."

Clara sat bolt upright. "Oh, Gawd Jake, don't. Promise ya won't.

154

If you come after'm he'd hurt ya, bad, or Uncle Ott'd git ya. Don' go near them, they're dirt mean. Promise!"

So he promised. She lay back in his arms, silent now, and he held her and played with her nipples, kissing them, saying that he wanted to be with her, protect her. She smiled up at him, looking into his eyes. "Jake, honey, let's run away an' get married."

"What?" The suggestion surprised him and he let go of her.

Clara misunderstood his quick movement and cried, "I thought you loved me."

"I do, Clara. I do." Clumsily, he tried to reassure her, but running off from his family wasn't even thinkable and marrying was what you did when you were man-grown and out on your own.

Clara was up now, rebuttoning her dress. Angry tears rolled down her cheeks. "All you wanted to do was mess 'round with me."

Jake grabbed at her hand. "Clara. No. I love ya. Please."

She pulled away and scrambled off through the underbrush.

Jake sat there for a long time trying to sort out his feelings. He wanted to be with Clara, wanted to protect her, but he wasn't about to run off, his family needed him. She could understand that.

The next day after work he headed straight for her camp, wanting to apologize, wanting to be close to her, wanting to make her understand, but when he got there she was gone. They were all gone. The Tarpin camp was abandoned, only the trash was left behind. Jake ran down to the river, to their hiding place. She wasn't there so he ran up to Bull's tarpaper shanty. No, the Tarpins hadn't left any word, they just packed up and pulled out, leaving behind a mess for Bull to clean up. Clara was gone. He had made her cry and she was gone.

8

The Jefferson County board of supervisors met each Tuesday in an oak-paneled chamber on the second floor of the granite courthouse. The rest of the time the high-vaulted chamber was as empty as a church sanctuary in midweek. Morning sunlight shone through the tall windows along the east wall, casting golden light patterns across the rows of public benches. Up in front, beyond the low railing that separated the public from their elected officials, past the vacant desks where the clerk and county attorney sat each Tuesday, there was a long table and around it five high-backed leather chairs, the seats of authority. All of the chairs were empty but one. Charles Gilmore, a dapper, silver-haired insurance broker wearing a neatly tailored blue summer suit, sat alone, idly tapping a pencil on the protective glass tabletop.

Congressman Alf Young, wearing a rumpled palm beach suit and Panama hat, stood looking out a nearby window that had been pushed partway open. The smell of fall was in the air. From where he stood Young could see three or four people in the courthouse park below and, over to the left, a few cars were passing by on Main Street. He also had a view of the Jefferson Grammar School, over across on the north side of Main. In the schoolyard some of the children were swinging and climbing the bars, others had chosen up sides and were playing Red Rover come over, running and shouting, cheering teammates who made it safely across the line without getting caught. It was a satisfying scene. Turning his head, Young spoke in that loud, braying voice of his. "You know,

Charley, Jefferson City is one of the prettiest towns in the valley."

Gilmore, who was chairman of the county board of supervisors and coveted Young's House seat, said nothing.

"You're lucky, living close to the people who elected you. Even in hard times, they haven't lost the spirit that's made this town something special." Congressman Young's words echoed through the chamber. "Let me tell you, I miss scenes like this when I'm back in Washington."

Gilmore frowned and swung the chair around. "For Christ's sake, Alf, you're not running for Congress again until next year, can the bullshit."

"Naw, I mean it, Charley." The congressman faced the window again. "I miss Jeff City."

"What brings you out this time?"

"The Central Valley Project." Young turned from the window. "We stopped over in Sacramento and the bureau people took us up to see how Shasta Dam was coming along. They're really moving the dirt and pouring concrete, you can already see what it's going to be like. Did you realize that reservoir's going to hold four and a half million acre-feet of water? Think of that, Charley, bringing that much Sacramento River water all the way down across the delta and into the Central Valley. You know, we sit back there and vote that money, all hundred and seventy million dollars of it, but we don't really appreciate what we're doing until we get a chance to see it. Tomorrow we're headed up to the San Joaquin River for a look at the Friant Dam site. Secretary Ickes is going to let the first contract sometime next week, you know, and work'll be starting by November. You coming with us?"

Gilmore nodded. "Wouldn't miss a chance to hear you give a speech."

"Great." Young ignored the sarcasm in Gilmore's voice. "You know that dam's going to be good for you people here, Charley, not only the water that'll be comin down the Friant-Kern Canal, but all those jobs too. Times like they are, that's really going to help out. Do you know there are thirty-four hundred men at work on the project now building Shasta and the big canals and hundreds more'll be hired for Friant. That's going to be fifteen million dollars well spent, I'll tell you. Yes sir. It'll put a lot of people back to work."

Charley Gilmore nodded in agreement. Alf Young might be an old windbag and a drunk, but he was right about one thing, times were still hard here in the valley. Hardly a week went by without some farmer or businessman going bankrupt. His own business was way off and even the old-line life companies were hurting, people just couldn't pay their premiums. It was rough, that was certain. Most people in town had hunkered down, cinched in their belts a notch or two and were toughing it out, but some just couldn't make it. Charley swung around in the chair, not liking such dark thoughts. He tried to be a quick-smiling man who saw the bright side of things. That was the ticket, look on the bright side.

"We can use those jobs, you're right about that, Alf, but you know, by God, tough as times are here in Jeff City, our folks are all pulling together, helping each other. Why, just last month the power company announced it was going to have to lay off half of its men. You know what happened? The crews got together and decided that rather than have half of the men put out of work, they'd all work half time, work one day on, take one day off, that way nobody'd get fired. Can you beat that? This is a good town, Alf. People here pull together."

"You don't have to tell me, Charley. They're good people. The best." Young turned back to the window. "Wonder what's keeping Titus? Any idea what he wants?"

"Hell, I don't know, talk about price supports on cotton or maybe it's all this labor trouble. You've heard about the strikes they had up around Marysville?"

Young nodded. "Up at Shasta, some of the boys from Farm Bureau were saying their workers wanted to keep on picking fruit but the CIO brought in a bunch of outside agitators and stirred things up."

"That's not all, the governor sided with the union."

Young came over and sat down. Idly, he spun a chair next to him around once, then again. "Remember, Charley, I warned you all about Olson and now it's my guess that John L. Lewis and Harry Bridges see a good chance to stir things up all over this valley, and they've got the Workers' Alliance to help them out."

"You're right. We've already had union trouble this spring, in the cotton. The growers finally had to raise the chopping wage a nickel to get anyone in the fields."

"Yeah, we heard something about that back in Washington. Tell me, how the hell did they pull it off?"

"Well, like you said, the real problems's the governor. I tell you, Alf, I've been a Democrat all my life, just like you, and if Olson's a Democrat, I'll kiss your ass. He's more radical than that pinko in the White House and he's brought in that radical lawyer Carey McWilliams, put him in charge of relief, or at least he's telling the SRA what to do."

"Heard about the wage hearings McWilliams held up in Madera and . . ."

"Hell, Alf, he held hearings right here too . . ."

"That's what I was about to say . . ."

". . . and those union agitators rounded up a bunch of Okies, had them parading around outside, yelling and waving flags while he brought in a couple of egghead economics professors from the university to tell us that the farmers could afford to pay twenty-seven cents an hour. Tell that to Arn Schounberger's widow. Anyway, McWilliams flat-out told the association that if they didn't raise the wage, the county had to keep those damned Okies on relief, instead of sending them to the fields like we'd normally do that time of year." Gilmore was stabbing his forefinger on the glass tabletop to make his points. "Alf, do you know that last winter we were forced to carry nearly two hundred families on welfare, thanks to Roosevelt and you people in Congress?"

"Charley." The congressman sat up, on the defensive now. "For Christ's sake, seventy-five percent of that money comes from the federal budget."

"That's only because we convinced you these damned migrants aren't our people. Feeding them isn't a local problem, it's a federal problem."

Young tried to say something else but Gilmore didn't stop talking.

"That damn McWilliams said he'd get our federal money cut off if we sent people out to work for less than twenty-seven cents an hour, threatened to tie us up in federal court for weeks, so the farmers said they'd pay a quarter, and that settled it. But the farmers didn't have any choice, they had to get the cotton chopped. That kind of thing never happened when Merrium was governor, so you see where the trouble is this time. The unions've got the governor doing their work for them."

"And that's got Titus on his war horse?"

Titus Wardlow came pushing through the double doors just as the congressman spoke. "Yeah, Alf, that's what's got me up on my fucking war horse." Wardlow strode down the aisle toward them, cigar clamped tight in his teeth. He brushed past Gilmore with a nod, quickly shook hands with the congressman, and flopped down in a chair. "We know the goddamn union's got at least a dozen agitators here in the county and one of those bastards is out there in my Camp Six right this fucking minute. The boys up in Fresno County say the same thing, the union's holding meetings all over the fuckin' valley, that's what, from Bakersfield clear to Madera. They want a dollar and a quarter a hundred for picking cotton and they're talking strike and that so-called governor is on their side, making speeches, encouraging them." Wardlow had the cigar stub in his hand now and was using it like a pointer, barking, "Alf, we need some help from you to head this thing off."

"Hell, Titus, you know I'll do what I can, but this is a local matter." Alf Young was uncomfortable around Titus Wardlow. He never knew quite what to expect from the grower.

Titus relighted his stogie, puffing hard, eyeing the congressman all the while. "Look, we know how to handle the union stuff, we've busted that up before, but this is the first time we've come up against a union that was backed by the governor of the fucking state. That's politics and that's where you come in. You told us before the election what a big Communist Olson was, well you were right. And I guess you heard what that fella Zack said, the one that quit the party, he told the Dies Committee yesterday that a bunch of those CIO unions are run by the fucking Communists, right out of Moscow. It was on the radio this morning, he said Russia wants to cripple the USA, in case of war. Well, it's happening right here, Alf, and we gotta head it off. We want you to get that Dies Committee out here, quick, get an investigation going that the fuckin' papers will pick up."

"I'm giving a talk to the Lions Club at noon. I can say I'd like to see the committee come in and investigate."

"Alf, dammit, I don't want a goddamn speech, I want somethin' big. I want the Dies Committee, want them right here in Jeff City. You understand?"

"I'm on the Agriculture Committee, you know. Maybe we could get something started there—"

"Fuck the Agriculture Committee. It's got to be Dies. Look, tell the son of a bitch that making statements about Olson from Washington doesn't do any good, tell him he'll be a big hero if he comes out and saves California agriculture, tell him that there's big bucks here at campaign time, I don't care what the fuck you tell him, just get Dies out here. And fast, we haven't got much time before we start picking." Titus turned abruptly to Gilmore. "Charley, if a strike does start we've gotta be ready for it. Windy's promised to deputize all of us at our next meeting, and we need some help from you and the board."

Gilmore straightened up in his chair, a frown wrinkling across his suntanned face. "Windy Scott's the sheriff, so he can do what he wants, but do you think that's wise? Deputizing a bunch of farmers? We've already given him money to hire extra men."

"Charley, if the CIO and that Workers Alliance oufit get the Okies and Mexicans stirred up, we could be in for real trouble again, like we were in 'thirty-three." Wardlow stared hard at the board chairman. "This isn't the time to be cautious, Charley. We've got to let them know we mean business, all of us. The sheriff can't do it alone, the American Legion's going to help out, but the Associated Farmers are the strongest bunch in this county and we can get all the help we need from every other chapter in the state. Right now we're setting up a phone network so that one call will bring out a hundred deputized men, armed and ready to go."

"Titus, let me warn you, as chairman of the board I'm not comfortable with a bunch of farmers running around the county with guns. If anything happens—"

"Charley, don't warn me!" Wardlow's face hardened and his words were measured. "I'm not asking, I'm telling you! And that means the Associated Farmers are telling you! We want you to put through a resolution asking Alf to get the Dies Committee to hold hearings here in Jeff City. You warn the committee that the Communists are already here, tell them about the threat to our crops, just the sort of thing you were talking about when I walked in. That ought to bring Dies quick enough."

Wardlow got up and was pacing now. "That brings up the next point. The sheriff needs a stockade, someplace where we can hold big bunches of strikers. The fairgrounds would be a good place for it and we've offered to build the stockade, but Windy said that wouldn't look good, to have the association involved. He said he'd already asked the board for money but he hasn't heard anything back. Why?"

"Titus, dammit, we don't have extra money to throw around just because there are a few union organizers out there. I don't think we can justify the expense of building a stockade. As an elected official I—"

"Charley! Get Windy the money!" Wardlow turned and headed out the door, trailing smoke, talking but not looking back. "I don't care how you do it! Just do it!"

Wardlow pushed out through the heavy doors and was striding down the marble walkway, headed for the stairs, when he heard his name called. He stopped and looked back.

"Mr. Wardlow! Oh, Mr. Wardlow!" It was one of the secretaries from the clerk's office. "There was a long-distance call for you, Mr. Wardlow." She hurried up, handing him a slip of paper. "A Mr. Axelrod's secretary called from St. Louis. That's the number, there. She said it wasn't urgent, but Mr. Axelrod would like you to call back when you get the chance."

Roxie. When she phoned, she put the calls through person-to-person, acting like she was Axelrod's secretary so that no one on his end would get suspicious. Grunting a curt thank you, he stuffed the slip into his shirt pocket, tucking it behind the cigars and pencils, and was down the stairs, out of the courthouse. Climbing into his mud-spattered pickup, he was still swearing to himself, goddamn politicians were always trying to cover their asses. He started the engine, jammed the shifting lever into reverse and backed out, ground the gears into first and lurched ahead, tires screeching out his anger. Dammit! He didn't need a strike, not now. His Devil's Den deal was right on schedule, he'd bought the land, tied up the railroad leases, drilled the first wells and leveled an initial thousand acres, putting in pipelines and drainways, but the costs were running higher than expected, much higher. It was the wells; they'd gone deep, but had to go even deeper to get to the water and that meant putting in bigger lift pumps. The extra costs were putting him in a real bind, but it was a problem he could handle, if nothing upset the balance right now. He had two thousand acres of cotton in the ground, half at El Adobe and the other half at Devil's Den, it was a damn good crop that should gin out at two bales to the acre and that would give him enough to make his first payments and develop more of the Devil's Den lands. But there was no room for a strike, higher costs would kill the deal. He'd gone over the figures yet another time this morning; the way it penciled out, paying the buck and a quarter demanded by the union, instead of the eighty cents a hundred set by the association, would cost him another eighty thousand dollars. There was no way he could do that and keep the deal alive, not with cotton selling for eight cents a pound, ginned.

Titus drove up Main toward the center of town, his mind on the union. The strike threat couldn't have come at a worse time. He braked for the blinking red light at Highway 99, shifted into second and rolled through the intersection, accelerating across the railroad tracks. It wasn't just the bank loans that worried him, Armor Cotton Oil's regional people had been around asking questions about the union efforts to organize the cotton pickers, wanting to know what the association was doing to head off the trouble. Armor financed his crops and ginned his cotton and they had signed onto his expansion plans, agreeing to finance the Devil's Den cotton crop and put up some money for new farm equipment. Now Armor's regional guys were saying the top brass in Los Angeles were getting nervous, they didn't want anything to do with any unions, not on deals they were financing. Wardlow had to keep them happy, he needed Armor for at least a couple more years, then he could dump them and build his own gins.

Wardlow glanced at his watch: ten fifteen. Time for coffee. The parking stalls at the curb in front of the Dixie Cup were full and a big power company line truck was double-parked out in front. Two linemen were up on tall ladders on either side of Main, unfurling a banner, snapping its hooks onto the high cable that was anchored to opposing buildings across Main. The red and white banner read:

WELCOME TO THE 1939 JEFFERSON COUNTY FAIR
OLD TIMERS DAY PARADE AND RODEO
October 5th–8th

Titus found a parking spot down past the theater, pulling in next to other dusty, mud-spattered pickups. As he walked back to the cafe, one of the linemen yelled down, "Hey, Titus. We gonna get to shoot ducks on your place this fall?"

"You bet. I'll have some of that grain land flooded again." He had the cafe door open. "And Andy, don't forget, I want one of those pups when that Stormy bitch of yours has her litter."

"Right." The lineman grinned. He was proud of his water spaniels. They had good, solid retriever blood in them and Stormy was the best. No matter how cold and foggy or how far out a duck or goose fell, she swam to it and brought it back to the blind without a tooth mark on it. "She's due most any time now and I promised you second pick, right after me."

"Good."

Wardlow had paused and was looking up at the lineman, blocking the doorway. A voice on the inside warned him, "Coming through, Titus."

Judge Barkham started to squeeze past.

"Rooster, what you doing in town?" Wardlow stepped back, and before the judge could respond, added, "I was coming out to see you this morning."

"What about?"

They were standing on the sidewalk. Wardlow took Rooster Barkham's elbow and steered the cocky little judge a few steps up the street, out of the lineman's hearing. Talking in a low voice, he explained, "I've got a damn labor agitator in one of my camps and I want the son of a bitch locked up."

"What's he done?" Judge Rooster Barkham was irritated by Wardlow's brash manners and lack of respect for his office.

"He's trying to stir up trouble, talks up at the union meetings, saying we're all a bunch of cheap bastards and the only way to whip us is by striking."

The judge had on a spiffy blue blazer, his favorite red bow tie and white slacks. He rocked back on his heels, chest out, hands in his pockets, frowning. "What'd you expect him to say? That he loves you all and he'd work for nothing?"

"Hell, Rooster, this is no joke." Damn! Dealing with Charley was one thing, dealing with Rooster Barkham was another situation altogether. Not only was he a Barkham, but he was popular all over the north end of the county and just couldn't be pushed. You could lean on him, but not too hard or the feisty little bastard would get his feathers all ruffled and then there was no way to work with him.

"I didn't say it was funny, Titus." Barkham puffed out his chest even further and stood his ground. "I don't like this business either, but as far as I know, talking's still not against the law. You catch that fellow breaking a law, then I'll issue a warrant and the sheriff can bring him into my court. This fellow, what's his name?"

"Sharp. Cletus Sharp."

"Okay, when this fellow Sharp does something besides talk, let me know."

"You're not going to give me a warrant?" Wardlow couldn't believe what he was hearing.

"Tell you what. Why don't you just order him off your place. Then if he gives you any trouble or if he comes back on your place, why he's trespassing, and that's against the law."

"Okay," Wardlow growled. "See ya in court."

The usual bunch of farmers hunched around the big table in the front window of the Dixie Cup having their morning coffee when Wardlow walked through the front door.

"Hey, anyone hear Gabriel Heater last night on the news?" Tiny Schmidtz didn't wait for any answer. "Said the goddamn Russians are going to side in with Hitler."

As Wardlow sat down, Gert brought over his coffee. Coffman, the cattleman from the hills, was talking now. "The Reds signed that treaty so they wouldn't have to worry about the Germans while they're trying to stop us from growing food here to help England."

"What do you mean?" George Yates asked, his young face worried by the talk of war and the Reds.

"It's all part of the Communist plan to take over the world, kid. First Europe, then us," Coffman said sternly.

"Know what CIO means?" Yates's face brightened and he paused, looking eagerly around the table. "It means, 'Come in Okies.' Get it? CIO means 'Come in Okies.' One of my kids picked that up in school the other day, isn't that somethin'?"

They all chuckled.

Wardlow pulled out a fresh cigar, bit off the end and fumbled in his pocket for a match. The slip with Axelrod's name and the St. Louis phone number on it fell out onto the table. He picked it up, looked at it briefly and pushed it back in his pocket, wondering why Roxanne was calling. She and Ax were off racing again and weren't due back in Bakersfield for another week. After the crash last year, Roxanne had been in that Oklahoma hospital for a couple of months before her husband Bart put her on a train in a special hospital bed and brought her home. He hired special nurses to look after her and stayed around for nearly a month after that, then was off again to Arabia. Wardlow dropped in on her whenever he was down that way, working on the Devil's Den deal. The new ranch was thirty-five miles west of Bakersfield and he'd built an airstrip out there first thing, then began constructing new equipment sheds and shops, housing for his foremen and crew bosses, labor camps and a small, comfortable house for himself. It had been nearly six months before Roxie was up and around enough to come out and see the place, but it wasn't long after that that she was back flying again. The crash didn't slow her down once she had climbed into the cockpit of a new midwing monoplane Axelrod found and Bart paid for, a Folkerts Special powered by another Menasco. She and Axelrod were back in competition. She had placed third in the Thompson on Labor Day and, afterwards, called him from Cleveland to say they'd be racing in St. Louis before they'd be home.

Wardlow took another swallow of coffee. His mind was back on Cletus Sharp, the union agitator. He wanted the bastard out of his camp and he meant to do it today. Puffing the cigar to life, he got up. "Maybe you fellas can afford to sit around all day, but I've got work to do."

Back on Main Street, Wardlow headed for the sheriff's office in the red-brick jail, over on Sixth Street, behind the courthouse. Wardlow parked in one of the slots reserved for official cars and went inside.

A gum-chewing deputy looked up. "Hello, Mr. Wardlow."

"Windy in?"

"No, but Captain Ramey's here." The deputy got up and stuck his head into a nearby office. "Titus Wardlow's here to see ya."

Wardlow wrinkled his nose at the smell of the place and relighted his cigar. Even at the counter, the air was fetid, a stinking mix of body odors, decaying food and urine coming from the crowded cell blocks and drunk tanks.

A big, jowly deputy with a heavy belly and broad butt waddled out, adjusting the weight of his gun belt. "Mornin', Titus, what can I do for ya?"

166

"Need a couple of deputies for an hour or two. Got some trouble in one of my camps."

"What's the problem?"

"Damn union agitator."

"What's he doin'?"

"Goddammit, Ramey, I'm not playin' questions and answers. Just give me the deputies."

"Maybe we better wait till the sheriff gets back."

"Where's he at?" Wardlow was already coming around the counter, headed for the phone.

"Home, I think."

Picking up the phone, he wiggled the hook. "Hello! Operator? Get me the sheriff. Yeah, at home." Chewing on his cigar, Wardlow eyed the big wall calendar: Saturday, September 30. Hell, the damn month was already gone. "Hello, Windy? Yeah. Say, I need a couple of deputies to toss a goddamn agitator out of one of my camps. Yeah, Rooster said I could toss his ass out. Okay, tell Ramey. He's afraid to shit 'less you say so, and don't forget to tell him which hand to wipe with."

Wardlow laughed at something the sheriff said and handed the phone to Ramey, who turned his back, mumbled, nodded and hung up. Ramey headed out back, yelling over his shoulder, "They'll meet you out front. I gotta call 'em in on the radio."

Twenty minutes later Wardlow was speeding west along Dairy Avenue, the two deputies following close behind in a black and white sedan. Across the river and north past the Quantrell School, Wardlow turned west again on Avenue Eighteen and glanced up to make sure the deputies were following. Two miles from the ranch headquarters, he slowed and turned down a dirt road that paralleled a cottonfield bursting with white lint; it was going to be a damn good crop. Wardlow's speeding pickup kicked up a roostertail of dust, blinding the deputies trying to follow him back toward Camp Six. The camp was laid out along two streets back by the canal, four rows of shanty cabins and tents with old cars and trucks parked beside them. There were a half dozen outhouses and twice that many fifty-gallon-drum garbage cans. The cans were full and the overflowing garbage was scattered everywhere.

Wardlow braked to a stop near the entrance to the camp and got out, dust swirling around him. He stood there beside the pickup looking over weathered, single-room cabins, tattered tents and makeshift shelters. There were fifty or sixty families living here, maybe more, all waiting for the harvest to start. The cabins were all full and every day more workers pulled in, pitched their tents and waited. Here and there women were washing clothes in old tubs or sweeping the bare ground, trying to make things neat. Children played in the dirt or scampered about the top of the canal bank. Several men squatted beside a battered Dodge truck. They had been talking but now, as they watched Wardlow drive up with the law, they were silent, unmoving. One of the men said something, and they shifted uncomfortably. Just behind them a blond teenage girl in a faded yellow dress came out of a lean-to and ran barefoot up the ditch-bank carrying a pail. She had hair the color of spun taffy and a lithe figure. Halfway up she stopped and, like a frightened deer sensing danger, looking back down at Wardlow and the sheriff's car.

A blond woman poked her head out of the lean-to and yelled at the girl, "Clara Tarpin! You git that water, now. Hear?"

The girl disappeared over the top of the canal bank and in a minute reappeared, leaning heavily against the weight of the full pail, trying not to slosh the water.

Wardlow called to the deputies. "Come on, let's get it over with."

As the lawmen climbed out of the patrol car, the men beside the old Dodge stood up and one of them, a stringy fellow wearing a shapeless hat, patched Levi's and a sleeveless shirt came out to Wardlow. The others hung back. Standing a respectful distance from the farmer, the man asked, "You want somethin', Mr. Wardlow?"

"Looking for Cletus Sharp."

"That's me."

"Sharp, I want you off my land. Pack up and get out!"

Bewildered, Cletus Sharp stood his ground. "You got no call to throw me out, Mr. Wardlow, we'uns ain't done nothin', just waitin' here to pick yor cotton when she's ready."

"No Red son of a bitch is goin' to pick my cotton. Now get off my land, you an' that trash you call family."

Sharp's jaw muscles tightened and his fists doubled. Hatred filled his pale gray eyes and beat through the veins at his temples, coiling him tight as a spring ready to snap. Just then four ragged children came running to him and gathered around his legs, clutching at his faded jeans, staring fearfully at Wardlow and the deputies. Without taking his eyes off Wardlow, Cletus Sharp brushed at the youngsters, trying to get them loose from his legs. He glanced down at the oldest, a child of nine, pleading, "Arlene, git these kids outa here. Go on back to yor maw. Please, honey, I got no time . . ."

Sensing the desperation in her father's voice, the girl grabbed at her brothers and sister and herded them safely away.

Sharp, his voice once more under control, looked Wardlow in the eye. "You got no right to call me and mine trash, Mr. Wardlow."

"Arrest him!"

The two deputies rushed Cletus Sharp, jerking him roughly about and slamming him over the hood of Wardlow's pickup. The lawmen had reacted so fast Sharp had no time to resist.

"Aw, God, no!" Sharp wilted as the deputies put handcuffs on him. "Don't. Please don't. Who's gonna feed my fambly? Please. My woman ain't well, she can't do for all them young uns."

The deputies pulled him upright and, one on each arm, pushed him toward the patrol car. Wardlow stepped in, confronting Sharp. "You should've kept your mouth shut. Ditch water's not good 'nuff for you, is it? Think I ought to build you shithouses, do you?" Wardlow grinned as he watched the surprised look on Sharp's face. "We know what you're saying, we know when you goddamn Reds hold your meetings and we know where. You should've packed up and left when I gave you the chance."

There was a scream in the camp and a fat woman in a washed-out dress waddled quickly toward them, her barrel legs moving awkwardly, her face flushed and desperate. "Wha'cha doin' to 'im? Wha'cha doin'?"

Wardlow barked at the deputies, "Take him to town and lock him up."

As the deputies dragged the man to the car, Sharp begged, "Please le'me talk to my woman first."

Wardlow blocked the woman before she could reach her husband, telling her loudly, "If you aren't packed up and off my land by nightfall, I'm goin' to have them pile your things and burn them."

The woman got past him and over to the patrol car. Sobbing, she clawed at the sedan's rolled-up windows, trying to talk to her husband who was locked inside.

Wardlow turned and yelled to the watching men and women in the camp, "Remember this! I will not tolerate any agitators or Communists on my land. You want to work for me, you stay away from the likes of him. Picking starts in a couple of weeks. Pay's eighty cents a hundred. Those that want to work, stay. Those that don't, get out. Now. Or I'll have the law throw you out."

Wardlow climbed into his pickup, slammed the door and drove off. The deputies, with Cletus Sharp in custody, followed along in his dust. Out on the country road, the lawmen turned back toward town.

Wardlow drove to the ranch headquarters. Stomping into his office, he told his secretary that he didn't want to be disturbed and banged the door shut. Collapsing in his chair, Wardlow put his boots up on the desktop and sat there, thinking. Had he been too damn hard on that Okie agitator? No! Goddammit! He had to stop this union thing before it got started. He pulled the message from Ax out of his pocket and put a call through to St. Louis. Had Roxie crashed again? Ax answered the phone, growling something at him, and then put Roxanne on the line.

"Titus! We won! Won the Belixir Trophy. I smoked Turner's ass." She was excited. "We'll be back on Thursday. Can you fly down for the weekend?"

"Maybe Friday night, but I've got to be out at Devil's Den early Saturday."

"Titus." She sensed the trouble in his voice. "What's the matter?"

"We got trouble here."

"What kind of trouble?"

"Union agitators. Tell you about it when I see you."

9

Lige had been right, Kakorian was a good boss. He paid well, was friendly and worked right along beside them doing whatever needed to be done. He provided a clean camp, out back by the barn; the washhouse and showers were smaller than those at Bull's Camp but better built and well kept up, and the outhouses easily passed Bessie's inspection.

They had been working steadily in the vines since late August, cutting grapes and spreading the bunches to dry on flat wooden trays. At night, after the supper dishes were done, Bessie got out her own little tally book and entered the day's wages, going over her accounts by lanternlight. By mid-September she'd managed to pay off half of the hospital bill and they were catching up on the house payments, but there were problems. The grape harvest was nearly over and they wouldn't start work in the cotton for a while yet. The good news was that Kakorian promised them a dollar a hundred in the cotton and that extra twenty cents would put another eighty or ninety dollars in the sock. Bessie snapped her tally book closed with a smile. For the first time since they'd come out to California she could see that they really had a chance now to get off the road; that extra money would do it. Come the end of October they'd pay off what they owed and move into that house.

Each morning Bessie noticed the school buses stopping out in front for the Kakorian boys. Two of them went into high school in Jeff City, the youngest went to country grammar school down the road a ways. Certain now that the house was really going to be theirs, she decided it was time for Jake and Susie to start back to school. She wanted Mary Ellen to finish up high school too, get her diploma, but her oldest daughter shook her head angrily and, with tears in her eyes, Mary Ellen said no, that was all over. Bessie nodded her understanding. It was different with Jake and Susie, she was determined they were at least going to finish grammar school.

Jake argued. "Ma, we gotta work an' put money by."

"Boy, you cain' miss out on any more yor schoolin'."

"But Ma . . ."

"Don' be givin' me no buts, yor startin' school Monday mornin' an' that's that, mister." Bessie gave him a loving swat on the behind. "An don' ya be gettin' in no fights, neither. Hear?"

The weather, hot all through the first half of September, had turned cool and blustery. Monday it rained.

Holding pieces of cardboard over their heads, Jake and Susie ran splashing through puddles up past the Kakorians' house and huddled close under one of the chinaberry trees out front, near the mailbox. Neither was dressed for a storm. Over his freshly laundered overalls and snap-button shirt Jake was wearing Ertie's old Levi's jacket. Susie didn't even have a coat. She wore one of Mary Ellen's old dresses and an old wool sweater of Bessie's that had been patched at the elbows.

The Kakorian boys were standing in the shelter of their wide front porch. Navo, the oldest, yelled, "Hey, come on up here an' wait!"

Jake and Susie scurried up the porch steps. "Thanks."

The Kakorians had on new Levi's, wool shirts and warm coats with pullover hoods. Navo was seventeen and Ara two years younger. Birge, who was twelve and in the sixth grade, was waiting for the Quantrill Grammar School bus. Ara stared boldly at Susie and asked if she was in high school. Shyly, Susie shook her head, saying she had to go to Quantrill because they'd gotten so far behind in their schooling. Jake felt angry and embarrassed. He was as old as Ara and should be going to high school too. Ara might work in the fields alongside him, but Jake felt a gulf between them; once he had gone to school as an equal; now he was behind and felt ragged. Seeing Ara interested in Susie made him even madder.

When the high school bus growled to a stop out front Navo and Ara ran down the porch steps and across the lawn, jumping on board. Ten minutes later the big yellow grammar school bus arrived, doors banging open, its windows all steamy. Inside, the bus was noisy and there was the wet smell of wool and lunches. Birge found a seat next to a friend, leaving Susie and Jake standing in the aisle as the bus doors slammed shut and the vehicle lurched forward.

Susie let the momentum carry her on to the rear, where the other camp kids were sitting. Jake followed, feeling shabby and belligerent, ready to sock somebody. Back home in Bitter Creek he had liked school, but not out here. They had tried to go to school once before, while they were at Kitahara's last winter, but he'd gotten into two fights with grower kids before the first week was up and he'd been thrown out. Now, as he followed Susie back to the rear of the bus, nobody said anything to him. He flopped into a seat beside her.

As the bus pulled into the driveway forty minutes later the bell atop the school was clanging. The big white school building was a handsome wood structure set up on high foundations, with round pillars supporting the covered entryway. Through the glass-paneled front doors a wide hallway led back between the classrooms to the office at the far end. Hurrying students filled the hallway with shouts and laughter as Susie made her way toward the office, Jake reluctantly following. The office door was open and two women worked behind a counter, one talking on the phone, the other filing folders. On the back wall a large clock ticked off the seconds, then buzzed and, up on the roof, the final bell clanged. Classroom doors closed. Classes started.

Standing at the counter, Susie cleared her throat once, then again, and when that got no response, she spoke up, " 'Scuse me, ma'am?"

The woman at the file cabinet looked up. She was a big, round-shouldered person, heavyset, with jet black hair pulled tight and piled high. Her eyebrows were plucked and penciled black in high arches; her puffy face, powdered white and heavily rouged, was a map of meanness. She wore a white nurse's uniform, draped like a tent over the great mass of her body, but what awed Jake the most was the size of her bosom, like two big watermelons under a cotton sack.

When she spoke her voice was gravel, raked raw by cigarettes. "Sit down there and wait, can't you see I'm busy?"

They sat on the bench in the outer office and waited. Finally the woman slammed a file drawer shut and strode to the counter, unsmiling. "Are you camp kids?"

They jumped up. "Yes'm."

"Names?"

"Robertson, he's Jake, I'm Susie."

"What grades were you in?" The woman reached under the counter for some forms.

"Jake, he was in the seventh an' I was in the sixth, back in Texas." Susie's voice quavered. "We ain' had much chance to go to school since leavin' there."

She jotted down the answers. "Where you living?"

"Mr. Kakorian's farm."

"How long are you staying?"

Susie shrugged. "Least till cotton's picked."

"Okay." The woman pushed the swinging gate open. "I'm Nurse Hobson and the law says I've got to examine you." She nodded to Susie. "Come on back." Jake started to follow, but the nurse stopped him. "You wait out here."

Herding Susie in front of her, Nurse Hobson went through a side door into a tiny adjoining office. In about five minutes Susie came back out, mad enough to cry. The nurse called Jake in. Her office smelled of medicines. It had white cupboards and drawers and there was a fold-out cot covered by a gray army blanket. The nurse leaned over her desk filling out forms. "Shut the door and take off those clothes."

"What?" Jake started backing away.

"Where are you going?" She had him by the arm.

Jake tried to pull away. "Wha'cha doin'?"

"Hold still!" She shook him, hard. "I've got to examine you for lice. All of you dirty little Okies've got lice or ringworm or worse."

Frightened by the woman's size and strength, Jake awkwardly slipped out of his overalls and shirt and stood there, stark naked and humiliated, trying to cover himself with his hands while she poked and rudely probed. When she was through he quickly dressed and fled the office. Susie was waiting on the bench. Jake plopped down beside her, whispering, "Le's git out of here."

"We cain't, Ma'd skin us alive. 'Sides, we don' even know where we're at, how we gonna git back to camp?"

The school secretary assigned them to a combined seventh- and eighth-grade class taught by Mr. Gomnitz, the school principal. Gomnitz was a gaunt, thin little man in an ill-fitting tweed suit who wore wire-rimmed spectacles. When Jake and Susie opened the door to his classroom and stood there, hesitantly, the teacher looked them over, then gestured toward the back of the room. "Find a seat back there somewhere." He watched them briefly, indifferently, then went on with the lesson.

Finding a desk next to the back wall, Jake scooted in and then studied the teacher, wondering what to expect. Gomnitz had a narrow, pleasant face and a high domed forehead that was sparsely covered by thin, light brown hair. A tiny brush mustache tickled his upper lip and his voice was soft, but not gentle. There was something about the sound of his voice that was cold and remote, especially when he looked toward the back of the room, where the camp kids sat. Looking quickly around, Jake could see maybe fifteen other camp kids in the back of the room, while up front there were another twenty youngsters, farmers' kids by the look of them. At recess several kids from the camps told Jake that, except for the nurse, Quantrill wasn't so bad. Sometimes Gomnitz whipped a kid with the big strap he had hanging in his office, but that was only if you shot your mouth off, or got in a fight with the farmer kids.

Jake and Susie quickly settled into the routine, up early and off to school. Each afternoon they were back in camp about the time their parents came in from the vineyards. They helped out with the chores and had supper. The first week of school passed quickly enough.

On Sunday, after their first week in school, the family had a day off and they planned to install a water system over at the house outside Hyattville. The Kakorian farm was only twenty-seven miles from their place—that's what they called it now, "their place"—and they had been driving over every chance they got, fixing the place up, even though they couldn't move in until fall. The idea for the water system came after James Earl had heard about a badly dented two-hundred-gallon water tank they might get cheap. James Earl looked it over and decided he and Jake could repair it and fix up a water system without too much trouble. Bessie was reluctant to spend the money, but gave in when they pointed out that to have such a system would be cheaper in the long run, since they wouldn't have to haul water so often.

The tank, rusty and stove in on one side, belonged to a Portagee dairyman over in Kings County, near Hanford, who wanted ten dollars for it. James Earl pointed out a jagged hole down in the bottom that had to be patched and offered five. They settled on seven dollars and Kakorian let them borrow the farm truck to haul the tank back to camp. Using tools from the farm shop, they sprung the tank back into round, welded up the hole and installed pipe outlets on either side. They worked on the tank evenings after Jake got home from school and by Saturday they had it ready. On Sunday they hauled the tank over to Hyattville. The Parsons came along too. With used lumber and pipe bought from Simmons, they built a platform close to the kitchen wall and plumbed a pipe into the sink, all by midafternoon. The sink, drainboard and cupboards were a surprise for Bessie. James Earl had found them in one of Simmons's wrecked houses and he'd bought them cheap.

That afternoon, after they'd finished, they had a picnic of sorts. Bessie and R'becky had brought some food over and Ertie had a jug that he and Lige were nipping on. After they'd eaten, Jake wandered around front and found Junior alone, sitting out on the front stoop, smoking.

"Wha'cha doin'?" Jake sat down beside him.

"Jus' thinkin'." Junior offered Jake a Lucky Strike.

Jake glanced nervously around as he took the cigarette and accepted a light from Junior. "Wha'cha thinkin' about?"

"Solidarity."

"Wha'cha mean?"

"Union guys stickin' together, no matter what." Junior took a deep drag, blew the smoke out his nostrils and talked about the power of workers sticking together and greedy farmers trying to squeeze more profits out of their crop by only paying eighty cents. "They talk 'bout losin' money, but that's bullshit. They can afford a dollar an' a quarter, the governor said so himself, by Gawd. He's on our side and he got them college fellers to figger it out. Damn farmers want their cotton picked, they can pay a buck and a quarter. If they don't, we strike! We gotta be tough, be ready to go to jail. Sometimes people gits killed in strikes, but that cain't make no difference, gotta stand up to 'em."

Jake was awed. "How ya know 'bout all that?"

"We was in a big strike once."

"Where somebody was killed?"

"Yup. Back in 'thirty-three. We was pickin' cotton out west of Pixley a ways when we seen the picket lines an' Pa, he ups and says to us, 'Let's hit 'em a lick, git their damn attention,' so we all walked out."

"Who got killed?"

"Couple of Mexicans. Farmers did it. Wounded a whole bunch of other people too, there at a big rally outside the train depot. Musta been a dozen of them farmers come a roarin' up in cars and jumped out, ever' one with a gun of some kind. Fired right smack into the crowd, ya could hear them guns just a pop-pop-popping an' people was runnin' and screamin'. Bullets whizzin' ever' which way. Nigger woman, she got plugged right through the cheeks of her ass, slug went clean through by Gawd. She run right by me, a screamin' an' the blood just squirtin'. Shootin' didn't last more'n a minute, I don' guess, then the farmers jumped back in their cars and tore out."

Jake was awed. "Law arrest them farmers?"

"Yeah, but only 'cause a fella from a big San Francisco news-paper was there when the shootin' started an' he took a whole bunch of pictures. When the story got out, there was such a stink they had to arrest them farmers, but they let 'em off 'cause the farmers said they was shot at first. That was a crock of shit." Junior took a last puff and flipped his cigarette butt away. "That strike was a regular bull bitch, but it got the job done. Them farmers raised the pay from sixty cents to six bits 'fore it was over."

Jake nodded. "So yor folks is union people."

"Not really. But Pa, for all his easygoin' ways, gets his dander up once in a while." Junior turned and looked directly at Jake. "What about yor folks?"

"I don' know."

"Seen yor pa at a union meeting couple nights ago."

That surprised Jake.

Junior chuckled. "He was with my pa."

Jake shook his head, remembering that Lige and Ertie had gone to town, and he wondered if his mother had any idea where they'd been.

He got his answer the next morning, early, before daylight. He heard his parents arguing. At first he didn't know what had awakened him, but then he heard their voices. Driven by the urgent need to piss, he grabbed up his clothes and was out of the tent in a hurry. The camp was dark except for the opaque glow of a lantern in their tent. As he scurried by, Jake could see the silhouette of his mother by the bed pulling on her shirt, and he could hear the anger in her voice. "Ertie Robertson, don' you be gettin' us mixed up in any of this union business!"

Ertie's shadow reared up the tent wall as he sat up. "Goddammit, woman, I didn't do nothin' but listen to what they was sayin'."

"Lige belong to that union?"

"Hell, no, he don' belong to no union."

"Well, Junior does. R'becky said so, an' she don' like it none, I'll tell you."

"Junior's a growed man. He kin do what he wants."

"Get us all in trouble, that's what. Was you drunk?"

"No goddammit, we wasn't drunk."

Jake hurried on to the outhouse and quickly relieved himself. Back outside, he headed for the sinks to wash up. Over in the corrals he heard a horse stomp impatiently, another snorted and trotted a few steps toward the barn. Nearby, a match flared and Jake saw his father standing there, lighting a cigarette. For an instant the glow highlighted Ertie's curling hat brim, his long, bony face and mustache. In that light he still looked like a cowboy. "Mornin', Pa."

"Ready?"

"In a minute."

While Jake splashed water on his face and ran a comb through his unruly hair, Ertie went over to the sedan, got his whiskey bottle out from under the front seat and took two big swallows, smacked his lips and took a third gulp before putting the bottle back. A horse nickered and stomped its feet again. Ertie headed for the barn. "Hurry up boy, it's comin' light."

"Be right there." Jake toweled off his face and hands.

Kakorian still used horses to pull the cultivators and French plows in the vineyards and to haul wagonloads of boxed raisins out of the vineyards. Dolly, one of the big Percheron mares, had a yearling colt. After seeing how Ertie handled the team, Kakorian had asked him if he'd like to train the young gelding. Ertie had allowed he would and, while he hadn't said much about it, Jake could see how his father's spirits had perked up. He'd even started calling the colt Socks, after one of his favorite horses back home.

Jake hurried after his father. "Pa? Is Mr. Kakorian really going to pay us a dollar a hundred?"

"Tha's what he said."

"But Junior heard the farmers' association was going to make'm all pay eighty cents."

Ertie didn't say anything.

"Pa, Junior said the union—"

"Listen." Ertie stopped and turned. "Junior Parsons's just full of piss 'n vinegar. Leave it be."

Jake silently toed the ground, not looking up.

Ertie's voice softened. "Look, Mr. Kakorian done tol' us he was payin' a dollar. Now come on, we got to harness them mares and I want to work that colt some this mornin'."

They turned and headed toward the barn.

"Junior said you an' Lige went to a union meetin' the other night."

"Wasn't much of a meetin', jus' some fellas Junior knowed."

"Pa, what's a Communist?"

"What?"

"A Communist? Junior says farmers hates Communists wors'n niggers even."

"Boy." He paused, impatient with his son but still trying to think of a good answer. "I don' rightly know, I guess ya could say Communists is Rooshan troublemakers." The colt nickered softly and stuck its head over the top rail as they walked by. Ertie reached up and rubbed the colt's ears.

"But Junior says the farmers're yellin' that there's Communists right here," Jake argued.

"Farmers is always yellin' 'Communist' this and 'Communist' that, they see 'em behind ever' bush."

"Ya ever seen one?"

"Damn, boy, yor a pester-bug this morning."

"Ya ever seen one, huh?"

"Hell, I wouldn't know what one looked like if it jumped up and bit me." Ertie started for the barn again.

"But Junior said—"

"Goddammit, boy, we got work to do." Ertie was in the barn now, opening up the tack room. He snapped on the lights and turned on the dusty old Philco radio that Kakorian kept up on a shelf.

The announcer's voice blared: ". . . Weather today will be clear and a bit cooler, with a high of ninety-five expected. Raisin-drying conditions will be good for another few days, but the forecast calls for unsettled weather by the weekend. Turning to market news, cotton prices are . . ."

Ertie hauled the harness out as Jake climbed up into the loft and began forking hay down into the mangers. Below him the mares nickered gently, expectantly, and the sounds of the radio announcer droned through farm price quotes and then the local news: "Chamber officials said the number of entries for the Old Timers Day Parade this year have already set a record . . ."

Jake pushed the last bit of hay down the chute, hurled the fork like a lance into the mow and climbed back down into the wide alleyway. In the tack room he stuck a curry comb in his back pockets, scooped up a measure of rolled oats and went to Dolly's stall. Opening the stall door, he shoved on the mare's big rump, "Dolly! Move over!" The gentle mare moved compliantly to give him more room as he dumped the feed in her box. Dolly nuzzled into the grain and began munching as Jake curried her sleek sides and legs, combing out the clods and burrs, still thinking about Junior and how much they could make if the farmers paid a buck and a quarter. Hell, at that wage he could pick maybe five dollars a day, in good cotton of course.

He finished up his chores, then headed back to camp. It was near full daylight now and his mother would really get after him if he was late for school. Quickly he changed into a clean pair of overalls and shirt, pulled on the scuffed hand-me-down shoes James Earl had given him, and was out of the tent.

Bessie had the camp stove hissing and there was a pot of mush on. Jake hungrily spooned out a bowl full.

"Molasses's there on the table." Bessie poured him a cup of coffee.

Susie came out of the tent, grabbed up her lunch sack and, ready for school, headed up past the Kakorians' house to wait for the bus there by the mailbox on the county road.

"Boy, ya better get a shake on, you'll miss the bus."

"Yes'm." Jake spooned up the last of his mush, grabbed his lunch sack and ran for the county road just as the bus pulled in, horn honking and brakes wheezing. He could see Susie and Birge Kakorian, the farmer's youngest son, climbing on. The door started to close, but Susie was by the driver, motioning, pointing to Jake running. The driver, a fat, ill-tempered man with a day's growth of graying whiskers, waited until Jake scrambled up the steps, then banged the door shut and gunned the engine. The lurch sent Susie and Jake stumbling down the aisle past the farmers' kids who always sat in front. Someone stuck a foot out, tripping Jake, sending him sprawling on the floor. For an instant he lay stunned, but then, hearing the snickers around him, he was up, fists cocked, trying to figure out who had tripped him up. Susie grabbed up his lunch sack and, before he could swing, she pulled him toward the rear of the bus. "Sit down or we'll get throwed off."

Jake shrugged off his sister's grasp, but he followed her, shoving past the rows of growers' kids, the look on his face daring anyone to try anything, anything at all. In the back, he slid into an empty seat and stared out the window, feeling challenged, yet fearful. Damn farmer kids. He leaned his head against the cool glass window and let himself bounce along, watching the farms and fields slide by, hardly noticing it when the bus lumbered up to the El Adobe Camp Six stop and wheezed to a stop. Without paying much attention, Jake watched a dozen camp kids line up as the door opened; then he saw her. Clara! She was standing there, one hand tugging anxiously at a strand of blond hair. His heart fluttered; he actually felt it, like a bird's wings inside him.

He jumped up and, as she climbed up into the bus, he yelled, "Clara!"

Heads swiveled and the youngsters stared at him, then at her. Clara had stopped, shocked. Then, laughing and crying, she pushed her way back and slid into the seat beside him.

Jake couldn't believe it. He took her hand and she squeezed back, hard. "Oh, Jake, I never thought I'd see ya again."

He wanted to kiss her, to hold her, but other kids were looking at them. Heads close together, Jake and Clara whispered their love. At school, she was in his class and they sat across the aisle from each other and at recess Jake led her back of the schoolhouse, clear back to the fence where there were some old eucalyptus trees and there, out of sight, they kissed and held each other.

School was a joy, with Clara there, and the week went rapidly by, but there was a problem. They were never alone and never together for very long, just at recess and on the bus rides. Camp Six, where Clara was living, was too far away from Kakorian's for them to be together in the afternoons. Then Jake got an idea; actually it was Susie who first mentioned it, but he seized on the plan. It was Friday and they were outside, at lunch, the four of them, Jake, Susie, Clara and Clara's brother Homer. They were out back sitting under the eucalyptus trees when Susie said she guessed they all could just walk off, for all that Gomnitz cared. He never paid any attention to them in class.

Jake let out a whoop. That was a great idea. Skip school. They did it, the four of them. Getting away was no problem since old Numb-nutz—that was the name that Susie'd come up with for the teacher—never paid attention to the camp kids once he'd taken roll. They headed for the sandy banks of the Palo Rojo, a couple of miles away, feeling adventuresome. At first they wandered aimlessly along under the oaks, hurling sticks into the near-dry river, then Homer, who was a bit younger, wanted to play hide-and-seek. Jake and Clara quickly agreed and slipped off into the willows; out of sight, they kissed eagerly, awkwardly. Jake fumbled with the front of her dress and Clara pushed him back a little, then quickly unbuttoned the top of her dress, pulling it down over her shoulders, letting him touch her again.

Just then her brother Homer had come crashing down through the willows, shouting, "Clara! Jake! Where are you guys? Come quick, we found a snake! Maybe a rattler!" Homer stood in the sandy river bottom looking wildly around. "Hey! Where are you guys?"

Back in the willows, Clara quickly pulled her dress up and, as they emerged, Homer yelled, "Come on," and ran back up the bank. They followed him.

Susie was holding up a small snake, clutching it behind the head. As Homer came running up she poked the reptile's head at him and he jumped back. Jake laughed at Homer, who was nearly a year younger, and awful dumb. "Hell, that ain' nothin' but an ol' gopher snake."

"Jake, gimme yor shirt," Susie ordered.

"Jeesus, what fer?"

"Wrap the snake up in it."

"Naw, you ain't, not my good shirt." Jake backed away from his sister. "Susie, he'll shit on it."

Susie scoffed. "You afraid?"

Still half afraid, Clara asked, "Wha'cha gonna do with it?"

"Take 'im home, put 'im in a box. Jake, hurry up."

Jake reluctantly took off his snap-button shirt and helped Susie wrap the snake inside, knotting the sleeves and shirttail into a kind of carrying sack. The idea of taking the snake home wasn't exciting at all, but he sure would like to stick it in the nurse's face at school, make her scream. Better yet, they could hide the snake in her desk so when she opened the drawer it would scare her to death. "Let's stick that goddamn snake in ol' Nurse Hobson's drawers, where—"

"Her drawers!" Surprise delighted Susie's face. "Jeesus Gawd, Jake, how ya goin' to do that? Jus' run up behind her and hike up her dress?"

"Susie!" Jake blushed, suddenly realizing what he had said. They all started laughing and Jake tried to explain, "I was . . ." He gasped for breath. "I was talkin' about her desk. Just think what she'll do when she opens up the drawer and sees this ol' snake a-hissin' at her."

"She'll piss 'er pants!" Susie giggled.

"Let's do 'er." Homer danced eagerly about.

"How we gonna get the snake in her office?" Clara asked. "It's locked, ain't it?"

"Sneak in her winda." Jake made up the plan as he talked. "She goes over to the Riverdale School ever' afternoon, but she leaves the winda open in her office 'cause it's hot in there. I seen that. She don' get back till after school's out, so we can Injun back inta school and I kin hike Susie up through the winda. Clara, you'n Homer'll be the lookouts."

And that's just the way it worked out. They waited for the final bell and then just walked onto the schoolyard as youngsters spilled out of the building headed for the buses. In the noise and confusion, they quickly ducked around back of the building and Jake boosted Susie through the window, then handed her the snake, still wrapped in his good snap-button blue denim shirt.

Susie was gone from the window for only a minute or two, then scrambled back through and jumped to the ground. "Le's get outa here."

"Ya do it?"

"Couldn't get her desk drawer open," she said breathlessly. "But I put it in the cabinet where she keeps that purple medicine she's always swabbin' on people."

"That's just as good." Jake started toward the back. "She likes nothin' better'n paintin' kids purple. Clara, come on. Homer, back this way. Quick."

They ducked out the back of the schoolyard and fled laughing and anticipating Nurse Hobson's reactions. Cutting across fields, they headed for El Adobe's Camp Six, where Clara and Homer were living. From there it was another mile and a half to Kakorian's.

They were halfway home when Jake suddenly stopped. "Susie! My shirt!"

Dumbstruck, Susie looked back at her brother.

"Where'd ya put it?"

"Gawd, Jake, I left it on the floor, by her desk."

"We gotta go back!"

"Jake, we can't."

"We gotta, that's my good shirt!" He turned to run.

Susie grabbed him. "She'll be there."

That was Friday. All day Saturday, as they worked emptying trays of dried raisins into the sweat boxes and hauling them to the barn, he'd fretted about the shirt. If Nurse Hobson gave it to old Numb-nutz and he found out whose it was, Jake was sure he'd get skinned alive. By Sunday he'd decided not to go back to school, then he wavered because he wanted to be around to hear what happened when Nurse Hobson opened the medicine cabinet and the snake slithered out. He didn't want to miss that. No sir.

Monday morning he was having second thoughts as he did his

chores. If they got caught, he'd get a strapping at least, maybe kicked out and then he wouldn't be able to see Clara every day. Jake forked the hay down to Dolly, then leaned on the pitchfork, worrying.

Down in the alleyway Ertie was easing the harness on the colt's back, gently talking to the animal. In the tack room the radio droned: "In the crime file on this Monday, October second, Sheriff Windy Scott told KMJ News that Cletus Sharp, the vagrant who was shot and killed by deputies on Saturday as he attempted to escape from custody, had been arrested for . . ."

"Boy," Ertie's voice broke into Jake's thoughts, "it's late, you better git on up to camp and git ready for school."

Susie and Birge Kakorian were pitching pennies as Jake came out to the bus stop. Forgetting his worries, Jake dropped his lunch sack on Kakorian's front lawn and dug out his milk money, five pennies. Birge stood, penny in hand, tongue clenched between his teeth, ready to pitch to the score line ten feet away.

"Keep yor toe behind the lag line," Susie yelled, distracting him.

"Susie!" Birge straightened up. "That ain' fair."

"Throw it," Susie taunted, hovering over the line, waiting for the toss.

Birge made his pitch, sailing the coin short.

"My turn," Jake barged in.

"Well pitch it then," Susie said, not arguing.

Jake toed up and lofted the coin high and flat. It hit and skidded almost up to the line, clearly beating Birge but not Susie. It was close. She shouted, "I win," and started to grab the pennies. Jake pushed her away. "Git a stick 'n measure, goddammit!"

Birge ran over to a chinaberry tree and broke off a small branch and stripped it of leaves. They crowded around as Birge carefully marked off Susie's throw then held the stick over Jake's penny. Jake won.

"Aw, shit." Susie turned away.

A half mile down the county road the yellow high school bus stopped in front of a neighboring farm, then started up again, coming toward them. Up at the house the front door banged open and Navo and Ara came running down the steps. Both were darkly handsome, like their father. Navo was quiet, Ara loquacious, a budding young football star at Jefferson High. Susie brushed a hand self-consciously at the skirt of her made-over dress, embarrassed, yet smiling brightly at Ara.

"Morning." Ara had trouble keeping his eyes off her budding breasts.

"Hi." Susie could think of nothing else to say and they both glanced at the approaching school bus. It rumbled up noisily and stopped in a cloud of dust. Navo got on, but Ara stood for a second with Susie.

"Wisht I was goin' with ya," she said impulsively.

"I do too." Ara smiled and climbed on the bus. The door slammed and it roared off.

Susie stood there, watching it pull away.

"Susie!" Jake yelled. He and Birge had thrown their pennies and Birge was the winner if Susie didn't pitch closer to the line, but she wasn't paying any attention. Jake, down on one knee looking at the pennies, shrugged, "Oh, hell, take the money. She's got the hots for Ara an' cain't think a nothin' else."

"Jake!" Susie screamed angrily and jumped on her brother, hitting him over the head with her fists as he scrambled to his feet, trying to get away. Susie stepped back and swung a roundhouse punch that missed and Jake turned to face her, fists clenched, ready. But as quickly as the attack started it was over. Susie turned away.

"You guys going to fight some more?" Birge asked, wide-eyed.

"Naw." Susie shook her head. "Not if'n he keeps his trap shut."

The Quantrill bus was fifteen minutes late, time enough for Jake to win a nickel from Birge and two more cents from Susie before the bus arrived, horn honking. Birge, clutching his lunchpail and books, took his usual seat up front.

Jake belligerently took his time going to the rear, silently daring any of the farmer kids to start something. When he sat down, Susie shoved in next to him. "Susie." Jake tried to push her away. "This is saved."

"I'll move when Clara gets on." She wanted to get Jake's mind off fighting. "Ya think ol' Nurse Hobson found the snake in her drawers yet?"

That got Jake's attention. "Aw, Gawd. Bet she found my shirt too an' they're onto us."

"Ain' no way they know who that shirt belongs to."

Jake sighed. "Maybe we kin steal it back."

"No sir." Susie looked at her brother, amazed. "I ain' goin' back in there, Jake Robertson."

"Scared?"

"Jeesus, Jake," Susie hissed. "If you wan' that ol' shirt so god-dang bad, git it yerself."

"Yor scared." Jake turned and looked out the window. Telephone poles blurred by and cottonfields stretched clear back to the distant line of trees that marked the meanderings of the Palo Rojo River.

The bus bounced hard through a chuckhole and squealed to a stop near the dirt road to Camp Six. There were maybe a dozen camp kids standing there, waiting. Jake spotted Clara and Homer crowding onto the bus, along with her cousins Frank and Danny who were low-down mean white trash. Homer was the first one back, his eyes wide with excitement. Sliding in behind Jake, he asked, "You guys hear what happened?"

Susie had changed seats, letting Clara in beside Jake. Clara was near tears. "Gawd, it was awful."

"What?"

Homer, anxious to be the first with the news, was talking fast, in a loud voice. "Laws shot down Cletus Sharp, killed him dead-er'n hell, right after they come an' arrested 'im Saturday. Ol' Wardlow hisself was there, yellin' about Cletus Sharp bein' a Red agitator. Deputies throwed him in the car, handcuffed."

"Shot him right there?" Jake asked.

"Nope. Shot him after they hauled him away. Said he tried to escape, but nobody saw it. Mrs. Sharp, she got word he'd been killed an' there was talk that he'd been arrested 'cause he'd stole a bunch of stuff but hell, that's all bullshit 'cause folks in camp heard ol' man Wardlow clear 'nuff warning that anyone else mixed up with the union would get the same. We heard that, didn't we, Clara?"

Clara nodded. "Oh Jake, that poor woman, with all them kids. Gawd I thought she was gonna die, way she was cryin' and carryin' on."

Homer kept right on talking. "She wen' to wailin' an' hollerin' somethin' fierce. Folks tried ta help 'er but she didn' wan' 'em around, blamed 'em for lettin' the laws take her man away an' kill 'im . . ."

"Oh fer Christ's sake, Homer, shuddup," Frank Tarpin snarled across the aisle. Frank was big and dirt-mean. "Cletus Sharp sure 'nuff got hisself into that mess with all that union talk. Argitators is troublemakers. Pap's right about that. Says all they do is get a feller into trouble, when he oughta be workin', feedin' his fambly."

"Yor pa don' know shit." Jake was so angry he forgot his fear of Frank. "A goddamn strike'd teach them fuckin' farmers a lesson!"

Frank clenched his fists and started to get up. Jake was on his feet, wild-eyed, daring a fight. Frank hesitated, his gaunt, narrow face and steely eyes calculating the risk.

The driver slowed and, one eye on the mirror, yelled, "What's goin' on back there!"

The farm kids had all turned and were watching. Frank glanced up front, then looked at Jake, hissing, "Not here, chickenshit. I'll git you later."

Jake stood there, ready to strike, not wanting to wait, feeling the fear creeping back into his gut. Clara grabbed his arm and pulled him back down. "Gawd, Jake, don' talk like that." She glanced toward the front of the bus where the farmers' kids sat. "They'll hear ya."

"I don' give a shit." His heart was pounding and he continued to glare at Frank.

"Jake, please don' be like that." She touched his face gently. "An' stay away from Frank an' Danny, they'll hurtcha."

Her touch distracted him and the anger began to subside, but he was troubled still. "Ain'chew mad?"

"Honey, they're mean, Frank an' Danny'll—"

Exasperated with her now, he pulled away. "Wasn't talkin' 'bout Frank, I ain' afraid of either of 'em. I was talkin' 'bout the laws killin' that fella. Don' that make ya mad?"

Clara didn't answer.

"Clara, they shot 'im down like a dog."

"Jake, I know ya don' like Frank, but what he said was right. Mr. Sharp come by our camp an' was tryin' to get Pa an' Uncle

Ott 'n them to come to the union meetin'. Grandpa, he run 'im off with a shotgun."

Jake just looked at her in disbelief. He couldn't understand why she was talking on like this when she ought to be fighting mad too. "You like bein' Okies? Bein' treated worse'n niggers?"

Tears filled her eyes. She blinked and wiped at them, then turned and looked out the dirty window, speaking softly. "Tha's a awful mean thang to say."

"Oh, Clara, I'm sorry." He reached out to touch her, but now she pulled away.

"We *are* Okies." The words squealed out in anguish. Embarrassed, but still angry, she looked around to see who had heard, then turned to Jake, lowering her voice. "I was born in a tie camp on Indian lan' an' we ain' never lived in a proper house but once, on a sharecrop, outa Fort Smith. Never even made a crop. We're trash, jus' trash."

Jake put his arm around her and this time Clara didn't resist. "Oh, Jake . . ." Her voice trailed off. She had on the same yellow dress that she'd worn when they had found the snake. He stared at the buttons and remembered how firm and round her breasts were, wanting to feel her soft skin against him again. Clara looked down at him and down at her own figure, realizing what he was thinking. She smiled and wiped away the tears.

Jake whispered, "You ain' trash. Don' never say that again. Hear?"

She nodded.

He glanced back to make sure no one could overhear, then asked, "Ya ever go skinny?"

"What?" Clara wrinkled her nose in a curious half-smile, cocking her head. "Wha'chew mean?"

"Get all naked an' go swimmin'."

"Jake!" She blushed and looked around, shaking her head no, but whispered back, "I would if it was jus' with you."

The bus driver, shifting down and braking, wheeled the bus into the school driveway. Jake looked out. Gomnitz was standing there on the porch in the same tweed suit he always wore, watching as the youngsters piled off the bus. He seemed to be looking for someone. Oh, shit. Jake's heart pounded as he walked with Clara up the steps and past the teacher. In the hallway the school secretary was singling out the camp kids, making them line up outside the office. Once they were in line no talking was allowed. Waiting there Jake was near panic. Was this just a routine inspection by Nurse Hobson, or a trap? Behind the nurse's closed door he could hear her sharp screeching voice, "Hold still! Turn around," and he was relieved because it sounded routine. The door opened, a boy came out and the voice ordered "Next" and he caught a glimpse of the nurse and could see the medicine cabinet was open. Then the door closed.

"Next." Jake went in and stood before the nurse, frightened. She grabbed his thin, bony jaw, turning his head this way and that, pulled at his ears, then made him drop his overalls and stand there, skinny naked. He didn't see his shirt until she ordered him to turn around. There it was, hanging on a coat rack. He gritted his teeth and held his breath. Nurse Hobson told him to pull up his pants and dismissed him. There was no reaction to the shirt, no sign of the snake. By midmorning recess, the door to the nurse's tiny clinic was locked and she had gone on her rounds.

At recess Jake huddled with Susie, Clara and Homer, puzzling over the problem. The snake could have simply crawled out and somehow escaped, or it might still be back in the cabinets. Maybe it was dead. That medicine in there smelled awful. Jake still wanted that shirt back. He pulled Susie aside. "Maybe we kin sneak in there now, 'fore the bell rings."

"Gawd, Jake, if'n we get caught, ol' Numb-nutz'll kill us."

"We gotta, Susie." Jake tugged her around the side of the school house.

"Maybe it's a trap."

Jake looked around. "Ain' nobody goin' to see us." They were standing under the nurse's office window, hesitating. Several children ran by without stopping. When they were gone, Jake held out his hands, making a stirrup, "Susie, come on."

She hesitated. "Wait, somebody's a-watchin' us." Susie stepped away from the building, her body alert. Then, without any warning, she doubled her fists and confronted Jake, yelling angrily, "Gimme my four cents! I won!"

Taken by surprise, Jake backed away just as Gomnitz came around the corner toward them.

"I said gimme my money!" Susie screamed and swung at her brother. "You cheated!"

Bewildered by Susie's actions and frightened by Gomnitz's approach, he jumped back. "Goddammit, I won. We measured."

Gomnitz stepped between them. "What's going on here?"

"Jeesus," Jake pleaded. "Them pennies's mine, not hers."

"What're you talking about?" The principal looked puzzled. "What pennies?"

Susie whined. "Make him gimme 'em back. He cheated when we was pitchin' pennies an' I don' have 'nuff for milk at lunch on accoun'a that."

"Did you cheat your own sister?" Gomnitz had ahold of Jake's arm.

Jake tried to pull away. "She's crazy, I won 'em fair'n square."

"Give her the money back, you know we don't tolerate gambling in this school."

Jake dug into his pocket, a look of pure hatred coming over his face as he handed the four pennies to his sister.

Gomnitz let him go. "Now you two get on back to the playground where I can keep an eye on you. Don't let me catch you sneakin' back around here again, you hear?"

"Yessir." Glad to be released, they ran back around the building and out onto the playground. Out of Gomnitz's sight, Susie started laughing. Jake, still angry, grabbed her. "Gimme my money back."

Susie stopped laughing.

"That's my money, goddammit."

"I know it. Here." Susie willingly gave him the coins. "I was jis' tryin' to fool ol' Numb-nutz, make him think we was fightin'. Gawd, Jake, think if he'd come around jis' a minute or two later. I'd a been inside."

"You ain' mad 'bout the money?" Jake was puzzled.

"Naw. I was jus' playactin'."

"Jeez, Susie," he laughed. "Ya had me fooled too, I thought ya'd gone crazy or somethin'."

Susie put a friendly arm around Jake. "I was scared spitless, him a peekin' 'round the corner that way. Feared he was gonna catch us."

"Jeez, I never even seen 'im."

The bell rang and the play yard emptied. Gomnitz stood by the door to his class, watching as they filed in and took their seats, the farmer kids up front, the camp kids in back. Late afternoons were social studies and Gomnitz passed out mimeographed maps of ancient Greece and Asia Minor. He instructed the class to color in the city-states, yellow for Athens, red for Sparta, green for Thebes, brown for Crete. The Aegean Sea, of course, should be blue. This was a test, not a game. The papers would be collected at the last bell.

Jake, right arm crooked over the map, tongue clenched between his teeth, worked over Sparta, starting at the borders and coloring inward. The task was boring, but he liked the subject, especially the mythology: Theseus, the mythical king of Athens, killed the man-eating Minotaur who lived in King Minos's labyrinth on the island of Crete. Jake took up a brown pencil and doodled in a monster on the island of Crete, wondering what a labyrinth was. He tried several times to sound the word silently, contorting his mouth and tongue around the syllables. They sure had funny names for things back in those times.

Susie was sitting behind Jake and she nudged him, whispering, "Which one's Corinth?"

Jake checked to see if Gomnitz was watching, then lifted his map and pointed.

Across the aisle Clara looked up and smiled briefly at Jake and his mind wandered from Theseus to Aphrodite. Head down, tongue still between his teeth, he continued his coloring, but his thoughts were of Clara.

A small, tightly folded piece of paper landed on his desk and he looked around. Clara smiled. He opened the note and read the message: "Tonight?"

He wrote back, "By the ditch," refolded the note, stuck it between his toes and stretched his leg across the aisle, keeping his eyes on the teacher all the while.

Clara retrieved the note, read it and then scribbled a quick answer, thought of something else and added a few more words. She folded the note and dropped her hand down.

Just as Jake clutched the note with his toes Gomnitz called out his name. "Jake Robertson!"

Jake froze. He'd concentrated so much on getting Clara's answer back he'd taken his eyes off the teacher.

"What you got there?" The teacher came down the aisle, hand extended.

"Ain' nothin'."

"Let me see it."

The whole class was watching.

Reluctantly, Jake handed up the note and Gomnitz elaborately unfolded it and turned to the class. "We have here a love note, of sorts, and . . ." He paused, saying half aloud, "What's this?" His mocking tone was gone and his face was stern. "What's this?"

Clara shrunk down in her seat.

Gomnitz ordered Jake to stand up and Jake obeyed.

The teacher faced Susie and Clara. "You too. All three of you go to my office. Right now."

Turning the class over to a student proctor, Gomnitz herded the three into his small office. Frantic, Jake whispered to Clara, "What'd ya put in that note?"

"You two, be quiet!" Gomnitz closed the office door. There, folded on top of Gomnitz's desk, was Jake's snap-button shirt. Picking it up, the teacher shook it in Jake's face. "This is yours, isn't it?"

Susie tried to step between them. "Please, Mr. Gomnitz, we didn' do nothin'."

"Then what were the two of you doin' out by that window? Answer me that, girl?" Not waiting for an answer, he put the shirt back on the desk and took the leather whipping strap from its peg on the wall.

"We didn' do nuthin'," Susie pleaded.

"He," Gomnitz pointed at Jake, "put that snake in Mrs. Hobson's drawer. I knew if we kept quiet someone would tip their hand." A thin smile on his face, the teacher ordered Jake to bend over and grab his ankles.

Susie pulled the principal's arm. "I did it, Mr. Gomnitz. Not him."

Gomnitz shook her off, but she came back at him, grabbing at his arm again, trying to stop him. Gomnitz tried to push her away. Hysterical now, Susie bit him on the hand, hard. The teacher yowled in pain and shoved her away, knocking her sprawling across the room.

Jake reached for Susie, pulling her to her feet, all the while yelling at Clara, "Run! Git the hell out of here!"

"Jake!" Susie grabbed up the shirt and tossed it to him as they all three bolted out of the office and down the front steps of the school before Gomnitz could stop them. The principal chased after them briefly, but then, panting and holding a handkerchief over his bleeding hand, he went back inside and called the sheriff's office.

With Jake in the lead, the three youngsters fled through the cottonfields, heading for the river. Finally, breathless, Jake flopped on the riverbank. Looking up at Clara, he asked, "What'n hell'd ya put in that note?"

Clara sobbed. "Jis' wanted to know what happened to that ol' snake."

That night Jake and Susie said nothing to Bessie or Ertie, figuring that in the morning they would just announce they'd quit school, hoping that would be the end of it. There was no way they were going back and face ol' Numb-nutz. It never even occurred to them that the teacher would call the sheriff, but just before supper a patrol car pulled into the Kakorian driveway and the deputies drove straight back, past the tank house toward the camp. Jake was washing up when he spotted the sheriff's car and saw Clara and Homer locked in the backseat. Jeesus Christ. Ducking around behind the washhouse he ran to warn Susie. "Jeesus, the law's got Clara and Homer and they're comin' to git us." Before she could say anything, he was pulling her and running out into the vineyard.

Kakorian saw the patrol car too. Curious, he headed for the camp to see what the trouble was. The deputies were out of the car, arguing with Ertie and Lige. The others were standing around nervously watching and listening.

"Goddammit, where are those two kids?" Sergeant Dobbs demanded. He was a big, dark man, handsome and muscled.

"Ain' seen 'em." Ertie looked around, shaking his head. "Don' know where they went off to. You know how kids are."

Under the vines, Susie started to laugh, and Jake hushed her, afraid they would be spotted.

"Officer, what'd ya wan' em for?" Lige asked.

"Keep outa this." Dobbs glared at Lige, and turned back on Ertie. "Listen, buster! I'll run yor ass in instead of those damn kids of yours."

"Name's Ertie Robertson." Ertie stood there defiantly. "An' ya got no right to come in here cussin' me or my kids. What the hell'd they do? Rob a bank?"

The deputies hadn't noticed Kakorian come up and didn't realize he was standing there, just behind them.

Dobbs reached for his billy. "Listen, you goddamn Okie, I'll teach you your rights!"

"Sergeant!" Kakorian's hard-edged voice surprised Dobbs.

The lawman spun around, his hand going for his gun, but when he saw the farmer, he let his hand fall to his side. "Oh, it's you, Mr. Kakorian. Sorry."

"Sergeant, what are you doing on my land?"

"We come after them two kids that attacked Gomnitz, over at the school."

"Attacked Gomnitz?"

"Yeah, the boy he hit him, an' the girl, she like to took his hand off when she bit him. He be lucky if he ain' poisoned." Dobbs snickered.

Jake whispered to Susie, "Jeez, I never hit him."

"Shhhh."

"Gomnitz needs your help against two kids?" Kakorian's skepticism was sharp. "Sergeant, I'd think the sheriff would have better things for you to do than chase kids for that fool Gomnitz."

"Sir?" Dobbs asked, "can we talk to you, private?"

They walked out of earshot and stood in a huddle. Dobbs was doing most of the talking. Susie wiggled back under the vines, uncomfortably. "Jeez, Jake, maybe we oughta get outa here."

"Where to?"

"I don' know."

"Why'd ya have to bite'm? I coulda taken the lickin'."

"Jake, look, Mr. Kakorian's laughing."

Sergeant Dobbs and his partner were standing there, frozen in anger, as the farmer shook his head and walked away, yelling back over his shoulder, "Dobbs, I'm going to call the sheriff. You just wait right there."

Ten minutes later Kakorian was back and orders came over the patrol car radio to forget the matter and turn the youngsters loose. Sergeant Dobbs opened the door and ordered Clara and Homer out.

Kakorian stepped up, confronting the lawmen again. "Sergeant, I think you ought to take them back to their camp. If you leave them here, I'll just have to call the sheriff again."

Dobbs told Clara and Homer to get back in the car, climbed in the front seat and slammed the door.

After the lawmen had gone, Kakorian took Ertie aside. "Look, you people are good workers, but I don't want any more trouble. Okay? I promised the sheriff the kids wouldn't go back to school."

"What the hell'd they do?" Ertie wasn't sure whether he should be angry or grateful.

"Pulled a fool prank on the nurse. Put a snake in one of the cabinets where she keeps medicine, nearly scared her out of her wits when she came in this morning and opened it up." Kakorian chuckled again, then turned serious. "Deputies said that when the principal caught them, the girl bit him and then your boy took a swing at him. A prank's a prank, but hitting a teacher is something else."

"Hell, maybe he had it comin'." Ertie felt defensive and proud.

"Maybe. I'm not saying any different, but just keep them away from that school. Okay? Goin' back there would only cause more trouble for your kids."

Ertie nodded. "Okay." They'd be better off staying away from the likes of those damn school people. He took out his Bull Durham and thoughtfully rolled a cigarette. "Mr. Kakorian, been meanin' to ask ya something."

"What's that?"

"We been hearing that the farmers' association's set the price of cotton-pickin' at eighty cents. That right?"

"Yes." Kakorian looked Ertie square in the eye. "Why?"

"You plannin' to drop wages to eighty cents?"

"No. I told you people I was paying a dollar and that's what I'll pay. I don't give a tinker's damn what the association says, they don't run this farm. I do." Kakorian fell silent for a moment, obviously irritated, then he asked, "You a part of that Workers Alliance or the CIO?"

"No sir, I ain't mixed up with them outfits."

"Good. I won't have anything to do with that bunch of Communists. They're out to destroy this country."

10

Colonel Remington M. Winchester was seated in the Hotel Californian dining room in Fresno having his breakfast, a poached egg
on wheat toast and two slices of crisp bacon, a glass of chilled
apple juice and coffee, black. Although he was an officer in the
United States Army on active duty in the California National
Guard, he wore civilian clothes while assigned as an adjutant to
Governor Olson. This morning he wore a sharply pressed brown
suit, subdued brown tie and cordovan shoes, polished to a high
gloss. A brown snap-brim hat with a tiny yellow and blue feather
in its band was set carefully beside him on the seat in his usual
booth in the hotel's main dining room. The high-ceilinged room
was large, comfortably formal, and he considered the food pass-
able, though not comparable to the fare at the Senator in Sacramento or San Francisco's Clift.

At the table, just to the left of his plate, he had neatly folded a
copy of the local paper, the *Fresno Bee*, and was reading as he
ate:

HITLER SUMMONS REICHSTAG
Soviet Deal to be Told

Berlin, Oct. 4, 1939 — Adolf Hitler, moving swiftly upon his
conquest of Poland and expanding his partnership with Soviet
Russia, is calling the Reichstag into session . . .

As an army regular, Colonel Winchester felt obliged to read all of the war news, not that he was a war-lover, but it was always best to keep informed. The colonel was a thinly handsome, sophisticated fellow with dark hair parted on the left and a trim little mustache. He thought of himself as an urbane, precise man who could quickly sort out a situation and make logical decisions, but now he was troubled and felt ill at ease. Following the shooting death of that migrant worker, Governor Olson had dispatched him to the San Joaquin Valley to scout out the farm labor unrest; it was a distasteful assignment. Civilian political squabbles were such disorderly affairs, and that shooting was particularly messy. What was the fellow's name? Winchester pulled out a little notebook. Sharp, yes, Cletus Sharp. Curious happening. No previous record. Shot while escaping from a police car. Well, solving that riddle wasn't his worry. The governor's instructions were simple enough, feel out both sides, see if there was any way to head off a strike.

Jefferson City was such a wretched town that he had chosen to stay in Fresno, a forty-five-minute drive to the north. When he could arrange it, he was seeing people here, at the hotel, on more neutral ground. Colonel Winchester glanced at his watch; there still was plenty of time. He was meeting Titus Wardlow here for coffee at nine fifteen. Colonel Winchester had come down early to enjoy a leisurely breakfast and review what he knew about this fellow Wardlow and the Associated Farmers. When he had phoned Wardlow, asking for the meeting, he had assured the farmer there were no tricks, the governor had sent him down on a fact-finding mission, nothing more. Actually, his instructions were a little more precise; the governor had decided to attend the Old Timers Day parade on Saturday, which was the day after tomorrow, and afterward he wanted to meet with the farmers, privately. The governor was being extremely naive, Colonel Winchester was certain of that. No one he had talked to here welcomed the idea of Olson coming to Jefferson County, but Olson was adamant, believing that by sitting down with the farmers he could make them understand his own resolve in this matter. He was the governor and he intended to see an end to this trouble. His parting words had been, "The farmers and their bankers are going to have to realize that this administration will function on behalf of the economically submerged part of the population."

At least Olson didn't beat about the bush. Colonel Winchester liked that directness, even though he disliked the man's politics. When Winchester had called to warn the governor that he was facing a hostile reception, Olson had thanked his adjutant but said he must come down anyway; his appearance at the parade would bring the issue out into the open, even if it meant a confrontation. And, after all, his political strength was in the cities and with organized labor, not on the farm, so it wasn't like he was losing any votes. There was a chance to settle this thing, Olson said, explaining that he'd talked with CIO leaders and was convinced the unions would be willing to negotiate; he hoped to bring the farmers to the table. Olson was right about one thing, the local union leaders and workers alike wanted to settle and would take a dollar a hundredweight, if they got union recognition as well, but Colonel Winchester was certain that they were underestimating this situation, and so was the governor. This was no minor skirmish over wages, this situation was shaping up as an all-out war between the CIO and industrialized agriculture.

Tactically, killing that migrant had been a big mistake, even if it had happened the way the sheriff said. That one act had given the enemy a cause to rally around. The CIO was committing its top organizers, sending them into the fields and labor camps; the unions were holding nightly rallies in the courthouse park and drawing big crowds; labor leaders and liberal churchmen in San Francisco and Los Angeles were holding solidarity rallies and drumming up urban support while the CIO was quietly leasing land for a strike camp, stockpiling tents, food and blankets, and building a war chest. Clearly they were planning a major strike that could shut down the entire San Joaquin Valley cotton harvest and attract national attention. The New Dealers in Congress were already making noises about strengthening the National Labor Relations Act and the CIO leaders saw this as a major opportunity for a showdown over farm labor issues. Farmworkers were the largest group of workers not covered by the 1935 act that had made it possible for industrial workers to unionize and force their bosses to the bargaining table. Now the Reuthers and other CIO leaders wanted Congress to bring migrant farmworkers into the act. Tactically, a big cotton strike made more sense now than ever before because there was a New Deal Democrat as governor of California, the biggest farm state in the country.

From his vantage point, Colonel Winchester could see there was a big hole in that union scenario. The unions had never won a farm labor strike before. There had been some minor victories, a few more pennies an hour in wages, but never recognition, never a contract, never a lasting presence, because the growers always had the government on their side. The strike would work this time only if the governor were a strong leader who had a firm grip on the state politically. Olson was a man of strong beliefs, but he was neither a powerful leader nor did he have much political control. A conservative coalition of Republicans and rural Democrats controlled the legislature, and State Attorney General Earl Warren was a conservative Republican and former law-and-order prosecutor from Alameda County. The governor's position was weak.

Colonel Winchester had warned Olson of all of this and, that duty done, he reminded himself that it was not his place to judge, or take issue. He had learned early in his career to put aside his own feelings and follow orders. With a big war shaping up in Europe, now wasn't the time to rock any boats. The governor, no matter what his politics, was still in command and he, Colonel Winchester, was just a soldier on a recon patrol.

Colonel Winchester turned to the second section and skimmed the news. Most of it was local: milk was going up to twelve cents a quart, delivered; the district attorney was investigating voter registration fraud. Tucked away in the back pages a headline caught his eye:

MIGRANT LABOR STUDY MADE
Transient Crop Workers' Plight More Serious

Washington, Oct 4 (AP) — From California to New Mexico, the migratory labor problem in the Southwest is growing more serious, the Works Project Administration reported today.

Present relief methods are insufficient to care for thousands of homeless families seeking employment, WPA investigators said. They charged that cotton farmers caused the problem by luring families from Oklahoma and Texas with false promises of good jobs and big earnings.

Rural sociologists estimate that between 200,000 and 300,000 Dust Bowl refugees have flooded into California alone since 1932 and that there are 10 workers for every available job. With a surplus of labor, cotton farmers are lowering the wages and the living quarters provided for migrants are inadequate, unsanitary and unhealthy according to the report . . .

The story was not unexpected. The WPA investigators had briefed the governor nearly two weeks ago, before they left for Washington.

Sipping his coffee, Colonel Winchester turned his attention on Titus Wardlow, thumbing through his notebook, reviewing what he knew about the man. Wardlow was forty-one, married to Barbara Ann Braddock, thirty-four; they had a son, George, twelve, and daughter, Carolyn, nine; Mrs. Wardlow and the children regularly attended the First Methodist Church in Jefferson City, but Wardlow seldom went, nor did he play golf or belong to any clubs. Wardlow's only diversions seemed to be that airplane and Roxanne Darling, the race pilot. That was just a rumor of course, the part about Roxanne Darling, but it was an interesting bit of intelligence. Wardlow's war record was impressive, two German aircraft and an observation balloon downed before he had been shot down over France. By all accounts, Wardlow was a tough, determined man who had close ties to big, corporate farm operators like Ward Smyth, president of Coco Oil's farming operations, and Stan Knudson, chief executive officer of White Creek Farms. Smyth and Knudson were powerful men who preferred to stay in the background and let the aggressive, hard-driving Wardlow take the lead.

And that brought Winchester's thoughts around to the Associated Farmers, a vigilante movement born during the violent, Communist-led strikes six years earlier. The association's strength came from its forty-two associated county chapters, each pledged to aid the others during labor unrest. The guiding forces behind the association were the California Farm Bureau and the powerful Agriculture Committee of the California Chamber of Commerce, the latter with strong ties to both the big banks and industrialized agribusiness interests based in Los Angeles and San Francisco. The association was headquartered in Sacramento and its executive director was Art Casperson, former head of the state Social Relief Agency under the previous administration and a man who had close ties to the legislature and the state justice system.

That was the overview. Within each county, the association worked closely with the sheriff, creating a paramilitary antilabor-strike force. The man who trained and coordinated these forces was Major D. Adam Shriver, U.S. Army (retired). Colonel Winchester knew and disliked Major Shriver, a blustering, arrogant martinet who had done nothing significant in twenty years in the service. However, Major Shriver did have some sense of logistics and tactics. He had proven this in the Salinas vegetable strikes in 1937, ruthlessly stamping out that rebellion. That was a plus for the farmers, but the situation now was different; with Olson as governor, the association could no longer call out the state highway patrol or the National Guard to help them, as they did in Salinas and later in the Stockton cannery strikes.

That didn't mean, however, that the guard or the highway patrol could be counted on to help the strikers. While the guard could be called out by Olson, politically that wouldn't be wise and, as for the highway patrol, its loyalty was questionable. The patrolmen were state policemen, true, but each county patrol unit was made up local fellows who were commanded by men who had risen up through the ranks. In the valley, their sympathies were with the farmers. Given that, and the political realities of Sacramento, the governor really didn't have all that much control over the situation.

Colonel Winchester glanced at his watch, then skimmed through the *Jefferson City Tribune*. A front-page story reported that the cotton harvest had already started in Kern County and the paper was predicting picking would begin in Jefferson County on October 10. No mention was made of the Workers Alliance or the CIO, but the coming weekend's celebration got a big play. A queen had been chosen for the Old Timers Day celebration and Ward Bigalow, a cattleman from the foothills, was to be grand marshal of the parade. Buried deep in the story was a brief mention that Governor Olson would be on the judges' stand.

"Winchester?"

"Yes?" Colonel Winchester glanced up.

"I'm Titus Wardlow." The farmer sat down without waiting to be invited. He didn't offer to shake hands, nor did he take off his hat, just pushed it back on his head and continued to chew on the cigar stuck in the corner of his mouth.

"Coffee?" Winchester signaled the waiter.

Wardlow grunted.

"Care for some breakfast?"

"No." Wardlow sounded brusque, even hostile. "What's on your mind, Winchester?"

"As I said on the phone, the governor sent me down here just to get a lay of the land. He wants me to find out what the issues are. As you know, he's going to be here for the parade Saturday, and he is hoping to meet with you and the other farmers."

"We've got nothing to talk about."

"Oh?" Winchester was irritated by the crude manner of the man. "Your association set the picking wage at eighty cents, the unions are asking one dollar and twenty-five cents. Is there room to negotiate?"

"No!" Wardlow took the cigar butt out of his mouth and, using it like a pointer, growled, "And you tell Olson that if he wants to settle this thing, he'd better get the fucking Communist unions out of here. They don't represent our workers and we sure as hell aren't about to sell our people out."

"Are you willing to hold an election? Let the workers vote on union recognition?"

"Recognize those Communists? Winchester, you got to be kidding." Wardlow shook his head in surprise. "Besides, our workers don't need an election, they're free to come talk to us anytime they want and they've told us they don't want anything to do with those damn agitators." Wardlow cocked his head a little to the side and squinted, like he was sizing up an adversary, measuring his reactions. "You've got to remember, farming isn't like running a goddamn factory, we can't shut down everytime somebody wants to talk. When our crops are ripe, we've got to pick and sell them right then, no matter what. We don't set the market price, like they do on cars, we take whatever we can get. We can't wait. The fruit's there, ripe. We gotta move it or lose it. When anybody threatens to strike us at harvest, we're going to fight. You can count on that!"

That was a long speech and Colonel Winchester, hoping Wardlow might be opening up a bit more, asked, "What about those university economists who say you could afford to pay one dollar and twenty-five cents and still make a profit?"

"Shit! Let 'em come on down and try it, on their own money. See how long they last." Wardlow struck a match and puffed his cigar back to life. "Look, you can tell that governor for us that the trouble is being stirred up by professional agitators who are out to cripple American agriculture. Tell him that. And if he's as good an American as he claims he is, he'll help us get those Reds out of here. Then we can talk about what the workers want, but not at harvest time. Strikes at harvest have got to be outlawed. Tell him that."

"All right, I will, but now I'm curious. You were paying as much as one dollar per hundredweight in nineteen thirty-six, why are you paying twenty percent less now?"

"Winchester, I didn't come here to argue." Wardlow got up and, leaning over the table, growled again, "You came for information, you got it. No recognition of the Communist unions! No negotiations! If there's a strike, we'll take care of it, our way!"

Wardlow turned and walked out.

11

The last sweatbox of raisins had been stacked in the barn and the weather had changed. Brisk winds swayed the towering sycamores and swirled through the short, round chinaberry trees up by the big house, sending flurries of yellowing leaves to the ground. In the Robertsons' camp there was time now to rest a bit and put things in order before the cotton harvest started. The sun was already well up as Mary Ellen and Billie Jo washed the breakfast dishes. Ertie and James Earl sat sipping the last of their coffee and Benjy snuggled between them sucking his thumb. Jake had been out sparking Clara much of the night and, sleepy-eyed, he sat at the table spooning down the last of his mush.

Bessie had a roaring fire going over in the washhouse stove, heating water for a big bunch of laundry piled up next to the tubs. Glancing over at the tents, she hollered, "Susie! You git up, right now!"

Jake grinned, watching his sister stumble out of the tent, making for the outhouse, her hair mussed and her shirttail flying.

Ertie sucked a last drag on his cigarette, crushed it out and got up. "Well, we gotta feed them horses and I'm goin' to work with the colt. Ya comin', boy?"

Jake scraped up a last bite. "Pa, can I drive Socks some this mornin'?"

"We'll see how he does."

They harnessed Socks and led the colt out into the big training corral. As Ertie hooked a thirty-foot lunge line into the colt's hal-

ter and got it started cantering around him in a circle, Jake
climbed the corral fence and sat on the top rail, watching. Once
Socks was limbered up, Ertie put the colt in a training bridle,
snapped long reins into the rings on the snaffle bit, and began
driving Socks, walking along behind the colt, working the reins,
turning the animal first one way then another.

Up at the main house the back door slammed and Kakorian
came down the steps, shrugging into his coat as he glanced up at
the thin layer of clouds. He was headed for the shop, where he
and James Earl were going to overhaul the tractor and get it in
shape to pull the cotton trailers, but he had to talk to Ertie first.

"Hi, Mr. Kakorian." Jake waved from his perch.

"Mornin', Jake." The farmer stopped and peered into the corral.
"Ertie, can I see ya a minute."

"Whoa." Ertie pulled back on the reins. "Whoa thar, son. That's
it." The colt stopped. "Jake, come on over. Easy now."

Jake eased down off the fence and walked slowly up to his father, taking the reins. Ertie helped him get Socks walking again
then limped along beside him as Jake clutched the reins uncertainly. Confused by Jake's tentative signals, the colt skittered
sideways in quick, dancing little steps, head cocked around, eyes
wide, pulling Jake along.

"Right rein." Ertie's voice was calm but demanding. "Git after
him! Pull on that rein! That's it. Keep pullin' him around, now
slack off, easy, easy. That's it! Now bring him on around the other
way." Ertie stayed beside his son until both the boy and the colt
began to settle down, then he went over to the farmer standing
just outside the corral gate. "Mornin', Mr. Kakorian."

"Mornin'. The colt's looking good. How's the boy doing?"

Ertie let himself out through the gate. "Oh, he's green, but he's
learnin'. Don' mind, do ya?"

"Not at all, long as you're here."

Ertie was pleased. "That colt's a winner. When he gets full-
growed he's gonna outpull anything in the county."

"Ertie, got a favor to ask of you. I promised Mrs. Kakorian we'd
let her Four-H Club fix up the big wagon for the parade tomorrow. They're coming over this afternoon, after school."

"Okay, I'll get it out for them. Ya want it up by the house?"

"Out in front of the barn's fine, but what I want you to do for
me in the morning early is hitch up the team and drive the wagon

into town. Parade starts at ten, so you'll have to leave by four-thirty." Kakorian took out his wallet. "Here's ten dollars."

Ertie looked at the money in surprise. Ten was nearly a week's wages. "What's that for?"

"A bonus, for working with the colt. Why don't you take the family in too, give 'em a treat. And don't worry about the wagon afterward, one of the boys can drive it back."

"Thanks." Ertie folded the bill and put it in his pocket.

"We'll meet you in town a little before ten, by the high school there on L, just off Main."

"I'll find it. Want me to drive the team in the parade too?"

"Why, no!" The question surprised Kakorian. He looked curiously at Ertie, shaking his head. "No thanks," he said, and headed for the shop, passing by Lige who was coming over to watch them work with the colt.

"Mornin', Mr. Kakorian, mornin', Ertie." Lige climbed up and sat on the fence, took out his pocketknife and tobacco plug and carefully sliced off a generous chew.

Ertie stared after Kakorian for a bit, then climbed up and perched beside Lige, showing him the ten. "See what he give me?"

"What fer?"

Ertie yelled at Jake. "Ease off that rein, ease off. When he's doin' wha'cha want, give 'im slack. That's it." Turning back to Lige, Ertie explained, "For workin' the colt, that an' he wants me to drive the team inta town tomorra so his kids can be in the parade. Wanna come along?"

"Sounds good to me, they got a dandy parade here."

"Ya know"—Ertie was thinking about Kakorian's response—"it's hard to figger that bird out."

"Kakorian?"

"Yeah. He works right alongside us, an' that makes ya want to like the man, but when I offered to drive the team in the parade you'd a thought I was some uppity nigger wantin' to come in the front door."

"Aw, he probably didn't mean nothin'."

"And I'll tell ya somethin' else, when I asked him if he was still gonna pay a dollar, he got mad, started askin' if I was in the union." Ertie shook his head. "Ya reckon there's Communists runnin' them unions, like he says?"

"Well, Junior ain' no Communist, I know that, an' that Cletus Sharp was just a workin' man, like you'n me." Lige spit a stream of tobacco juice. "Seems like a man ought not have to die for speakin' out when things is wrong."

"That's the damn truth." Ertie rolled a cigarette. "What d'ya reckon's goin' to happen?"

"Junior says the people's scared and mad at the same time." Lige moved his cud around, worked up a big spit, and let fly again. "He's been to them rallies in the park and he said it sounded like folks's ready to strike."

"People'll say most anythin' when they're worked up." Ertie lit his cigarette and inhaled deeply. "Sometimes they're like a bunch a dumb sheep, all jumpin' this way an' that, but it seems like they don' do nothin' but make a lot of noise."

Lige just chewed on his cud for a while, then spit angrily, dribbling juice on his chin. "Shit!"

"What's stickin' in yor craw?"

"Well"—Lige wiped his chin with the back of his hand—"I guess I don' see 'em as dumb sheep."

"Aw, hell, all I meant was that talkin' an' yellin' at a meetin' don't get nothin' done."

Lige was serious now, very serious. "Them folks is jus' like you'n me, Ertie. An' ever' once in a while they gits mad enough to do somethin'. You'll see."

"Figgerin' on joinin'?"

"Been thinkin' on it, right 'nuff."

Ertie shifted his weight uncomfortably. "But yor the one tha' always goes 'round trouble."

"I never said that."

"Hell, tha's 'xactly what ya said back at Bull's Camp, said ya never—"

"What I said was that I don' go askin' for trouble by workin' for them contractors or outfits like that El Adobe, but this here's different. There's times when folks's just gotta do somethin' 'cause things is so bad, an' this looks like one of them times."

"What makes ya say that?"

"Thangs is different now, what with this new governor comin' right out for higher wages. Junior says he's sent some high mucky-muck 'round to try an' git them farmers ta hike up the wage." Lige looked right at Ertie now. "An' don' forget, this ain't just some local union, this here's the CIO that whupped Henry Ford's ass back in Dee-troit."

"Got yor mind made up, ain'cha?"

Lige was silent.

"Figgerin' on joinin'?"

"Hell, I don' know." Lige looked off toward the shop. "Kakorian's a good man an' I never knowed him to go back on his word. I jus' don' know, Ertie."

On Saturday morning dark gray clouds hung low in the sky and the streets in Jeff City were damp. It had stormed during the night and the air was heavy with the threat of more rain. Even so, hundreds of people lined Main Street waiting for the parade. Most were dressed in western outfits, the men and boys wearing cowboy hats and bright, silky snap-button shirts, the women and girls in bonnets and long pioneer dresses. They crowded the sidewalks and stood three deep along the curbs all the way from the high school clear down Main past the courthouse and into the center of town where spectators jammed the second-story windows and lined the rooftops. Balloon salesmen and trinket vendors walked along the street hawking wares and two motorcycle cops prowled the parade route, keeping the street wide open.

The judges' platform, draped in patriotic bunting, was set up at the usual location on the lawn in front of the Jefferson Elementary School, directly across Main from the courthouse and park. A workman pushed his way through rows of empty chairs to the microphone and switched it on. "Testing. Testing." The words echoed and the mike squealed. "You folks across the street there hear me okay?"

People at the curb waved and someone yelled, "Give us a speech, Henry!"

That got a laugh. There was a stir at the back of the crowd surrounding the platform and several uniformed cops pushed slowly through the throng, clearing the way for Governor Olson, Congressman Young, several city councilmen and county supervisors. The governor was wearing a dark suit and a white cowboy hat. As he climbed the platform stairs and came into view the crowd fell silent.

Olson quietly, quickly shook hands with the other dignitaries and took his seat. Silver-haired Charles Gilmore wasn't wearing a hat, but he was neatly dressed in Levi's and a brown silk shirt and had a yellow scarf tied around his neck. He stepped to the microphone. "Cowboys and cowgirls, as chairman of the county board of supervisors, let me say howdy and welcome you to the Old Timers Day parade. Today we've got a special guest with us, the governor of the great state of California, Culbert Olson!" Gilmore stepped aside, clapping his hands. "Governor Olson!"

Flashbulbs popped and there was a scattering of applause as Olson waved and stepped up to the microphone with a big smile. "Thank you, Charley. Thank you all for inviting me to this great county to help you celebrate your rich and colorful history and to pay honor to those men and women who pioneered this land."

A farmer close down front yelled, "Aw, sit down!"

Olson paused. Below him, a couple of news photographers sensed trouble and pushed through the crowd, trying for a better angle. One turned and focused his big press camera on the angry faces, with the governor in the background.

"These are troubled times," Olson continued, "and I know there are those among you who disagree with the efforts of this administration to bring some economic stability to those thousands of displaced, impoverished men and women who want nothing more than a chance to earn a living for their families. But it is my fervent hope that our differences will not hinder my sincere efforts to get the cotton growers and the representatives of the workers to the bargaining table where they can negotiate a fair and reasonable wage agreement so that you can get on with the harvest of your bountiful crops. Thank you." The governor turned and sat down.

Anger stirred the crowd. People shouted and booed as Gilmore, caught unawares by the brevity of the governor's remarks, stepped up to the microphone, hands raised. "Settle down! Settle down!" No one paid any attention, so he called for help. "Congressman Alf Young, say a few words. Alf, come on up here. Ladies and gents, Congressman Alf Young!"

"Look yonder!" Alf Young brayed into the microphone and pointed up at the big clock in the granite tower atop the courthouse. Heads turned, necks craned. Young grinned and kept pointing. "Look yonder! When that clock strikes ten, the parade starts. That means you all don't have but just a few more minutes to have to listen to us politicians jawing up here." There was applause and laughter. Young knew his people and their moods. "This ain't a day for serious palavering, this here is a day to have fun." Skillfully he joked and humored them back into their pioneering good cheer.

Down at the west end of town, a block off Main, the parade was assembling in front of the high school. Neighing horses and yelling people were milling everywhere, trucks and tractors pulled decorated floats slowly through the bedlam. A half dozen school bands were noisily warming up. The Lions Club was in charge and fifteen or twenty harried men wearing those yellow army-style overseas caps trimmed in purple, with matching yellow and purple vests emblazoned with the club logo, were frantically shouting orders and directing traffic, trying to sort things out and get the parade started.

Jake, wearing freshly laundered jeans and his snap-button shirt, pushed through the crowds, Susie following right behind him, yelling, "See 'em?"

"Na." Jake jumped up on the bed of a truck, looking over the pandemonium. "Don' see 'em nowhere."

Ertie and Lige had driven the team in, while the rest of them came in by car and truck, found a good viewing spot near the beginning of the parade route and sent Jake and Susie to scout the men out and bring them back.

Nearby the Jefferson High band struck up, horns blowing, drums banging, cymbals clashing. The parade was starting.

"We'll never find 'em." Jake looked frantically around.

"Let's go back." Susie grabbed her brother and they pushed their way through the crowds to the curb just as the band wheeled briskly out onto Main Street, red and gold uniforms sparkling bright. The American Legion color guard fell in behind the band, smartly marching four abreast, two Legionnaires with Enfield rifles at right-shoulder arms flanking the standard-bearers. As Old Glory and the state flag passed by, people along the street came patriotically to attention, hands over their hearts. Policemen controlling the intersections saluted smartly.

"Come on!" Jake dashed across the street right behind the color guard, running hard. A policeman shouted, "Stop!" Jake instinctively darted away from the shout, Susie on his heels. The policeman ran a few steps after them, but they disappeared into the crowd, leaving an eddy of angry people behind. With so many people jamming the sidewalks, it took them a few minutes to spot the family and wiggle their way to a spot at the curb. Lige and Ertie were both there, sipping on a bottle of whiskey.

Out in the street, six Old Timers were riding past, each seated royally in a brand-new convertible automobile. The tops were down and, as each car passed, people pointed: "Lookee, there's old Jess Barnes! His daddy built the Blue Pine Mill up there in the hills and flumed the rough-cut lumber out to the railroad just north of town. And there, in that next car, why it's Tom Crain, who's eighty-three if he's a day and still running his cattle back in the high country. Ain't that Big John Turner, there in that green Chevy? Sure it is and by gollies, there's Horace Starbuck, look at that old curmudgeon! Why he come to Jeff City in 'seventy-eight, just got down off the train, without a dime in his pockets. Now look at him, rich as the Barkhams, they say."

The Associated Farmers float pulled into view, a big one built by the high school aggies on a flatbed trailer pulled by a new John Deere tractor. The students had fashioned a replica of the county, complete with cottonfields, a miniature gin, tiny vineyards and orchards; there were toy tractors and haybalers in the fields and, on the banks of the blue-painted Palo Rojo River, a model of Jeff City, complete with trains and trucks and a replica of the water tower at Ninth and D streets. In the center of the float, standing back-to-back on a raised platform, were two Legionnaires, their rifles smartly thrust out at parade rest. Above them a banner proclaimed the parade's theme:

PROTECT FREE ENTERPRISE!

A small two-wheel trailer had been hooked to the rear of the float and a gallows had been constructed on the trailer. Swinging from the hangman's rope was an overalls-clad dummy with a crudely lettered sign pinned to its ragged shirt. The sign read: CIO AGITATOR.

As the little trailer bumped along behind, waves of laughter and applause signaled the crowd's approval.

Not far behind, Sheriff Windy Scott rode a heavy-chested steel-dust stallion with great, proud balls. The sheriff was a tall, cigar-chewing man in dark glasses; once a bare-knuckle fighter, he had a battered face and a big, laughing smile. The sheriff wore a black Stetson, a fancy black shirt with silver piping, and black batwing chaps with silver conchos. Silver Mexican spurs jingled at his boot heels and around his waist was slung a silver-studded gunbelt holstering two nickel-plated Colt .45s. Behind Sheriff Scott, riding six abreast, came the Jefferson County sheriff's posse, all decked out in black hats with silver bands, white silk shirts with black yokes and cuffs; each posseman carried a holstered pistol.

Behind the posse came more floats and bands and marching troops of Boy Scouts and Future Farmers. Among the groups of horsemen were a dozen real cowboys from the rodeo and, as soon as they rounded the corner and came into view, Jake sensed a change in his father. Ertie edged out closer to the curb and looked them over. Then, excited, he turned and slapped Lige on the shoulder. "Look, there's Smoky. Smoky Day."

"Who?"

Ertie stepped out, off the curb, and yelled, "Hey, Injun!"

Several of the cowboys looked at Ertie and one pulled his horse up in surprise, a grin breaking all over his dark face. The cowboy reined his horse over to Ertie and leaned down, his hand outstretched. "Gawddamn, hoss! I thought you was dead."

"Not likely." Ertie laughed as he shook hands.

"Where ya been?" Smoky stepped down out of the saddle. "I come by Sweetwater a time or two, but ya'all was gone."

Ertie offered Smoky his bottle and, as the cowboy took a swig, he explained, "Been out here nearly three years."

"Ain' heard of ya rodeoin' none. Ya quit?" Smoky sensed immediately that that was the wrong question and switched the subject. "Hey, got the kids with ya?" Looking around, he spotted Jake and Susie. "There they are. I'd know that little gal's sorrel hair anywhere and Jake, there. Why hoss, that boy's hard to hide, he's as ugly as you."

Jake's face turned red with pleasure and he glanced around self-consciously.

Smoky looked up the street. "Hey! Gotta catch up." He reached into a shirt pocket. "Here's some passes. Come out an' gimme a hand in the chutes. I gotta tough horse drawed."

"I'll be thar." Ertie watched Smoky swing back up in the saddle and spur the horse into a trot, its steel shoes ringing on the pavement.

After being singled out by a real cowboy in front of all these town people, just watching the parade seemed boring. Restless now, Jake whispered to Susie, "Wanna go see the governor?"

"Where's he at?"

"By the park. Junior said that's where he's gonna be."

She grinned her agreement and they slipped away, free. Jake pulled out a pack of Lucky Strikes.

"Where'd ya git 'em?"

"Junior." Jake took one and handed her the green-and-red pack, then helped her light up. She puffed, coughed and sputtered, then regaining composure, she dangled the cigarette in the corner of her mouth, the way Ertie did.

They had maybe ten blocks to go and pushing through the crowds was such a struggle Jake turned up a side street. "Come on, get there quicker this way." They ran to the next street over and skipped along the quiet avenue lined with big houses set back on neatly kept lawns and shaded by graceful old trees, their leaves yellowed and falling. One of the houses, a rambling, cream-colored stucco with a red tile roof and a large bay window, attracted Susie's attention. She stopped. "Don' ya wish we lived there?" And, before he could answer, she ran up the curving front walk.

"Susie! No!"

Ignoring his warning, she peered in the big front window. "Jeez, Jake! Come look! It's like a picture book!"

"Susie!" Jake looked nervously around. "Come on!"

Reluctantly, she came away, then they were off again, running. Crossing H, Jake turned back toward the parade route. "This way." They found the judges' stand but the crowds were too thick for a good look at Olson. Susie pointed across the street to the park. "We can skin up a tree over there, then we can see it all."

"Okay." They took off across the street, scurrying between floats and disappearing in the crowd standing along the borders of the park. They shinnied up a big sycamore and, perched above the crowd, they had a good view. People were cheering and shouting, musical brass-and-drum sounds filled the air and the announcer's voice boomed out the identity of each unit in the passing parade. Out in the street two hardworking news photographers, lugging big four-by-five cameras and cumbersome bags, were flashing pictures.

"Which one's the governor?" Susie wondered.

"That feller there, one with the white hair and brown shirt, with the yella scarf, bet that's him."

A town-kid higher up in the tree yelled down, "Ain't neither. Governor's the one with the white cowboy hat on."

Jake looked up, scowling, not sure if he was being challenged or not. They clung to their perch for a while, then dropped out of the tree and wandered around. The park was a big one, heavily forested and neatly groomed; there were cement walkways, open grassy areas and, in the very center, there was a bandstand and rows of benches.

"That's where the union meets," Jake said importantly.

"How ya know that?" Susie was skeptical.

"Junior tol' me. Said fellas get up and give speeches, said if ever I wanted to come, jus' come on ahead."

Off in a far corner of the park they discovered a small zoo, of sorts; there was a caged black bear sprawled asleep in its own fecal wastes, a monkey cage where a half dozen listless primates lolled about, toying with their flaccid cocks, and a slimy green pool where a small alligator snoozed.

"Damn thang looks dead," Jake said disgustedly.

"Jake, there's some parrots." Susie skipped over to an aviary holding brightly colored macaws, feathered in reds, blues and yellows. "Ain' they purty."

"Purty." The word was squawked back at her by a green Amazon sitting higher up in the aviary, its yellow head cocked sideways. Three more Amazons were perched there.

Susie called, "Purty bird."

The Amazon answered, "Purty bird."

Jake hollered, "Hey you!"

The bird, more aggressive than the rest, answered, "Hey you," then fluttered down, landing on a perch close to them. A second Amazon followed.

Laughing, Susie tried, "Hello, dummy," and the first bird watched her, cocking its head sideways again. She repeated the words.

The bird imitated her, "Hello. Dummy." They talked to the parrots for a while, then Susie tugged at Jake. "Come on, let's see what else we can find," and they were off, running through the park.

Suddenly, Jake stopped. "There's Junior!"

"Where?"

"Over there, with that bunch of guys."

Junior and a couple dozen other men, all of them from the camps, were unfurling banners or holding placards with slogans that read, WE WANT WORK, NOT RELIEF or FAIR PAY FOR A DAY'S WORK. Two of the men unrolled a twelve-foot cotton sack and inked boldly across the banner were the words: STRIKE — WORKERS ALLIANCE & CIO-UCAPAWA — STRIKE.

Jake tugged on Junior's sleeve. "Whatcha doin'?"

"Wouldn't let us in the parade, so we're goin' to surprise 'em, right in front of the governor and those press photographers." He handed Jake a black armband. "Here, why don' ya join us." Junior turned to Susie. "Sorry, we ain' lettin' no women in this. It might get rough."

Junior, who seemed to be boss, was yelling instructions, hurrying the workers, forming them up. There must have been forty of them, by Jake's reckoning. Excited, but frightened too, he started to tie the armband on, then hesitated.

"Go ahead, if ya wanna." Susie was clearly disappointed.

"Naw." Jake impulsively seized the opportunity to escape. "If you cain't, I don' wanna neither." He stuffed the armband in his pocket and they hung back, following along at a distance as Junior led the union men across the park and circled around behind the courthouse. The plan was to come out on H Street, which crossed Main a block upstream from the judges' stand. Marching along H in ranks ten and twelve abreast, with Junior and a burly fellow named Ike out in front carrying the cotton-sack banner, they came up behind the crowds watching the parade. The workers began chanting: "Strike! Strike! Strike!"

Startled parade watchers turned and looked back in disbelief. Marching toward them were stern-faced cotton pickers, angry men in worn-out overalls or tattered jeans, their faded, hard-worn clothing stitched and patched. The townspeople fell away, like the sea parting, giving these ruffians room to march through and turn onto Main, all the while continuing the chant: "Strike! Strike!"

The workers broke into the parade right behind the Lions Club Float, crowding in ahead of Boy Scouts from Troop Three who had been marching behind their own color bearers, but were standing there staring wide-eyed at the chanting workers. Behind them the parade came to a dead stop, each entry crowding into the one in front like a freight train with the emergency brakes set. Up ahead, the queen of the Lions Club float—a cherubic blonde, all pink and white with a rhinestone crown in her golden hair—clapped both hands to her mouth and screamed, certain those Okies intended to rape her.

"Strike! Strike! Strike!" The workers came abreast of the judges, marching directly into the cameras. Flashbulbs popped. Onlookers and lawmen alike were stunned by the suddenness of it all.

A deputy yelled into his radio, "Help! Get us help! There's a riot!" Every police radio along the parade route crackled the warning and they heard it in the jail as well.

Sergeant Dodd and two of his deputies had been posted in front of the judges' stand; they charged into the street yelling, "Halt! Halt!" trying to block the marchers.

But Junior and the workers wouldn't stop.

Far up the parade route sirens sounded and motorcycle patrolmen came roaring back through the floats and marching units, narrowly missing the gawkers who were spilling out into the street. A startled tractor driver watched the cops careen by and drove his rig squarely into the float in front, upsetting the grandmotherly members of the Jeff City knitting circle, knocking one poor woman clear out of her rocking chair, skirts flying.

Deputies came running out of the jail and across the park, not waiting for Captain Ramey, who waddled fatly along behind, his gun belt a-jiggle.

The highway patrolmen surrounding the judges' stand held their ground, protecting the governor, while a half dozen city police and deputies rushed to Sergeant Dodd's aid, billy clubs swinging. Junior ducked, dropping the banner and pushing himself away, arms raised protectively. A club whacked him in the head and Junior felt the crushing weight of another deputy piling on his back; his arm was jerked back in a hammerlock just as he fell. Other workers tried to get him free, but more lawmen swung into action, clubbing one worker unconscious, flailing at others. Blood oozed from a downed striker's nose.

Jake fought to get through to Junior just as a cop raised his club, determined to bash in Junior's skull. "Stop!" Jake screamed and hurled himself at the lawman, knocking him off balance. Someone knocked Jake sprawling, hands grabbed at him as he scrambled to his feet. An arm locked around his throat and he could feel the muscles choking off his wind; whoever had him was strong, too strong. Terrified, Jake wiggled and kicked but was lifted off his feet and hurled to the ground, WHAM! And one of his arms was cranked painfully up behind him. "Hold still, you little shit!" He heard the ratchet sound of handcuffs and kicked wildly, squirming free. He rolled over and saw the deputy on his knees, reaching with the handcuffs. Jake kicked hard at the man's balls, felt his heel sink into the soft groin and heard the man's stunned groan. Jake was up, running. All around him men were yelling and fighting, pushing and grabbing. Jake got knocked sideways, tripped and fell again. Terror consumed him as he scrambled back out of the way, trying to get free. Where was Susie? Frantic, he looked around. She was gone. Then suddenly she was beside him, wildly grabbing and pulling on him, shouting, "Jeesus, let's get outa here!"

Running, jumping over hedges, darting across lawns and sidewalks, they fled into a quiet neighborhood. Safe, Susie leaned against a car at the curb, trying to catch her breath. "Jake, yor crazy. Fightin' a law like that."

"What happened to Junior?" Jake, his lungs heaving for air, looked at the tattered sleeve of his shirt. His pants were torn and he had a skinned knee that stung like crazy.

"Cop clubbed 'im down and two of 'em put handcuffs on 'im. Then somebody grabbed at me, so I run."

They were walking now, headed back to where the cars were parked. "Jeesus, Susie, what's goin' to happen to 'im?"

"Jail, if they don' kill 'im."

"Aw, don' say that."

"Killed ol' Cletus Sharp, didn' they?" Susie stopped her brother. "Jake, ya shouldn' oughta jumped in like that. What if they'd killed ya, or tossed ya in jail."

Jake scoffed, pleased with himself. "Got away, didn't I?" They walked along the empty sidewalks, quiet for a while, then Jake asked, "Why they hate us so much?"

"Hell, I don' know."

"Too bad they ain' all like Mr. Kakorian."

"Yeah, he's nice."

"An so's Ara, ain' he?" Jake gave Susie a playful shove. Twice now he'd seen her sneaking out nights and guessed she was meeting him somewhere, in the barn probably.

"Jake!" She blushed, but said nothing more.

Their parents and the Parsons were all by the cars, waiting. "You kids down at the fracas?" Ertie asked.

R'becky and Maybelle crowded around them, worried. "Where's Junior? Ya seen 'im?"

Bessie had ahold of Jake's overalls suspenders, tugging at them. "What happened to you? Ya been fightin'?"

"Cops got Junior," Susie told Maybelle. "Clubbed 'im down and grabbed 'im 'fore he could get away."

"What?" Lige had just taken a swallow of whiskey and it was halfway down when he heard what she'd said. He choked. "They what?"

The center of attention now, she tried to explain. "Jake tried to knock the laws off'n him, but he couldn't. They got 'im, just clubbed him down and hauled him off."

Still gasping, Lige asked, "What'd he do?"

Bessie hadn't let go of Jake and he was trying to pull free, at the same time answering Lige, "Junior tol' me the cops wouldn't give 'em leave to be in the parade, but they just did 'er anyways. Busted right in, shoutin' about the strike, right there in front of the governor, by Gawd."

Bessie gave him a shake. "Don' you swear, young man. Was you with 'em? Was you?"

"No, Ma! I wasn' with 'em." Jake couldn't escape Bessie's grip.

"Where'd they take 'im?" Maybelle pleaded to know.

"Ma, le' me go." Jake struggled to get away.

"Was he hurt?" Maybelle pleaded again.

"Dammit, woman!" Ertie slammed his hand down on the car fender. "Let 'im go, so's he can tell us what happened."

Bessie let go and Lige gently took Jake by the shoulders, facing him squarely. "Where's Junior now?"

"I don' know. Susie saw 'im last."

Susie shrugged. "Jail, I guess. They had 'im handcuffed, I seen that."

"Was he bad hurt?" Maybelle asked again.

"Didn' seem bad hurt."

Junior was in jail, along with several other union men, but the jailor wouldn't let Lige or R'becky see him. A deputy said to come back on Monday, after the judge set the bail. Back outside, they tried to decide what to do next.

"Likely he won' get more'n a day or two for fightin' an' the judge'll let 'im out." Ertie offered his friend a drink and suggested that since there was nothing they could do to help Junior, they ought to go on to the rodeo. He had passes enough for everyone.

Bessie shook her head no. The union trouble had spoiled the day for her. The Parsons just wanted to get on back to camp and Lige offered to take Bessie and anyone else back with them. James Earl said he'd be glad to drive Maybelle and the twins back in Junior's car. Jake and Susie wanted to see the fair and go to the rodeo too, so it was agreed they'd stay with Ertie. As Bessie started to put Benjy up in the truck, Susie yelled, "Ma, leave 'im with us. We'll take 'im on the merry-go-round, won' we, Pa?"

"Shor we will."

Out at the fairgrounds the parking lots were filling fast and throngs of noisy people were crowding through the turnstiles. The ticket taker looked at Ertie's passes suspiciously, then shrugged, tore off the stubs and handed them back. Inside the main entrance, the bunting-draped exhibit halls and livestock barns were off to the left, the rodeo arena and grandstand were straight ahead, the carnival off to the right. Ertie headed for the rodeo arena and the contestants' gate, to the fenced-off area behind the bucking chutes. Big stock trucks, dusty cars, pickups and horse trailers were parked all around the horse barns. Nearby, just inside a wire fence, were the bucking chutes and pens of bucking horses and bulls.

Jake and Susie followed along behind Ertie, each hanging onto one of Benjy's hands, swinging him between them. A deputy guarded the contestants' gate. Ertie held out the pass stubs, but the deputy shook his head. "You can't come in here, this is for the cowboys."

"Mister"—Ertie pushed his hat back and reached for his cigarette papers—"I was give them passes by Smoky Day. Now he's a cowboy, an' so was I, oncet. Them passes is good."

"Nope. Ya can't come in," the deputy snarled.

"Call the chute boss over, he'll okay it."

"Look, I told ya no, goddammit. Now you an' your Okie kids get the hell out of the way, let them cowboys through."

Two young bronc riders had come up and were waiting behind Ertie. He turned to them. "Say, fellers, would ya tell Smoky Day that Ertie Robertson's out here an' this jasper won' let'm in."

"You Ertie Robertson?" One of the cowboys put his saddle down and shook hands. "Why I was to Laramie Plains when you win the bronc ridin' on that Midnight horse. Gawd, I was just a kid then." The cowboy pushed the gate open, ignoring the deputy. "Come on in with us."

"Hey." The deputy tried to stop them. "Hey, you can't do that."

The cowboy pushed the deputy roughly aside. "Listen, buster, he's from Texas, but I'm from Oklahoma an' I don' like the way you talk. I say that this here's a cowboy an' he done showed you his passes, now you get the fuck out of the way." He pushed on past the deputy, who just stood there, uncertain what to do.

The word *fuck* was no sooner out than the young cowboy sheepishly glanced back at Susie, embarrassed. Once they were through the gate the blushing cowboy turned to both Susie and Ertie. "I'm awful sorry. That word just slipped out."

Ertie nodded and Susie bashfully mumbled, "It's okay."

They found Smoky back behind the chutes dusting rosin on the swells of his bronc saddle and rubbing it in until it squeaked. Most of the cowboys were youngsters who didn't know Ertie, but the well-known bronc riders like Smoky and Burle Maulkey knew him. They'd ranged widely together across the country, riding in the big rodeos in Chicago and Boston and New York's Madison Square Garden. Sometimes they came west in the fall to ride in San Francisco's Cow Palace and maybe do some stunt work in the movies. Along the way they stopped off at the smaller rodeos in towns like Visalia and Jefferson City. These big-time bronc riders slapped Ertie on the back and shook his hand, but Jake could sense that his father felt like an outsider, happy, yet at the same time uneasy because he was no longer one of them.

All around them there was the clang of the bells on the bull ropes and the sounds of horses rattling down through the chutes, gates were slammed shut and men were yelling and swearing as they moved the stock. At first Benjy hung back, clinging to Jake or Susie's side, but, as he became used to the noise and swirl around him, he slipped away, attracted by the bulls in a nearby pen. No one paid much attention until he climbed the fence and started down the inside.

A startled cowboy shouted, "Hey kid, don't!" Another bull rider grabbed Benjy's pants just as he went over the top rail.

Embarrassed, Jake retrieved his brother from the cowboys just as someone called his name.

"Jake?"

Surprised, Jake stopped and looked at a gaudy blond woman in red riding pants and red spangled blouse that sparkled over her large, round breasts. She wore white boots and a white belt with an enormous silver and gold trophy buckle.

"You're Jake?"

Susie was standing just behind the woman. "This here's Dixie Lee, the trick rider. 'Member her?"

"Gosh, you two have grown." Dixie Lee patted Jake's head. "Why I ain' seen you since I don' know when."

Jake looked at Dixie Lee and felt an old anger return. He didn't like this woman.

"You probably don't even recollect me, do you?"

"Yes'm, I do. You was a friend of Pa's."

"I hope I still am. And this is Benjy." She reached over and gave the boy's hair a brush. "I was just askin' Susie here to warm up my horse."

Jake pushed Benjy gently forward. "Kin she take Benjy along? He kin sit up behin' 'er, double."

"Why shor."

Susie gave Jake a murderous look but didn't say anything. Dixie brought her white horse over and helped Susie up into the trick-riding saddle, then boosted Benjy up behind his sister and showed him where to hang on. Susie gave the horse a kick and rode out into the arena, joining the procession of bulldoggers and ropers who were walking their horses around, warming them up.

Free of Benjy, Jake followed Dixie back over to where Ertie was lounging against the chutes talking with Smoky.

"Hey, Dixie, how ya been?" Ertie stood up and put his arm around the trick rider, giving her a friendly pat on the butt.

"Doin' fine. Where'n hell you been?"

"Out here in California."

"Doin' what?"

"I'm a goddamn prune picker." He tried to make it light, but it didn't come off.

"I heard about your wreck."

"Yeah. That bronc was supposed to be a hell of a circus horse. Did you know that?"

Dixie looked puzzled.

"Fella that owned that horse had been training him to do a somersault in the air. Think about it. Me an' that horse would be famous right today, if only he'd made it all the way around and landed on his feet. Trouble was, that goddamn knothead'd only learned half the trick, so we landed upside down instead."

"Ertie"—Dixie Lee was laughing, but sadly shaking her head—"you never was much for tellin' jokes."

"Hell, it's better'n cryin'. How you been makin' out?"

"Can't complain. Damn, it's good to see you again. Wha'cha doin' tonight?"

Ertie winked at Smoky. "She's just as fast on the track as ever, ain' she?"

Jake felt the old anger again as the trick rider moved in on his father. He turned and started to walk away, his face clouded over. Ertie glanced at him and his own expression changed. "Where ya goin', boy?"

"Nowhere," Jake shrugged.

Ertie dug out his purse and handed Jake some change. "Buy yourself a soda, get one for Susie and Benjy too."

Jake took the money and drifted away as Ertie turned back to Dixie. "Smoky here was tellin' me about this new Turtle Association thang. I cain' hardly believe it."

"It was the year after you got crippled up," Smoky continued the story. "We was at the Boston Gardens and a bunch of us cowboys got together an' decided we'd had enough of the colonel's ways. We wasn't goin' to contest until that goddamn ol' tightwad put up more prize money."

"Can ya beat that?" Ertie was amazed.

Ertie had bought another bottle on the way to the rodeo and now Smoky reached for it, took a drink and went on, "Well, you 'member how thangs was, all them damn promoters wanted to hog most of the money up front an' give us the hind tit. Well, by Gawd we tol' the colonel we wanted all our entry fees added to the purse, and not only that, but we wanted a bigger purse to boot. If he didn't like it, he could go straight to hell and we'd go on to New York. He'd have no cowboys. That was it. No money, no cowboys. Would you believe it? We called a strike, an' shit, it worked. The colonel he threw a fit, called us ever'thang you could think of an' we just spit in his eye and grinned. Come time for the show to open, he caved in. It worked so good we struck again at Ogden and Tucson too, and . . ."

Ertie shook his head. "A goddamn union. For cowboys?"

"Well, there was some who didn' cotton to the sound of that word *union* so we call it the Cowboys Turtle Association. Turtles, for short."

"Why the hell Turtles?"

" 'Cause we was so goddamn slow catchin' on to the idea that the promoters couldn't have no rodeo without cowboys."

Jake wandered out back by the horse barns, found an out-of-the-way corner and sat there brooding about Dixie Lee and his father. Back then, back when Ertie was rodeoin' all over the country, he traveled alone much of the time. It wasn't unusual for him to be gone two or three weeks, but when the rodeos were close by he took Jake and Susie with him on weekends and everyone back of the chutes looked after them, got them sodas and cotton candy. Dixie Lee had been his father's girlfriend then and, since he was only six or seven, that hadn't seemed much different to Jake than seeing Ertie with his cowboy friends. Then, early in the spring of 1932, Ertie had started staying away longer and finally he was gone altogether. They got letters from places like Cody, Wyoming and Calgary, clear up in Canada, quickly scrawled messages indicating that Ertie was hitting a lucky streak and had a chance at a world championship if he kept going. Each letter contained some of his winnings, more money than they'd seen in a long while, but they never knew from one week to the next where he'd be or when he was coming back. Ertie was gone all that summer and fall, returning late in November, unannounced. There were hugs and excitement and apologies and talk about Madison Square Garden and how he failed to place in finals. After a while Jake noticed that his mother wasn't saying much, nor did she look as happy as he thought she should because Pa was back.

Bessie had said little for days, just went furiously about her work, banging cupboard doors, slamming pots and kettles around, storming in her silent not-so-silent way. Finally, late one night, after they'd all gone to bed, Jake heard them talking. He couldn't hear the words, only the angry sound of their voices, sounds that went on, relentlessly, for an hour, then another. After that Ertie stayed much closer to home, working harder to make a go of the horse and mule business. He put in more hay and grain for Mr. Perkins and contracted out his team of Morgans to the government to work on the Lake Sweetwater dam. He still competed in local rodeos, once more taking Jake and Susie along, but something had changed. Somehow his father was no longer quite as wild in the saddle, nor was he as playful in that roughhousing way cowboys have. At first Jake thought it was because his father hadn't won the championship, and he'd gone out of his way to let Ertie know that it was okay not to have won. He loved his father just as much, anyway. That had choked Ertie up and he hugged Jake, then made some joke about old bronc riders and Jake was happy again.

They saw Dixie Lee once or twice at nearby rodeos, but she was no longer friendly. Then, at the rodeo in Big Springs, she and Ertie were yelling at each other and Dixie Lee came after him with a riding crop. And that was when Jake learned that Dixie Lee had something to do with Ertie's being gone so long that summer. As he sat by the horse barns thinking about the trick rider he could still remember her lashing out at Ertie and his father grabbing her arm. She was swearing and he was yelling back, "You knowed I was married."

"But you was rodeoin' full time. I thought you'd left her."

"I never tol' you that. I was havin' a run at the world title."

"But you wen' to Boston an' New York with me, not her!"

"Dixie, not here, not in front of the kids, goddammit."

But both Jake and Susie heard those words and they'd talked about it afterward. Susie, who seemed to know more about such things, said, "Pa was sleepin' with her, but he ain' no more, an' she's mad."

Now, seeing Dixie Lee again and her being so friendly, he worried that his father might take after her again and that made him mad. There were men who hung around rodeos, boozy, washed-up cowboys who worked the chutes for day wages or drove trucks for the stock contractor; sometimes they traveled with a woman like Dixie Lee, living off of what she made. Jake sat there, doodling in the dirt with a long stem of hay, not paying any attention to the sounds of the rodeo, puzzling over this idea that his father had once gone off with Dixie Lee, leaving them. But he had come back. And things had been okay again, at least until that horse had turned over on him.

"Jake! Jake!" Susie came running up with Benjy in tow. "Where ya been? Been lookin' all over for ya!"

"What d'ya want?" Jake was cross.

"Lookee." Susie held up a dollar bill. "Pa gimme this an' said we could go to the carnival and ride the loop-de-loops, said to take Benjy on the Ferris wheel. S'posed to meet 'im back here by the chutes in a couple of hours."

Jake got up and brushed the dirt off his overalls. "Okay." But his heart wasn't in it, not at first.

Benjy, sensing Susie's excitement, squealed with laughter and began tugging on her and motioning for Jake to hurry. Susie laughed. "Come on, Benjy, we'll ride the Ferris wheel."

And they did, three times. Susie held Benjy while Jake rode the loop-the-loop and forgot about Dixie Lee. They ate hot dogs and cotton candy and got lost in the house of mirrors and let Benjy ride the merry-go-round by himself. The crowds swirled happily around them as they hiked down the sawdust lane between the pitch booths and cootch shows, stopping to watch a man swallow swords and flaming torches. They threw baseballs and finally, when the money was all gone, they just walked along, gawking.

That's when Susie spotted Ara Kakorian, with some town kids.

"Jake, keep Benjy."

"Okay."

She ran to join Ara.

Jake took a firm grip on Benjy's hand and wandered on down the midway. As they passed the Ferris wheel again, Benjy dug in his heels and begged, "Ride! Ride!" pointing up at the swirling lights. Jake dragged him on past, but the same thing happened when Benjy saw the bumper cars. "Benjy, we ain' got no more money." Jake squatted beside his little brother, trying to make him understand, but the boy just clouded up and fussed, pointing and pleading for another ride. Angrily, Jake stood up and pulled Benjy along, trying to ignore the fussing.

They had been by themselves for maybe fifteen minutes when Susie caught up with them again, angry and hurt, her eyes rimming with tears.

"What happened?"

Gritting her teeth, she said nothing.

"Susie, what happened?"

She hissed, "Ara! He acted like he hardly knowed me! Him an' his goddamn town friends. Didn' wan' me with 'em."

Jake put his arm around her shoulder and tried to pull her close, but she pulled away, angry. He shrugged. "Come on, let's go find Pa. Benjy's pooped."

"Time is it?"

"Don' know." Jake asked a passing adult, "Mister, what time is it?"

The man walked on by, not answering. Susie went over to a ring-toss booth and came back. "Said it was a'most five-thirty."

No one was back of the chutes and there were only a few cowboys around the horse barns when they got back. None of them knew Ertie, but when Jake asked for Smoky Day they said he was probably in town, since his car was gone. It had started sprinkling rain and Jake told Susie to wait in the barns with Benjy while he ran out to the parking lot. The '32 sedan was there, locked and Ertie had the keys. Discouraged and feeling abandoned, Jake walked back to the barns, ignoring the rain that was coming down harder now. "He ain' at the car."

"Le's ask over thar at the rodeo office." Susie darted over to a house trailer that was parked by the contractor's stock trucks.

The rodeo secretary looked up from her tally books, saying she'd seen Ertie talking with Dixie Lee. "Maybe they're over in her trailer." The secretary got up and looked out the door, pointing. "It's the red one with the white trim. Boy, why don' you run over there and let your sister and little brother stay in here, out of the rain."

Jake nodded. He hated the idea of his father being with that woman. Head down, he started for the trailer but had gone only a few steps when he heard a car horn honking. A big Buick touring car was roaring across the parking lots, splashing through the puddles. It turned down the lane between the chutes and the stables toward him. The top was still down and Smoky was at the wheel. Ertie was up front with him. In the back were three more cowboys and a couple of young girls sitting on their laps, laughing and hanging on.

"Susie!" Jake's spirits soared. "Here's Pa!"

The Buick skidded to a stop and Smoky yelled, "Come on kids, pile in. We'll drive ya back to your car."

When he pulled up beside the sedan and let them out it was raining hard. Ertie quickly opened the car, letting them in, and then he turned back to Smoky, who wasn't saying anything. They shook hands, holding the grip, then let go. "Well, hoss, see ya down the road." Smoky put the car in gear and let the clutch out slowly, saying, "An' Ertie, don' never give up. Fight them bastards."

12

Anxious to see Clara, Jake pedaled hard, sending his bicycle zipping along the country roads, past fields of cotton bursting white. The bike was a red Deluxe Hawthorne Comet, almost exactly like the one in the Monkey Ward catalogue that Bull had left in the outhouse for wipes. Jake had torn that page out and saved that picture, marveling at the bike's beauty; new, the Comet had fenders, a headlight, chain guard, a carriage rack over the rear fender and cost $25.88. His Comet wasn't new, not by a long shot: the front forks weren't true and the bike didn't have any fenders or a headlight or chain guard anymore, but the bike was his and, while owning a bike wasn't as good as having a car, it did let him get around now that he was a *man* who was getting laid regularly. Yes, he'd fucked. Been fucked. Really. And not just once, either. Having crossed over that threshold, he looked back in wonder, hardly believing that *it* had happened, but all the same, feeling much much older.

It had happened unexpectedly that first day he'd pedaled proudly over to show Clara his bicycle and taken her for a ride. She had perched sideways on the bar between his arms, laughing, her hair blowing and tickling his face. They had ridden down to the river and there, back in the willows, they had wiggled out of their clothes and, naked, they'd held each other close, her warm, satiny-smooth skin exciting him. His hard cock poked awkwardly between them and he nervously, uncertainly humped and struggled, trying to get the damn thing between her legs. She giggled and pulled away, rolling on her back, raising and spreading her knees so that he could poke it in. For an instant, he saw her cunt, mysteriously slitted and folded, then he was on her and in her, *fucking*. And afterward she'd sworn it was the first time for her and wanted to know if he'd ever done it before and before he could answer she'd said, "Now we're married." He only nodded. Lying there in the tangle of clothing, a bit disappointed because it was over so quickly, he wasn't certain what men did right after they fucked; he felt naked and exposed. Quickly pulling on his tattered overalls, he had looked around to see if anyone had been watching.

Since that first time, they'd fucked twice more and she'd let him look at her cunt and she'd played with his cock and even kissed it and said it was hers forever. She was right about that, it was hers whenever she wanted. His crotch fairly tingled as he pedaled along thinking about fucking and about how important the bike was now. The Comet made it so much easier to be with Clara.

The first time Jake had seen the bike it was hanging on the wall out in the equipment shed, all twisted and bent like a giant pretzel. The bike belonged to Ara, he'd left it lying in the driveway and Mr. Kakorian had backed over it with the pickup. Afterward they'd hung the wrecked bike on the wall in the far corner of the shed where Kakorian stored old bits and pieces of broken machinery that might one day provide a usable part or two for some repair job. Jake had no thought of repairing the bike, not right then. That idea came to him much later, as he was hoofing it back from a visit with Clara the day after they put the snake in Nurse Hobson's cupboard. It was late and, walking along barefoot, frustrated and hungry because he'd missed supper, he was wishing he had a car of his own, or even a bicycle. Bicycle! The next day he went back into the shed and examined the wreck more closely; the front wheel was badly bent, the forks and frame were sprung, a pedal was broken, but the rear wheel and coaster brake weren't damaged. Maybe the Comet could be fixed up.

Ara wanted five dollars for the wreck. Jake bargained him down to three and the bike was his. The next problem was getting the money to pay Ara and buy the parts he needed. Mr. Kakorian was paying James Earl to work on the tractor and he'd found odd jobs for Ertie and Lige to keep busy, so Jake asked him if there was some extra work he could do to raise money to buy the bike. The farmer looked at him, then nodded. "Tell you what, those stalls need to be shoveled out and the manure spread on Mrs. Kakorian's garden. I'll pay you twenty cents an hour."

Since he'd been kicked out of school, he shoveled out the stalls during the day and after supper he got James Earl to help him straighten out the frame and front forks. Mr. Kakorian let them work on the bike in the shop and use whatever tools they needed. For the next couple of days he shoveled stalls and worked on the bike, making do with what he had. The shit-shoveling job lasted three days and, after paying off Ara, he had a dollar fifty-five left.

Late that evening Kakorian came out to the shop to see why the lights were still on and found Jake, angry and near tears, painstakingly trying to refit the main pedal shaft into the frame. Tiny ball bearings kept slipping out of a badly damaged race, frustrating the effort. It was obvious that without a new bearing race he couldn't fix the bike, but Jake wouldn't give up. Kakorian stood there watching him for a few minutes, then patted Jake on the back and told the boy that since he had to go into town the next day anyway, he would drop by the bike shop to see if they had any secondhand bearings. He asked, "Is there anything else you need?"

Wiping the grease from his hands, Jake dug into his pocket and handed the farmer his savings, a dollar fifty-five. "If there's 'nuff left over, I need a pedal too."

"How about replacing this?" Kakorian held up the bent front wheel, inspecting it. "It's pretty well shot."

Jake didn't know whether the farmer was ridiculing him or not. He didn't have enough money for that. "I been tryin' to straighten it out."

The next day Kakorian returned with the parts and a used front wheel. "Fellow at the bike shop had this laying out on his scrap heap. Said there was no charge." Kakorian gave Jake fifteen cents change.

Surprised, Jake grinned. "Gee, thanks."

He finished the repairs Wednesday afternoon and rode right over to Clara's. He went back Thursday and Friday and would have gone back Saturday but for the parade and rodeo. Now, as he rode toward their rendezvous, he was full of yesterday's events, eager to tell her about his close scrape with the law and how Junior was in jail, certain she would be impressed. Their rendezvous spot was in a cottonfield, by a big irrigation pump and standpipe. The spot was only a mile down the ditch-bank from her camp, but it was way back in the field, at the end of a dirt lane. Hidden by the ditch-bank and the waist-high cotton all around, their little clearing was sheltered and warm in the afternoon sunlight. He rode up, calling her name. "Clara!"

There were only the sound of birds in the cottonwoods on the other side of the canal and the hum of the electric transformer on the power pole above the pump.

"Clara!" Leaning the bike up against the pump stand, he scrambled up the ditch-bank and looked around. No one was in sight. Shrugging, he ran down off the bank, got the folded cotton sack off the bike rack and spread it at the base of the concrete standpipe, making a couch. Sitting there, leaning back against the concrete pipe, he lit a cigarette and idly picked at a frayed hole in the knee of his overalls, running his fingers through the white threads, twisting them, thinking about the parade and the fight with the law.

Coming along the ditch-bank, Clara saw him there, sitting in the sun, smoke curling from his cigarette. She thought he was handsome, even if he had those homely freckles and big ears. It was obvious he didn't know she was there on the bank above him. With an impish grin, she ran down off the bank and pounced on him. "Boo!"

Startled, Jake tried to jump up but Clara was all over him, laughing. They rolled over and over, wrestling, playing, then, shedding their clothes, they made love, urgently, quickly. Afterward Clara stood up, naked and beautiful, ordering him off the cotton-sack couch. She took it by the corners and gave it a good shaking to get the dirt clods off, then neatly spread it again, asking, "Where were ya yesterday?"

"Wen' to the parade an' rodeo." He told her about the fight and what had happened to Junior. They had snuggled back down on the sack but now Clara sat up, pushed him away, worried, scolding him for getting involved. "Jake, ya coulda got hurt or throwed in jail too."

"A feller's gotta stand up for his friends." He reached over and tweaked one of her titties gently.

She slapped his hand away. "Jake, be serious!" Slipping the dress over her head, she wiggled into it and smoothed it down over her legs. "I don' want ya hurt an' I don' want us split up again. Honey, don' pay no 'tention to them union guys. Ain' nothin' gonna make them farmers change. We gotta look out for ourselves, gotta work so's we can get 'nuff money to get married, be on our own."

"Hell, Clara, them farmers cain' get no cotton in without us to pick it," Jake argued as he pulled on his overalls. "A strike'll make 'em come around."

"Jake, don' mess with 'em, they killed Cletus Sharp."

"Ya sound jis' like my ma." Jake shook his head. "She's sore at me an' Susie for gettin' mixed up in that fracas."

Clara was exasperated. "I s'pose ya joined the union too?"

"Aim to!"

"Jake Robertson, yor crazy!" She jumped up, brushing the sand and stickers from her dress.

"Clara! Don' be mad."

Jake reached up for her. She let him pull her back down. "Jake, don' get messed up in no union! Please! Yor ma's right, all that'll do is get ya in trouble."

"Ma don' know ever'thang."

"Sounds to me like she's got right good sense, workin' to get that house an' all."

"Aw, that ain' nothin' but an ol' railroad car."

"Damn you, Jake Robertson, you was the one braggin' how ya'd fixed up the water tank, an' all. I'd give anythin' to live in a house that's got a kitchen an' a sittin' room where ever' Christmas ya kin have a pretty tree all decorated."

"Christmas tree?" Jake was puzzled.

"We ain' never had a Christmas tree." Clara was sad now. "Oh, I got to help decorate one once, down in Arvin, at the government camp. Them church people from town come out an' give a big party there in the community hall an' they brung along the biggest ol' pine tree ya ever saw an' let us help hang pretty thangs on it. They give us candy an' I got a doll. Weren't new, I knowed that, but she was purty an' had a nice dress. I called her Mandy, after my baby sister."

"What happened to her?"

"She died." Clara wiped away a tear.

The whole mood had changed and Jake felt sad too, for Clara. "I mean, what happened to the doll?"

"Got lost some'eres."

"I'm sorry." Jake held Clara close, trying to comfort her. "We had them Jeesus Christers come 'round one Christmas time, tried ta give us a handout. Pa, he chased them off, tol' 'em to go straight to hell. Ma didn't want no charity, neither, but she got mad at him swearin' and being mean to them Christers, said they was only tryin' to be Christian. Pa, he jus' went off an' got drunk."

"Jake, promise ya won't join that union." Clara was on her knees now, pleading.

"Clara, I tol' ya we all gotta fight back or thangs ain' never gonna get any better. Junior says—"

She was yelling now. "I don' care what Junior says. You don' love me or ya wouldn't talk like that. You keep messin' 'round an' you'll get ever'body fired an' we won' see each other again, ever. I hate that union, hate it worse'n poison. Hate Junior too."

Jake sat up, yelling back, "You got no call to talk 'bout him like that. Least he's doin' somethin' about it. We don' fight back we ain' nothin' but white trash."

"Who you callin' trash?" She was up on her feet now. "You go to hell, Jake Robertson! You an' Junior an' that goddamn union."

Jake was up too. "Clara! I din' call you trash, what I said was that if . . ."

Clara clapped her hands over her ears, shaking her head and screaming, "Go to hell!"

". . . we don' fight back we'll all keep on livin' like trash."

She stormed up the canal bank and ran.

Ever since the Old Timers Day parade, union organizers had been roaming the county, spreading the word: The time had come to strike! And they had good news. Help was on the way. Inspired by the news photos and stories of the parade riots that had made the front pages in the east, the whole CIO organization, including the auto workers in Flint and Detroit, had committed to helping the cotton pickers.

The cotton harvest was set to begin on Tuesday, October 10th. That was the day after tomorrow. The union was calling the workers to a rally in the courthouse park tomorrow evening for a strike vote: the workers themselves were to decide whether to take eighty cents or hold out for a dollar and a quarter and demand union recognition.

When Jake rode back into camp after his fight with Clara, he saw Ertie and Lige off by the barn with Mr. Kakorian but he was so upset he didn't pay much attention. He wished Junior was here, instead of in jail, he needed somebody to talk to. He didn't want to lose Clara, but dang it, he wasn't going to miss the strike and he didn't see how he could have it both ways.

That evening at supper, Ertie told them that Mr. Kakorian had decided to start picking his cotton in the morning, instead of on Tuesday like the rest of the association, and that he was paying a dollar, like he promised.

The news caught Jake by surprise. He didn't say anything about the union or the strike vote tomorrow night; instead he asked, "We workin'?"

There was a silence and everyone looked at Ertie. He stabbed his fork into a piece of sidemeat. "Yeah, we're workin'."

"How 'bout the Parsons?" Bessie was worried.

"Them too. Lige an' me talked it over an' figgered since Kakorian's kept his end of the bargain, we ain' got no call to go against 'im."

Bessie sighed and a faint smile crossed her face.

Jake shoveled up the last of his beans in silence, wiped the plate clean with a chunk of cornbread and left the table, angry and worried about Junior. It was like they'd abandoned him, there in jail. What if everybody went to work tomorrow, before the union had a chance to hold the strike vote? He wandered out back of the barn, kicking clods. Finally he picked up a clod and hurled it hard against the back of the barn. *Wham!* Then another: *Bam!*

They were out in the cottonfields early the next morning and Mr. Kakorian gave them a little speech about how he was paying what he promised and didn't give a tinker's damn what the Associated Farmers said about it. Lige told the farmer that Junior had gone off fishing with some friends after the parade and likely they'd thought work didn't start until Tuesday. Kakorian nodded his understanding and said, "Let's pick cotton."

It was afternoon before Junior showed up. A car dropped him off out on the county road and Lige met his son by the scales and took him around back of the high-sided cotton trailer where they talked for a long time. Junior went into camp to clean up and change clothes, then he was out in the field, picking.

Jake, wanting to hear what had happened to his friend, paced his work so that he finished his row just as Junior started his second. Jake dropped into the row beside Junior. First off, Jake wanted to hear about jail and was Junior hurt bad.

"I got whacked on the head pretty hard." Junior worked steadily, pulling handfuls of cotton from the bolls and stuffing them in his sack. "An' they kicked us 'round some in jail, but not too bad. Mostly it was crowded and smelled bad in thar."

The union had bailed them out. But Junior didn't want to talk jail now, he was more concerned about the pending strike, telling Jake, "I'm between a rock and a hard place, a union man with a strike comin' up an' here I am workin'."

"Strike vote ain' till tonight." Jake was leaning over his row, working swiftly, dragging the sack behind.

"Don' matter, we ought not be workin'." Junior straightened up and rubbed his back, then bent back over his row. "Yor family gonna go to the rally tonight?"

"Naw. My Pa'n yorn both decided we'd all stay on workin' 'cause Mr. Kakorian's payin' a dollar, like he said." Jake was worried. "If they do vote to strike, what're you gonna do?"

At first Junior didn't answer, then he shook his head. "I ain' sure. Pa said I'd best move out if I was a striker, but Maybelle, she ain' too happy 'bout goin' over to the strike camp."

"Strike camp?"

"Yeah, we vote a strike, farmers's goin' to be throwin' ever'-body out that's in the union. So the union's leased forty acres out near Collins Corner. It's got well water and we're settin' up a regular camp for strikers."

"Where ya get the money for that?"

"Movie fella from Hollywood. He just up an' leased the land in his own name, so's they didn't know it was the union doin' it. Then he give us the money to fix 'er up."

"There gonna be a lot of folks come to the rally tonight?"

"You bet!"

Jake wished that he was on his own, like Junior, so he could go to the rally and become a striker.

By midafternoon Jake had his third hundred picked and had to weigh up. Hefting the bulky mattress of a load up on his shoulder, he staggered out of the field and over to the cotton trailers.

Mrs. Kakorian was weighing Susie's sack on the scale that hung from the big wooden tripod. "That's sixty-three pounds."

Susie got under the sack and, using her shoulder, lifted it off the scale and, balancing the sack there precariously, she started up the ladder that leaned against the side of the cotton trailer.

"Wait up, I'll help ya." Jake hooked his sack on the scale for Mrs. Kakorian, waited while she noted the weight and gave him his weight tickets. Working together, he and Susie lifted their twelve-foot-long sacks up the ladder and shook them out in the cotton trailer. When they got back down, Jake looked around to make sure no one could hear, then asked Susie, "Wanna go to the union rally tonight?"

"You crazy? Ma'd never hear of such a thang."

"Mean, sneak off. Junior'll give us a ride in. We can tell Ma we're goin' over to visit Clara an' Homer."

"Hey! Sure." Susie was excited by the idea. "We can say Junior is givin' us a ride over to their camp."

Since Jake was sparking Clara and the four of them had been friends in school, the plan worked, no questions asked. Junior's Chevy was a noisy old clunker with a rusted-out muffler. As they sped out of camp, Junior yelled over the clattering engine noises, "You guys ain' goin' to get me in trouble with your folks, are ya?"

"Naw, they think yor takin' us over ta Clara's," Jake grinned and yelled back. The car windows were rolled down and he stuck his hand out, deflecting fresh air onto his face.

Driving in Dairy Avenue they saw carloads of other workers headed for the rally and, in town, as they approached the park, the streets were crowded with more old jalopies and trucks. Junior turned right on H just before they got to the courthouse, cutting south to avoid the congestion, and found a parking spot a couple of blocks away. Walking back, past the jail and sheriff's office and into the park, Jake could see hundreds of people, maybe thousands. With Junior in the lead, they headed for the bandstand, moving quickly through the crowds. " 'Scuse me, please. Comin' through. 'Scuse me."

The sun had just set and the electric lights strung overhead along the walks were glowing, casting pale shadows in the dusky light. People were milling about, greeting each other, laughing and talking. Children were everywhere, running and playing, or clinging to their parents, wide-eyed. Some folks had spread blankets out on the grass and were eating their suppers, like they were at a giant potluck social.

Susie tugged at her brother's arm. "Jeez, ever see so many people?"

Up on the bandstand a guitar player, backed up by a banjo picker and a fiddler, was playing a union favorite and folks gathered around were clapping and singing.

The rows of benches in front of the bandstand were nearly full and more people were taking seats all the time, and not just white folks, either. Looking around, Jake saw lots of Mexicans and niggers too.

Junior was headed toward the bandstand and a small knot of men and women huddled there. He told Jake and Susie to wait for him by a big tree, and in a few minutes he came back. "Look, I'm goin' to be busy for a while. I'll meetcha right here, by this ol' cedar tree when the meetin's over. Okay? We'll be lookin' out for ya if there's any trouble."

"Trouble?"

"Like at the parade."

"Junior?"

"Yeah, Susie?"

"How'd ya get so many people here?"

"Had organizers a-goin' all over the county, talking with folks, tellin' 'em 'bout the strike vote."

"Was Cletus Sharp an organizer?"

"Yup."

"Are you?"

"Sometimes. Look, I gotta go now. I'll meet ya right here, okay?"

Junior was gone and they stood there, uncertain. The park looked different now. During the parade it had been nearly empty and seemed big, but now it was crowded and seemed smaller, somehow. Two uniformed deputies were patrolling nervously around the edges of the crowd, nightsticks in hand, and prowl cars circled the park slowly, the city cops watching the crowd gathering.

Jake pointed. "Susie, look, yonder." Over across Main, on the lawn in front of the Jefferson Grammar School where the judges' stand had been, there was a small crowd gathering, townspeople by the looks of them, and farmers too, maybe thirty or forty of them.

The union leaders were taking their places on the bandstand now, two white guys, a Mexican and a big, fierce-looking black man, tall and muscular with grizzled gray hair. The black man had on freshly laundered overalls and a white shirt with the sleeves rolled up and Jake could see that part of his right arm had been amputated, just below the elbow. The Mexican, a quiet, dark man with curly black hair and a tiny mustache, stood off to one side, alone and nervous. The two white men had their heads together and, when the music ended, one of the white men stepped uncertainly up to the microphone, clutching a notepad. In his forties, he was a heavyset fellow in a brown shirt and black Frisco jeans. He had wavy white hair and a red face, open and friendly. Trying not to show any nervousness, he studied his notes for a second or two, then spoke. "Folks, I want ya all to gather 'round 'cause it's time to get this here meeting started. Come on down closer. Can ya hear me in the back there? Okay. Fine, that's it, come on up close."

He waited as the audience gathered, urging the more reluctant ones in back to move in closer, then introduced himself. "I'm Carl Jones. Folks just call me C. J. and I'm from Grady County, Oklahoma. I'm standin' up hear 'cause I was elected president of this here strike committee an' I'm supposed to lead the meetin' tonight. We're gonna talk about us workin' folks an' the starvin' wages these here farmers is payin' an', after the speechifyin' an' all the jawin's done, we're goin' to take us a vote whether or not we're gonna strike."

At the word *strike* there was applause and shouts of approval.

"First off, so's there ain' no misunderstandin's 'bout whose runnin' thangs, le' me tell ya that this here strike committee's made up of workin' people, jis' like you an' me. This here's Tommy Joad"—he pointed to the other white man—"an' that feller there's Librado Chavez. Big fella next to 'im is Thad Greene. You'll be hearin' from them in jist a minute or two, but I wan'cha to know that ever' county in this whole valley has got a committee like this an' all of them committees makes up the strike council that's part of this here union local that's been chartered by the United Cannery, Agricultural, Packing and Allied Workers of America.

"Now that name's a mouthful to have to say, so we just call 'er U-ca-pa-wa for short. U-ca-pa-wa belongs to the CIO an' old John L. Lewis hisself tol' me that if we vote to strike, he's gonna stand a hundred percent behind us . . ."

Susie grabbed Jake's arm. "Come on, let's see if that parrot'll talk to us some more."

As they wiggled their way out of the crowd, C. J.'s voice boomed over the public address system. "Folks, I want ya to meet a feller who's been out here workin' in the fields, who's walked the picket lines and had his head bashed in by company goons before he even knowed what a union was. His name's Tommy Joad an' he's one of our U-ca-pa-wa organizers."

There was polite applause and Joad's voice sounded across the park: "Thanks, C. J. Glad to be here. First, I wanna . . ." The microphone squealed and Joad stepped back, then, pointing to the mike, he said, "Don' s'pose this here's a growers' microphone do ya?"

After the laughter died down, Joad got serious. "I wanna tell ya right off, I'm one of them cussed outside agitators. Like C. J. here, I come from Oklahoma. My folks was 'croppers, had a forty not far outa Sallisaw, an' jus' like many of you, we come out to California 'cause we didn' see no other choice. We come to pick their crops, not to be starved and cheated. Now I ain' one ta cry 'bout what's happened in the past, but I jus' wanted ya to know who I was when ya see me comin' 'round.

"I didn' start out to be no union organizer, Lord knows, but I don' see no other way for us workin' people to get ahead. Farmers's organized. They got their marketin' associations that tell the grocery store guy how much he's gotta pay for a sack of spuds, an' then there's the Associated Farmers that sets the wages they're gonna pay us. Well, by gollies, we ought to get together an' tell 'em it'll take a dollar an' a quarter for us to go to work."

The people applauded and cheered.

"Fella tol' me once that if we was all to stand up together an' hook our arms together, takin' a strong holt, why there weren't nobody could push us around. The guy that tol' me that, his name was Casy. Was a preacher oncet, before join' the union. Him an' them folks he was with was strikin'. They'd been pickin' peaches for a nickel a box, then it was two and a half cents an' they was starvin' so they stood up and said, 'No, sir, we ain' going to work for no starvin' two and a half cents.' Well, the goons run 'em all off that farm an' hired a bunch of scabs, me an' my family included. We didn't know nothin' about unions or strikes then, an' we was gettin' a nickel, while Casy an' them was out on the picket line. Then one night, late, them goons raided the strike camp, they busted Casy in the head and killed 'im. That was the night they broke the strike. The next day they dropped the pickin' rate back to two and a half cents, and there was lots of people so hungry they tried to make do on that.

"That was two years ago. Them strikers didn' belong to no union. They was just people, like us, who tried to get somethin' better, an' they stood up an' tried to take that step. They didn't have no big union behind 'em, like we do, but they started somethin' an' by gollies, we in the CIO are gonna finish it. We got us a new governor, one that's on our side. With his help we pushed cotton-choppin' wages up this las' spring an' now them cotton farmers wants to push wages back down again. But we ain' gonna let 'em do it. We're tellin' em, 'Hell no.' "

The crowd broke into cheers and applause and somebody started chanting, "Hell no! Hell no! Hell no!" And the crowd picked it up, "Hell no!"

Jake and Susie were almost to the parrot cage when they heard the crowd's response. Jake stopped. "They're really goin' at it. Maybe we oughta git back over there 'fore we miss somethin'."

"Naw, they're jis' yellin' an' shoutin' like preachers get 'em doin' sometimes. Come on," Susie said impatiently, "let's get them parrots talkin' again."

Almost all of the people were crowded around the bandstand and only a handful of youngsters were hanging around the park's scruffy little zoo. The walkways were lighted by strings of overhead bulbs and Jake could see other kids standing by the animal cages or ducking in and out of the light and shadows, playing tag. Mostly they were white camp kids, but some were Mexicans and it seemed strange to see them up close, their jet black hair slicked back, their skin brown as butternut. Two of the Mexican kids were looking at the parrots and talking excitedly in Spanish.

Susie ran up, looking for the most talkative Amazon. Spotting the bird, she called out, "Hello, Dummy."

The two Mexican kids looked at her suspiciously.

Jake dug a biscuit out of his pocket, broke off a morsel and held it up to the wire close to where the Amazon was perched. "Hey Dummy."

The bird cocked its head to one side, eyeing the bribe. It scooted over closer, squawking, "Hey Dummy."

Jake repeated the process and each time the bird responded he gave it a crumb. The Mexicans, who were a bit younger and smaller, watched in fascination, speaking softly between themselves. Several other youngsters stopped what they were doing and came over to the cage.

Susie grabbed for Jake's biscuit. "Le'me try."

"Le'me try!" the parrot responded.

Jake pulled his hand away before his sister could snatch the biscuit. She protested, "Jake!"

"Jake!" a second bird responded. Two more had moved in close on the perch, interested in the food.

"Susie, I only got a li'l bit left."

"Gimme some!" she demanded.

"Gimme some!" the first parrot squawked.

Grudgingly, Jake broke a piece of the biscuit for her and they each chummed the birds some more. Several were talking now and Jake got the first bird to say "Numb-nutz." But then he was out of biscuit crumbs. "Aw, shit."

"Aw shit," a parrot mimicked him.

Jake was dumbstruck. Some of the kids snickered and one of them yelled, "Shit!"

"Shit!" the parrot screeched, ducking its head back and forth anxiously begging for crumbs. Susie pushed her last crumb through the wire. Jake, recognizing that the possibilities here were endless, ran over to a trash barrel and started pawing through it, looking desperately for something else to feed the parrots.

Halfway down in the trash barrel, Jake let out a shout. "Got some!" He'd found a half slice of bread and was running back. Suddenly he stopped, frozen.

The two deputies were coming down the path toward them. One shouted, "What the hell're you kids doin'?"

The bigger Mexican grabbed his brother's arm, pulling hard. *"Vámonos,* César! *Córrete!"*

Everybody scattered. Jake and Susie scurried into the dark bushes, then headed back into the crowds around the bandstand, looking back nervously. The lawmen weren't in sight.

Up at the microphone, C. J. was introducing another speaker. "Folks, this here's Thad Greene. He used to work at the Dairyland Gin till he got his arm caught in the compress. They fired him 'cause a one-arm man ain' no use to 'em no more. So he went to preachin' an' organizing for the union. I want ya all to hear what he has to say. Come on up here, Thad!"

"Thank ya, C. J." The black man came to the mike with authority, raised his face to Heaven and shouted in a deep, vibrant voice, *"Lawrd!* Hear our cry!" He looked out over the crowd as he paced his delivery, seeking a rhythm. "The *farmers* and the *bankers* say *they* are *Christians!"*

He paused briefly, still sensing the mood. "And they say that *they* are the righteous and that we are low-down and mean. They call us *niggers!* and *Okies!* And they say our brown brothers are *spics!* They claim to be God-fearing Christians defending themselves against Communists! And outside agitators! But I say to you, these greedy men are not Christians! They are *liars!"*

The blacks in the crowd responded, "Tell 'em, brother."

"They are *thieves!"*

"Yes Lord!"

"And *killers!"*

"Amen!!"

Jake nudged Susie. "Christ, you ever hear a nigger talk like that before?"

"No."

Jake couldn't believe it. "Susie, he's talkin' 'bout white men."

The preacher was hitting his stride now. *"Jesus Christ* our *Lord* was a working man."

"Praise God."

"He worked with His hands like we do."

"Amen, brother."

"If He was to walk right by here today, what would He say? *He'd say things are wrong here!* By His teaching Christians love other people, they don't *cheat* them, an' *rob* them and *starve* them and then call them names."

Applause.

"But we're not going to take it any more!"

"No. No!"

"We are going to *rise up!* and *walk out!* Out of those fields, and join *together* to form a *union!* and *demand* what is rightfully ours!"

The words thundered across the park and the crowd applauded, nearly drowning out the wail of a distant siren. At the back of the crowd Jake heard the siren and looked around just as the sheriff's car came tearing up Main and screeched to a stop at the curb in front of the school, its red spotlights glowing brightly. Sheriff Scott climbed quickly out of the car and slammed the door. He was wearing his working uniform, tan blouse and pants, pearl-gray Stetson, heavy Sam Brown gunbelt with extra cartridges, handcuffs, a billy and his nickel-plated .45 in a tie-down holster.

"Jeesus H. Christ. Look 'at 'em." Jake stared at the crowd of townspeople and farmers that had grown by a hundred or more and was swarming like angry hornets, buzzing mad. The sheriff waded into their midst. The two deputies left the park, running across the street to join the sheriff.

"Come on." Susie wanted a closer look at the trouble. They ran to the park's edge and stood in the shadow of a large elm, watching. "Damn, they're mad. Wisht we could hear what they're yellin' 'bout."

"Maybe we could sneak into them bushes over there." Jake pointed to the growth around the school building. "Hide right there."

"Jake, they'd see us crossin' the street."

"Not if we cross down there." Jake pointed to the far end of the park, down by the highway. "Come on!"

Keeping to the shadows, they ran a block and a half and, coming out of the park where Main intersected Highway 99, they crossed over and snuck back down the other side of the street, past the county library, dark now with the silent stone lions guarding the front steps. The library grounds and the schoolyard were separated by a dark side street. Both sides of this street were lined with parked pickups and patrol cars. The streetlight on the corner illuminated the farmers and townspeople on the school lawn and across Main Jake and Susie could hear the rally loudspeaker. Jake signaled for Susie to follow him and he darted across the sidewalk and crouched down behind a pickup. The streetlight didn't penetrate the shadows this far back and there was no one in sight. Bent low, they scampered across the dark side street and hid behind a car, safe for the time being.

"Jake," Susie whispered in his ear, "let's go back."

"Shhhh. We kin injun up closer." Crouching low, he ducked across the side yard and, dropping to his hands and knees, wormed into the hedge that grew close along the side of the building. Reluctantly, Susie followed. Once in among the bushes, they were screened from view and, like stalking Indians, they crept along in the shadows until they could clearly hear the angry voices.

"Goddammit, Windy, no nigger's goin' to talk like that about white men. I say we're goin' in there and clean those Communist sons a bitches out and then we're going to lynch that black motherfucker."

Jake and Susie lay flat in the soft earth, shouldered in close against the cement foundations, looking at the man who had just spoken. He was huge, with fists as big as hams; in one hand he held a gleaming white ax handle. "Susie, that's one of them that jumped us in the parade."

"Sssshh."

Jake wiggled forward a few more feet and Susie kept close to him. They had reached the corner of the building and could see the people gathered not only on the corner, but along in front of the school as well.

The big man was standing toe-to-toe with the sheriff, yelling. Then Titus Wardlow pushed between them, shoving the big man back. "Tiny, goddammit! You're not going to do a fucking thing!"

Looking down on Wardlow's growling face, Tiny wouldn't give up. "Titus, we're going to flush them out. Now get out of the fucking way." Tiny brushed Wardlow aside with the powerful sweep of his arm and looked at the other farmers. "Who's with me?"

Angry grumbles of assent were heard all around. Many of the farmers and some of the townspeople were ready for war. Most were armed with clubs and whips made out of radiator fan belts; a few had pistols stuck in their waistbands. But Wardlow wasn't having any of it. He closed with the big man, giving Tiny a hard push backward. "Goddammit, I said no! Not now!" Each sentence was punctuated with another push on the big man's chest. "Not this way! When we do it, it's going to be organized and legal and there'll be no fucking slipups."

The big man backed up only so far, then stopped. He brushed Wardlow's hands aside. "Titus, you heard what that nigger son of a bitch said, him an' them other goddamn Reds. They're whippin' up a strike, for Christ's sake. We gotta bust this up right goddamn now."

"Listen you big dumb bastard!" Wardlow threw down his cigar, and was right up in Tiny's face. "You go stormin' in there an' kill somebody an' the shit will really hit the fan. With all the pressure the governor's getting after that damn parade, he'd have to declare martial law and we'd have the fucking National Guard in here for Christ's sake!

"Tiny, goddammit, I don't like this any better than you do, but we're going to do it the association's way! That's what they sent Shriver in here for, so we're going to listen to him! And we're going to wait! You got that? We wait until they strike, then we move. Legally! And with the help of the sheriff and the highway patrol. When those goddamn strikers get in their cars and head for the fields to picket, we've got 'em for breaking the anti-caravan law and even if a few carloads slip past us we'll get them on the picket lines and throw their asses in jail. Legally! That's why we got the board to pass those ordinances against caravaning and picketing and got Windy here to deputize all of us. The association doesn't want you or anyone else fucking it up. So we're going to do it their way! Is that clear?"

They stood there nose-to-nose, yelling, the bulldog and the bull. "Goddammit, Tiny, is that clear?"

Then it was over. Backing off, the big man nodded angrily. "Yeah, Titus, that's damn clear."

"And you deal with that nigger later, after all of this is over." Wardlow took out another cigar, bit the end off and spit it out. "Windy, if any one of these guys tries to cross Main Street, stop 'em." Wardlow lit his cigar.

As the match flared, Jake and Susie got a good look at the controlled anger and determination on Wardlow's face and it sent a chill through them. Wardlow took several quick puffs, then turned and walked back to where he'd parked his pickup, passing so close by Jake and Susie they could smell the cigar smoke. They froze, staying crouched down with their backs against the cold schoolhouse wall, watching as Wardlow drove off.

The farmers and townspeople milled about now, their anger defused by Wardlow's orders. The sheriff instructed his deputies to keep an eye on things until the rally broke up across the street, then he too climbed back into his car, turned off the red spotlights and drove away. Others were leaving also, but many of the men stayed around, standing in little knots and clusters, talking away their unused adrenaline, arguing over what had just happened. Crouched in the bushes, Jake and Susie could only hear snatches of conversations.

"Goddamn, Titus has a lot of balls, standing up to Tiny like that."

"Hell, they're friends."

"But it's not like him to take orders like that."

"Who, Tiny?"

"No, goddammit, I mean Titus. What the hell's got into him, letting that little tin soldier run things?"

"Hell, Clem, what Titus said makes sense."

"The hell it does. We should've hit 'em tonight."

"Leastways, we should get that nigger."

A deputy sheriff cradling a sawed-off riot gun on one arm, added, "That nigger's goin' to get himself killed, sure enough. But you boys heard the sheriff. Not tonight!"

"Still say we oughta lynch the bastard."

"Shit, just shoot the black son of a bitch, like we done that other agitator, the white one."

A bank clerk asked the deputy, "Sam, what the hell did happen to that Okie?"

The question focused all attention on the deputy, who, shifting the shotgun's weight, told them, "He'd wiggled out of the handcuffs somehow, got one hand free, opened the door, jumped out just as they come up to a stop sign, just jumped and ran out across the field. Wouldn't stop when they yelled at him, so Elmer let him have it. Said he meant to wing him."

Somebody snorted. "Wing him, hell. Elmer don't miss." And

there were murmurs of acknowledgment because Deputy Elmer Snodgrass was probably the best pistol on the force, if not in the county.

Susie whispered, "Let's get out of here."

"D'ju hear what he said?"

"Come on, Jake, let's get out of here."

But Jake didn't move.

She tugged at him, hissing, "Come on."

Jake pulled angrily away, not taking his eyes off the deputy. He hated them, every one. Sons of bitches! Susie grabbed his arm again but this time her grip signaled terror, not just fear. Jake looked at his sister. Her head was turned and she was staring down the front of the school building at the dark, shadowy figure of a man crouched in the bushes like they were, not fifty feet away and looking straight at them. It was crazy. Jake blinked and looked again and he could still see the man's weasel-sharp features, eyes almost shining; the fellow, whoever he was, didn't move, but he was tensed up like a coiled spring, ready to fight or flee. Susie let go of Jake's arm and scooted back and Jake, his heart pounding, followed. How long had that man been there, staring at them? Crawling quickly away they retreated, then they were up on their feet and stumbling out to the curb, where they crouched behind a pickup, staring back to see if they were being followed.

"D'ju see 'im?" Susie whispered, trying to catch her breath.

"Gawd, yeah. Jis' sittin' thar like a varmint in a trap."

"Who was he?"

"Shit, how'd I know?"

Sure the man wasn't following them, they slipped between the front end of a pickup and the rear bumper of a sheriff's patrol car, ready to recross the side street and duck into the shadows of the library. Jake hesitated, looking at the patrol car. Maybe it was the one that the deputies drove when they'd picked up Cletus Sharp an' killed 'im. Anger mingled with his fear. He wanted to do something to get back at them and he looked around for a rock or something to smash the windows. That would make too much noise. He pulled out his knife, pried open the razor-sharp skinning blade and quickly, viciously stabbed a tire and yanked it out, slashing deep through the rubber. The whooshing escape of air thundered in his ears and he ran to the front of the patrol car, stabbing and slashing another tire, ignoring the sounds and, in his frenzy, not hearing the angry shouts.

"Hey!" The deputy and a couple of farmers were running toward the patrol car. "What the hell's goin' on there!" And another voice yelled, "Jeesus, Harv, there he is, by your car." Someone else shouted, "He's cutting your tires!"

"Stop!" The deputy's shotgun was up.

Jake darted across the street, headed between two parked cars like a rabbit diving for its hole.

BOOM! The shotgun thundered.

A car window exploded.

Ducking low, Jake was between the cars and on the far side yelling for Susie to run just as the deputy fired. He felt the stinging shower of glass and heard the rattle of shotgun pellets hitting the car. Later, when he thought back on it, Jake would remember seeing the back window of the car blowing out just above his head, but now he was running as hard as he could, following Susie through the library yard and around the corner, ducking and bulling through the bushes, running for their lives, trying to stay in the dark. They fled down an alley, stumbled over garbage cans and finally, two blocks away, they collapsed in the shadows, cowering, listening. There was the sound of sirens again, but no pursuit, no immediate danger.

"What the hell'd you do that for?" Susie demanded.

Jake didn't answer her.

"Jake?" She looked at him. "Gawd, Jake, yor bleeding!"

A shard of glass had cut his forehead and another had nicked his ear. Both were tiny wounds, but bleeding made them look worse. He let Susie daub at them with his shirttail as she scolded him. "What the hell'd ya do that for? We damn near got killed."

"Le'me 'lone." Jake pulled away, sobbing, trying to catch his breath.

Susie put her arm around him, confused, not knowing what to do. They sat there on the ground, huddling together, not talking. After a while she urged him, "Come on, Junior'll be lookin' for us." Susie helped Jake up and they walked out to the highway, then circled around through the city so that they came up on the park from the opposite side. The sound of the gunfire and sirens had broken up the rally, but people were still standing around.

Junior was with a group of men near the bandstand and as they walked up, Jake whispered to her, "Susie, we better not say nothin' to Junior 'bout this."

She nodded agreement. As they approached one of the fellows was saying, "Hell, nobody knows what went on over there."

"Christ no. Heard the shot, then a little while later we seen the deputies dragging Ron across the street. Had him handcuffed and he was bleedin' some, his nose I think. Couldn't tell if he was shot, but it looked more like he'd been worked over."

"Damn, an' he was a good man, too. How the hell they catch 'im?"

"No way to tell, till we get the lawyer in to see 'im. Shit, he jus' got out of jail, didn't he? Wasn't he with them at the parade?"

"Yeah."

"Dammit, I tol' him not to go sneakin' round over thar. Was too dangerous." C. J. hiked up his jeans and angrily spat tobacco juice.

"Yeah, but without what he heard when he snuck into that farmer's meetin' the other night, we might've been up shit creek out at the strike camp."

Jake and Susie stood there listening, but it was hard to make out what the union guys were talking about. When Junior did spot them, he paid little attention to them, other than to tell them to stick close by, and it wasn't until they were on the way home that he explained what had happened. One of the union's top organizers, a fellow named Ron Blue, had been arrested. "They got him over there, across the street from the park, where the farmers was. We heard the shot an' then seen them deputies. They had him cuffed and was dragging him to jail."

The news was stunning. A union guy had been arrested, and he was hurt, maybe shot. Jake asked, "What'd he look like?"

Junior glanced at Jake curiously. "Short little fella, skinny. Had shaggy hair, a pointy nose and hardly no chin."

"What was he doin' over thar?" Jake tried not to give away his feelings of panic.

"Spyin' on the farmers." Junior looked over at Jake. "Say, what happened to you? That a cut on yor head?"

"Jis' a scratch. Was messin' around, playin' kick-the-can with some kids an' I run into a stob on a bush." Jake changed the subject. "Didja vote a strike?"

"Yeah, weren't ya there?"

"Tol' ya, we was playin' kick-the-can over by the monkey cages, then we heard the shot." Jake was panicky now, certain the man they'd seen was the union organizer. Things were happening too fast. "Junior, you gonna strike tomarra?"

"Yeah."

Curious about the arrested organizer, Susie asked, "Was he really a spy?"

"Ron? Yeah, he'd go anywhere. Do anything. He took it on hisself to keep track of what them farmers was a-doin'. Nobody told 'im he had to do none of them thangs, he just did 'em. Like the time he slipped the latch on one of them basement windas in the Eagles Hall, where them farmers meets. He tol' us later that he figgered the basement was empty, bein' dark like that, an' so he just slipped through that winda and injuned up them stairs, said he was behind a stage of some kind and he cracked a door and could see a hundred, maybe two hundred farmers and he sure got an earful."

Junior slowed for a curve and shifted down, the clatter and smoke from the engine filling the car. He shifted back into third and drove easily, talking loudly over the engine noise. "Said them farmers was mad as hops about that Hollywood fella helpin' the union get the strike camp and they was talkin' about burning the camp down. Soon as people moves in, said they're goin' to git the county health doctor to condemn the place so's they can burn it down, but we're outfoxing them. That camp's so spic-an'-span, even your ma wouldn't be able to find nothin' wrong and we got fellas that's checkin' to make shor that there ain' no rules broke so that county doctor won't find nothin' wrong. Show 'em they ain' dealing with trash."

13

The jail was crammed full of strikers, the drunk tanks and holding cells downstairs were crowded, the cell blocks on the second floor overflowing, even the runways and corridors were jam-packed. A noisy mob of protesting strikers was gathering outside the jail and those prisoners closest to the windows pressed their angry faces against the bars and shouted down to their comrades who were free, egging the demonstration on. A driving rain drenched the mob. Thunder clapped, then rumbled away like wagons crossing a wooden bridge and, for an instant, the storm drowned out the noise of the mob.

Upstairs in the courthouse, Charles Gilmore stood at the rain-spattered boardroom windows, staring down at the mob as it surged around the stone walls, "Look at 'em! Dr. Pebble's right, they're not even human."

Sheriff Scott had been across the hall in superior court; now he too stood at the windows in the boardroom, surveying the scene below. "It's a damn good thing that new wing of the jail's built out of solid granite and concrete."

"Windy, I had no idea you could round up that many in one morning." Gilmore looked pleased. "I mean, by God, man, those ordinances are really proving their worth, aren't they?"

The ordinances outlawing both car caravans and picketing had been quietly passed by the board weeks earlier. Unaware of the new laws, the union had gathered its forces in the park early that morning and sent them out in car caravans to find workers in the fields and set up picket lines. Those first caravans drove right into the road blocks Windy Scott set up outside of town and the armed posses trailing along behind the caravans closed the trap, attacking from the rear, jerking workers out of their cars at gunpoint, beating them with clubs, herding and crowding them into slat-sided cattle trucks.

Before it was over, they'd arrested a hundred fifty, maybe more, but the posses hadn't gotten anywhere near all of the strikers. Many had broken out of the trap and escaped, others had taken back roads and weren't even stopped. However, the sudden, brutal attack stunned the union forces and, as word of the jailings spread, the strikers returned and rallied in the park under lowering skies. Hundreds were gathered there and their anger grew into a grumbling protest that swelled until its fury matched the gathering storm. Ignoring the rain, somebody shouted, "Bust 'em out!" The words sparked through the crowd, flashing it to action. "Bust 'em out!" The mob broke from the park and rushed the nearby jail.

Up in the board room Wardlow was beside the sheriff now, growling, "Where the hell are your men?"

"Downstairs. We're setting up a command post in the basement, should be fifteen or twenty there right now with plenty of tear gas and riot gear."

Wardlow looked at the sheriff. "Who's in the jail?"

"Ramey."

"Shit!"

"He'll be all right. Got ten deputies, plenty of food and water and enough ammunition to fight off a goddamn army." The sheriff resented Wardlow butting in. "Our only problem'll be feeding and watering that many prisoners."

Down below they could see the union leaders desperately trying to regain control of the strikers, shouting and pushing people, ordering them to return to the park.

Wardlow grunted. "What's happening across the hall?"

"That Commie lawyer, Wirin, from the ACLU's over there trying to get Judge Murphy to overrule Rooster and turn the strikers loose." Sheriff Scott shook his head. "Constable over there in Hyattville phoned, said Rooster really laid into Wirin, told him no big-city Jew lawyer could come into his court and try to bamboozle him. It was against the law to caravan or picket without a permit and if the ACLU didn't like it they could just go to hell. So Wirin's over here appealing to Judge Murphy."

"Appealing?" Wardlow asked sharply.

"Don' worry. Murphy's telling 'im there's nothin' in the damn Constitution that says a union's got a right to parade their damn cars around this county without a permit."

Gilmore patted Windy on the back. "We got 'em now. Every time they get in their cars, we arrest 'em."

"Oh, shut up, Charley." Wardlow turned from the window. "Windy, what are you going to do about that mob down there?"

"What do you suggest?" The sheriff didn't hide his irritation.

"Hell, arrest 'em."

"Where the fuck will I put 'em, Titus? The jail's full."

"Put 'em in the goddamn stockade." Wardlow bristled.

"It ain't finished yet."

"What!" Wardlow couldn't believe it. "It was supposed to be ready last week!"

"Couldn't do it, goddammit!" Windy Scott yelled back and the two men glared at each other.

"Why not?" Wardlow demanded.

"Because I don't have any fucking money. The board there"— Windy Scott pointed at Gilmore—"won't give me enough to hire extra help so I've been using jail trustees and scrounging materials. Friday we ran out of wire and roofing paper."

"Shit!" Wardlow turned on Gilmore. "Charley! What the fuck's the matter with you guys?"

"Titus, I've told you before." Gilmore drew himself up defensively. "I'm responsible to all the taxpayers of this county. Windy got a thousand dollars and that's all we can—"

"Shit." Disgusted, Wardlow turned back to the sheriff. "Windy, what do you need?"

"Hog wire. A dozen more rolls. And some more roofing paper, maybe ten rolls."

"Okay, I'll get the stuff out to you and send ya some men."

"That might not be legal," Gilmore worried.

"Bullshit," Wardlow snarled, "this is an emergency, Charley. We need that stockade, quick. If we don't break up those caravans before they get picket lines up, this thing could get away from us, and that wouldn't be good for any of us."

Gilmore didn't say anything.

"Would it, Charley?"

"No," Gilmore sulked, but gave in. "You're right."

"Windy, how long will it take you to finish it?"

"Couple of days."

"What about them, down there?" Wardlow looked out the window again, pointing.

"Hell, they can't hurt much milling around in the rain like that. If it gets serious, we'll hit 'em with tear gas, bust 'em up."

"Okay." Wardlow started to leave, then stopped. "Charley, there's another thing. You know that Armenian that farms out on Avenue Fifteen 'n half, east of my place?"

"Kakorian? Yeah, I know him. Why?"

"Friend of yours?"

"I carry his insurance, we talk business, that's all."

"Hear he started picking yesterday and he's paying a dollar a hundred. That's not good." Wardlow paused, then got to the point. "Why don't you go out and see him, suggest that he get in line, like everybody else." Not waiting for an answer, Wardlow stormed out, wishing now that he'd let Tiny and the others tear up that rally last night.

Rain came down hard, pelting and chilling the mob around the jail, drowning their fury. In twos and threes and then in bunches they turned in sullen frustration and walked back into the park. They'd been beaten, the strike had been broken before it got started. In the park the drenched strike leaders huddled around a table in the cold rain arguing.

Tommy Joad was angry and worried. "Dammit, we gotta do somethin' right now or it's all over!"

"But what?" C. J. snapped back. "They got us boxed up. Look over yonder, the damn jail's full now an' . . ."

"Tha's it!" Thad Greene's black face broke into a great big grin, white teeth flashing. "The jail's full. We got 'em between a rock an' a hard place." He could see they didn't understand, so he pointed to the mobs of wet strikers. "Look, there's more of us here than that jail can ever hold. They can't lock us all up 'cause they got no place to put that many people."

"Thad's right." Joad was excited now. "An' if nobody bails out, why shit, the jailhouse stays crammed full, so they cain' use it no more."

Chavez and the others on the strike committee agreed. C. J. nodded his approval, then chuckled. "Now all we gotta do is convince them folks that goin' to jail is fun."

That didn't prove difficult at all. When Tommy Joad and C. J. announced the plan over the public address system there was no reaction, at first, but then as the idea of going to jail on purpose sank in, the crowd began to buzz and strikers began to grin at the thought of such an audacious, defiant act. Why shit, this was a damn good way to say Fuck You in capital letters. Word of the union's plan spread quickly.

The second day of the strike dawned clear and windy. By sunup the park was full of strikers and most of them were ready to go to jail; even the mothers and grandmothers were arguing that they had the right to go to jail and somebody else could stay out and watch the children. On Wirin's advice, the pickets were told to refuse bail and sign nothing if arrested. No resistance was to be offered, nor were they to cooperate in any way, even if they were told to leave the jail. Once more the strike caravans headed for the fields and again they were followed and more strikers were arrested. These were herded into a makeshift jail in the basement of the courthouse, but picket lines were going up all over the county and more workers were joining the strike. Especially sweet were the victories at El Adobe, where two big crews walked out of the fields.

The tables had turned. Unable to detain the strikers, the growers were on the defensive. All they could do now was confront the strikers on the picket lines, keeping the union as far away from the pickers in the fields as they could. Knowing how uncontrollable these growers could be, Major Shriver was afraid someone else would get gunned down and then the shit would really hit the fan.

Shortly after noon Shriver put a call through to the association's headquarters in Sacramento, explaining to Casperson that it would be the day after tomorrow before the stockade was ready.

"Jesus Christ!" There was a pause. "All right, let me make a few calls and I'll get back to you by three." When he called back that afternoon, Casperson said their only choice was to empty out the damn jail and start arresting the strike leaders. "If we cut off the snake's head, the rest will die."

"Emptying the jail won't be easy," Shriver warned. "That damn judge set bail at two hundred fifty dollars each, and told the ACLU to go to hell."

"Well, try."

"Okay. By the way, the ACLU's appealing. Judge Murphy turned them down yesterday and Wirin's up in district court in Fresno today."

"I know, I know." Casperson was exasperated. "Major, we've got to have that jail space by tomorrow. Lean on that judge."

Shriver talked to Rooster Barkham on Thursday. Rooster refused to release the prisoners, but he did drop the bail to fifty dollars. The jailed pickets refused bond. That same day Wirin took his appeal directly to the California supreme court in San Francisco, after the appellate court in Fresno refused to hear the case. The high court agreed to hear the case on Friday.

For the farmers, the strike was getting out of hand. Thursday morning the Jeff City *Tribune* reported more workers had walked out of the fields and the paper estimated that half the cotton harvest was shut down. Lawmen and growers were protecting those workers who stayed in the fields, the *Tribune* reported, and new workers were being recruited from as far away as Texas and Louisiana and would be arriving soon.

Editorially, the paper called on the governor to step in and order the strikers to return to the harvest because there was clear evidence that the strike was being led by outside agitators. If the truth were known, local workers wanted no part of this Communist-led union; its only support was coming from the CIO unions and from liberal churches in the big cities that for years had supported the California Migrant Ministry's charitable efforts. In the past that church support had been welcome, but since young agitators from Union Seminary in New York City had taken over the migrant ministry and gotten mixed up in this union business, such charity only played into the hands of the Communists, the editor declared.

By the third day the strike had built up its own momentum. Each morning before dawn more strikers assembled in the park as the union organizers announced the day's plan and dispatched the caravans, instructing the picket captains to take their people to designated targets scouted out the afternoon before. No longer were the instructions announced over the public address system for everyone, including grower spies, to hear. Now only the picket captains were told which fields to target and the strikers followed the leaders. So did the sheriff's patrol cars and, soon after a picket line was set, pickuploads of farmers came roaring onto the beleaguered farm. The growers set up a counterpicket line, standing just inside the property line, shielding the strike-breaking workers.

The strikers picketed until midafternoon, then returned to the strike camp to eat, rest and clean up; in the evening they drove or hitched a ride to the nightly rally in the park. The park tables and benches around the bandstand became the unofficial union headquarters, where, as the day's light faded and the air chilled, hundreds of workers met with union organizers and picket captains to talk over the day's results, new members were signed up, scouts reported in and the next day's actions were quietly planned.

Major Shriver drew up new field operational plans and established his command post in the Eagles Hall, not far from the park. He strengthened the telephone network that alerted the farmers about when and where picket lines were appearing, and he prepositioned squads of deputized farmers at strategic places around the county to shorten their response time. Tempers were short along the picket line as club-carrying farmers tried to face down pickets who challenged and provoked them; the strikers insulted and defied the farmers, yelled at the workers, trying to coax them out and, failing that, screamed obscenities at them, called them scabs. The growers stood there, red-faced, grim-lipped, heeding Shriver's warning that if they moved violently, illegally, Governor Olson would send in National Guard troops.

"We're holding our own," Shriver reported to Casperson, and predicted, "The stockade should be ready tomorrow."

Casperson had good news too: more workers were on the way.

Early Friday morning six heavy trucks with Louisiana plates rolled down out of Tehachapi Pass on Highway 58, headed toward Bakersfield. Road grime and dust covered the big rigs. They were flatbeds with high board sides and canvas-covered tops; scores of black field hands rode inside, crowded on narrow benches. At Bakersfield the convoy turned north up Highway 99 and forty minutes later the weary drivers picked up a police escort as they crossed into Jefferson County. Two motorcycle cops took the lead and two carloads of sheriff's deputies followed along behind. As the convoy lumbered into Jeff City and headed west out Main, pedestrians stared at the sullen faces of the road-weary black workers riding uncomfortably in the trucks.

The convoy passed out of town, headed west on Dairy Avenue, the drivers pressing down hard on the gas to keep up with their escort. At Road 17 the convoy slowed and turned north, crossed the Palo Rojo River bridge and sped on toward the sprawling white buildings of the El Adobe Ranch headquarters.

The county road in front of the ranch office and store was lined with battered jalopies and mobs of banner-waving strikers milling about the ranch entrance. The union, tipped off by a sympathetic crew boss that scabs were being trucked in, was ready. At the sight of the approaching trucks a yell went up from the pickets; picket captains scrambled up atop cars and shouted into their megaphones, giving orders, shaping up the picket line, drawing it across the front of the ranch entrance.

Opposite them were the barricades thrown up by the ranch hands; fifty-gallon oil drums had been rolled out and chained together with steel cable, two pickup trucks were parked broadside in the entryway and a dozen men stood at the ready behind the barricade, each armed with a riot gun. Up on the veranda of the office building there were two dozen more armed men, each wearing a white armband that identified him as an Associated Farmers posseman.

The convoy approached the ranch entrance, sirens screaming, red lights flashing. The motorcycle cops slowed and turned into the mob, a spearhead trying to force through the massed pickets. The frightened lead driver shifted down and tightened his grip on the steering wheel, following the cops. Ranch guards quickly moved the pickups to let the convoy through, but the crush of pickets surged into the gap, choking off the entrance, sealing it with their bodies. The motorcycles were engulfed by the crowd; one of the cops lost his hat and was nearly knocked from his cycle, but gunning ahead, he managed to break through in a roar, scattering pickets aside. Terrified, the second cop broke through too, but they had failed to clear a path for the trucks. The mob swirled around the trucks, ripping at the canvas cover, screaming obscenities at the cowering workers inside. Frantically, the first driver plowed ahead, his truck breeching the human mass like a bull-nosed scow forcing the waves. A rock smashed through the windshield, showering the driver with glass. The big truck's fenders bowled workers over, scattering them. A man went down, unseen; he scrambled to get clear, but the steel bumper knocked him sprawling under the wheels, screaming. The sound was lost in the riotous noise. Strikers surging around the back of the vehicle stumbled over the crushed man. Someone yanked him clear of the other trucks bulling through the mob.

It wasn't until the last truck had broken safely through the line that people heard the shouts for help and saw two men kneeling beside the crumpled figure on the ground. One leg was grotesquely bent and blood oozed through the pantleg that had been torn by a protruding bone. The victim moaned. Somebody yelled for a doctor and a picket captain shouted into his megaphone, "Git back! Give 'im room! Git back!" A jalopy truck was brought up. Carefully the man was lifted onto its flat bed, where a woman cradled his head and shoulders while two other strikers held his leg, immobilizing it as best they could. "Take 'im to the county hospital," someone yelled.

Up on the veranda Shriver stood next to Wardlow watching. "Damn, it looks like one of 'em got run over."

"Serves the bastard right," Wardlow snapped.

"It could mean more trouble."

"Shit. From who?"

"The press. The governor."

Wardlow tried to control his anger. "Goddammit, the bastards were trespassing."

"Calm down, Wardlow, I'm just thinking out loud, anticipating. We've got to keep on top of this thing." Major Shriver toyed with the riding crop he always carried. "Oh, I forgot to tell you, Casperson called, said another two hundred workers will be in later tonight, from Juarez."

"Mexicans?"

"Yes."

"Dammit, I told him I wanted more niggers. You ought to know we can't mix niggers and Mexicans in our camps."

"I ordered the Mexicans, they're closer. If you don't have workers in your fields it'll look like El Adobe's losing control and if that happens, we're in real trouble."

Wardlow relit his cigar, puffing angrily.

"Look, Wardlow"—Shriver faced the farmer—"I know what I'm doing, I broke that strike in Salinas. We whipped them before they got started. With the stockade we would have stopped this strike in its tracks, but it wasn't finished and your people didn't keep their heads about them either."

"Wha'cha mean by that?"

"Killing that Sharp fellow wasn't very smart."

"Shit, he jumped out of the goddamn car and ran."

"Wardlow, I was warned that you were a hothead, that all of you out here on the west side were hotheads."

"Oh, fuck Casperson!"

"It wasn't Casperson, but that's beside the point. The point is that the strike's just about over down in Kern County. They listened to us and it went like clockwork. Same in Kings, but you people here let the ball get away from you."

"Shit, they're havin' hell in Fresno and Madera too, just like us. Stockade'll be ready by tomorrow and we'll start locking the bastards up."

"Not if Wirin gets a court order, you won't."

"What d'ya mean?"

"None of those anti-caravan ordinances are constitutional. You should know that."

"So what? Judge Murphy threw Wirin's appeal out."

"That's exactly what he wanted." The officer slapped his riding crop hard on his boot-top for emphasis. "Wirin's smart, and he's not afraid of your blustering or your courts. He had to get that appeal thrown out locally so he could get the case before the state supreme court, that's where he has to be if he's going to win."

"Yeah, but that'll take time."

"Like hell. He's arguing before the supreme court today in San Francisco and his chances of getting a restraining order are damn good. If he wins, your damn stockade will be useless."

"You some kind of lawyer?"

"The association has the advice of some very good lawyers and I listen to them. You should too. I've got one of our attorneys with me today. Name's Kincaid, Cyrus Kincaid." The major looked at Wardlow, expecting the farmer to react to the name. When he didn't, Shriver added, "From Los Angeles." Still Wardlow showed no sign of recognition. Shriver mentally shrugged, once more amazed at how rustic these valley farmers were. "Kincaid's in town with the district attorney right now explaining some alternatives we think will work. We're opposing Wirin, of course, and we've even got the attorney general to come in on our side, but Kincaid doesn't see much chance for us to prevail."

Wardlow sensed Shriver's contempt and he could see that the arrogant little shit never even tumbled to the fact that he, Wardlow, knew Kincaid. Titus Wardlow might have mud on his fucking boots, but he wasn't a hayseed, not by a long shot. Kincaid was a senior partner of a big Los Angeles law firm and Armor Cotton Oil was Kincaid's client. Wardlow had met Kincaid while putting the railroad land deal together, but he'd had no idea that Kincaid was also advising the association. That was a surprise. He hadn't reacted when Shriver had mentioned Kincaid's name because he wanted to let this new element play itself out a bit further, see what Kincaid's involvement meant.

Still misreading Wardlow's reactions, Shriver thought he had the advantage and was pressing it. "You people here don't seem to realize that this isn't just a local strike. The CIO and John L. Lewis mean to win this one. That's why they hauled some of the local rabble up to the CIO convention in San Francisco this past weekend, showing the big-city press that the CIO is organizing the cotton pickers. There's talk that Lewis himself will come down to walk the picket lines. If he does, that'll mean *The New York Times*, the Chicago papers, all the national press will be here.

"That's not all. We hear that the Reuthers have the auto workers contributing buckets of money to the strike and Bridges is supporting it too. That means you won't be shipping any cotton across West Coast docks." Shriver puffed up to his full height, snapping his crop on his cavalry boots. "Mister, this is nineteen thirty-nine and the Communists know that they've got a governor on their side. That rabble out there knows it, too." Shriver pointed across the yard to the picket lines. "But remember this, the governor is weak. Weak and vulnerable. The legislature opposes him on this issue and he doesn't dare call out the troops, not unless he absolutely has to. He'll bluff as far as he can. That's why Winchester's nosing around here. Winchester goes by the book. If we make a mistake, he'll let the governor know. So whatever we do, we've got to make it look good, look like we're the victims.

"On that score, I suggest you have somebody call the county hospital and tell them to take damn good care of that fellow that got run over. Then, even if he dies, it was an accident and you tried to help. It was clearly their own fault, but you farmers wanted to make sure he was treated well."

Wardlow chewed on his cigar, furious. How could he have let himself get in a position like this, having to listen to a goddamn worm in a fucking stuffed shirt? Somebody ought to step on the little shit, squash him flat.

Two hours later Wardlow sat at the big table in the board of supervisors' chamber, still angry. Around him were the district attorney, the sheriff, Charley Gilmore and a couple of others. Standing in the background, looking out the window, was Cyrus Kincaid, a tall, handsome man in an immaculately tailored gray suit. Kincaid was urbane, a quiet man with silver-gray hair, neatly barbered; his hands were soft and delicately shaped, with long fingers and manicured nails. When Shriver introduced Wardlow to Kincaid before the meeting, neither man had given any sign of having met before.

Major Shriver was presiding, with Wardlow and Windy Scott on his right, Gilmore and District Attorney Harlan Haggers on his left. Haggers was a jovial fat man of enormous girth who wore a rumpled brown suit.

"Well, now, the first order of business is to clear the jail." Shriver looked around the table, letting the words establish his authority. "Mr. Kincaid here informs us that the prisoners have no right to refuse release. They can refuse to sign a pledge to appear in court, but even so, the judge can still let them out. Wardlow, I'll leave it up to you to convince the judge that this is vital to his interests as well as ours.

"The next step is to cut off the snake's head. By that I mean arrest the strike leaders. We have a list of nearly a hundred who should be taken in." The major paused, enjoying the reaction to this last fact. "Don't look surprised, we have an undercover operative working on the inside. He's from the state Criminal Identification Department and has been a member of the Workers Alliance for nearly two years. He's here in Jefferson County now, reporting regularly to CID in Sacramento. We don't know who he is, but we're getting his reports through Casperson.

"I think I should once again point out that this isn't just a local strike by a ragamuffin bunch of cotton pickers, this is a major effort by the Red unions to take over agriculture. A war, if you will. The enemy has probed our front all up and down the valley and, quite frankly, they've found a weak spot here in the center of our line. Jefferson County is now the focus of their attack. You should also know that what is happening here is being watched very closely by the association, at the very top, and there are some who are not happy with what they've seen. But I'm digressing."

Wardlow bit down hard on his cigar, his eyes squinting hatred as he rocked the chair gently back and forth, watching Shriver. The little bastard wasn't subtle, and maybe that was an advantage.

Major Shriver went on. "Earlier this season, the CID operative was on the picket lines up in the Marysville peach harvest and he found evidence of the Red plot. Here, let me show you some of the literature he uncovered." Shriver tossed two pamphlets out on the table. A third he held up. "I'll read a little of this to you: 'There is no way out of the general crisis of capitalism other than the overthrow of the exploiting classes by the proletariat; the workers must confiscate the banks, the factories, the mines, the stocks and goods of the capitalists, the lands of the landlords and the church. . . . The Communist Party must raise before the toilers in the United States the revolutionary way out of the crisis . . . only the destruction of the capitalist system can free the millions of toilers.'

"There you have it. They want to confiscate your lands, your banks, your very way of life. That's clear enough, isn't it? These were found in a CIO organizer's suitcase. Many of these same organizers are right here in Jefferson County, now. You've got one of them in jail for slashing the tires on a police car. He was using the name Ron Blue, but CID has identified him as Aaron Bluestein, a professional agitator whose record dates clear back to the International Workers of the World. Gentlemen, what we have here is incontrovertible evidence of the Communist conspiracy. These fiends are conspiring to take over the farms and to overthrow the government and, my friends, that is against the law. The crime is criminal syndicalism, a felony. Mr. Kincaid here has been helping the district attorney draft the charges against Mr. Bluestein, charges that he conspired to violate the California Criminal Syndicalism Act. Bluestein is the example. Mr. Kincaid advises us that in future arrests it would be best to apprehend each of these agitators after they are heard giving speeches or seen meeting with workers or as they lead them on the picket lines. In other words, catch them in some act of advocating overthrow of the American system, like you did with Bluestein. His arrest was a big break for us, that kind of overt terror tactic will prove our case in court. We need more such arrests, but just arresting the leaders is not enough. That strike camp must be eliminated, the picket lines broken up, but we've got to do it legally. We are not going to give the governor any excuses to come in here.

"The strikers know we're trucking in hundreds of outside workers to take their jobs. When they see their leaders in jail and their camp burned down they'll go back to work. If we do this right and there are no more slipups, the whole thing should be over within a week. Are there any questions?"

As the meeting broke up and Shriver turned to leave, Kincaid called after the officer, "I'll be with you in a minute, Major, I want a word here with Mr. Wardlow."

Shriver stopped and started to come back.

"No, no. I'll catch up with you. I'll only be a second here." The silver-haired attorney waited as Shriver walked through the swinging double doors toward the elevator. "Titus, we'd like to have a meeting with you at Armor's office in Bakersfield tomorrow morning, if that's possible."

"What for?"

"We'd better not talk here. Can you make it?"

"Let's see, tomorrow's Saturday." He stalled. The request caught him by surprise and he wanted time to think things through. "I've got to meet the county health officer in the morning, about that strike camp, how about afternoon?"

"How late?"

"Four-thirty okay?"

"I think that'll work." Kincaid was irritated by the idea of having to stay over in Bakersfield, but he didn't let it show. "If there're problems, I'll leave word at your office."

That afternoon, late, Wardlow had a drink with Rooster. They drove out to Bebe's, a favored steak house and bar on the highway north of town, and over a pitcher of martinis he convinced Rooster that the union really wanted to keep the jail full and that it would shock the hell out of them if all the strikers were turned loose. Rooster liked the idea so much he called the jail right then and released the prisoners, all that is except Bluestein, who'd slashed the deputy sheriff's tires.

Early the next morning Wardlow dropped by Dr. Pebble's house and, over coffee, they agreed the Collins Corner strike camp was a public health hazard that should be abated. The only question was how soon?

"Kincaid said you'd have to give them a warning first, then we can burn them out if they don't close down." Wardlow took out a fresh cigar. "Why don't you take a couple of deputies and inspect the camp this afternoon? Catch 'em by surprise."

"I was going to play tennis." Dr. Pebble hesitated, but looking at Wardlow's expression, changed his mind. "Okay, I'll do it. You coming along?"

"No. I've got to fly to Bakersfield. Besides," Wardlow chuckled, "I don't think it'd look too good if I was with you."

From the Collins Corner store and gas station it was just a half mile west down Avenue Twenty-six to the strike camp. The camp had a single entrance and the gate was open, but as Dr. Pebble drove up, followed by two deputies in a squad car, he was stopped by two unarmed union guards standing in the driveway. One of the guards, an older, shaggy man in tan workpants and shirt, came up to Dr. Pebble's county car and peered in. "Wha'cha fellers want?"

The sheriff's deputies were quickly out of their squad car, slamming the doors and adjusting their gunbelts. One of the deputies yelled at the younger guard who still stood in front of the doctor's car, "You, there! Stand aside and let us through."

"Y'all got a warrant?" The older guard straightened up, looking at the lawmen.

"Listen, goddammit, Dr. Pebble here is the county health officer. He don' need no warrant to make a health inspection. We're comin' in."

The older guard stood his ground. "This here's private property. If ya come in, ya'll be breaking the law. The doc here, he's welcome, but lawmen ain' got no authority here 'less there's a law bein' violated. Doctor, if ya'll just wait here for a minute, we'll get somebody to take ya 'round the camp."

The younger guard nodded and went off at a trot.

"All right." Dr. Pebble ordered the deputies to back off and then sat in his car, waiting, watching. Beyond the fence he could see orderly rows of tents set out along wide dirt streets. It was a big camp, laid out as neatly as any city. Even from the outside he could see water lines had been installed and pit privies constructed, all according to the specifications spelled out in the county health handbook that he had authored. By his guess, there were a thousand families living here, yet there was no sign of disorder or trash problems.

Within a few minutes the young guard was back with two other fellows, one a small, swarthy man with a full black beard, the other a fair-haired, lean fellow with high, wide cheekbones, dark brown eyes and prominent yellow teeth. The young guard pointed to the taller man. "This here's Tommy Joad, he talks for the union, an' that there is Doc Abraham, he does our doctorin'."

A deputy crowded up to Joad. "Listen you, we're comin' in."

"Mister, we know who Dr. Pebble is, an' he's welcome to look the camp over, but the law don't set one foot on this here property 'less'n they have a warrant. You try an' we'll call the governor's office."

"Wait for me here," Dr. Pebble ordered as he opened the car door and got out. Clipboard in hand, he walked into the camp with Joad and Dr. Abraham, asking the black-haired, bearded young physician, "Where'd you train?"

"Harvard. And you, sir?"

"I don't see that as any of your business. What do you do here?"

"Practice medicine. I'm assisted by two public health nurses."

Joad chuckled. "Doc, here, he's right proud of that 'ere clinic of his. Come on, we'll show ya that, an' the whole shebang, right down to the crappers. Ain' no finer crappers for miles around. Better'n them over to El Adobe. Ya know, Doc Pebble, if'n I was you, I'd take a look at old man Wardlow's camps. They're jus' plain damn filthy."

The inspection was a flop. Dr. Pebble couldn't turn up a single violation. He phoned Wardlow with the news, catching him just before he took off for Bakersfield.

"Titus?"

"Yeah?"

"That camp's clean as a whistle. There wasn't a thing I could write them for, not one."

"Goddammit. I didn't send you out there to give them a fucking kiss. I want you to declare that place a health hazard. I know how those goddamn Okies live. They sure as hell have trashed my camps."

"Titus, I can't. They're going by the book. My book." Dr. Pebble sounded helpless. He explained, "It's not the Okies who are running things out there. They've got a medical doctor and two public health nurses and a bunch of professional agitators. I'm telling you, there are no violations."

"Shit!" Wardlow slammed the phone down. He sat there, puffing and chewing on his cigar, mad at himself, mad at Shriver and those bastards who were pulling that little shit's strings. Damn! Wardlow hated being manipulated, by anyone, but there was no way in hell that he could put the Devil's Den together without Armor and American First. And now with Kincaid to worry about, he felt roped in even tighter. Fuck it! He slammed a fist against the desktop as he got up and headed for the hangar.

That evening, after the meeting with Armor and the bankers, Titus and Roxanne had a late dinner in a small Basque restaurant in East Bakersfield. An old waiter in a white apron set out a bottle of homemade red wine, hot bread and butter and pointed to the menu on a blackboard across the room, behind the bar.

The fare was simple, various kinds of lamb and beef, soup and beans and vegetables. The narrow dining room was dominated by a long table crowded with happy, noisy shepherds who spent their infrequent holidays here and in the hotel above. Roxie and Titus had a small table in back, where no one would notice them. He asked for a double Scotch and Roxie poured herself a glass of wine and listened.

First off, Grady Armor hadn't been at the meeting. He'd sent one of his pencil pushers to hold hands with that little shit from the bank, a fucking kid vice president with an MBA from Stanford. When Kincaid introduced the banker, he'd winked at Titus, signaling that they shared the same thoughts, but that was a ploy too. "They let Kincaid do most of the talking. Boy, he's smooth. He said he was on my side and that it was the bankers who were worried. What would their stockholders think if the bank became entangled in a messy labor situation? That's what he called it, 'a messy labor situation.' Shit!"

The waiter set out steaming platters of meat and bowls of beans and steamed vegetables. Titus picked at his food and kept talking. Roxie poured them both wine, surprised by what she was hearing. It wasn't the words themselves, but the way he was saying them. She sensed fear there, deep down under the blustering anger. He was vulnerable and afraid. But dammit, when you were flying flat-out, throttle pushed to the firewall, there was no time for fear, fear was the betrayer, the fatal weakness.

"Fuck 'em!" She was mad at him now for letting such feelings show. "Goddammit, you've got the land leased, you got the damn loans, what more do you need? Tell 'em to go to hell and go for it. Don't look back."

Her anger made him madder still. "Goddammit, this isn't some fucking race!"

"Don't yell at me, you son of a bitch, I'm not the one snapping at your ass." She was up from the table. "Where's the goddamn can?"

He pointed toward the back. "Through that door." As she left the table, Wardlow lit a cigar, puffing up blue smoke. How the fuck could he explain it to her? Grady Armor and the goddamn bankers had him in a box. He didn't want to take their fucking orders, but he had to work on their money. If they'd just get off his ass, he could get the goddamn strike settled his way, quick and dirty. But no, they had made it clear: no more violence. Yes, they agreed, the strike had to be ended quickly; that was why

Shriver had been sent to Jefferson County. They were calling the shots and they wanted no public exposure, no more front-page pictures and stories. He shrugged; they were the real power. One day he'd be up there in their league playing hardball against those assholes, but for now he had to bite his tongue.

Roxie came out of the bathroom, calmer now, and curious. "Why are they so shy about busting a few heads?"

"Politics. They've got the legislature in their pocket and the governor's weak, but if they give him an issue, he can get a lot stronger, fast. They don't give a shit about a few farmers down here in the valley, but they are afraid of the unions. The problem is they want to pussyfoot around, pass laws, make it all nice and clean and the union'll just go away. But that's bullshit! And now the goddamn strike's out of hand because they've screwed up."

He was up and flying early the next morning, still angry and tired. Obsessively, his mind was back on Shriver and Kincaid and how they'd taken over the association and were using him, using all of the farmers. They even had their own spy inside the union, a CID man. That really pissed him off, their keeping that a secret for so long. Those fuckheads! He pushed the Spartan to full throttle. Taking out his anger and frustration, he dove, building up speed, then pulled up into a loop and, winging over at the top, dove back down and pulled up, completing a Cuban Eight. He dove again and leveled off a few feet above the fields, flying flat-out, skimming the tops of farmhouses, popping up over power lines and dropping back down into the fields, engine roaring. By the time he landed at the ranch, he'd made up his mind; he had put up with their shit too long. It was time to retake control, but first he needed to get some measure of the situation inside the union and to do that, he needed a spy of his own, one who would report to him, not the major.

He stormed into the office. "Ruth!"

The secretary was already up, expectant.

"I want to see that big Okie crew boss."

"Jethro Hammer?"

"Yeah." He banged through the swinging gate and the door to his private office, slamming it behind him.

Hammer's crew was picking in a field a couple of miles from the office and it wasn't long before Wardlow heard the big man's boots clomping down the porch. Ruth stuck her head in the door. "He's here."

"Send 'im in."

Jethro Hammer's huge frame filled the doorway behind the secretary.

"Come on in, Hammer. Cigar?"

"Thanks." The crew boss took the cigar and sat down in an oak chair. He was a tall, heavy man who weighed nearly two fifty. Dressed in rough work clothes, he was in his early thirties, blond, with clear blue eyes and a ruddy complexion. "What can I do for ya?"

"Got somethin' I want you to do."

"Will if'n I can."

"We gotta have some way of finding out what those goddamn Reds are going to be doing next and the only way I can see to do it is have a spy in their camp."

Hammer looked at the farmer, not saying anything.

"You had a guy on your crew that fingered that union agitator in Camp Six, didn't you?"

"Yeah. Guy named Tarpin."

"He came to you, told you about it?"

"Naw, not 'xactly. He was shootin' his mouth off one day around camp, sayin' how he hated them Communists, that sort of thang. I asked him what he was talkin' about and he told me. He's got a big mouth."

"Trust 'im?"

Jethro Hammer was balling and unballing his huge fists, and he shifted his weight uncomfortably. "Look, Mr. Wardlow, I work for ya, so I'll do what ya say, but I still don't like the way that fella got killed and in a way—"

"Aw shit, forget it."

"But it was me that told ya that he was a union man."

"Hammer, it was that Tarpin guy who named him. You had no way to know the son of a bitch would jump and run. Goddammit forget it. Now tell me, do you trust that Tarpin fellow or not?"

"Hell no I don' trust 'im, not him ner any of that clan."

"Clan?"

"Yeah. Dolph Tarpin, the one-eyed fella that was shootin' off his mouth, he's one of three boys. There's him, his two brothers an' their ol' man. Them an' their families, they're all trash, the whole bunch, but that Dolph, he's the worst."

"What makes you say that?"

"Way he treats his wife'n kids. I stopped him from beatin' one of them boys. He had him down an' was kickin' him."

"Hell, I'm not looking for a saint. Go bring him in, I want to talk to him."

"Right now?"

"Yeah."

Hammer had been right, Dolph Tarpin was a mean-looking hard case, standing there in front of the desk. Wardlow didn't ask him to sit down, just explained that he was looking for someone to pose as a union sympathizer and move into the strike camp. Tarpin backed away, shaking his head no, but when Wardlow offered to pay him twenty-five dollars, cash, right then, and twenty-five a week, Tarpin tried to haggle the price up. "What about my pa an' the rest of 'em. Gotta pay them somethin' too."

"You miserable son of a bitch." Wardlow took the cigar out of his mouth. "I'm offering you more money than you've ever made in your fucking life. You either do it, or get your ass off my ranch, the whole fucking bunch of you. Now which is it?"

"What about my wife and kids?"

"Hell, take the whole bunch, just like you'd been thrown off my place."

"Pa an' Ott an' 'em others?"

"The whole bunch."

"What'll I tell 'em? They know I hate the goddamn union."

"I don't give a shit what you tell them." Wardlow pulled fifty dollars out of his wallet, counted out half and said, "There's the first twenty-five. Hammer here'll give you the second half once you're in the strike camp."

Tarpin's one good eye blinked and he acted like a junkyard dog that'd just been kicked, but wanted the bone being held out to him. "I'll take it." He snatched up the money.

"Just you remember, if those union goons find out you're spying

272

you'll be lucky if they just beat the shit out of you. And if you try to fuck me up with them goddamn union Reds, I'll nail your dirty hide to the fucking barn. Do you understand me?"

"Yes sir, I hate them Communists 's much as you, Mr. Wardlow." Tarpin nodded, backing out. "An' so does Pa 'n the others."

14

Jake felt guilty picking cotton on the day the strike started. He was certain all of the cottonfields were empty except Kakorian's, that everybody else had walked out. Over in the camp he heard the sound of Junior's old Chevy starting. Looking up he saw Junior drive out, his family and all of his belongings packed in the car. Junior was a striker. That's what he'd told Mr. Kakorian yesterday as they all were leaving the field. He had just walked up and said, "Mr. Kakorian, I'm stickin' to the union."

Kakorian's dark face had hardened and he'd looked back over at Lige and Ertie, suspicious.

"They ain' in this, Mr. Kakorian," Junior had assured the farmer. "It was my pa there that tol' me I'd best move out."

Kakorian had only nodded, still looking at Lige and Ertie. "You two in this?"

Before either could answer, Bessie spoke up, "No sir! We come here to work, and that's what we aim to do."

No one else said anything and Kakorian seemed satisfied. He even tried to change Junior's mind. "Boy, you're making a big mistake. I hate to lose a good worker, but I won't ever hire you back if you join those Communists."

Junior hung his head and toed the ground. "You been decent to us, Mr. Kakorian, but I gotta do it. We ain' never gonna be nothin' but tramps if'n we don' stand up for decent wages and a clean place to live."

"But you've got that here." Kakorian had looked at Junior for the longest time, then turned and walked away.

Jake waved as the Chevy turned out on to the road.

Junior honked.

Jake watched until the car was out of sight, then, glancing up at the heavy clouds scudding low across the sky, he bent back to his work, his mind on the union and the crazy events of the night before. He could still see the dark figure of Ron Blue crouched in the shadows by the school, hear the shotgun blast and feel the terror again as the car window exploded.

Near midmorning he felt the first raindrops, leaden splatters that thumped his back and fluttered through the leaves around him. The air was heavy with the fresh, wet smell of the storm that came thundering over them. Kakorian yelled to Lige and Ertie, asking them to help him lash a tarp over the partially filled cotton trailer, ordering the rest of them out of the field. "Get on home!"

They ran for camp. A short while later Ertie came limping in out of the storm, soaking wet, water spilling from the curl of his hat brim. First thing, he grabbed up his whiskey bottle and took a long, shuddering drink, then rolled a cigarette. Rain drummed on the awning over the kitchen, the wind whipped the canvas and blew cold sprays across the kitchen. Bessie put the coffeepot on the little kitchen stove and had a kettle of beans warming. Using kerosene, James Earl got a roaring campfire started just out from under the rain fly and, protected by the awning, the others gathered close to the blazing wood. Rain spattered and hissed in the flames.

Benjy whined and tugged at his mother's arm, cold and hungry. Bessie hugged him close. "Mary Ellen, fix 'im a piece of cornbread 'n molasses, then get 'im out of those wet clothes. Billie Jo, you and Susie get them tents straightened up, see that thangs ain' gettin' wet. Hear?"

Ertie poured himself a steaming cup of coffee, laced it with whiskey and sat down on an overturned nail keg by the fire, smoking and sipping the hot drink, relishing its warmth. Jake pulled up another stool and sat by his father, wishing for a cigarette and some whiskey in his coffee.

James Earl squatted on his hams nearby, poking at the fire.

"That Junior's a fool for goin' off like that. Way I figger it, he broke his word to Mr. Kakorian."

"Didn' neither," Jake blurted out.

Ertie took a drag on his cigarette, not saying anything.

"He shor as hell did." James Earl shifted his weight and looked belligerently at his young brother. "He agreed to work for a dollar, like the rest of us. Mr. Kakorian ain' dropped the pay so Junior had no call to walk off."

"Pa," Jake looked to his father, "ya think Junior did wrong?"

Ertie sucked a last drag on the cigarette and hurled it into the fire. "Hell, I don' know, boy!" He got up and, taking the bottle with him, headed for the tent. "Gotta get outa these wet clothes."

Ertie felt trapped. It was true, Kakorian hadn't gone back on his word, so what had changed? Nothing. He had to admit that, but even a dollar wasn't much of a wage, and that was a fact. Maybe they ought to just say to hell with it all and head out, go south to work in the winter vegetables down in the Imperial Valley. But shit, it was only October. Work down there didn't start for another couple of months and even then the pay was worse than up here.

A sharp wind shook the ridge poles violently, snapping and popping the canvas.

Out at the stove Bessie spooned out steaming bowls of beans and set out scalding cups of coffee. They all ate quickly, standing around the fire, then holed up in the tents to wait out the storm.

Bessie lay on the bed, a blanket pulled over her, leafing through a back issue of Mrs. Kakorian's *Woman's Home Companion.* Turning the pages, Bessie skimmed the advertisements for Bon Ami, the best cleanser for all housework, Ipana toothpaste for the perfect smile, and gentle Ivory soap. The ad for Armstrong's linoleum floors pictured a beautiful bathroom all done in blue, a sky-blue bathtub and flush toilet, all clean and shiny, spic-and-span blue floors. Bessie felt a great sadness, lying there in the dank, gray canvas tent, so crowded by the bed and boxes she could hardly have moved around even if the floor weren't muddy. The sharp pain of it almost overwhelmed her.

She pushed those feelings hard back into a numb corner of her being and turned the page, escaping the blue bathroom.

There on the next page was another teasing come-on, a bright red and yellow pitch for an "Exciting Crisco Slogan Contest" offering not one, but two five-thousand-dollar prizes. Crisco asked, "Are you one of the good cooks who's crazy about New Creamier Crisco? Do you stir up a cake in a jiffy now and get a cake so light and delicious that your family raves about it?" To win one of those five-thousand-dollar prizes you just had to write ten little words or less saying why Crisco was the best shortening ever, that's all, and there was a picture of a lady who had won five thousand dollars in last spring's contest, "Just when I needed the money the most."

Bessie rolled over, facing the wet-splotched canvas wall. She too needed the money the most, right now. The storm meant they were losing a day's wages, maybe two, and they couldn't afford that loss, not if they were going to pay off what they owed. Buying a cook stove for the house had been a mistake, they could have made do with the camp stove. She should have put her foot down, but the boys'd been so good about fixing up the kitchen and putting in the sinks and cupboards, she'd let them talk her into getting the stove. They were making good money, James Earl and Jake had argued, and besides, it was only a small stove. They'd spotted the stove in a secondhand store and it was a bargain at nineteen fifty, even if one leg was missing. They propped bricks under that corner and bought a new flue with a damper and some secondhand stovepipe. All told they'd spent near twenty-five dollars, more than a month's worth of house payments.

Wind shook the tent again and the rain was coming down steady now, reminding her that winter was not far off. With winter coming, they needed more time to put money by for the cold, foggy months when there was no work; Bessie wished now that when they'd signed the papers on the house they'd asked Judge Barkham to put the due date back to the last of November, after the cotton was all picked. October thirty-first was too soon. Anxiously she put the magazine aside and got out her tally book and pencil. The numbers told the story: With the hospital bill and what they still owed on the down payment, plus catching up on the regular monthly payment, they needed one hundred thirteen dollars, plus enough to buy groceries. On the other side of the tiny ledger, she expected the family could earn near three hundred dollars in the coming three weeks, if it didn't storm more and they all stayed healthy. That meant if nothing went wrong, nothing at all, there'd be enough to get them in the house. There was no give in those numbers, no room for accidents or a strike that could knock them out of work for God knows how long.

It was the strike threat that worried her, that and the approaching winter. She hadn't been able to put money aside to carry them through until work opened up again in late March; pruning would help, but what they made at that wouldn't be near enough. There was the cost of gasoline because they'd be living at home and driving a good ways to work and then they had to make the regular house payments. That was twelve sixty-eight a month. Bessie added in the food costs and other family expenses, knowing even before she got a total that they needed to put by four hundred dollars if they were going to get through the winter. Well the first worry was the house; they'd get the payments caught up, then see about getting through the winter after they were sure of having a roof over their heads.

It was a gamble. She knew that. Bessie snapped the tally book closed, determined they were going to move into that house. With the Lord's help and seven good, strong workers, they'd make it. Yesterday's picking tallies totaled just over ten dollars. The first day out and Jake was already picking close to three hundred pounds. That boy! Not yet sixteen and doing man's work when he ought to be in school. This was a hard-scrabble life that made the young ones grow up so awful fast. Just a boy, but already acting like a man, chasing after that girl, picking more cotton than most grown men.

Wednesday was clear and windy. By early afternoon the cotton was dry and they were back in the fields picking again. Thursday passed without any signs of the strike. On Friday morning, as Jake came into the barn to feed the horses, he heard the radio announcer chattering away: "The weather today is going to be clear and warming as a high pressure moves in off the coast . . ." Jake climbed up into the loft and forked hay to mares, scrambled back down the ladder and went into the tack room to get their grain, listening for news of the strike. The announcer machine-gunned through the market reports, then turned to the news: "This is the fourth day of the cotton strike and officials now estimate that as many as eight thousand pickers have walked off the job throughout the San Joaquin Valley. Here in Jefferson County the sheriff's office estimates that seventy-five percent of the cotton harvest has been shut down and, according to Associated Farmers spokesman Arthur Casperson in Sacramento, Jefferson County is now the focus of the Communist union's attack on all California agriculture.

"In other strike news, Sheriff Windy Scott has informed KMJ that Ronald Blue, the union agitator jailed Tuesday night on charges of destroying public property and vandalism, is really the well-known Communist activist and ex-convict Aaron Bluestein. Bluestein, forty-five, is also wanted by authorities in Yuba County on felony charges connected with the Marysville labor unrest during the peach harvest . . ."

Ron Blue. Aaron Bluestein. Jake wanted to talk to Junior, but he couldn't. Junior was living at the strike camp down in the south part of the county and was all the time busy with the strike, or so Jake guessed because he hadn't seen hide nor hair of his friend since Junior pulled out on Tuesday. Finished with his chores and breakfast, Jake went into the fields still thinking about what he'd heard on the radio. Aaron Bluestein was a Communist, whatever that was, and it sounded like he was sure enough headed back to San Quentin State Prison, unless somebody could spring him from that jail.

Working along, Jake mulled over ways of busting Aaron Bluestein out of jail. The simplest would be to hide that big nickel plated .44-40 down inside his overalls and walk right into the jail house. They'd never suspect a kid who was coming to visit a prisoner and when they weren't looking he'd pull that big hawgleg out and go to blazing away. The slugs would be zinging and whanging around the jail and the damn deputies would be running to save their asses and by Gawd if they stood their ground, BLAM! They'd be dead. The fantasy was richly satisfying and he relished each action, adding little details. He was the swashbuckling young cowboy fighting the bad guys. Scooping up the keys from a jailor's body, he unlocked the cells and the prisoners, once freed, were slapping him on the back and laughing, telling him he was a real hard case. Some of them joined his gang and together they fought farmers, and, like John Dillinger, robbed banks and gave money to the families that were going hungry and couldn't pay off their mortgages. Then, remembering that most folks didn't even have mortgages, he and his gang were helping them find little places of their own so they wouldn't have to be Okies no more. Clara was with him, fighting by his side, and they were like Bonnie and Clyde, only he had no idea where they'd be able to get a machine gun.

Sometime just before noon, a caravan of old jalopies slowed, then pulled off the county road and parked across from the Kakorian farm. Strikers climbed out of their cars and trucks, doors slammed and pickets milled around in the road, unfurling red banners, handing out homemade picket signs. Thirty, maybe thirty-five strikers spread out along the roadway. A picket captain was standing on the bed of a truck, shouting orders; another was up on the roof of a car. He raised a megaphone and yelled out across the cotton rows, "Strike! Come out! Stand with us against the growers!"

Surprised by the booming words, Jake looked up. The picket line was spreading out along the edge of the field and the people were yelling and chanting: "Strike! Strike! Come out! Don't work!"

Jake stood there. Several rows over he could see his father and Lige were talking to Mr. Kakorian, who was gesturing with his hands, pointing at the picket lines and then back toward his house.

"Hey, you all in there, come on out!" the pickets yelled. "Come out, there's a strike! Don't be scabs. Dirty scabs!"

Ertie and Lige nodded and the farmer left the field on the run. Ertie and Lige motioned for them all to go back to work and it wasn't long before they heard the sirens and saw three pickuploads of farmers following a sheriff's patrol car. Dust boiled up along the edge of the road as the pickups and patrol car skidded to a stop. The armed farmers jumped out and, taking a quick look at the situation, they went into the cottonfield, clubs and whips at the ready, deploying themselves in a line confronting the pickets.

Jake watched the picket captains standing atop the truck and the coupe and he could hear them yelling through their megaphones, warning the strikers to stay on the road, encouraging them to stand up to the growers. Off to one side, the two deputies had stayed in the patrol car and Jake could see one was talking on the radio. The lawman nodded, as if agreeing to some command, put the mike down, and the deputies climbed out of the car, unlimbering their truncheons. They beckoned to one of the farmers and, after a brief huddle, four more farmers were singled out to help the lawmen. Their targets were the strike leaders atop the truck and coupe. Led by the deputies, the five farmers pushed through the picket line, daring the strikers to even so much as raise their hands. Meeting no resistance crossing the road, they split up, one deputy leading three farmers to the truck, the others going for the striker up on the coupe.

A deputy yelled to the picket captain on the truck, "You! Up there. Get down. Now!"

The picket captain ignored the lawmen, ordering his pickets, "Stay in line! Don't move."

Two farmers swung ax handles at the picket captain's legs. He jumped back, but the third farmer had run around the truck and was there on the other side. With one hand, he swung his ax handle at the captain's knees, cutting him down like a stalk of wheat.

Two other farmers had jumped up on the coupe's running boards and were clubbing that striker, knocking his legs out from under him. The striker's megaphone flew up in the air and he tumbled down over the hood and onto the ground. A deputy pinned him to the pavement and handcuffed him.

The picket captain had been jerked off the truck and he too was handcuffed, but not subdued. He screamed, "Fuck you!" and spit at one of the deputies.

All of the other strikers, caught between the ranks of farmers in the field and the vigilantes and deputies, stood frozen, uncertain. Farmers yelled threats and insults, trying to coax them into a free-for-all that would break up the picket line.

Seeing what was happening, the picket captain yelled to his people, "Stay'n line. Git back! Stay outa this!"

A deputy jabbed his truncheon into the picket captain's gut, knocking the wind out of the man. As the striker sagged, gasping for air, the deputy jerked him over to the patrol car and stuffed him into the backseat. The second strike leader was pushed into the car and the door slammed. The deputies conferred with the farmers briefly, then jumped into their car and sped off with the prisoners, siren wailing. The farmer-vigilantes stayed on the farm and Kakorian was with them now, confronting the leaderless strikers who had broken ranks and were milling angrily about, not quite certain what to do. A young striker not much older than Jake grabbed up a fallen megaphone and started yelling, "Git back in line! 'Member what Sam said! Stay in line! We gotta show 'em!"

And a shout went up, "Strike! Strike!" Some of the strikers began to reform the picket line, confronting the farmers. Others hesitated.

Jake, sensing the critical moment, threw off his cotton sack and raced across the rows to his father. "Pa, we gotta do somethin', quick!"

Ertie either didn't hear Jake, or was ignoring his son, his attention riveted on the strike line. Hatred sparkled in his eyes.

"Pa! Goddammit, we gotta strike! Now! Ya seen what they done."

Ertie shrugged out of his cotton sack and, for an instant, it looked like he was ready to walk out.

Out on the road the pickets were milling around again, angry. A few screamed at the farmers and hurled insults at Jake and the others, calling Bessie and the girls "dirty scab bitches."

Ignoring the insults, Jake tried to urge his father. "Kakorian's in it too, see 'im standin' there with the rest of them bastards."

Bessie came hurrying up. "Boy, go on back to work. This ain' none of our doin'."

"Hell it ain't!"

"Jake Robertson, you git back to work, right now. Mr. Kakorian ain't gone back on his word, an' neither will we."

Jake looked at his father.

Enraged, Ertie stood there immobile, caught between the twin furies of his hatred for those club-swinging farmers and his anger over the pickets' insults. Nobody talked about his wife and daughters that way, goddammit. Fuck 'em! As for the damn farmers, he'd kill any son of a bitch that come at him with a club, but this wasn't his fight. "Go back to work, all of ya!" he yelled, turning furiously back to picking cotton.

Disgusted, Jake stomped back through the rows, but he couldn't pick, not now. They should have walked out, hit back. Dropping to his knees Jake punched the near-full cotton sack, punched it hard again and again, pounding it with his fists like his father should've done those damn farmers. Once he would have done it too, would have fought 'em then told 'em to go straight to hell and walked off, but not now. It was like he didn't know his Pa anymore and it seemed like the family was sinking deeper in a quicksand bog that had no bottom. Exhausted by his furies, Jake collapsed onto the sack, sobbing.

How long he lay there he couldn't say, but suddenly he realized the field was silent. The strikers were gone. So were the farmers and with them went the chance to get even. Slowly, sadly he went back to picking, wishing he could make his parents see that alone, nobody could win this thing. The only way to get free was to strike. Somehow he had to convince his father, because if Ertie ordered it, his mother had no choice but to go along. And, after they'd won the strike, there'd be time enough to make money and pay off the railroad house.

Sometime later the sound of his mother's voice surprised him. "What?"

She was picking in the row next to his and stood now, looking at him, speaking softly. "Boy, I know ya think Junior's a-doin' the right thang, but a strike right now ain' nothin' but trouble for us."

"But Ma, we ain' trash." Angry tears burned his eyes. "I ain' goin' to be treated that away. Junior says that—"

"Hush." Bessie slipped out of her sack and stepped through the row and put her arms around him. "Yor right, we ain' trash an' we ain' goin' on livin' like trash. We almost got us our own place again, a home where we can be people. I know it's been hard, but honey, we're goin' ta make it." She squeezed him. "We gotta be strong. Ain' nobody goin' help us, no union, nobody. All we got's ourselves, an' with God's help, we'll get off this ol' road, put roots down. You understand?"

Sunday was a day off, a chance to work on the house. With the help of the Parsons, they were digging a trench out back for the sink drain and gravel-packed leach line. While James Earl plumbed the drainpipe out of the house, Junior and the rest of the men piled into Lige's truck and headed up along the river to find the gravel. That took most of the morning, but not long after noon the truck rumbled in off the county road and wheeled around back of the house, brakes squealing. The men climbed out, slamming doors behind them.

Bessie, R'becky and the girls had a spread of food ready for them, beans flavored with chunks of hamhock, cornbread and molasses and coffee strong enough to float a flatiron. Bessie yelled to them, "Come on, let's eat before y'all shovel off that load."

There was no furniture in the house yet, so they sat on the floor or ate standing at the drainboard. At first there was little talk, just the sound of spoons scraping and mouths smacking, but after the last bit of cornbread had sopped up the bean juice and they were on their second cups of coffee Jake told Junior about how the pickets had come to Kakorian's place.

Junior lit a cigarette. "Hell, what'd ya expect?"

"Junior Parsons, you got no call to be swearing," R'becky admonished her son sharply.

"Sorry, Ma. But y'all gotta expect picketing. We stop wherever they see anybody workin'."

"Ya always call womenfolk names?" Ertie asked in disgust.

That stopped the conversation.

Junior looked puzzled. "What d'ya mean?"

"Some of them pickets was cussin' yor ma there an' Bessie an' the girls, callin' names, that's what I mean!" Ertie eyed Junior coldly.

Junior hung his head for a moment, then looked Ertie right back. "I'm sorry 'bout that. They ain' supposed to say nothin' like that, but ya gotta remember, some of them folks was beaten up, throwed in jail to make a union an' when they see y'all workin', breakin' their strike, they gits mad. They got no call to say names, I ain' makin' 'xcuses, but ya gotta understand how they feel too."

Ertie just looked at him, not saying anything.

Lige tried to shift the conversation. "Son, don' it matter that Kakorian's payin' a dollar?"

"Some of us think we oughta leave little farmers like him alone, them few that's payin' higher wages, but most folks don' think it's fair, y'all workin' and them not."

"What's fair 'bout walkin' out on a man that's treated ya right? Goin' back on yor word to 'im?" Bessie spoke harshly, surprising even herself. "Sorry. But it's gotta be said. We got payments to make. We can't go off strikin' for somethin' we already got. That don' make sense."

"I ain' sayin' y'all should strike." Junior backed off, not wanting to start an argument. "It's jus' that we got orders to picket wherever thar's people workin'."

"What happened to them two fellas they arrested, the ones with the bullhorns?" Jake asked.

"Got 'em in jail. They—"

"Stop it." R'becky cut Junior off. "There's too much of this strike talk. I'm tired of it."

Lige put his plate and cup in the dishpan and picked up a bucket, starting to pour water over the dishes. "We best be unloadin' that truck."

Bessie was quickly up, taking the bucket from Lige. "Leave that be. You men go on. Jake there can fetch me another bucket of water from the neighbors' tank, they said to use what we needed."

By early afternoon they had graveled in the perforated drainpipe and all that remained was to backfill dirt into the trench. Junior couldn't stay. Apologetically he said he had to get back to the strike camp to get some things, they had a big rally planned that evening in the park. "Y'all're welcome to come. It ain' like you'd be joinin' up or anything. Just come an' listen, that's all. Lots of folks do."

No one took Junior up on his invitation but Jake, and he had to do it on the quiet, catching Junior as he, Maybelle and the twins went out the front door. "Can I go along?"

"Folks know about it?"

"I can tell 'em you're droppin' me off at Kakorian's and I'm gonna ride my bike over to see Clara."

"Okay by me."

Jake ran back into the house. "Ma? Pa? Junior says he'll gimme a ride back to Mr. Kakorian's if it's okay with you. Can I please? I wanna go see Clara."

"Shor, go ahead." Ertie nodded.

Jake looked pleadingly at his mother.

She smiled sadly. "Go on."

Jake dashed back out front, opened the rumble seat in the trunk of Junior's coupe and jumped in. Sitting back there reminded him of riding in the open cockpit of an airplane and when the twins saw him climbing into the rumble seat, they begged to join him. Junior grinned and lifted them up over the rear fender to Jake who plunked them down, one on either side, and put an arm around each child. "Hang on!"

The girls giggled and clung excitedly to Jake's arms. As they drove off, Jake looked back and saw Susie standing there by the house, looking mad and hurt. Damn, he'd clean forgot her in the scramble to get permission to go.

It was nearly an hour's ride to the strike camp. Driving through the front gate, Jake was awed by the size of the layout. The camp really was a tent city, like Junior had said, with blocks and blocks of tents and old cars and trucks parked along the dirt streets and there were people everywhere, going about their Sunday-afternoon chores or just lazying around. Junior's tent was three streets down from the main gate and off to the east side, near a dirt playing field. A noisy crowd was watching and cheering a softball game. Out beyond the playing field Jake could see two big circus tents and rows of tables and benches, all set out under canvas awnings.

Junior pulled up in front of his tent and stopped. As he helped the girls down from the rumble seat, Jake asked, "What's them two big tents an' tables over thar?"

"One's the commissary, where folks gits groceries, an' the other one's the kitchen tent. Ever' mornin' and evenin' they feed folks there that ain' cookin' for theirselves."

"It's all free?"

"Shor. Strikers ain' makin' no money to buy groceries." Junior turned toward his camp. "Won' be but a minute."

Jake drifted off a ways, gawking at the camp. He knew from talking to Junior and hearing the radio that the strike was big, but Christ, he'd had no idea it was this big.

Junior came back carrying boxes of leaflets. He dumped them in the rumble seat, slammed the trunk closed and climbed back in the car, yelling at Jake, "Come on!"

Surprised, Jake asked, "Ain' Maybelle and the kids comin'?"

"No. Get in." Junior stepped on the starter button and the old Chevy growled, backfired with a loud BANG and clattered to life in a billow of blue smoke. As they drove out of camp, Junior yelled over the engine noise, explaining that Maybelle didn't like taking the twins to the rallies because they didn't get home until late and then too, it could get dangerous.

"Ya expecting a big crowd this evenin'?" Jake yelled.

"Yeah!"

"Heard on the radio that the unions got seventy-five percent of the harvest shut down. That right?"

"More, maybe. Ain' no way of knowin'." Junior glanced over at Jake. "Jus' about time ya figger ya've got thangs shut down on a place, ya find a whole bunch of scabs workin' off somewheres else. Some of these farms's so big ya never know where they'll be workin' next."

"What happened to that fella Ron Blue?"

"Still in jail. Looks bad for 'im."

"I know, I heard on the radio that his real name's Aaron Bluestein or somethin' like that, an' he's got a record."

"Yeah, that's right. Did two years in San Quentin a while back. Busted 'im for union work, like they did this time." Junior pulled out a pack of cigarettes and gave Jake one.

"How come ya called 'im Ron Blue, then?"

" 'Cause he didn't want the laws to know who he was."

"He tell ya that?" Jake asked.

"Yeah, he got throwed in jail with us at the parade. Remember?" Junior inhaled deeply and blew the smoke out through his nose. "That was scary, I'll tell ya. None of us'd ever been in jail before, 'cept for Aaron. He kept talkin' to us when the guards couldn't hear, warned us not never to fight back, not in jail. Jus' go along easy. He shor knowed the ropes."

Junior stopped talking for a minute, then went on, "When they locked us up in that cell, that was when Aaron tol' us who he really was. Round the union, he was always kinda quiet like and we thought he was standoffish, but there in jail he'd talk, if ya asked him somethin'. Tell ya anythin' ya wanted to know.

"We had a lot of time to talk, le'me tell ya." Junior seemed so used to the car noise he didn't notice that they had to yell to be heard. "Turned out Aaron, he was from New York City. His daddy was a professor at some college or other, but Aaron he quit college and joined up with an outfit called the International Workers of the World, took up with an old-time organizer named Blackie Ford."

Jake had difficulty hearing parts of the monologue because of the engine clatter and roar of the broken muffler, but as they drove across the county a picture of Aaron Bluestein began to emerge. Junior told how Aaron had been with Ford up in the Dakota wheat harvests in 1913 and they'd ridden freight trains into California, landing in Sacramento. From there they hitched their way to the hop harvest up near Wheatland. There were maybe two thousand people squatting in a godawful camp on a ranch out of town a ways and maybe work enough for half that many. That starved-out camp was hell, the way Junior described it, and he said Ford, Aaron and another fella were there, trying to organize a strike when a posse came storming down on them, shooting. They killed a little boy who was going for a pail of water. Some of the workers in camp had guns too and they started shooting back. When the gunfight was over another worker and two lawmen lay dead. Blackie Ford was captured and sentenced to life for murder, even though he never carried a gun. Aaron got away, but a couple years later he was arrested in another strike and sent up. Now that they had him jailed again, likely they'd throw the key away this time, Junior said.

"Hell, he didn't do . . ." Jake shouted, but didn't finish the sentence.

Junior glanced over at Jake, but when he didn't say anything more Junior went on, "Way Aaron figgers it, them two town kids he saw in the bushes thar that night, they must of cut them tires."

"You talk to him?" Jake had a fearful knot in his stomach.

"Naw, but Mr. Wirin, our lawyer, got in to see 'im, said Aaron wasn't sure what'd happened, but it wasn't till after he'd seen them kids that all hell broke loose."

The knot in Jake's gut cinched down tighter. He wanted to tell Junior, confess that he'd been the one who cut the tires, but he was afraid to go to jail.

They were quiet for a while, then Junior started talking again about the union and how much profits the farmers were making. Jake sat there listening and watching the farmlands whizz by the window. When Junior got to going on like this there wasn't any stopping him. Jake squirmed in the seat, uncomfortable because he wanted to come clean, but he couldn't find the words to confess his part in the arrest of Aaron Bluestein. So he kept quiet.

They arrived in Jeff City at sunset. The evening was cool and there was the smell of burning leaves in the air. Not far from the park a rattletrap truck loaded with strikers had conked out smack-dab in the middle of Main Street. The driver was out bending over the front bumper, trying to crank-start the engine as traffic detoured slowly around the disabled vehicle. Up in the back of the truck two dozen cotton pickers were leaning over the sideboards shouting strike slogans at the passing cars. Junior tooted his horn in support of the stranded strikers and edged past the truck. Turning south on H, he drove along the park's western edge. The streets were crowded with workers and their families heading into the park.

"Look at 'em all," Jake yelled.

"Folks is comin' in from Fresno and Tulare counties too. Union thought it'd be a good idea to have a big get-together right here in Jeff City, let them farmers see we got the people on our side."

Junior turned left, passed the jail and turned right again onto a side street. There were cars everywhere and it was three blocks before they could find a place to park. Junior pulled into the curb and switched off the engine. Jake impulsively shouted over the dying engine noise, "Gotta tell ya somethin'!"

The engine backfired and was silent.

"It was me!" Jake yelled in the startling quiet. Embarrassed, he lowered his voice and tried again, almost whispering now, "It was me that slashed them tires that night, not Mr. Bluestein."

Junior nodded wisely. "I wondered maybe it was somethin' like that. After Aaron said he'd seen two kids over there in the bushes, I 'membered you and Susie'd come runnin' up lookin' all scared."

"I meant to tell ya before, honest, but . . ." Jake squirmed in the seat. "This mean I gotta go to jail?"

"Don' know, Jake. We gotta talk to C. J. and Mr. Wirin." They were silent for a while, then Junior asked, "What were you doin' thar anyways?"

"Ah, shit, me an' Susie was jis' tryin' to see what was goin' on. Didn' mean no harm, but when I heared them laws laughin' 'bout shootin' down that Cletus Sharp fella like he wasn't no more'n a damn dog, I got mad."

"They said somethin' 'bout the shootin'?"

"Yeah, that's what got me so mad. I never meant to do nothin' like that."

Junior opened the car door. "Come on, let's go."

"Junior?"

"Yeah?"

"I wisht I hadn't done it."

"Wisht ya hadn't neither. Come on." Junior got out and opened up the trunk. "Here, help me carry some of them boxes and we'll go find Mr. Wirin, see what they says."

They cut through an alley and, coming out on the next street, Jake saw a large gray-green building, a meeting hall or church of some kind. There were a few mud-spattered pickups and fancy cars in the parking lot behind the building and, although it wasn't dark yet, the lights were on inside.

"What's goin' on over thar?" Jake hurried, trying to keep up with Junior.

"That there's the Eagles Club, where the farmers hold their meetin's."

"That the place Mr. Bluestein snuck into?"

"Yup."

Crossing Sixth Street they could see fifteen or twenty uniformed deputies standing around out in front of the jail. Two white motorcycles roared by, ridden by state highway patrolmen uniformed in tan and wearing high black boots.

In the park the lights were on and people were milling about or standing in groups, talking or listening to a lively group of fiddlers, banjo players and guitar pickers up on the bandstand playing a jaunty tune.

Back of the bandstand the union had roped off an area and set up chairs and tables. "There's C. J." Junior set his boxes down on one of the tables. "Come on."

Apprehensive now, Jake put his load down and followed.

Junior pulled the union leader aside. "Seen Al Wirin? Gotta talk to ya both."

"What's up?" C. J. eyed Jake curiously.

"It's about Aaron. Let's find Al, then I'll tell ya both at once. Oh, this here's Jake, Jake Robertson."

"Howdy, boy."

Jake shook C. J.'s big, callused hand.

Wirin was over on the far side of the bandstand, talking to some workers. C. J. caught his eye and as the lawyer came over, introduced him. "Al, ya remember Junior, and this 'ere's Jake Robertson. Judgin' by his hands, he's still pickin' cotton."

The lawyer shook Jake's hand. "How much can you pick, boy?"

"Made near three fifty yesterday."

C. J. shot a questioning look at Junior.

Junior nodded and gave Jake a friendly pat on the back. "He ain' foolin'. Jake here's a hell of a cotton picker."

"Boy, don't ya know there's a strike on?"

"Yessir." Jake looked up at C. J., feeling miserable.

"What was it you wanted, C. J. ?" Wirin's voice was soft, but impatient. He was a thin, studious little man in a rumpled suit who had an intense, furiously quiet way about him.

C. J. looked at Jake. "Go ahead, tell 'im, boy."

"Sir"—Jake's voice quavered—"it was me that slashed them tars," the words were rushing, "but I never shot out no windas. Deputies was shootin' at me. Was them that blowed out the winda." Jake gulped and added, "Wisht I hadn' done it, but sir, they was laughin' about killin' that fella an'—"

"Who was laughing about the killing?"

"Them laws."

"Did they say why he was shot?"

"Naw, they was—"

"Think. Really think about it for a minute. Did you hear them say what happened before they shot Cletus Sharp?"

Jake shook his head. "Naw, all I 'member is a city cop was standin' with a deputy an' they'd heard that big nigger from the union givin' his speech. It made 'em mad an' the cop he said that the nigger was gonna get hisself killed talkin' that-a-way. Said they oughta shoot 'im jus' like they done that Okie."

Wirin nodded. "Did they say who shot him?"

"I don' 'member no names. Susie—she's my sister—she was grabbin' at me, sayin' we gotta get out of there. An' I wisht I'd just run, but damn, I jis' had ta get back at 'em, so I cut up their tars, only I didn' know it would make so much noise and I got scared and took off runnin' . . ." Jake's voice trailed off.

"Well, that lets Aaron off the hook," C. J. said.

Wirin looked at C. J. "What do you mean?"

"Gives him an alibi, when he comes up for trial."

"Not necessarily. Even if the district attorney's office believed Jake, do you think they'd drop the charges against Aaron? Not likely. They'd say that Aaron put the boy up to it and charge him with conspiracy anyway." Wirin turned to Jake. "Come on, son, I want to talk to you. Alone."

The lawyer took Jake off a ways and sat down on the grass, directing Jake to sit beside him. Jake obeyed, still frightened. The lawyer seemed different now, more friendly somehow, and when he spoke the words weren't so impatient. "Jake, I want you to understand that I am Aaron's attorney. That means I must do everything I can to help him. I also want you to know that what you have told me is privileged. That means what you have said is just between you and me, and no one else. Ethically, I am not allowed to talk about what you said to anyone, not even the law. Do you understand?"

Jake nodded, although he really didn't understand what was happening.

"What you've told me is a big help because now I know what happened. That will help me defend Aaron. And, knowing that you know what happened, I must ask you to think about whether you can testify in court when Aaron goes to trial. I can't force you to testify, that must be your choice. At this point, I don't even know if your testimony would be helpful. Nor can I tell you what to do. When we decide what we are going to do I will talk to you again, and at that time I think it would be wise if we got you a lawyer of your own."

"Mister, I ain' got no money for lawyers." Jake's voice was desperate now.

Wirin laughed, kindly. "I know that. The ACLU, the people I work for, will send one up from Los Angeles, if I ask. There'll be no charge. You said your sister was with you? You can tell her what we've talked about, but make sure that she understands that none of this should be discussed with anyone else. Until we decide what to do, we'll keep this to ourselves. Okay?"

Jake gulped. "Do I have to go to jail?"

Wirin laughed. "No, I don't think so."

"Kin ya tell Mr. Bluestein I'm sorry?"

"You can tell him yourself, when we get him out."

"Get 'im out?" Jake's voice had real enthusiasm in it.

"We're going to try." Wirin got up and led the way back to where they'd left Junior and C. J.

As they walked up, a man leaned over the bandstand railing and yelled at C. J., "You gonna start this meetin'? Or do you wan' me to?"

"Hold yor pants on, I'll be there in a minute." C. J. faced Jake and put both hands on the boy's shoulders. "Boy, what you done was understandable, but dumb. I ain't talkin' right or wrong. I'm sayin' what you done caused more problems for Aaron and the union than it solved. Can ya see that?"

"Yes sir."

"Since you're a friend of Junior's here, ya may be thinkin' 'bout joinin' up with the union. That's fine. We want everyone to join, but I don' wanna hear that ya done any more dumb things like slashing tars. Okay?"

"Yes sir."

C. J. slapped him on the back—"Good"—and went up the stairs to start the meeting.

Junior had gone off somewhere and Jake was alone. Really alone and sorry he'd gone off without Susie. He drifted aimlessly through the crowd, paying little attention to the sounds of the meeting booming over the public address system. Somebody named Reuther had been introduced, and he was at the microphone giving a speech: ". . . the Congress appropriated money for the farmers' welfare, only they called it a 'crop subsidy' and Roosevelt is spending millions building dams and canals and fixing up highways right here in this valley and the politicians call that 'progress.' But when they have to cough up a miserable little bit of money to feed hungry people they call that 'relief' or 'welfare' . . ."

Jake headed for the parrots' cage, shuffling along slowly.

Someone called his name. "Jake?"

He looked around, surprised.

"Jake?" Clara ran up.

"Wha'cha doin' here?"

She was in his arms, happy tears streaming down her face, explaining that she was living in the strike camp. Her whole family had moved out of Camp Six so fast there'd been no way to let him know where she was going.

"Yor living in the strike camp?"

"Yeah, 'cause Pa, he got into it with that big crew boss over that bunch a niggers they put down at one end of our camp. Had them niggers workin' right in the same fields as us too. Grandpa, he refused to pick cotton, said he wouldn't go into no damn field with them niggers. That's when that crew boss told Grandpa he'd either pick cotton or git the hell out. Pa, he jumped right in, grabbed up a stick and was threatenin' to brain the crew boss but that fella's so big he jerked the stick away from Pa, slapped 'im down an' tol' us to git out of camp.

"Grandpa was so mad he grabbed up his shotgun, swearin' he would kill that big lard-ass crew boss." Clara giggled. "That's what he called 'im, a lard-ass. But Grandpa, he clean forgot he ain' got no more shells for that 'ere gun an' that crew boss fella, he wasn't afeard, noway, just jerked that shotgun away from Grandpa and smashed it against a big cast-iron pot Ma had settin' by the fire. Gawd it was funny, Grandpa and Pa backin' off, that big crew boss comin' at 'em swearin' he'd pound sand up their asses with a shovel if they wasn't outa camp by suppertime.

"We was out of there quick as we could pack up and all the time Pa, he was sayin' that by Gawd we'd help the union shut the whole harvest down. That'd fix Wardlow an' that big, dumb ox and so we moved right over to the strikers' camp. But Jake, honey, I was worried sick. How was I gonna find ya?" Clara had been talking rapidly. Suddenly she stopped, then asked, "Wha'cha doin' here?"

"Come with Junior." Jake took her hand. "Come on." He led her over into the dark and they kissed and talked. He told her about Aaron Bluestein and talking with Mr. Wirin, the union attorney, and she hushed him and clung to him with a kind of urgency that wasn't sexual, pleading with him not to say anything to anyone else. "Jake, honey, ya shouldn't even a tol' me."

"But Clara, that man's in jail 'cause of me."

"No he ain'. They're a-puttin' all them agitators in jail. Just lookin' for excuses. He'd been arrested one way or 'nother. Honey, it ain' yor fault an' if they find out, they'd just put ya in jail right along with 'im." Clara hugged him hard. "Oh, Jake, I'm so scared of losin' you."

Jake couldn't think of anything to say, but he was wondering if she could come stay with them. What would Ma say? Well, at least they had a mailing address now. "Look, no matter what happens, if we get split up, you gotta promise you'll write me a letter an' send it to the Hyattville post office. Just write it to me, general delivery, then that way I'd know where ya was an' could maybe come git ya."

"Oh, Jake!" She kissed him again, happy suddenly.

Her sudden burst of enthusiasm was infecting. Jake tugged on her hand. "Come on, I gotta show ya somethin'!"

They took off running.

"Whar we goin'?"

"I'll show ya." He ran along the path to the aviary and pointed. "Here!"

"What?"

"Parrots."

"I seen 'em."

"Heard 'em talk?" Jake looked for the green and yellow Amazon that had been the most talkative. "There! There's the one. Hey, Numb-nutz."

The bird cocked its head at the sound of Jake's voice.

"Numb-nutz," Jake called again.

Clara giggled.

The bird flew to a perch close to Jake, "Awk! Numb-nutz!"

Clara laughed. "Oh, Jake!"

"Oh, Jake!" the parrot mimicked her words.

Jake ran to a nearby trash can, rummaged through it.

"What're ya doin'?"

"Lookin' for somethin' to feed it." He found a nearly empty box of Crackerjacks and ran back to the cage. The parrot snapped at the offerings as Jake chummed it. "Shitty bird!"

Clara giggled.

"Shitty bird!" The Amazon cocked his head and imitated Clara's giggle.

Clara was laughing now. "Jake!"

"Jake!" the parrot mimicked.

Jake grinned and, feeding the bird more Crackerjacks, he tried for the big one: "Fuck you!"

"Fuck you!"

Several other youngsters were gathering around as Jake fed the parrot more Crackerjacks, attracting other Amazons and brilliant-hued macaws. The birds clustered around, begging.

"Awk! Fuck you."

Suddenly fear was in Clara's voice. "Jake!"

"Jake!" A parrot sounded the fear.

Clara was looking down the path that curved in toward the center of the park. Two deputies were patrolling toward them.

Jake grabbed Clara's arm. "Let's git out of here." They ducked around the cage and into the bushes.

An Amazon squawked, "Fuck you!"

The other kids scattered.

Ten feet away the deputies heard the parrot and stopped dead. There was no mistaking the words. The taller deputy shook his head in disbelief. "Christ, did you hear that?"

"Christ," a parrot screeched, and others sidled up, hoping the deputies had more Crackerjacks. "Fuck you!"

The second deputy, a short, chubby fellow with a happy face, started laughing and slapping his taller partner on the back. "Shit, Harv, I think that one bird's hot for your pants."

"Shit, Harv! Awk. Fuck you."

"George, that ain't funny." Deputy Harv was embarrassed and angry. "It was them damn Okie kids. They been teachin' these here birds to cuss."

"Shit, Harv!"

"Fuck you!"

The chubby deputy was laughing so hard he damn near peed his pants. Grabbing his crotch, he doubled over, trying to catch his breath, but he couldn't stop laughing, "Haw haw haw haw."

"Dammit, George, it ain't funny. What if there's women and kids around. We gotta tell the sergeant about this."

"Shitty bird!"

"Oh shit." The words wooshed out of George and he wiped the tears out of his eyes. "Should have seen the look on your face when that bird said . . ."

"Don't say it," Harv hissed at his partner, hand to his own mouth in warning. "Don' say nothin'. Let's get out of here. We got to report this to the sergeant."

The deputies took off for the command post.

"Fuck you! Awk!" The parrots, feeling cheated, set up a ruckus, trying to call the deputies back. "Fuck you!"

Jake and Clara were hiding in the bushes not far away, laughing and holding their sides. "Oh, God Jake, didja see the way that tall skinny one looked?"

Jake gasped for breath, tears streaming down his face.

"They gonna bring that sergeant back, ya reckon?"

"I wanna see that."

"No." Clara had stopped laughing. "Let's git outa here 'fore they catch us."

"Aw, Clara, le's see if that sergeant comes over."

"Jake!" Clara was exasperated. "Come on!"

It was dark now as they made their way through the crowd. Passing into the deep shadow of a tall elm, Jake stopped and pulled Clara to him and kissed her, feeling the warmth of her body pressed close. They kissed, deeply, and his hands cupped the rounds of her butt.

"Jake, don't." She pulled away. "Thar's too many people watchin'."

"They cain' see us." He pulled her close again.

"No, let's find some'eres else."

Trucks roared by on the highway and the voices of the union speakers echoed through the park. Clara led the way out of the park and down an alley. They found her father's worn-out sedan and there on the broken springs in the backseat they made love and talked and made love again and planned how they could be together.

She clutched him closer to her. "Jake?"

"Yeah?"

She looked into his eyes, pleading. "Le's run off'n get married. We kin do it. I know we can."

Jake hugged her, frightened and hurting too. "Clara, I don' wanna lose ya, but how can we run off? We got no money, no car."

"We can hitch. Get jobs an' buy us a car. Ma, she wasn't no older'n me when she married Pa." Clara's voice quavered.

"Yeah, but you said he was way older'n her."

"Don' ya wanna git married?"

"Shor I do. Honest." And he meant it. When she had first proposed, back at Bull's Camp, the thought of marriage had startled him. But now he yearned to be with her and that meant marriage, he was certain of it, even daydreamed about it sometimes, thinking they would live in a house and he'd work in a garage, fixing cars, but the idea of going off on his own right now with a wife and maybe having babies was too unsettling. Besides, they wouldn't ever be any better off if they didn't win this damn strike. Maybe when it was over, then they could plan something, he argued, explaining, "Clara, the only way them farmers is gonna pay us what we got comin' is if we fight 'em. Union's gotta win this strike."

Clara pushed him away, angered by the way he always slipped away from the idea of marriage.

They sat there in silence, both uncomfortable, uncertain. Jake thought of how Camp Six had been a long bike ride from Kakorian's and how getting to the strike camp that way was out of the question. Collins Corners was way down in the south part of the county. But if he was living at the strike camp too they could be together every night. Jake suddenly sat up. "If I joined the union too, I could stay with Junior."

"Would he let ya?"

"Shor he would. I could help the union, like Aaron Bluestein did."

"What do ya mean?"

"Spy on the farmers."

"Jake, you're crazy."

"No, I could do 'er. Come on, I'll show ya. It ain' far."

Jake knew they were only a few blocks from the Eagles Hall, but it took him a while to find the right street. "There! That's the place, up the street there."

"Where? Wha'cha talkin' 'bout?"

"That building there, that's it." The Eagles Hall was all lit up and now there were a lot more cars and pickups in the parking lot and along the street. "Farmers's havin' a big meetin' there right now. Come on." He had her hand, leading the way. The night was dark and they stayed on the opposite side of the street, keeping to the shadows.

"Jake, wha'cha gonna do?" Clara was whispering, even though they were still a half block away.

"Injun up an' slip through one of them basement windows, jis' like Mr. Bluestein."

"No you ain'! This is crazier'n puttin' that snake in the nurse's office. Jake, they'll kill ya if they catch ya."

"Clara, I gotta. Don' ya see. It's me that got 'im in jail, so's the least I kin do is try to do his job." They were directly across the street from the Eagles Hall now.

Through the windows he could see that the main auditorium on the first floor was jam-packed with farmers and out front, on the porch, there were a whole bunch of strangers hanging around. Even in the pale, shadowy light of the streetlamp, Jake could see these fellows weren't from around here, they had on city clothes.

Jake glanced up and down the street. No one was coming either way. He turned to Clara. "You stay here an' look out. If they catch me, you run tell Junior, or C. J."

"Jake! No!" Clara was trying to keep her voice down. "I don' even know no C. J. an' ain't sure which one Junior is. Come on, let's get out of here."

But Jake didn't wait. He ducked off, running low, his shadow flickering across the street. He slipped between parked pickups and was quickly in the dark of the building, his back pressed against the wall.

The hall was a long shoebox of a building with false parapets, one of those structures that had the first floor raised four or five feet above ground level, leaving space underneath for a large basement that had windows. The top halves of the basement windows were above ground level and were dark; the lower halves were recessed in cement wells that collected fallen leaves and debris. That was the way Aaron snuck in, through one of these basement windows, but which one? Jake pressed against the wall, wondering. Overhead he could hear people moving about in the main auditorium and the scraping of chairs on the wooden floor. Light from the first-floor windows cast yellow patterns and shadows across the sidewalk and lawn. Jake quickly let himself down into one of the window wells, feeling for the bottom with his feet, hoping there was no broken glass down there. The window well was only waist deep and the bottom was soft with decaying leaves. He knelt and felt the steel window frame, trying to find a way to pull it open. The window wouldn't budge. He got out his pocket-knife, opened the long blade and slipped it through the crack, feeling for the catch. Still no luck.

Out on the sidewalk shoe leather scraped cement and he heard voices, arguing. Jake crouched deep in the window well, holding his breath as two men walked by, one swearing, saying, "Fuck 'em. Let's get on back and have a drink," but the other said, "No. We gotta hang around." The sounds of the shoes faded. Jake put his knife away and raised up cautiously, peeking quickly around. Heart pounding, mouth dry as cotton, he hoisted himself up out of the well. Maybe Aaron had left another one of the windows unlatched. He lowered himself into the next recess and the next, trying each window, but they were all locked. Furtively, he slipped around the back corner of the building and crouched there. Above him there was a wooden stairway going up to the rear entrance to the main floor; in front of him a stairwell led down to the basement door and a rack full of garbage cans. The main-floor windows were dark, indicating there was some kind of room or partition between this entrance and the well-lighted meeting hall up front. Jake ducked quickly down into the protective darkness of the lower area and tried the basement door. It was locked. How the hell did Bluestein get in? Pocketknife out, he tried to force the door lock. It was quiet back here and the scratching, digging knife blade scraped loudly.

Overhead the meeting noises were softly muted. Then they were suddenly louder, as if someone had turned the volume up, and footsteps thudded across the floor above him. Bolts rattled in the upstairs back door and it banged open. Jake scrunched down between the garbage cans, peering up, not daring to breathe. Two men were standing directly over him, on the back stoop.

"Titus, you can't leave them out."

"The hell I can't. Look, Major, I said no goddamn reporters. They've got no right to come pushing in here, it's a private meeting."

"But it's the—"

"I don't give a good goddamn if they *are* from *The New York Times* or the *San Francisco News*. Fuck 'em."

"But you've let Sam James from the Jeff City *Tribune* in to cover the meeting and they know it."

"Sam's okay," Wardlow growled. "All those fucking big-city reporters want are headlines to sell their goddamn newspapers."

"You keep them out and you'll have headlines. Every major paper in the country's out there. *The New York Times, Chicago Daily News, San Francisco News*, the whole bunch."

"Why? That's what I want to know."

"Reuther brought them. They were all at the CIO convention up in San Francisco and he sees a chance to get his name in the paper, so he's sold them on the idea there's a story here. Titus, those are the big guns out there. If they think you're hiding something, you'll have headlines, all right. The union's already had them out on the picket lines and in the strike camp."

A match flared and Jake could smell cigar smoke.

"But listen, Titus, you can use the press. You've got Colonel Winchester in there to hear what the farmers have to say, what better way to send a message to the governor than the front page of *The New York Times*. Use Professor Grogin's figures, show them that it takes nine cents to grow cotton and pick it, but the market price is only eight cents. Show them that it is the Communists who are running this strike, you've got one in jail and that evidence from Marysville.

"Let Winchester know in no uncertain terms that you want the governor to put a stop to this strike once and for all, before the situation gets out of control and local authorities have to act to put down this rebellion, legally and by the book. This is a perfect opportunity, you've got Winchester here anyway, and he'll deliver any message you give him. But think about it, which is going to pressure the governor more, a quiet report from a staff aide? Or headlines from coast to coast? That's the national press out there, use them. Their story will make the wires: beleaguered farmers trying to save their crops. Give it to them in simple terms: heroic farmers who feed and clothe America threatened by an unfair strike. Remember, you're not opposed to unions, you are on the side of the working man. Hell, you work beside them in the fields and you are willing to be fair with them. But the time to talk is later, not now, during the harvest. Strikes at harvest are unfair, the Communists know that is when farmers are the most vulnerable . . ."

"All right, all right! Shut up for a minute, will you?" Wardlow had an idea and needed to think it out. Yeah, he could use the press, but not quite the way Shriver thought.

"It'll work, I tell you."

"Okay! They can come in!" Wardlow barked, but now he had a grin on his face. Once he made his move, the die would be cast. There was nothing Shriver or Kincaid could do. Wardlow grunted in satisfaction and turned to go back inside.

"One more thing." Major Shriver held him back. "Remember, let the others talk, you just set the tone and then let Winchester hear their anger. You're the reasoned leader, trying to control them. Make sure that comes through and I guarantee you the message will get to the governor before Winchester can report back."

Footsteps scraped on the wooden porch, the back door opened and banged closed and the bolt was shoved home.

Jake's heart was thumping, he could hear it. The farmers were planning something big and they wanted to make it look like it was the governor's fault. Jake slipped away, anxious to tell Clara and Junior what he'd heard.

15

Except for the pale glow from the streetlight hanging over the intersection, the neighborhood was dark. Some of the light reached the front steps of the Eagles Hall, where a half dozen men stood smoking and talking. By the looks of them, they were all from out of town. Two or three had on double-breasted suits that looked slept in, the others wore sport coats or blazers. Cigarettes dangled from the corners of their mouths and they wore their hats pushed back with a casual insolence that set them apart.

Among them there was the one exception, a neatly tailored fellow who wore no hat. He was a rather tall, angular man in his early fifties who combed his wavy, iron-gray hair straight back. He was outfitted in a crisp poplin safari jacket and matching tan pants with large patch pockets; his shirt was open at the collar and he had a powder blue scarf tucked in around his neck. He was a handsome man with a ruddy face and a trim little mustache and, like the others, he was smoking, but his cigarette was neatly placed in an ivory holder that he clenched between his teeth. He was Roderick Munn, from *The New York Times*.

"Are those clods going to let us in?" asked a tweedy-looking photographer who was holding a big box camera. A heavy bag full of film holders and flashbulbs sagged from his shoulder.

"Hell, we got a story, no matter what they do," grinned a bespectacled little man with a thin face.

Cigarettes glowed and smoke drifted over the idle reporters and photographers. They'd spent most of yesterday on the picket lines with the CIO's Walter Reuther. Up early again this morning, they'd tagged after the jaunty union leader as he tried without success to talk with farmers and county officials. One of the reporters had learned that Colonel Winchester was meeting with the farmers in the Eagles Hall that night and, since Reuther was giving a speech to the workers in the park, the newsmen decided it was best to split up and pool their efforts. Some stayed with Reuther, the others followed Winchester—but found their way into the Eagles Hall barred. They were locked out.

"How long we been out here cooling our heels?"

"Nearly a half hour."

"Hey Rod," somebody called to the man in the safari suit. "What'd Reuther say about going back?"

"The bus will leave from the park right after the rally. We're going back to Fresno and we can file from the hotel," Munn said, adding, "Walter's planning to fly back to San Francisco in the morning."

There was more silence and pacing, then one of the reporters swore, "Jesus Christ! I got a nine-o'clock deadline. What time is it, anyway?"

"Seven-thirty."

"There's a pay phone in that gas station on the highway, across from the park."

A cameraman held his Speed Graphic up and, in the weak light of the street lamp, checked the settings and made sure the shutter was cocked. He took the big flashbulb out of the pan, stuck the end in his mouth to wet it and then reinserted the bulb. Everything was ready. He yawned and looked at his watch again.

Without warning, the front doors banged open and there in the doorway stood Titus Wardlow, cigar stub clamped in his teeth, snarling, "All right! You guys can come in!"

Cameras flashed, freezing Wardlow in their instant glare, stripping any civility, leaving only hatred and distrust. The next morning newspaper readers from San Francisco to New York would see an Associated Press wire photo showing the scowling face of California agriculture; the headlines would read:

FARMERS TO FIGHT BACK
WARN THEY WILL TAKE LAW IN OWN HANDS

But in that instant when the doors flew open and the cameras flashed, the newsmen were startled by the abruptness of Wardlow's appearance. They bristled, instinctively ready to snarl back, and it took a second or two for them to realize they were being invited inside.

"I'm Roderick Munn, from *The New York Times*," the tall, hatless reporter in the safari suit extended his hand to Wardlow. It was a simple, regal ceremony, worked the world over, the introduction and handshake, followed by those imperious words, "from *The New York Times*."

Wardlow ignored the proffered hand. "Go on in."

Once inside, the newsmen hesitated, uncertain of their reception. They moved to one side, standing against the wall, getting their bearings, judging the room and what it might hold. There was no fear, only caution in a strange, hostile environment. These were, after all, the nation's top labor writers, most of them had covered labor uprisings, bloody ones, and in this room they were looking at some of the same farmers who had run them out of the fields yesterday and had refused to talk this morning.

There were perhaps two hundred farmers in the hall, some sitting, some standing or milling slowly about the room, rugged, sunburned men, freshly scrubbed and wearing clean shirts, men who didn't fit comfortably indoors. As Wardlow came back into the room, many of them turned and stared at the newsmen. Munn and a reporter named Rose from the *San Francisco News* followed in Wardlow's wake, trying to have a word with the farmer. Somewhere along the way they picked up Major Shriver, an unnoticed escort.

"Mr. Wardlow?" The *Times* man had managed to outflank the farmer and now stood in front of him, blocking the way. "You *are* Mr. Wardlow, president of the Jefferson County Associated Farmers?"

Wardlow nodded, chewing on his cigar.

"As I tried to tell you back there, I am Roderick Munn, from *The New York Times*." This time Munn didn't try to shake hands, only nodded toward the second reporter. "And this is George Rose, of the *San Francisco News*. I wonder if we might ask you a few questions?"

Wardlow squinted through cigar smoke, saying nothing.

"We understand you are meeting here tonight with the governor's representative, Colonel Winchester?"

"Uh-huh." Wardlow nodded and rolled the cigar from one side of his mouth to the other, still eyeing the reporters.

"What's the purpose of the meeting? Are you negotiating some kind of agreement or settlement to the strike?"

Wardlow took the cigar out of his mouth and, thrusting it like a rapier, he snapped, "Get this straight! There's no strike here! Our workers want to work and we mean to protect their right to work."

The *Times* man stepped back, trying to avoid the soggy cigar. "No strike?" He couldn't conceal his disbelief.

"That's right! Go ask the workers, they'd be back in the fields picking tomorrow morning, if it weren't for the outside agitators that are causing all the trouble. Ask the sheriff. We've got a dozen of those Communists in jail right now. Red agitators, every one. Now you print that." Wardlow jabbed the soggy butt of his cigar at the newsman.

Munn retreated. "But . . ."

Wardlow brushed past Munn. "I got a meeting to run."

"Mr. Munn." Shriver stepped up and introduced himself. "I'm Major Shriver, a consultant to the Associated Farmers. Maybe I can be of help. First, let me assure you the association wants to cooperate with the press. I realize Mr. Wardlow there has been a bit brusque, but you must forgive him, he and the other farmers here have millions of dollars invested in that cotton crop and they see this as a war. The Communist-led CIO unions are out to break them. As you know, the Congress wisely exempted farm labor from the National Labor Relations Act in nineteen thirty-five because farmers are so vulnerable at harvest and because food and fiber are so vital to our national interests."

"Major." Munn had his pad out and was taking notes. "We'd like to interview Wardlow. George here and I were out on the picket lines yesterday and it was obvious that most of those strikers were bona fide cotton pickers."

"Munn, is it?" Shriver stood snappily before the newsman. "Well, Mr. Munn, please understand that Wardlow didn't mean there weren't some workers on the picket lines. Of course there are. What he said was that the real workers don't want a strike, they'd be back in the fields tomorrow morning if it weren't for the outside agitators, the Communists who are skillful, clever manipulators—"

"Major"—the newsman was impatient now—"as much as I appreciate your view of things, I want to report the farmers' side, and to do that I must talk to farmers."

Shriver nodded. "I assure you that after the meeting I'll get you with Wardlow and some of the others."

"Thanks." Munn turned away.

Shriver watched Munn and Rose work slowly through the crowd, stopping and questioning a farmer here and there. They were like vultures, but they had power and Wardlow hadn't handled them well. That was troubling. Shriver made a mental note to let Casperson know they were going to have to put Wardlow under a tighter rein.

Wardlow was up on the stage, adjusting the microphone. "This thing on?"

"Yes," a half dozen people shouted.

"Okay, grab a seat. We're going to get started."

Behind Wardlow there were two rows of chairs, all empty except for the one occupied by Colonel Winchester. Winchester was dressed in a neatly tailored dark blue suit, starched white shirt and a deep blue tie with wire-thin diagonal yellow stripes. His dark blue hat, with its yellow feather, and carefully folded navy blue overcoat were neatly stacked on a nearby chair.

"Let's get started." Wardlow thrust his face up close to the microphone. "Before I introduce Winchester, there, let me tell you how we're going to run things. He's going to say a few words, then we're going to let any of you that wants to say something come up to that microphone on the floor there and talk. Colonel Winchester"—Wardlow turned and extended an arm out to the officer—"come on up, the floor's yours."

Winchester stood taller than Wardlow and as he walked up to the mike there was a smattering of polite applause that quickly died in embarrassment. Unintimidated, Winchester stood at parade rest, arms behind his back, and spoke quietly, firmly. "Gentlemen, as many of you know, I'm here representing Governor Olson. It is his belief that reasonable men can negotiate their differences . . ."

The word *negotiate* triggered a scattering of boos.

"... in a labor dispute."

A redneck in overalls was up yelling, "There ain't no labor dispute here!" He was cheered and applauded.

Winchester glanced back to see if Wardlow was going to order the crowd to silence. When he didn't, Winchester simply waited until the noise died down and then went on. "This spring the governor's fact-finding commission, after careful study, determined that cotton growers could afford to pay a dollar twenty-five cents a hundred pounds and still make a profit . . ."

The room erupted in more boos and catcalls. Wardlow got to his feet and took over the microphone, yelling, "Sit down and shut up! You listen to what the guy has to say. Then we'll tell 'im what we have to say to the governor."

When order was restored Winchester eyed the hostile audience, controlling his own temper. "I want you to know, that as an officer in the United States Army assigned to the California National Guard and detached to the governor's staff, I resent your conduct. I have my orders and I intend to follow them. I am not here to make a speech . . ."

Applause broke out across the room, but quickly died.

"... I am here to assess the situation and report back to the governor. To fully understand what is happening here in Jefferson County, I intend to listen to what you have to say and convey that information to the governor. However, if I am interrupted one more time, I will consider that your message to the governor and I will leave."

Winchester looked over the audience, then continued. "The governor's commission concluded that reducing the picking wage to eighty cents was not economically justified. The fact of the matter is that there are a few small farmers in this county who are paying one dollar a hundred pounds picked. I've talked with them and they tell me that they expect to make a profit.

"The union's position is that the average worker picking two hundred pounds of cotton a day cannot make a living working at the current wage scale. And they have offered evidence to prove this contention.

"Now we, or I should say, the governor wants to hear your position and your demands. If you have information that refutes the commission's findings, we need to see those facts. And the governor has authorized me to tell you that he is willing to provide a mediator to help you settle this dispute, if both sides will agree to sit down and talk.

"That is all that I have to say. I will turn the mike back over to President Wardlow here, reserving the right to ask questions, if I may."

Wardlow stepped back up to the microphone. "All right. We've heard you out. Now, before opening it up for comments from the floor, I've got a few things to say. First, we are not negotiating with those Red agitators . . ."

Applause interrupted him.

". . . nor do we want any outside mediators or interference of any kind. As for your commission findings, we have our own study, done by growers, using University of California figures and applying them to this year's prices. Our figures show the cost of producing six hundred forty pounds of cotton per acre would require a market price of nine cents a pound of lint cotton to let the grower break even. And that is paying eighty cents for picking, not a dollar and a quarter. These figures show that we are paying pickers more than we should, if we expect to break even."

More applause and a few whistles filled the room.

"Now," he turned to the growers, "I'll let you talk to the colonel here. Who's got something to say?"

Suddenly the room was quiet. The only sounds were a few coughs and the nervous scraping of chairs. People craned their necks and looked around to see who would be the first up. Finally a redheaded farmer in Levi's and a western plaid shirt stood up. "I say we—"

Wardlow cut him off. "Red, come on down front to the mike and say your name so the boys from the press over there know who's talking."

There was the sound of the farmer's cowboy boots thudding down the aisle. He stopped in front of the mike and, looking at Winchester, started speaking rapidly. "My name's Red Barnes and I'm a cotton grower. Like Titus said, we don't want no mediation or interference of any kind from you or the governor. If the governor wants to stop this strike, then he'd better send in the state cops or your National Guard and start rounding up them agitators so our workers can go back into the fields."

The farmers cheered and applauded Red Barnes as he walked back to his seat.

Another farmer went to the mike, a swarthy little man with gray hair and a perpetual worried look. "My name's Aram Hagopian and I grow grapes and some cotton too. I just want to say that I come to this country with my uncle and my mother when I was just a kid. That's all that was left of my family, just me, my mother and my uncle Garabed, because the Turks murdered my father and my brothers. We escaped to Greece, then we come to Yettum, there in Tulare County. I bought my first land in Jefferson County thirty-two years ago. It was good land and we worked hard for what we got and now they want to take it away from us, the Communists. I got my bills to pay and we didn't do so good in the raisins this year and if we pay any more to these cotton pickers we'll go broke. We work hard, we don't take welfare from nobody. They want work, they got work. If they don't want work, then get them to hell out of here. That's all I gotta say."

Again the hall broke into noisy approval as the old Armenian went back to his place. The audience's angry juices were stirring and Wardlow, judging the mood, let several more speakers come to the mike. He could see Shriver trying to signal him to cut off the talk before it got out of hand and, lighting the stump of his cigar, he grinned a little to himself, thinking, Squirm, you little son of a bitch. Finally Wardlow cut off the speakers. "All right! That's enough!"

Turning to Winchester, he barked, "You've heard them, Colonel. Now you can tell Governor Olson that if he doesn't stop this invasion of radicals, *we will*! You tell the governor that, tell him that we won't take any more. If these illegal work stoppages aren't halted, if these Reds aren't dealt with by you and the governor, we are going in there and clean them out."

The audience was on its feet clapping and yelling encouragement. Wardlow stood there puffing on his cigar, his bulldog face wrinkled in an ugly grin. "That"—he waved his hand toward the audience, giving it his blessing—"that, Colonel Winchester, is your message."

Winchester turned and walked to the back of the stage, gathering up his hat and coat. Wardlow turned back to the microphone. "All right! All right! Settle down. We're going to take a five-minute break. Meeting's adjourned for five minutes."

The reporters were quickly making their way through the mob toward Colonel Winchester, who was coming down the steps at the side of the stage and turning to go out the back way.

"Colonel Winchester? Hold up, would you?"

Winchester looked at the reporters and paused.

"Sir," Rose asked, "what message are you going to take back to the governor?"

"Exactly what you heard here tonight."

"Can you put it in your own words, sir?"

"You saw it, heard it."

"What are you going to recommend?" Munn asked.

"I don't know. It's a little too early to tell."

"You said that some small farmers were paying a dollar an hour?"

"No." Winchester clearly wanted to break this off and leave. "I said they were paying one dollar a hundred pounds of cotton picked."

"And they can still make a profit?"

"That's what they said."

"Is this a legitimate strike? A bona fide labor dispute?" another reporter yelled.

"If you mean, 'Are there cotton pickers on strike?' then certainly, there are workers out on the picket lines and obvious differences of opinion over what wage ought to be paid. Look, gentlemen, I really am not at liberty to discuss this with you until after I have reported to the governor, then I'm sure he will have something to say." Winchester turned quickly and left through the rear of the building.

Shriver had kept an eye on the reporters and when he saw them heading back for Wardlow, he moved in ahead of them, reaching the farmer first. He took Wardlow's elbow. "Titus, I need a word with you now, before you talk to the reporters."

Farmers and Legionnaires were crowding around Wardlow, yelling and laughing and slapping him and each other on the back. At the rear of the crowd Munn was politely pushing his way through, leading the other reporters.

Wardlow felt the major's grip on his elbow and heard Shriver's words. He pulled his elbow away, snarling, "Fuck 'em."

"The press." Shriver nodded toward the oncoming Munn. "I want to talk to you before they do."

"I said fuck 'em. I got nothing more to say."

Munn was close enough to hear Wardlow. Unruffled, he asked, "You have no comment then?"

Wardlow growled, "No comment."

"Fine." There was a faint smile of pleasure on the newsman's face, just a hint that he had been handed something of value.

Rose had muscled in beside Munn. "You're certain? No additional thoughts? No explanations about why you big farmers agreed to pay eighty cents but some of the small farmers are paying a dollar and, we're told by Colonel Winchester, they make a profit? No comment on that?"

Wardlow turned away. Munn looked at Rose and winked and the San Francisco reporter grinned as he started for the front door. "Let's get out of here."

"Yeah." Munn was shaking his head and looking around the room, amused and a bit bewildered. "These farmers are a strange bunch, aren't they?"

"Hell, you easterners aren't used to our wild and woolly ways." Rose was out the door and down the steps, headed for the pay phone down by the service station.

After Winchester and the reporters had left, Shriver confronted Wardlow. "You agreed to the format, it was to be the farmers who laid it on Winchester, not you. They were going to show their anger, and you were supposed to be controlling them, holding back the wild horses, as it were. Why in hell didn't you stick to the plan?"

Wardlow took the cigar out of his mouth, inspecting it. Here it was, the showdown, and he relished it. Squinting into Shriver's eyes, Wardlow let him have both barrels. "Listen, you little son of a bitch, I don't care if God himself sent you down here, you are just a flunky. We followed your advice, and the strike's gotten out of hand. If we'd have done it our way, crushed it that first night, it would all be over now. Instead, that goddamn union's got most of the harvest shut down from here north to Madera.

"You've been holding us back, when we should have snuffed this thing out right at the start, burned their goddamn camps, run them out of the park. Well, we're through listening to you. We're going to do just what I told that Winchester fellow we were going to do, only he doesn't know that we know the union's planning something big. I said we'd give the governor a couple of days, well that's because two days from now we're going to surprise the hell out of those sons of bitches. Before we're through, they'll think they've run into a fucking buzz saw."

"What are you talking about?"

"That spy we got in the union camp, out at Collins Corner—"

"What spy?" Shriver cut in, demanding to know.

Wardlow's face wrinkled into a grin. "Oh, don't look so goddamn surprised. We got word that the union is planning a mass demonstration day after tomorrow or Wednesday at the latest. They've picked out Coco Oil and they're going to throw everything they have at us in one big push, try and put the fear of God in us by shutting down the biggest farmer around. Well, we're going to be ready for them. And we got help coming from Madera, Fresno and Kings counties, too."

Shriver looked surprised.

Wardlow laughed. "Look, Junior, I was running things long before you showed up. I don't have to raise my hand to go take a shit."

"But we're supposed to be coordinating what each county does so no one goes off on his own," Shriver yelled back. "I'm calling Casperson right now."

"I've already talked to him, but not until after I phoned a few more members of my board. We had a little rump session and decided we've got to end this thing, once and for all. And we're going to do it fast. No more of this goddamn pussy-footing around."

"You can't just go off on your own. You don't know what you're doing," Shriver fumed.

"The fuck we don't. You and Casperson forgot something, buster. When we set up the Associated Farmers, it was the local county chapters, not the state office, that was to run things." Wardlow looked menacingly at the officer, snapping at him, "Now that's what I told Casperson. And I also told him to get you the fuck out of here. From now on, we're running this show ourselves."

It was a big gamble, Wardlow knew that, but he was certain he could trounce the union, grab off a quick, crushing victory and that would be it. The strike would be over. By God, that would send a clear enough message to the walnut-paneled boardrooms in Los Angeles, let them know it was the farmers who were running things here in Jefferson County. More importantly, it would wipe out the threat to the Devil's Den deal. America First and Armor might not like the tactics, but goddammit, they couldn't argue with results. It would be over and America First's fears would be put aside. Their money would be safe, the project on schedule. Success! That's what counted.

The next morning, Wardlow and a half dozen other farmers sat around a long worktable in the Eagles Hall, planning the defense of Coco Oil's vast farming operations. Their primary problem was logistics. The oil company farmed a hundred sixty-one sections. That was just over one hundred thousand acres, but it wasn't located all in one place. The company's various farming units were scattered all over the west side of Jefferson and Kings counties. A union attack could be expected anyplace where they were picking cotton or ginning—or the union might raid the company's ranch headquarters. It could throw picket lines up around some of the camps, but which ones? Coco Oil had eighteen farm labor camps, all of them big ones.

Tactically, all they could do was plan, then wait and see where the union moved its people. They brought in a secretary, and a larger phone bank was being installed. It would be manned by Legionnaires. Windy Scott transferred his radio communications center to the hall and assigned Captain Ramey to keep the post staffed around the clock. In the event of trouble the deputy would alert the association and the command post would be quickly activated. The phone network was tested, and staging areas were established at key spots around Coco Oil's land. Squads of farmers and lawmen would be positioned at these locations so that when the alert sounded, they could respond anywhere they were needed. They had the stockade now, so Windy had been told to arrest every striker his deputies could get their hands on.

By evening they were as ready as they'd ever be. And hopefully the spy would pick up some more information, giving them an even better edge. Wardlow had offered him a hundred-dollar bill if he could pinpoint the time and place the union forces would strike.

16

Jake signed up with the union Sunday evening. The very next morning Mr. Kakorian pulled him out of the field and asked him to haul the cotton trailers to the gin. That meant driving the Oliver tractor and getting paid wages, even if it was just for a few hours. So now he was a tractor driver as well as a card-carrying member of the union. Monday was also the day the crisis started; Jake would see that later, when he looked back on what happened, but at the time he was caught up in the thrill of the new job and troublesome thoughts about scabbing on the union.

The first hint of trouble came after he'd made one run to Armor Cotton Oil's Palo Rojo River gin and was headed back to the farm, pulling the empty trailer along the county roads. Sitting high in the tractor seat, he wheeled around the last corner and came bumping down the road toward the Kakorian place. There parked by the edge of the field next to the cotton trailers was a big car, one of those powerful black Cadillacs with glittering chrome, like the big shots drove. Nearby, Titus Wardlow and a puffy-faced city fellow in a brown, pinstriped suit were standing in the field talking to Mr. Kakorian.

Jake slowed the tractor and pulled around in back of the Cadillac, parking the empty trailer next to the tripod holding the scale. Letting the engine idle, he climbed down and uncoupled the hitch, all the while glancing at the three men. Even though they were only a few feet away, the noisy tractor engine kept him from overhearing their conversation, most of it anyway, but it was obvious that Wardlow was trying to bully Mr. Kakorian. Jake heard Wardlow yell something that sounded like "Pay eighty cents or else . . ." Those were the words, he was sure of it, but he didn't hear the rest of the sentence. Whatever was said, the fellow in the brown suit was in on it because he was nodding.

Mr. Kakorian was angry. Fists clenched, he stood his ground, yelling back, "Go to hell!" Jake didn't actually hear the words so much as he saw Mr. Kakorian say them. It wasn't hard to see that he wasn't knuckling under to Wardlow or that other fellow, who looked like a banker.

The man in the brown suit looked over at Jake, suspicious. His oddly round, unfriendly face was so soft it sagged in jowly folds and his squinty black eyes were glittering cold. Instinctively, Jake hated the man. Climbing back up onto the tractor, he gunned the engine and maneuvered over to hook up a full trailer. Once more he idled the engine, climbed down and hooked onto the trailer. Hitch pin in place, he climbed back into the driver's seat and, glancing over at the three men again, he shifted into first gear. What he saw was startling: Mr. Kakorian, arm outstretched and jabbing a pointed finger at the road, was ordering them off his land. Distracted, Jake let the clutch out without advancing the throttle. The tractor lurched weakly and the engine died. Embarrassed, he quickly restarted the engine and gave it full throttle. The big wheels bit into the soft earth and the tractor jumped forward, was jerked back by the tug of the load and lurched forward again, snapping and banging the hitch.

It wasn't a smooth start, but the trailer was rolling. Jake pulled out onto the blacktop and, passing by the three men, he saw that it was Wardlow and the man in the brown suit who were backing off, not Mr. Kakorian. Suddenly the union card in Jake's pocket was troubling. How could he go against a man who was standing up to that son of a bitch Wardlow? Mr. Kakorian had told Ertie he wouldn't be pushed around and it was obvious he'd meant what he'd said. Jake-the-tractor-driver was happy. Mr. Kakorian was a good man to work for and he would probably pay him twenty-five cents an hour, maybe even thirty. Chugging down the road with the cold October wind in his face, Jake felt grown up. Tractor work could lead to a steady job, maybe.

The Quantrill School was on the way to the gin and, as he chugged by, the playground was full of kids, some on the swings and parallel bars, others playing Red Rover come over, running and screaming. When the youngsters heard the tractor they turned and watched. A few pointed and yelled. Pride surged through him. Not yet sixteen and he was a tractor driver and they were just *kids*. He sat tall in the seat and looked straight ahead, never acknowledging that he was being watched, sorry only that he didn't have a cigarette dangling from the corner of his mouth.

By the time he arrived at the gin, there was a line of trailers pulled by pickups and tractors, all waiting to be emptied. He queued up behind the last rig and idled the tractor's engine. Getting down, he walked around a bit, but it was a cold, cloudy day and the blustering wind chilled him, so he came back to the tractor and stood close to the engine, warming himself. It was past noon before he was unloaded and headed back for the last trailer.

The black Cadillac was gone and, as he pulled in, he saw Mr. Kakorian next to the tripod scale talking with his wife. Mrs. Kakorian, bundled in a sweater, was sitting at the card table she used as a desk for the weight records and pay slips. Sometimes she picked cotton too, but mostly she knitted or worked on farm accounts while she waited for the pickers to weigh up. Now she was looking up apprehensively at her husband who was standing there, arms folded angrily across his chest. Jake's arrival interrupted whatever it was they were discussing. As he unhooked the empty trailer and started to hitch up the final load Mrs. Kakorian called to him. He idled the tractor and cupped an ear.

"Shut that thing off and come eat your lunch!"

"It's gonna rain," he yelled back.

The farmer looked at the cloudy sky, then shouted, "That'll keep. Come on and get something to eat."

Jake climbed down and did as he was told. Sitting on the tongue of the empty cotton trailer, munching on a cold biscuit and a bit of side meat, Jake could see the Kakorians had resumed the discussion. Again he was the outsider, unable to hear what was being said. Mr. Kakorian was shaking his head no, and motioning toward the field where the pickers were bent double at the work. His wife was distressed and she obviously disagreed with whatever it was her husband had said. She had the ledger books open and was pointing to something. Mr. Kakorian shrugged helplessly and turned away, anger still scowled across his face. He climbed into his pickup, slammed the door and drove off, headed for town.

Jake took a swallow of water from the jug and sat there for a few minutes, watching the farmer's wife and wondering what was going on. Why were they fighting? Impulsively, he got up and walked over to the table where Mrs. Kakorian sat staring after her husband. "Ma'am, what'd them fellas want?"

"What fellows?"

"The ones that was here in the big car this mornin'."

Irritated by the question, she snapped, "That's none of your business."

"Sorry," Jake mumbled and quickly went back to work.

In camp that evening after work it was cold. They all stood close to a roaring fire, trying to keep warm as they spooned up steaming bowls of stew, washing it down with hot coffee. In between bites, Jake told them about Wardlow and the man in the brown suit.

"We seen 'em too." Ertie poured more whiskey into his coffee.

"Did ya hear what they said?" Bessie worried.

"Couldn't hear much"—Jake shook his head—"but they was talking about the pay, said something about eighty cents, but Mr. Kakorian, he was standin' right up to 'im, told Wardlow to go to hell."

"Who was the fella in the brown suit?" Billie Jo asked.

Jake shrugged.

Bessie put her cup down. "Mr. Kakorian was standin' up to 'im ya said?"

"Sure was. Ordered 'em right off the place, I seen that."

Bessie smiled, trying to look reassured. "I tol' ya thangs'd work out."

They finished supper hurriedly and, lighting the lamps, Bessie and Susie started cleaning up after the meal. Ertie stood close to the warming fire, sipping his coffee.

It rained during the night and the next morning Kakorian sent Navo down to tell them that picking wouldn't start until the cotton dried out, maybe afternoon sometime. Jake helped Ertie feed the stock, but there was little else to do and the corrals were too sloppy to work with the colt. Ertie got out both the .22 rifle and the nickel-plated pistol and sat at the table cleaning and oiling them. He liked the feel of cold steel and the smooth, precise actions. Both the rifle and the pistol had strong, delicately balanced triggers that conveyed a sense of purpose and power.

In a few minutes, Lige came over and sat down. "How do ya like that? Kakorian throwin' Wardlow off his land yesterday." Lige picked up the nickel-plated pistol and idly spun the cylinder. "Tol' ya he was a good man."

"Yup." Ertie nodded, concentrating on fitting the rolling block back in the .22.

Down at the other end of the table Mary Ellen and Susie were playing jumping jacks, a matchstick game that Ertie had made for them by punching holes in a large square of cardboard. The holes were punched out on a crosshatch grid and the matchsticks were stuck in the holes. The game was played like checkers, kind of; the idea was to capture as many opponent's sticks as you could by jumping over them. Susie had Benjy up on her lap and was letting him make some of the jumps.

Jake was in the tent, lying on his bed reading another Lancy Boyd story in an old copy of *Range Wars*. This story was called "Code of the West" and was a yarn about how the young rancher was tracking down the renegade rustlers who had raided the horse herds, killing off one of the cowpunchers that the small ranchers in the valley had hired to ride their range. In that stolen cavy of horses was the Ringold mare, a blooded mustang that Lancy had captured out on Ringold Mesa two years back. A gold-sorrel with sturdy legs and powerful, well-muscled rounds, she'd been running with a band of wild horses when Lancy had first caught sight of her galloping across the mesa. Instantly, Lancy had known he wanted her, but lasooing that mare turned out to take a lot of hard riding and every bit of skill he had. When he'd finally got his rope on her, the fight had begun.

The sun was out and the tent was warm. Outside, Jake heard his father say something and Lige Parsons responded, then he heard a third voice that sounded like Mr. Kakorian, but he couldn't make out what the farmer was saying. Jake continued reading:

The Ringold mare wasn't just another horse, no sir, she had Spanish Barb blood in her, Lancy could see it in her conformation and her spirit, the way she fought. He'd spent weeks breaking her, working her gently, trying not to extinguish that wild spirit that made her so much horse. He also bred her to Pie, his tough little Morgan stud. She was carrying a foal when the renegades ran off with the horses. Lancy meant to get the Ringold mare back and see the rustlers hung. If they made a fight of it, he was ready.

The voices outside the tent were louder now and Mr. Kakorian was saying, "From now on it's eighty cents a hundred." Jake heard the words "eighty cents a hundred" but didn't react at first because his mind was still on the story; then, suddenly, the meaning of what he had just heard rang clear. Jesus Christ! He tossed the magazine aside and was up and out the flap of the tent.

The farmer was standing just under the fly, next to the table, confronted by Ertie and Lige. The rest of the family and the Parsons were gathered around, dumbstruck.

Ertie had finished cleaning the rifle and pistol and had been sharpening his pocketknife when Kakorian came into camp. Now Ertie was standing, the whetstone in one hand, the open knife in the other. His jaw muscles were clamped down tight.

Lige again asked, "You're goin' back on your word?" This time it wasn't so much a question as a statement to be verified.

"I didn't want to drop the wage, but I've got no choice. I'm sorry. You're good workers, all of you, and I'll try to make it up to you in other ways . . ."

"But Mr. Kakorian," Jake shouted, not believing what he'd heard, "you told 'em to go to hell an' threw them off your place, I saw ya!"

Ertie snapped the blade shut and put the knife in his pocket. "Kakorian, you tol' us ya didn' give a damn what them other farmers's payin'."

"Look, this isn't a debate. The pay is eighty cents. I don't like it either, but that's it. Period." Kakorian turned and walked away, his back stiff, his step angry.

They watched him in silence.

"Whatever happened, he got pushed into it." Lige sat back down at the table, fiddling idly with the nickel-plated pistol.

"So what? That son of a bitch ain' no different than ever' other farmer." Ertie sat down on the nail keg, got back up, circled about the camp aimlessly, then turned and walked away, headed for the barn.

"Hol' on." Lige got up. "I'll go with ya."

Jake started to go too, but Bessie took ahold of his arm. "Leave 'em be. It ain' like we lost our jobs. We'll just have to work harder."

"Ma! He went back on his word! That extry twenty cents means close to two hundred dollars, time the cotton's all in."

"Well, we'll jus' work harder, that's all."

Susie sided with Jake. "But Ma, it ain't fair."

"An' workin' harder ain' goin' do no good, Ma." Jake pulled away. "There's only so much cotton out there, no matter how hard we work. When she's picked, she's picked."

"Ma's right." James Earl quickly sided with Bessie and so did Mary Ellen. "We'll all work harder."

"Oh, crap!" Jake turned on his older sister.

"Mister, don' you be talkin' like that!" Bessie snapped, angry now. She knew Jake was right about the money, but she didn't want to face it. "We'll just go out an' get another job when we're done here."

"Ma, what're ya talkin' 'bout?" Jake was exasperated. "There ain' no jobs when cotton's over, not till prunin' time an' that ain' till January."

"Jake!" James Earl confronted his brother. "Don' ya be usin' that tone a voice with Ma!"

Bessie hushed James Earl. "I'll handle this."

Jake insisted, "Ma, there ain' no winter work between now'n then. Onlyest way to get that money back is to strike."

"Boy, hush your mouth. We ain't strikers." Bessie was afraid of the strike. It meant no work at all and she was certain they would make it somehow, if they could just keep working. "We'll just have to find more work this winter."

"But Ma, if we force them farmers to pay us a dollar'n-quarter we'd more'n make up what we lose strikin' in a few days. Junior tol' me the union's got something big started that'll shut down the whole harvest anyway. Then nobody'll be workin' till the farmers give us better pay."

"Yor wrong, Mr. Smarty Pants, we'll be working. I ain' goin' to let this family get caught up in nothin' like that. We're goin' to be workin' and putting money by so's we'll have a place of our own this winter."

Jake wouldn't give up. "Ma, folks is strikin', thousands of 'em, folks jis' like us."

"Who'd pay for the groceries, us not workin'?"

Eager now, Jake explained, "We'd live in the strike camp. Union's got lots of groceries an' it don't cost nothin' 'cause it's all donated by them big unions and people from the cities, church people mostly. Some of 'em even come to help us."

"Us?" Now Bessie was looking hard at her son. "Boy, how come you know so much about this here union?"

"He's been sneakin' off to union meetings," Mary Ellen sneered.

Jake squared off with his older sister. "Junior took me. What of it?"

"What meetin's?" Bessie shook her son. "Boy, was you goin' to union meetings?"

Jake realized that he'd gone too far. Now he was in trouble. "Yes'm. But only a couple of times, just to listen."

Bessie gave him another shake. "Jacob Elroy Robertson, yor gonna git us fired, sure."

"Ma!" Jake pulled away, frustrated. "Ain' you heard none of what I said?"

"I heard, boy. An' I say we're goin' to stay right here an' work."

"Ma's right." James Earl stood beside Bessie now. "We gotta chance to get that house an' we gotta take it. Jake—"

Jake turned away. "No! I'm strikin' an' I don' care what you all do. I can move in with Junior." He fled to the barn.

Lige and Ertie were in the tack room passing a jug back and forth as Jake stormed in. "Whoa, boy." Ertie put his arm out to Jake. "Come, set."

Jake flopped down on a pile of empty feed sacks. Ertie held out the Bull Durham. "Wanna smoke?"

Surprised, Jake took the little sack and clumsily built a cigarette, lit it and, imitating his father, inhaled deeply. It was like sucking on a blowtorch. Jake coughed up the smoke, eyes squirting tears.

"Ain' like them tailor-mades you been sneakin', is it?" Ertie chuckled. "Ease up on it, boy. Take little draughts till ya get used to it."

Jake nodded. "Pa, what're we gonna do?"

Lige reached for the whiskey and took a pull on the jug. "Tha's jus' what we was talkin' 'bout."

Ertie sat staring at his own cigarette, turning it in his gnarled fingers. "We ought to quit. Just say 'to hell with it' and leave. Go on down the road."

"Why don'cha?" Lige was a little drunk. He gave the jug a shake, sadly noting it was near empty as he handed the last drink to Ertie.

Ertie was quiet for a spell, then he tried to explain. "Two reasons. First, we got too damn much money 'n sweat tied up in that house to jus' walk away from it." He paused, then added, "Then, goddammit, I wanna get back at them bastards, give 'em back some of that shit they done give us. Packin' up an' goin' down the road jus' ain' gonna git *that* job done."

"Pa? You talkin' 'bout joinin' the union?"

Ertie lifted the jug to his mouth, took the last swallow and sighed, smacking his lips. "I don' know, boy. I jus' wanna get back at 'em somehow."

Excitement returned to Jake's voice. "Junior says the union's goin' to shut the harvest clean down. That'll hurt 'em. Make 'em pay more."

Lige nodded. "I'll say this, I ain' never seen a union so strong as this one. This here's the CIO, an' don' forgit the governor's sayin' we oughta get a dollar'n-quarter too."

"Ya sayin' we oughta strike?"

Lige nodded. "There's times when a man's gotta let them bastards know they cain't walk all over 'im."

"Yeah, but just yellin' an' shoutin' an' waving goddamn signs around out there on the road sure ain't my idea of gettin' even. A two-by-four up alongside the head would git the job done a whole lot quicker."

"But Pa, it ain' just picketin', it's refusing to work. If we don't work, none of us, then them farmers don' get no cotton picked. That hurts 'em. 'Member what Smoky said them Turtles did, back at the Boston Garden? Woulda shut down the whole rodeo."

Ertie squinted at his son. "But them was cowboys, rawhide tough men. Once they set their minds to som'thin' they'd go to hell 'fore they'd quit."

"Ertie, if yor sayin' folks out here's weak, yor dead wrong." Lige was getting to his feet, a bit unsteady. "I tol' you once before these folks, they ain' a bunch of sheep. They're people, jus' like you an' me, an' this time they're mad clean through, goin' to do something about it. Only yor too goddamn stubborn to see it. I'm strikin', goddammit. The man went back on his word an' I'm strikin'."

There was a surprised silence and Lige swayed a little, standing there looking down on Ertie.

A grin spread over Ertie's bony face and he held up the empty jug. "Well, by Gawd, here's to the fuckin' strike!"

"Pa?" Jake couldn't believe he'd heard right. "We joinin' the strike?"

"That's what I said."

Jake reached into his pocket and pulled out his union card. "Lookee here."

"What's that?"

"My union card."

"Well, Jeesus H. Christ." Ertie grinned and slapped his son on the back. "How about that?"

Suddenly, Jake's face clouded over. "Pa, what're ya gonna tell Ma?"

"Lemme worry about yor ma, okay?"

Jake nodded, grinning. This was his pa, all right. Just like old times.

The argument started as soon as he limped back into camp. When Ertie said they were going out on strike, Bessie said, "No we're not."

Surprised, Ertie laughed and said, "The hell we're not. We're gonna join that union and go out on strike."

"Ertie. I mean it. This family's got work and a chance to put down some roots and I ain't goin' to let that go." She stepped inside the tent and let the flap fall behind her.

"Whoa up thar woman!" Ertie bulled inside after her. "This ain't somethin' I'm gonna argue about. I just ain' gonna git walked on no more. I ain' gonna be cheated. Nobody's gonna pay me brass money. It's time we stood up to them bastards."

Bessie was standing in the middle of the tent, her fists doubled and jammed down on her hips, her jaw set. "I'm going to have us a home. I mean it, Ertie. You go off strikin', you'll do it alone. Ain't nothing I can do 'bout that. Lord knows, it won't be the first time you've gone off."

"Woman, yor my wife and ya go wherever I go."

"Yes, I'm your wife, but when ya went off rodeoin', ya never took me along. An' when ya come back all crippled up, I was there to take care of ya. You go on, if ya have ta. I'll be here, workin', or I'll be over to the house whenever ya come back."

Bessie stormed past Ertie, going back outside.

"We're with ya, Ma." Mary Ellen put her arm around Bessie and hugged her. James Earl agreed. "Strikin' only means trouble."

That's when Billie Jo got into it, squaring off on James Earl. "When're ya goin' to stand up and fight back? Them farmers walk all over us, they killed Li'l Beth, as shor as they'd used a gun. I hate 'em, hate what they done to us. We ain' trash, but ya let 'em treat us like ignorant trash!"

Ertie had come out of the tent and, hearing Billie Jo, he grinned. " 'At a girl!"

Billie Jo whirled on him. "You ain' no damn better, gettin' drunk all the time, quittin' when thangs don' go right. It's 'bout time you stood up and fought back. I want out of this." She turned and was talking to Bessie now. "Same as you do, ma'am. You all been good to me, like a family, but cain' ya see, they ain' never goin' to let ya up, 'less you fight back?"

"Girl," Bessie spoke forcefully, "this strike ain' gonna change nothin'. Only thang that'll change is what we can change ourselves. Ain' nobody gonna do it for us. An' that's God's bitter truth. We gotta chance to get off'n that road, stop bein' tramps. We can have a home again. Ain' no union gonna help us do that. This here strike'll be gone in a few days. Maybe the pay'll go up some, likely it'll stay the same an' some folks'll have busted heads or be in jail like Junior was, or maybe they'll be dead."

Bessie looked at them. "I ain' goin' on no strike. I'm goin' to stay right here an' work as long as I can. If Mr. Kakorian throws me off, I'll find work some'eres else and when this season's over, I'm goin' to move into that house. Any of you that wants to stay with me, welcome. The rest of ya go on an' do what ya have to an' when it's over, you know where to find me."

And that was the way it happened. Bessie stayed on the Kakorian farm and worked, so did Mary Ellen and James Earl. Because

James Earl stayed, Billie Jo stayed behind, not that she liked the idea but she had no other choice. That afternoon the four of them went back out into the fields, taking Benjy with them. For a long time Bessie stood there in the cotton, heartsick. The strike was folly and now it was splitting up her family. Deep down, she was frightened and filled with a dark sense of foreboding, but she couldn't give up. Dear Lord, her soul whispered, please protect this family and bring us safely back together.

It had been decided that Ertie, Jake and Susie would take the Model A and a tent. Because they didn't plan to be gone long, they packed lightly. They had no more than struck the tent when Archie Parsons came over carrying a bedroll and a cardboard box full of his belongings. Looking around, he asked for Mary Ellen. Susie said she and the others had gone to the fields. Archie nodded, quietly saying that he wasn't going to strike, asking if he could put his stuff somewhere.

"Sure." Susie motioned toward the kitchen tent and watched as he dropped off his belongings and headed out to the cotton.

All the other Parsons were on strike. R'becky didn't like the idea, but she told Bessie her place was with Lige. They were family and had to stick together. "It might be different if we had a place of our own, like you all. But we ain't. All we got is each other," she said.

R'becky assured Bessie she would look out for Ertie and the rest. "I'll make sure they get fed an' that Susie keeps the laundry done."

As they were packing, Jake noticed his father slip the big nickel-plated pistol into his bedroll. When everything was loaded, Jake climbed behind the wheel and took the lead, since he knew the way. Lige followed along and they headed south across the county to Collins Corner. Feeling important, Jake wheeled up to the strike camp gate and announced to the guards that they were joining the strike. One of the guards pointed out the headquarters tents. "Just park over there by them other cars an' go on in, jus' tell 'em ya want to join the strike an' they'll git ya signed up."

The camp offices were in two big pyramid tents that were set wall-to-wall and connected, like two rooms. People were hurrying in and out as Jake followed Ertie and Lige inside. The rooms were dark, crowded and smelled of stale cigarette smoke, sweat and moldy canvas. Gasoline lanterns hung from overhead hooks, hissing and sputtering, casting eery blue-white light and deep shadows. Plank desks and worktables were piled with books and pamphlets, everywhere there were half-empty coffee cups, ashtrays spilling cigarette butts and empty soda-pop bottles. The two telephones were constantly busy. Four frazzled, overworked volunteers sat on folding camp chairs behind the makeshift desks answering questions and filling out forms. A dozen strikers milled about or stood in lines, waiting.

Lige leaned over a table near the entrance and asked, "Where we s'posed to sign up?"

Irritably, a young, fresh-faced college girl with long, wispy hair looked up from her paperwork. "Sign up for what?"

Confused, Lige mumbled, "Guy out there said we was supposed to sign up."

"Oh. You're new. Okay, over there." She pointed across the tent. "That fellow with the wire-rim glasses, he'll help you."

The fellow she pointed to was a bald, wizened little monk of a man with a fringe of frizzled white hair and a prune-wrinkled face.

Ertie and Lige got in line behind two other men.

"Pa." Jake tugged at Ertie's sleeve and nodded toward the man behind the desk. "Ain' he the feller that we was camped next to at El Adobe, that first summer?"

The prune-faced man was giving the two fellows ahead of them directions. "Streets is numbered and lettered, the letters run north an' south, numbers east and west. Yor next to each other on Ninth, between C and D. Just go down A there till ya get to Ninth and turn left. Can't miss it." As the two men left, he looked up at Lige, then at Ertie standing next to him. "Help you fellas?"

"We just got in. Want to join up," Lige explained.

"Why shor, glad to have ya." The man stared at Ertie and Jake. "Say, don' I know you fellas? Wasn't you up to Marysville, in the peach strike?"

"Naw." Ertie shook his head.

The man's puzzled look broke into a wrinkled grin. "Now I recollect. Ertie. Ertie Robertson. Yor the fella that don' take brass money. I'm Will Henry, remember? We was camped right across from ya at El Adobe." Will Henry stood up and they shook hands.

Ertie nodded. "This here's Lige Parsons."

"Glad to know ya." Will Henry sat back down, grinning. "He ever tell ya 'bout throwin' Wardlow's brass money back at 'im?"

Lige grinned. "Yup."

"Well, glad to have you boys." Will Henry pulled out a clipboard and some forms. "Reckon you'll need two camps?"

"If we can git 'em," Lige said. "Ertie here and his two young 'uns needs one, an' I got my family out in the truck. We needs another, side by each, if that's okay."

"I got two spots down at C and Eighth, one just across from the other, that ought to do."

"We'll take 'em," Lige said. "How much?"

"Nothin', friend. We only ask that ya keep everything clean as a pin. There's a block committee that'll be by to tell ya all the rules and sign ya up for duties." Will Henry was back to business.

"Duties?" Ertie asked.

"Yup. There's garbage pickup, latrine detail, kitchen help, commissary duty. It's kinda like the army, but that'll be explained to ya. It's real important that we keep this place fit to live in. Can't give them county officials any excuse to shut us down. They already tried it once, but we passed muster, you bet. Got real doctors and nurses lookin' after things." Will Henry pushed the papers toward them. "Just fill these out an' sign 'em an' you're all set. An' friend"—Will Henry looked at Ertie again—"like I said, I'm real glad ya joined up. Shorely am."

"Say," Lige asked, "where can I find Junior Parsons?"

"Parsons? I shoulda knowed. He's yor boy, ain' he? He's camped just down the road a ways, A and Eighth, 'cross from the mess tent and commissary, by that big field. Can't miss it. Glad to have the whole Parsons family."

As Lige and Ertie headed out of the tent, Jake hung behind. "Mr. Will, kin ya tell me where the Tarpin family's camped?"

"Why shor." Using his finger, he went down the list, then looked at the map. "Back in the far corner, D-Ten."

"Thanks." Jake ran out the door.

It was late afternoon and wood smoke hung blue over streets that were noisy with playing children. Women were busy cooking and men were sitting about, talking and smoking. Old jalopies were parked everywhere. Lige and Jake drove slowly down the dirt street dodging youngsters and marveling at the orderliness of the tent city. At Eighth they spotted Junior splitting wood and Maybelle leaning over a fire, stirring a pot. The twins were chasing each other in and out of the tent, giggling.

Junior looked up, recognizing the sound of his parents' truck. A big grin spread over his face. "Maybelle, look! There's Pa and the family. And the Robertsons too."

R'becky clambered down out of the truck and was hugging and kissing Junior and Maybelle. The little girls, arms outstretched, were squealing and jumping. "Grampa! Grampa! Gimme up!"

Jake, Susie and Ertie stayed in the pickup, watching. Junior noticed them and came over. "Come on, get out. You folks are welcome. Where's the rest of the family?"

"They stayed with Kakorian," Jake said, shrugging self-consciously.

Ertie leaned over and looked out the window past Jake. "We'll go on down an' get camp set up. Tell Lige we'll see 'im there."

Lige overheard Ertie and came over to the car. "Go ahead. We'll be down directly."

"Well, you come on back for supper, ya hear?" Junior insisted, adding, "We got plenty an' I 'xpect Ma'll throw somethin' in the pot too. We'll eat in 'bout an hour, leave for the rally 'bout six."

Ertie asked, "Ya have a rally ever' night?"

"Yeah. Not ever'one comes, but most do. We want to show them farmers that we got the people's support in this thang, and the park's the place to do it."

By the time they finished supper it was near sunset. The men sat around smoking and talking while the women started slicking up the dishes. Maybelle urged the others, "You all go on an' get ready. I can wash these up."

R'becky was surprised. "Ain' you goin' to the rally?"

"No. I stay with the girls an' some other folks drops off their kids for me to watch," Maybelle explained.

"Well, then, I'll stay and he'p out," R'becky said.

Susie edged away, not wanting to miss out on going to the rally. She found Jake sitting off to one side, listening to Junior who was telling Lige and Ertie how the union worked, how the rallies and the picket lines were set up.

"We goin' out strikin' in the mornin'?" Jake asked.

"Sure, we go out every morning."

"How do we know where to go?"

"I'll talk to C. J. and get you assigned to my picket line if I can.

But whoever's line yor on, he'll give ya the place to meet and then ya just go from there."

"How many picket lines ya got?" Susie asked.

"Maybe ten or fifteen, it's hard to keep track. We figger near five or six hundred people are goin' out ever' morning to picket."

"Wow! They all go to different farms?"

"Yeah, mostly, but at the big farms there'll be more than one picket line." Junior was enthusiastic. "We're winning this thang. Really winning it, most ever' cotton picker in the whole county is with us."

"You said the union had somethin' big planned." Jake was excited. "That tomorrow?"

"Can't say. That's secret. Seems like the farmers always know where we're goin' to be, so we don't say nothin' until the last minute now. Otherwise they can head us off or get to the fields quicker'n we do and then stand 'twixt us and them scabs. So we ain' sayin' ahead of time where we're goin' or what we're gonna do."

Jake was up and pacing around. "How long 'fore we go to the rally?"

Junior glanced at his pocketwatch. "Half hour, maybe. Gotta be thar by six-thirty. Why?"

"Wan' ta find Clara. Can I, Pa?"

Ertie nodded, grinning. "Shor."

"Be back in twen'y minutes." Jake ran off, anxious to see Clara and tell her what had happened.

17

Down in the southwest corner of the county, Wardlow and Sheriff Windy Scott sat at the big desk in the darkened Dixieland gin office. It was still a half hour before dawn and the trap was set: out back a hundred good men were hiding in the big gin building, each armed with a club or whip; two other posses were hidden on nearby farms, ready to close in behind the strikers when they drove into the gin yard. All they had to do now was wait.

Out the front windows Wardlow and the sheriff had a good view of the crossroads and, dark as it was, they'd be able to spot any caravan headlights a long way off. Satisfied, Wardlow struck a match and puffed up a glowing coal on the stub of his cigar, then rocked back, putting his feet up on the desk. "Windy, we got 'em this time."

"Can you trust that goddamn Okie?"

"Hell yes. He'd kill his own mother for a hundred dollars."

"And he said they'd meet here? At the gin?"

"Relax, for Christ's sake. That's their plan, they'll all gather here in the gin yard and then go hit Coco Oil's headquarters camp just after daylight."

"We only got two hundred men." The sheriff sounded uneasy.

"Shit, Windy, those strikers'll be expecting trouble at Coco's front drive, not here. When we jump them and slam the gate, they'll stampede. It'll be just like a rabbit drive, all we have to do is club 'em down."

"What do ya figger that Captain McNulty'll do?" The sheriff

sucked on his own cigar and the glow softly illuminated his pushed-in boxer's face.

"Sitting up there in Jeff City he can't do a damn thing. By the time he finds out what's happening, it'll be all over. Besides, you're the law here, not him. Stop worrying." Wardlow swung around in the creaking old desk chair and looked out the window. Except for the single floodlight over the gin yard, it was black-dark out and there was no sign of traffic on the county roads.

Captain McNulty commanded the twenty-five California highway patrolmen Governor Olson had dispatched to Jefferson County to keep the peace. Having outside lawmen here could cause problems, true, but the fact that Olson had only sent in a squad of motorcycle cops instead of a full company of National Guardsmen was another sign that the governor had no balls for this fight. McNulty, on the other hand, was a tough customer. Wardlow sensed that the first time he'd seen the officer. McNulty was a tall, powerfully built man of deceptively boyish good looks with unruly sandy brown hair. He had been dealt a no-win hand by the governor, yet he didn't flinch. From the very start McNulty made it clear that they would have to deal with him if trouble broke out.

Colonel Winchester had set up that first meeting to introduce the new officer. "McNulty, I want you to meet Sheriff Scott and Police Chief Dan Scheid. You know Lieutenant Harris, of course, head of the local highway patrol detachment, and over there is Titus Wardlow, president of the Jefferson County Associated Farmers."

Lieutenant Gabby Harris, a paunchy man with long black sideburns, didn't offer to shake hands. Instead he demanded to know, "What's your jurisdiction here, McNulty?"

Ignoring the belligerent tone, McNulty explained, "As long as the farmers don't take the law into their own hands, we will not interfere, but if anyone breaks the law, we will make arrests. If there are disturbances, we will put a stop to them by any means necessary." The last words were spoken with a deliberate, powerful emphasis. McNulty opened his briefcase and took out a document, handing it to Harris. "You and your men are now under my command. Is that clear?"

"Now captain," Sheriff Scott tried to head off trouble, "these farmers have taken about all they are going to take. Their camps were raided, their workers frightened out of the fields. They have the right to defend their own property."

"I have no problem with that, if they do it legally. But they will not be allowed to break the law. Is that clear?"

"Captain, I don't think you understand," Chief Scheid added. "Farmers are our best people. They are churchgoing, patriotic Americans who fought for this country. They're not lazy white trash who breed like rabbits and lay around on welfare. Farmers produce food and pay taxes. The trouble's caused by those outside agitators who've stirred up the Okies and we mean to run those Communists out of this—"

"You are not running anyone out!" McNulty's flint-edged voice cut the chief off. The captain turned to Gabby Harris. "Lieutenant, you and your six men are under my command. You will do as I order."

"Bullshit!" Harris unpinned his badge and threw it on the table. "The sheriff here'll deputize me and my men, won't you, Windy?"

"Damn right! Consider yourselves hired." The sheriff turned to McNulty. "I'm still the law in this county, Captain. And Dan here has jurisdiction in Jeff City. You have no authority off the state highways and county roads."

"Generally that's true, but Sheriff, despite what your county attorney may have told you, I do have full authority to quell any breach of the peace. I don't want to have to take such action and my men will not interfere with the duties of your officers, or yours either, Chief, but we will be at the ready and will act if we have to. Is that understood?"

No, McNulty wasn't a man to back down when it came to trouble.

The sheriff was up, pacing. He stopped and looked out the window. "It's startin' to get light out, they oughta be here by now. Reckon that night watchman warned 'em?"

They had sent the night watchman home early but, wanting to have everything look normal around the gin yard, they'd told the old black man to leave his car parked outside the office in its usual place and walk back to his shack. It was only a mile or so and he was still getting paid for a full night's work.

"Don't worry, Tucker's a good nigger. Minds his own business. Likely he's in bed right now pounding out another kid. Give him some pussy and a sip of wine and he's happy."

The sheriff continued to pace the floor. Pulling out his Colt .45 pistol, he spun the cylinder, checking the loads, and reholstered the six-shooter.

"For Christ's sake, Windy, relax. They'll be along." Wardlow chewed on his cigar and went over the plan again, mentally checking off the details. It had been a scramble, but they were ready, and all because of just that one phone call, that one tiny bit of information that gave them the edge. The setup was perfect: they were in a remote part of the county, far from McNulty's highway patrolmen; the three posses were poised and each group was in phone contact with the gin office. Wardlow picked up the phone and clicked the receiver. "Hello! Hello, May! Get me two-five-one-W." He waited, chewing his cigar. "Tiny? See any sight of 'em? Well, keep an eye out." He slammed the phone down.

"Want me to scout around a bit?"

"Windy, sit down, goddammit! The last thing I want is to have you out running around scaring them off. They'll be here."

Junior Parsons drove his old Chevy through the chilly darkness. Beside him, crowded in the middle, Jake squirmed with anxious excitement. He was a striker on the way to a picket line and next to him was C. J., the union's president. C. J. twisted around in the seat and stuck his head out the window, looking back, checking on the caravan. Straightening around, he yelled, "Yup, they're all comin' right along."

"Tol' ya I could see 'em in the mirror," Junior shouted.

Jake turned and tried to look out the rear window, but his view was blocked by three more strikers crowded in the rumble seat, their stark figures silhouetted by the yellow headlights behind them. Lige Parsons was next in line, driving a truckload of strikers. Ertie and Susie were riding with Lige and behind them the caravan was strung out for a quarter of a mile, a jalopy parade of old cars and trucks packed full of men and women.

"Any sign of the law followin' us?" Junior asked.

"Naw!" C. J. yelled across the cab. "By now ever' farmer in the county should be over guardin' Coco Oil."

Jake looked puzzled and started to say something, but C. J. was still talking. "When you get up here to Road Seventeen, stop. Wanna make sure nobody misses the turn."

Worried, Jake blurted, "This ain' the way to Coco Oil. That's way south of here."

"We know." Junior grinned.

Jake was confused. "What d'ya mean ya know? C. J. jus' said the farmers'd be guardin' Coco Oil an' I thought—"

"You're right. They'll be waitin' for us at Coco Oil, but that ain' where we're goin'!" C. J. yelled, explaining, "We've got some pickets goin' that way, but that's just to outfox them farmers while the big bunch of us hit El Adobe."

"See"—Junior slapped Jake on the leg—"we didn't even tell the picket captains about El Adobe. They still don't know where we're goin', not for sure. Told 'em to bring all their people to the Palo Rojo bridge on Road Seventeen. That's the meeting place.

"But we did let it get out that we had somethin' big goin' an' that we're headed for Coco Oil. We knowed the farmers was bound to hear 'cause they've been more than just a little bit lucky at showing up where we're picketing. So we're givin' 'em a fake, got Tommy Joad and Thad Greene leading a good bunch of boys down that way. They should be all be meeting at the Dixieland gin right about now. From there they'll make a big run at Coco Oil's headquarters down the road, mix it up a little with them farmers, then get the hell out. Meantime we teach ol' man Wardlow a lesson he ain' never likely to forget. An' this time it ain' just us alone, got a whole bunch of strikers comin' in from Fresno County to help out."

"Jeesus H. Christ," Jake whistled. "We was at El Adobe couple summers ago! Cheated us on the box count an' tried to pay us off in their goddamn brass money!"

"Where'd ya stay?" C. J. asked.

"Headquarters camp, behind the packin' shed."

"Know the layout there?"

"Sure, I know 'er."

"Good, we may need ya to help us." C. J. nodded, adding, "Wardlow, he closed up his other cotton camps and brought all them workers into the headquarters camp, niggers, Mexicans, an' what whites he's got left. Got 'em sleepin' all over the place, even in the packing sheds. Two days ago they got four big busloads of Mexican women from down south of El Paso. Government just opened the border and let them come to the farmers' buses."

"How the hell ya know all of that?" Jake was surprised.

"Couple of them El Adobe crew bosses is friendly to us."

"Here's the turn." Junior slowed and stuck his arm out the window, signaling as he pulled off onto the shoulder. C. J. jumped out and Jake followed right after him. The caravan had come to a stop and C. J. jumped up on the running board of Lige's truck. "Bridge's up ahead 'bout two miles, maybe a little more, you'll see some folks is already there. Pull in behind 'em an' don' let no one go on, jus' get 'em all lined up an' ready."

A worker in Lige's truck hollered down, "This ain' the way to Coco Oil, where we goin'?"

"Tell ya when we get to the bridge. Okay? Move out."

As Lige shifted into low and pulled away, Jake waved to Ertie and Susie.

C. J. stood out in the road directing the battered old cars and rattletrap trucks north toward the bridge, then, after the last car turned and chugged off, he came over to Jake. "In a little bit Junior and me've gotta git up to the bridge. I want ya to stay here at the corner and make sure people get headed north up Seventeen. Okay?"

"Sure!" Eager to help, Jake was nevertheless afraid he might be stranded out here and miss the action.

C. J. slapped him on the back. "Don' worry, Junior'll come pick you up 'fore we head out."

Jake grinned and nodded.

Junior lit a cigarette and leaned against the car, talking to the three men in back. C. J. took out his Bull Durham and built a smoke, lit it and then looked at his watch in the matchlight.

"How we doin' on time?" one of the men in the rumble seat asked.

"Right on schedule."

Jake wanted a smoke too, but no one offered him any tobacco.

Another of the workers in the rumble seat asked, "How many ya figger'll show up?"

C. J. sucked up a deep drag on his cigarette. "Figger maybe five or six hundred. Maybe more. Pretty much depends on how many of 'em comes in from Fresno."

"Wonder if Tom 'n them's at Dixieland yet," Junior said to no one in particular.

"Tell ya, I'm worried 'bout them, an' that's for shor." C. J. shook his head.

The men in the rumble seat were peering at Junior and C. J., puzzled. One asked, "What the hell you fellers talkin' 'bout?"

Junior explained the diversion tactics.

Someone asked, "How many strikers went to Dixieland?"

"Fifty or sixty," C. J. answered, explaining, "They was tryin' to get as many cars as they could, make it look big, keep them farmers and laws riled up long 'nuff to give us a good run at El Adobe. Then, when them farmers come a-chargin' back over here, we got another little trick or two up our sleeves."

"Wha'cha mean?"

C. J. put out his cigarette. "You'll see. We got some more surprises for them farmers."

The talk died down and they smoked in silence until they heard vehicles and, in the distance, saw a string of headlights coming north on Seventeen. The lead car slowed when they spotted C. J. out in the intersection, arm raised. He yelled to the driver, "When ya git up thar to the bridge, hold up and wait for us. It's just a couple miles on up the road."

As the long caravan growled past, strikers stuck their heads and arms out, shouting and banging on the sides of the vehicles. After the last car had passed by, C. J. came back and hunkered down next to Junior and they waited, talking idly until someone spotted a long string of headlights coming toward them from the west.

"That'll be the bunch from Fresno." Junior reached into his car and turned on the headlights, illuminating C. J., who was back out in the intersection signaling the drivers to head north. Engines whined and growled as drivers clutched and downshifted, slowing then turning ponderously on heavily laden springs. A dozen cars and nearly as many overloaded trucks lumbered by, their beds jammed with cheering strikers.

"Come on, Junior," C. J. hollered as the last truck turned the corner. "We gotta get to the bridge." He climbed into the Chevy, yelling to Jake, "Junior'll come back an' get ya directly."

Jake watched the car's single red taillight until it disappeared. Overhead there was the soft flapping sound of an owl's wings, then nothing more disturbed the dark morning quiet. He was alone. Jake walked out into the intersection, looked around, then came back to where the car had been parked. He waited. Standing, turning this way and that, shuffling, walking back out into the intersection, he waited. How long, he had no idea. Headlights flashed far in the distance and a fast approaching car came zimming along the road, flashing past in a blink and he was alone again. Jake sat beside the road, clutching his knees up against his chest, watching the dark morning pale and the first bright streaks of sunlight break above the black Sierra Nevada; those mountains were so beautiful and remote. Once they had gone hunting there in the high country. That had been the fall before Li'l Beth died and Ertie'd said there was bound to be meat up in those mountains. They'd seen plenty of deer sign but, before they'd even gotten a shot, an angry rancher had ridden them down and thrown them off the land, swearing the next time he caught any goddamn Okies on his range he'd shoot them like varmints.

It was coming full light now and the air was very still. Convinced he had been forgotten, Jake got up and paced impatiently, then sat back down, but he couldn't remain still. Impulsively he got back up and set out for the bridge at a trot, then stopped short. He was leaving his post. No matter what, he wasn't supposed to go off on his own, that's what C. J. had told him. Jake turned and trudged back to the crossroads, so lost in his lonely frustration that he didn't hear the approaching caravan until it was almost on him. The lead vehicle was a 1933 ton-and-a-half Chevy with high side racks; following along behind were eight other jalopies. The truckdriver slowed when he saw Jake and hung his head out. "Sonny, ya seen any strikers out this-a-way?"

"Shor, lots of 'em, right yonder." Jake pointed north. "Up by the bridge, it hain't but a couple of miles, an' you'll fin' 'em."

"Thanks, I thought we was plumb lost."

"Hey, mister," Jake yelled as the truck started forward, "tell 'em not to forgit to come back an' git me."

It was ten, maybe fifteen minutes before Jake spotted a car speeding toward him. Junior skidded to a stop, shouting, "Hurry up! They've already started for the ranch!"

Jake jumped in and Junior spun the car around, quickly shifting through the gears as they sped up the road and across the bridge, gas pedal to the floor. It wasn't long before they could see El Adobe's headquarters compound in the distance. Most of the caravan was already parked along the roadsides and strikers were piling out of the cars and trucks, milling around in the road, unfurling banners, carrying picket signs and flags. Everybody was yelling at somebody else, trying to find out where to go and what to do. Junior slowed and, honking his horn, drove cautiously through the mob, making his way slowly past the airport. Massed like this, the mob of strikers jammed the road clear up beyond the permanent employee housing and crowded into the wide parking area and driveway in front of the store.

"Christ, we gotta git this thing organized." Junior honked again, nudging the car through the crowd. "Do you see Pa's truck?"

"No," Jake yelled back, his eyes searching the crowds. "Wait! There it is, an' there's my pa over thar!"

Junior pulled off the road and nosed the Chevy in between two other cars. "Grab that bullhorn! We gotta get our people together!"

Our people. Jake liked the sound of it. They ran along beside the parked cars, ducking and dodging through the crowds, heading for Lige's truck. Standing up on the cab, C. J. was yelling into a megaphone: "All right! All right, everybody settle down! Get with your picket captains and follow 'em. Harley! Get your people over there, in front of the store. Pete! Dammit, come on. Get 'em together."

Junior yelled up at C. J., "Tell my people to gather here back of Pa's truck."

C. J. nodded. "All of Junior Parsons' pickets, get over here to Lige Parsons' truck. That's the one I'm standin' on. Junior Parsons' pickets, over here! Behind the truck!"

Lige and Ertie were leaning against the truck and Susie was sitting up in the cab, pretending to drive.

Excited, Jake yelled, "Pa, ever see so many people?"

Turning to Lige, Jake pointed. "Right yonder's the pay winda where Pa throwed their damn brass money back at 'em. Cheated us here too, on the box count. How much was it, Pa?"

"Near a dollar."

"Now we'll get back at 'em. Hope we see that Dago crew boss again. Don' you, Pa?"

Ertie grinned. "You excited, boy?"

Jake scrambled up on the truck and looked out over the mob of pickets. There was no sign of Wardlow and it was easy to see that the ranch had been taken by surprise. Foremen and office clerks were hastily setting up barricades, rolling out the oil drums and linking the cable. The two deputies assigned to the ranch full-time pulled their patrol cars sideways in the lane between the store and the office building. Shotgun-carrying guards were rushed into position and stood glaring menacingly as the strikers mobbed up along the entrance to the farm.

There on the porch of the store stood the fat woman who clerked behind the counter, and next to her was the man in the green eyeshade. And on the veranda of the office building, across the lane from the store, men were hurrying about or just standing there watching as the picket lines were forming. Back in on the ranch, past the shops and packing shed, Jake saw the familiar camp cabins and tents. Parked back there in the driveway were the crew buses and trucks standing empty, their tailgate ladders down, ready to load workers for the fields.

Along the picket line somebody started yelling, "Strike! Strike!" and the chant spread. "Strike! Strike! Strike!"

Mexican strikers joined in, *"Huelga! Huelga! Hay huelga aquí! Esquirol afuera!"*

Junior had all of his people together now and three of his assistants were passing out white cardboard picket signs. Jake reached out. "Gimme one."

He got a big placard that read: CIO ON STRIKE in bold red letters. Underneath in smaller letters, COTTON FARMERS UNFAIR. Nothing was written on the back.

"That shor ain' much of a sign," Susie scoffed.

Jake tried to ignore her and listen as Junior strung his pickets out in front of the store and gas pumps.

Susie grabbed him. "Le's make a better sign, print it on the back of this one."

"How?" Jake liked the idea but was stumped.

"I don' know. But we oughta think of somethin'."

"Somethin' 'bout brass money!" Jake was enthusiastic now. "How 'bout 'No Brass Money'?"

"What're we gonna write with?"

"How da I know?"

"Come on!" Susie went to Lige's truck and rummaged around behind the seat where he kept spare parts and a toolbox. She found a heavy pencil stub, like carpenters use, and, using a fender for a desktop, she blocked out the words: NO BRASS MONEY.

"Make it bigger!" Jake coached her. "Bigger. Yeah. That's good."

All around them the chanting was growing louder. "Strike! Strike! Strike!"

Susie handed Jake the sign. "How's that?"

"Good, come on!" They wiggled through the mob and found Ertie. "Pa! Pa! Lookee!"

Ertie grinned. "Let me borrow it for a minute." Holding the sign high, Ertie whistled shrilly, like herders do when they signal working cow dogs, and he yelled, "Hey you! Green Eyeshade! Yeah, you!" and waved the picket sign.

"No Brass Money!" Jake yelled, and Susie echoed the words.

Other strikers nearby picked up the chant. "No Brass Money! No Brass Money!"

All of the noise on the picket lines could be heard back in the camp where the strikebreakers were gathering in clumps and gaggles. The crew bosses were trying to get them loaded into the buses and trucks, but the workers were hesitating, trying to get a better idea of what was going on up by the store and office buildings.

C. J. yelled something at Junior, who nodded and motioned for Jake to follow him back away from the picket line. "Come on!"

Jake gave the picket sign to Susie and followed Junior back out of the crowd to where C. J. was standing. The strike leader put a hand on Jake's shoulder. "Is there any way for them to haul them scabs out 'cept drive 'em through us, here in the front?"

Jake nodded and pointed. "The haul road that runs north from the packin' shed. It's just over back of the store there and goes along behind them foremen's houses. They could get out to the county road from there or they could head east and come out on Fifteen an' a Half. When we was at Kakorian's I used to ride my bike down through there goin' to see my girl."

Jake paused, thinking. Then he turned and pointed straight down between the shops and packing shed. "Past the camp, thar, thar's a bridge over the canal. They could take 'em out that way, back through the peaches. If ya know your way, ya can hit a road that turns south along a ditch. Ya can make it out onto Eighteen, way over there, but it ain' a main haul, hardly wide enough for a truck to get down through there. It'd be hard to get them buses out that way, big as they are."

"Any other ways out?"

"Don' think so."

"Good." C. J. looked relieved. "We got the north and east sides blocked. And we got a small bunch of Mexicans over there on Road Eighteen. It ain' likely them scabs'd try to get out that way."

"What if they do?"

"Send 'em help, quick as we can."

"Who's leadin' 'em?" Junior asked.

"Manuel Padilla."

That worried Junior. "That means real trouble if them crew bosses try to go out that way 'cause them Mexicans's apt to kill somebody."

"Well, I didn' have nobody else to send. I warned 'im not to get into any rough stuff."

"Damnit, C. J., yor forgettin' that it was Manuel's brother that got run over that first day. I tell ya, he's got blood in his eye. That's certain."

C. J. shrugged. "Well, ain' nothin' I can do about it now." The union leader was staring down the lane at the crew bosses loading their workers. "I sure wish we knew what they were going to try." He turned to Jake. "Ya said ya know that layout back there?"

"Yes sir."

"Could ya injun your way back there for a quick look-see?"

"Yes sir."

"C. J. . . ." Junior started to protest.

"Listen, Junior, he's just a kid so they won't suspect nothin'. He knows the layout and could give us an idea how many people they got that's goin' to work an' which way they're headed." The union leader turned back to Jake. "Can you do 'er, boy? Might be dangerous."

"I can do 'er."

"Good. Jus' use yor eyeballs quick an' skin right back out fast as ya can. Okay?"

Jake nodded. "I kin sneak 'round back of the store"—he pointed—"back where they got that swimmin' pool, then up along the railroad tracks back of the icehouse thar."

"Okay, but be careful." C. J. gave him a friendly pat. "An' hurry, we ain' got much time."

The first part was easy. Jake slipped through the line of pickets and ducked behind the store, keeping to the long row of oleander bushes that screened his movements back as far as the north haul road. He stopped there, crouching in the bushes. In the background he could hear the pickets yelling and chanting. Off to his left were the spacious lawns around the ranch houses. Ahead was the packing shed and beyond that the icehouse; the railroad spur paralleling the two large buildings was empty now, but during the summer rail cars were spotted along the packing house dock for loading and then pushed in under the overhead steel scaffolding alongside the icehouse to be iced down for the long trip east. The crews that handled the ice worked on catwalks over the cars. The scaffolding and catwalks were empty now and looked like a giant erector set bolted to the side of the brick building.

Climbing up into the scaffolding looked easy enough—there was a steel ladder up to the walkways over the tracks; from there he could cross over on the ice conveyor and go up to the roof using those braces that were bolted against the building. Once on the roof he'd have a good view of the whole camp and the farm roads leading out the back way.

Jake made his move: a quick dash across the railroad tracks, up the steel ladder to the catwalks, over the guard rail and across the conveyor; he grabbed a firm hold on a cross brace and slowly stood up, balancing on the two-inch I-beam. Still holding on to the brace with his left hand, he reached up with his right hand for the second horizontal I-beam, but it was beyond his grasp. He'd have to jump for it; if he missed it was a thirty-foot fall. Time was short and he could see no other way up. Gritting his teeth, he jumped, hands grasping the cold steel. He hung there for a second, then skinned up and over the beam, just like he'd done hundreds of times on the school playground. From there he was over the wall and onto the roof. Like a crab, he crawled out almost to the roof's edge, lay down and wiggled forward until he could see the camp below.

Christ! Look at 'em! He remembered the camp was big, but not this big. Niggers and Mexicans everywhere. He'd never seen the likes of it, white families in the cabins and by the looks of it all the Mexican women were staying in the packing shed, must be two hundred of them standing out in the lane near the buses. The women looked frightened. Guards and crew pushers were herding them onto the buses, grabbing and pushing them. When the first bus was loaded, a shotgun-carrying guard got on with the driver;

the bus door slammed shut and the bus headed out the back way, over the bridge and turned right along the canal, heading for the narrow roads back through the peaches. The second bus pulled out and followed the first, heading out the back way through the peaches toward Avenue Eighteen.

Jake crawled back from the edge and ran quickly back over the roof. But, when he looked down, he froze. Coming up had been scary, but Jesus, how was he going to get back down? Forcing himself to move, he lay down flat and tentatively rolled over on his stomach, letting his legs over the edge, and scooched out, legs dangling, feet trying to find the I-beam. It wasn't there. He scrambled back up on the roof and looked over; the beam was there. Fixing the location in his mind, he rolled over on his stomach and, legs over the side, lowered himself, heart pounding. His toes touched the top beam and he balanced there for an instant, then cautiously squatted down, using the brick wall for balance. So far, so good. He let himself down onto the bar, swung upside down, hanging by his hands and legs, then let his legs drop, feeling for the beam below with his toes. Remembering how he'd had to jump for the bar on the way up, he guessed his toes were no more than two or three inches from the I-beam. But if he missed! His hands were cramping in pain. He had to try something else. Kicking wildly, he swung his body sideways, hooked a leg around the steel upright, grabbed ahold of it and slid down. Safe. He let himself down to the ice chute, quickly climbed over the conveyor belt and onto the catwalk and scrambled down the ladder, caution forgotten. On the ground, he ran down the railroad tracks in the shadow of the packing shed.

"Stop!"

The shout came from behind him. Running and stumbling as he looked back he saw a shotgun-carrying guard a long way back and heard the man yell, "Stop, or I'll shoot!"

Jake sprinted past the end of the packing shed. Ahead was the haul road and the oleanders, but instinctively he ducked left, around the corner of the packing shed, just as the guard fired.

For the second time Jake heard the rattle of buckshot pellets against a hard surface, but he was already safely around the corner. Ducking and dodging through old crates and stacks of boxes, Jake ran hard, trying to get away without thinking of where he was going. Looking ahead at the last instant, he stopped dead.

Shit! With the guard behind him there was only one way out and that was right into the center of the headquarters compound, out into the lane between the sheds and shops. He'd have to run like hell straight past the store and through the barricades to reach safety. There was no other choice. Just like in a game of Red Rover, he had to make a run for the safety line, but this time it wasn't the kids on the Bitter Creek schoolgrounds daring him to come over, no sir. It was the goons and they wanted to tag him out with guns or clubs.

The single shotgun blast had everyone, guards and strikers alike, looking toward the packing shed as Jake bolted into sight, pounding down the dirt lane, running as hard as he could for the barricades and the safety of the picket line. Behind him, the guard couldn't shoot for fear of hitting his own people; ahead, the guards at the barricades were caught in an instant of astonishment; then, realizing they had the boy in a trap, they came quickly toward Jake, feet outspread, ready to grab him. Jake ran straight at them. At the last instant he feinted left toward the office and ducked back to the right toward the store; leaping up on the porch like a high hurdler, running the length of the porch, he bowled the fat clerk out of the way and ran past the man in the green eyeshade, escaping down the steps. Crashing between the gas pumps, he sent cans and pails flying and darted safely across the picket line. Red Rover had made it over.

At the first sight of him running the strikers had fallen silent, but only for an instant; then they were cheering him on, and a roar of approval went up as he faked the guards out and ran down the porch. Panting for breath, Jake found C. J. and blurted out, "They're goin' out the back way! Over the canal, toward Eighteen."

"You all right, boy?"

"Yeah." Jake was doubled over, hands on his knees, trying to catch his breath.

Susie and Ertie were beside him now, concerned.

"I'm okay, I tell ya. Just winded."

"Boy"—Ertie had an arm around Jake's shoulders—"you'd a made a hell of a bullfighter. Way you ducked and dodged out there."

C. J. yelled, "Barney, get your people over along Avenue Eighteen, you'll see Manuel's pickets there. Back 'em up, see that those scabs don' get out. Junior! Get yor people over there too. An' Junior, tell that Mexican I don' want nobody killed. Understand? We'll stay here, case they double back this way."

"Okay!" Junior looked around for Lige. "Pa, you'n Ertie get them people loaded up. Bert! Dennis! Get your people over to Avenue Eighteen." Junior was stabbing at the air with his finger, pointing the directions. "Get on over as fast as ya can!"

"Pa, we're goin' with Junior." Jake grabbed Susie's hand. "Come on."

Manuel Padilla had placed his pickets along Avenue Eighteen to block the narrow dirt road that came out of the peach orchard. In effect he was crossing the T and his position was a strong one, but the assignment was not as important as being up at the main entrance. That was a disappointment. He was guarding an insignificant road, a narrow track bounded by the trees on the left and a high canal bank on the right, not a likely escape route. The Mexicans were restless because there was no one to confront. After hearing what sounded like a shotgun blast in the distance, a few started talking about going around front, where the action was, but Manuel Padilla would have none of that. Although he too wanted action, he ordered them to stay. It was their duty.

There was a noise in the orchard and somebody shouted for silence. Back in the trees they heard the lumbering growl of low gears and the scrape of tree branches on metal, ominous sounds like unseen tanks approaching through a forest. Padilla sent his scouts running into the trees; quickly they were back, warning that buses and crew trucks were coming this way through the orchard. Excitement electrified the atmosphere and the pickets crowded into the dirt road and up on the ditch-bank, tense, waiting. They were the ones who would have the action. Two hundred yards down the road they saw the white fender and hood of a bus nose slowly out from the trees and begin its clumsy turn onto the dirt road, coming toward them.

A shout went up: *"Viva la huelga! Viva la causa!"*

The road was so narrow the driver couldn't complete the turn. Fender against the canal bank, he stopped, backed up and tried again, cramping the wheels and gunning the engine. The bus came lurching slowly around and the driver shifted into second, step-

ping on the gas. A second bus inched through the turn and followed, bouncing ponderously along; behind it came another bus
and a crew truck loaded with blacks. The strikers charged screaming and yelling, a mob so forceful the lead driver jammed on the
brakes. The guard yanked open the door and, shotgun ready,
started to get out, but a hail of rocks and clods drove him back
inside. The mob was shouting at the women in the buses, "*Es-
quiroles y putas! Huelga! Huelga!*"

Frightened, but not wanting to run over anyone, the lead driver
tried to force the bus through the mob. The windshield shattered,
suddenly, explosively, showering him with glass shards, and the
bus's front wheels bounced through a deep chuckhole, wrenching
the steering wheel from his grasp; the bus turned sharply up the
ditch-bank and stalled, stranded high at a rakish angle. The women
workers screamed and the driver frantically tried to restart the
engine. Pickets swarmed around the front of the bus, rocking it,
trying to tip it over. Other strikers pushed past the first bus and
swarmed around the second and the third vehicles that were now
trapped in the lane. Black workers were leaping from the crew
truck and fleeing.

This was the scene Jake saw as the union reinforcements arrived. Junior was out of the car running, Jake following him into
the fight. Up ahead, a big, burly picket ripped a limb off a tree
and began using it as a club. Jake caught a glimpse of Ertie, tire
iron in hand, smashing out the bus headlights and beating on the
hood.

Jake laughed and yelled, "No more brass money!"

But his father couldn't hear him in the din and Jake was pushed
along, caught up in the mob's frenzy. He grabbed a clod and hurled
it and sought another and another and was carried past the first
bus by the swarm of pickets. Pandemonium engulfed these vehicles, another windshield shattered amid the screams and shouts
of trapped workers and strikers. A dozen pickets teamed up on
one side of the second bus and were rocking it, shouting "Push!
Push! Push!" trying to tip it over. The emergency door in back
flew open and the guard and driver fled. Inside the bus terrified
women workers were screaming. More strikers ran to the side of
the bus, joining in the effort.

The driver of the lead bus had gotten the engine started again,
there was the frantic sound of clashing gears as the bus lurched

back down off the ditch-bank and shot forward, the gas pedal mashed to the floor. Junior jumped aside as the bus bowled through the strikers and careened out onto the road, speeding away.

Shocked by the wild scene, Junior struggled to get through the mob; he had to stop them from tipping the second bus over. He lunged ahead, shouting, "Stop it! Stop it!"

Jake saw Junior fighting his way through the pickets and cheered, thinking his friend was encouraging the strikers. Back in the orchard Jake could see other buses and trucks stalled along the haul roads, blocked by the actions at the front of the column. Jake grabbed Junior's arm. "Look! Look! We got 'em stopped!"

The door of the third bus was standing open and the driver was gone, but the guard stood his ground, shotgun leveled, keeping the strikers back as thirty women scrambled out the door and fled. The guard fired a warning shot: BOOM! And he too ran. Back in the orchard gears clashed, engines revved as some of the drivers tried frantically to back up and turn around, but the earth was too soft and the trees too thick for them to break out before they were surrounded by strikers. Workers were abandoning the vehicles and running.

Manuel Padilla was up on the ditch-bank, gleefully watching the efforts to overturn the second bus and yelling encouragement through his bullhorn, *"Dale! Dales en la madre! Viva la huelga! Viva la causa!"*

Junior, frustrated because he couldn't get control of the mob, whirled and ran up the ditch-bank, grabbing for the bullhorn. "We gotta stop it!"

Surprised, Manuel hung onto the bullhorn, pulling it from Junior's grasp.

"Dammit, C. J. doesn't want any violence. Christ, Manuel! Those are just women in there."

"Putas! That's what they are, whores!" He turned and shouted over the megaphone, *"Pinche putas! Vendidas!"*

Junior was raging at Manuel, "Ya always fight women?"

The words were like a slap. Anger flashed in Manuel's eyes.

But Junior hadn't waited to see the reaction. He jumped down the ditch-bank and waded into the pickets again, pulling them back away from the vehicle, trying to clear the doorway so the women could get off the bus. "Get back, let 'em off. Get back!"

Then Manuel was beside him, *"Cálmala! Cálmala! Retíranse, hombres."*

Others took up the message—*"Cálmala, cálmala"*—and slowly, begrudgingly the strikers backed away a few steps, but stood there menacingly. A few of the women had escaped out the rear exit but most still huddled in terror, clinging to the seats. Junior forced the door open and motioned for the women to get out, but they only cowered there in the bus.

Manuel stepped up and in Spanish told the women they were safe, that they would be unharmed if they would get off the bus. The women came quickly out, fleeing through the orchard. Junior climbed back up on the ditch-bank, surveying the scene. The battle was over, the strikers were moving back out on the road. Satisfied, Junior found Jake and handed him his keys. "Take my car and go tell C. J. we got the road blocked."

"Anythin' else?"

"Jus' tell 'im ain' nobody comin' out this way an' we knocked at least a half dozen of them buses and trucks out of commission. And Jake, tell 'im nobody got killed." Junior grinned in relief.

"Okay."

Back around in front of the ranch headquarters Jake parked as close as he could get to the store and reported to C. J.

"Anyone hurt?"

"No, but them Mexicans went wild, tried to tip over a busload of women, but Junior got 'em stopped."

"Good. Anything else?"

"They wrecked some of the buses, smashed out the windows, ripped the wires off the engines. Ain' nobody goin' to drive out that way for a while."

"Good job."

"Wan' me to go back over thar?"

C. J. glanced at his watch. They had been at El Adobe for more than an hour now and word was bound to have reached the farmers. "Not yet. Stick close and listen."

"C. J. ?"

"What?"

"Am I doin' all right?"

"Shor, boy. You're doin' just dandy."

C. J. sent runners to tell the picket captains they were breaking off the confrontation, immediately. It was time to implement the third phase of their plan. Strikers standing near C. J. overheard the orders and were surprised. One grumbled, "Hell, C. J., we got this place bottled up. They can't get out if we stay."

More strikers were gathering around to hear what was going on. Someone else yelled, "We leave, they'll jus' load up them damn scabs and go pick cotton."

"Listen!" C. J. held up his hand for quiet. "We been here long enough. Likely every farmer and lawman in the county's heard what's goin' on here. When they show up, with Wardlow leadin' 'em, there'll be one hell of a fight if we're still around."

"Goddammit, C. J., we don' have to turn tail, there's more'n enough of us. We can fight 'em!"

A cheer went up.

"Sure, we can fight here and maybe we can whup 'em, but we got a better plan. We ain' tol' nobody but the picket captains 'cause we want to surprise them farmers. Why do you think Wardlow and all of them farmers aren't here right now? How come they ain' showed up?"

He let the question soak in, then explained, "We planned this so's the farmers'd think we was attacking Coco Oil. Sent a bunch of our boys over thar to draw them away from us here. By the looks of thangs, they done their job.

"But the idea was that when ol' man Wardlow got wind of us hittin' him here, why he'd come a stormin' this way, madder'n a scalded dog. Well le' me ask ya all somethin' else. What if he shows up with his bully boys but we ain' here? What if we've done split up an' are attackin' ever' other place we can find workers?

"The farmers'll be here. The whole bunch of 'em. An' we'll be out thar, where the workers is. I mean, boys, they'll never catch up to us. Before this day's done, I guarantee ya, the harvest'll be shut down."

The disagreement had dissolved into silence and the silence erupted in cheers.

"Okay, then, listen up! Stay with your picket captains and do what they say. We've scouted out ranches where there's workers in the fields. R'member, we don't want no violent stuff. Sweet-talk them folks into joinin' us if ya can. If ya can't, try to scare 'em out, but I don' want nobody hurt. That won't do us no good."

Once the third phase of the plan was in motion, C. J. called to Jake. "Where'd ya park the car?"

"Over thar, 'cross the road."

"Let's go. I'll ride along with you and Junior for a while, then later I may want to light out, if Junior'll lend me his car and a driver." C. J. gave Jake a by now familiar pat on the back. "That okay with you?"

"Want me to drive you?" Jake couldn't quite believe what he was hearing.

"Shor, if it's okay with Junior."

They were climbing into the Chevy now and Jake slammed the door, pleased as punch. He was a sure-enough union man and now he was the union president's driver. Wow! To hell with brass money.

18

A phone rang in the empty office. Early morning sunlight streamed through the windows casting rectangles of light on the vacant desk. A cigar butt smoldered in the ashtray, wisping curls of smoke rising blue through the yellow sunlight. The phone rang again.

Out in the gin yard the fight was over and the farmers milled about, excited by their easy victory. Some were still happily attacking the strikers' abandoned cars, bashing headlights and windows, slashing tires. Others taunted a dozen prisoners who stood roped together, hands tied behind their backs. Lying on the ground in front of the prisoners were the bodies of three semiconscious strikers, broken and bleeding. All three were black men. Trussed up like hogs, their bodies had been smeared with foul-smelling chicken manure. Red paint had been poured over their nappy heads. A handful of vigilantes, armed now with buckets and swabs, were smearing more chicken slops on the rest of the prisoners and slapping their faces with red paint.

Disgusted, Windy Scott turned and walked clear of the mob. There was no need to treat prisoners like that. The sheriff was also troubled by the morning's action—it had been too easy. They had caught the union by surprise, that was certain, but there'd been so few strikers, less than a hundred actually, and many of them had driven into the gin yard alone, in separate cars. That too was odd.

The farmers had closed the trap so fast some of the strikers hadn't even had time to get out of their cars. The posses converged quickly on the caravan and started smashing windows and grabbing door handles, jerking union men out of their jalopies. The strikers fought hard, once out of their cars, and they stuck together, rallying around Thad Greene. That big nigger was bull-strong, Windy Scott had to give him that. The sheriff had seen him grab up one man after another with that stump of an arm, using it like a giant clamp, pinning his victims while he smashed them senseless with that one big fist, all the while roaring insults. Only when the strikers were overwhelmed did Greene sound the retreat, his black face scowling in rage, his voice thundering: "Git-outa-here! Run! Scatter! Git-outa-here!" Those who hadn't been knocked senseless made a run for it; some got back to their jalopies and roared off, but most fled into the fields.

Ignoring the mob behind him, the sheriff walked toward the gin office, wondering why there had been so few strikers if this was really the union's big push.

The phone was ringing in the gin office, signaling trouble. Hurrying through the door, he grabbed the receiver off the hook and yelled into the horn, "Yeah?"

"Sheriff?"

"Yeah?"

"Oh, God, where ya been? We been tryin' to raise ya for nearly a half hour."

"Ramey?"

"Yeah." The captain's voice sounded frantic. "We finally dispatched a car out to warn ya. He there yet?"

"What the hell are you talking about? Ramey! What's happened?"

"Union's attacked El Adobe. More'n a thousand of 'em, and they wrecked the place, maybe killed some people," Ramey blabbered, near hysteria. "They jumped the place just after dawn. We been tryin' to get ahold of ya ever since . . ."

"Ramey! For Christ's sake calm down!" Sheriff Scott's jaw clamped down tight on the cigar butt and he swore to himself, wishing he had the guts to fire Ramey. But he couldn't fire him, the fat-ass bastard had some damned important political connections.

"Sheriff? Ya there?"

"Ramey, is the union still out there? At El Adobe?"

"Yeah."

"Who've you got out there?"

"Just two deputies. Elmer's in the office, there, where I can reach 'im. Dan's out back somewheres. Last we heard he said all hell'd broke loose."

"Shit!" The sheriff slammed the receiver back on the hook, thought for a second, then picked the phone up. "Central? Ring El Adobe!"

Sheriff Scott paced impatiently, holding the receiver to his ear with one hand, the transmitter gripped in the other. "Hello! Who's this? Well, get me Deputy Snodgrass. Elmer? What's happening out there?"

"The place is surrounded." The deputy sounded frightened. "I ain' never seen so many goddamn strikers."

Sheriff Scott interrupted. "You hear from Dan?"

"He's just comin' in now."

"Put him on." The sheriff was still pacing. "Dan? What's happening?"

"Sheriff, all hell's broke loose."

The sheriff rolled his eyes and snarled, "What the fuck does that mean?"

"Well, this mornin' they filled up all them buses with them Mexican women, from Juarez, an' the niggers they got down in Lou'siana, an' started out the back way, through the peach orchards there . . ."

"For Christ's sake, Dan, what happened?"

"I'm tryin' to tell ya, sheriff. They was goin' out that back way there, like I said, and I was followin' 'em when all at once them Mexican strikers jumped us, just run right at them buses."

"Why didn't you stop 'em?"

"Couldn't! It was like we'd knocked down a hornet nest, they was swarmin' so thick all over us, smashin' the windows, trying to tip the buses over. They run 'Dobe's guards off an' went after me, ripped the antenna clean off my car. I almost didn't get out of there."

The sheriff snapped, "Union still there?"

"Hell yes. Can't ya hear 'em outside? Sheriff, ya gotta get us help quick."

"All right, sit tight! We'll be there soon as we can." Sheriff Scott hung up and stood there for a second or two, thinking. A

354

damn sucker play. That's why so few strikers showed up here, the union'd outfoxed them. Sheriff Scott was out the door and striding through the gin yard, yelling at Wardlow. "Titus! They've hit El Adobe!"

"What?" Wardlow scowled.

"Suckered us over here and then hit your place. A thousand strikers. They knocked out your buses and trucks and bottled up the place. Crews never got out of camp."

"Shit!" Wardlow spun around and looked at the noisy mob, wanting to get their attention. He turned back to the sheriff. "Fire off a couple rounds!"

Sheriff Scott was surprised. "What for?"

"Get their fucking attention."

With a quick, fluid motion that was always surprising, the sheriff drew his Colt .45 and fired in the air: BLAM! BLAM!

The mob was suddenly silent.

"Listen up!" The sheriff shouted. "The union's hit El Adobe!"

Hundreds of angry voices reacted in disbelief. Sheriff Scott held up his hands for quiet: "Just got word! About a thousand pickets hit El Adobe just after dawn. The raid down here was a feint to pull us away."

"Quiet down!" Wardlow barked. "We got to catch them at my place!"

"What about the prisoners?" someone yelled.

"Load 'em in the truck. Windy'll send some of his men into town with them! The rest follow us to El Adobe!"

Sirens wailing, the posse raced north across the county, a parade of pickups and farm trucks loaded with men determined to lift the siege at El Adobe. However, when they got there, the county road in front of the ranch was empty; the strikers were gone.

Wardlow scrambled out of the sheriff's car and ran up the steps to the veranda just as the two deputies came out of the office.

"Sheriff?" Deputy Elmer Snodgrass yelled. "They're gone!"

"How long ago?" Wardlow growled.

"Fifteen, maybe twen'y minutes."

"Mr. Wardlow." The money changer in the green eyeshade was standing nearby. "I heared some of 'em talkin' like they was goin' off in little bunches, hit different farms."

"Where? They say where?"

"Didn't hear no names."

"Damn!" Wardlow looked around at the farmers and lawmen. "Okay!" He had his hands up, signaling for quiet. "Okay. We got problems. The union's scattered and is likely striking every place they find workers."

There were mutterings and rumbles of discontent. Several farmers were already heading for their pickup trucks.

Wardlow yelled after them. "If you get hit by pickets, call the network. If you can't get through, get word to the sheriff's office and we'll send you some help. Okay? Rest of you Jeff County farmers go on home. Holler if you need help. You guys from Fresno County, stick around until we get this thing sorted out, will you?"

There were nods and grunts of agreement.

Wardlow motioned to the sheriff. "Windy, come on in. We gotta make plans."

In the office, Wardlow collapsed in the chair behind his desk, pushed his hat back and picked up the phone. "Gimme six-two-three-J." He waited, chewing on his cigar. "What d'ya mean they don't answer? Goddammit, ring it again." There was no answer at the Eagles Hall. He slammed the receiver back on the hook. Damn! He'd forgotten that Shriver was gone, had left right after the big meeting in front of the reporters, and they hadn't left anyone behind this morning to man the office there.

The sheriff was on the phone at a second, smaller desk. "Yeah? Yeah, how many of them? Okay. Right, yeah, you did the right thing. I'll call ya back." He yelled across to Wardlow. "Union's hit Smuthers' place and another bunch's over at Aldrich's, out near Frye's Corners." The sheriff was up and on his way out the door.

"Wait a goddamn minute! Phone network's not working, we gotta set up some kind of command post, get this thing reorganized."

"Hell, they can just call the office, dispatcher'll keep track."

"All right. Windy, run it for me yourself, will you?"

"Sure."

"Use the boardroom. Run some more phones in there. Operators can push the calls there. I'm goin' up in the Spartan an' have a look around and then I'll land at the Jeff City airport. Have somebody waiting for me in, say"—he looked at his watch—"half hour. No, make it forty-five minutes. Okay?"

"Want me to send help to Smuthers and Aldrich?"

"Yeah. Have your men take some of those Fresno farmers along. Tell the rest to hang around here until we know where we'll need 'em." Wardlow was out the door and down the steps. "Olander!" He yelled at one of the Fresno growers, "I'm goin' up for a look. Want to come on along?"

Aloft, he flew an expanding search pattern, looking for strike caravans or picket lines. From the air the valley looked peaceful enough. The orchards were yellow now and losing their foliage, the grain and hay lands were barren and for miles they could see empty cottonfields, flagged white, ready for harvest.

"There!" Olander was pointing off to the right. "Down there, about two o'clock."

Wardlow banked the Spartan into a tight turn, studying the farm and the workers in the field. "Looks like Kakorian's place." Pushing the controls over, he dove into a low-level fly-by, the big radial engine thundering. "Look at those fucking strikers, goin' right into the field."

"Look, that fella's holdin' 'em off with a shotgun!"

"That's Kakorian."

"There's a bunch of kids in that field."

"Town kids. Schools let 'em out to pick for us when we need them." Wardlow orbited the field.

"That shotgun's got those strikers stopped, but he needs help," Olander shouted over the engine noise.

Wardlow leveled out and began gaining altitude, flying away, starting the search again.

Olander looked worried. "Aren't we goin' to help that fella Kakorian?"

"Not a goddamn thing we can do, 'less you've got a machine gun in your hip pocket."

Wardlow glanced at his instruments and pulled the power back to cruise, then let his gaze sweep the farmlands below. Several times they saw strike caravans and more picket lines around cottonfields. In one field the pickers were walking out and joining the strikers as the Spartan circled overhead. Wardlow made up his mind right there: fighting the strike on the picket lines wasn't getting the job done, they had to root those union bastards out of the damn park and bust up their camp. Drive them out!

Aggressively Wardlow banked the ship over, added power and headed for the Jeff City airport.

Colonel Winchester stood at the window in the boardroom watching hundreds of strikers gathering in the park for the evening rally. The farmers had seriously underestimated their opponents today and, as a military man, he had to give the union leadership high marks for their successful guerrilla tactics—but the fight wasn't over. Not by a long shot. The union forces were vulnerable. Their big strike camp was almost indefensible and Wardlow, his pride wounded by the beating at El Adobe, would show no restraint now.

The confrontation that Winchester had predicted was shaping up and he was powerless to stop it. At midday he had called the governor and warned him that there was just no way that twenty-five motorcycle policemen could handle this situation. Olson, after a long pause, had replied, "Colonel, my hands are tied. I can't send troops against the farmers. Politically, I'm on a tightrope. The Republicans have control of the legislature and many of the people in my own party sympathize with the farmers. They wouldn't stand for such a move. No, I'm afraid the highway patrol will have to suffice. Don't worry, Captain McNulty's a good man."

That was true enough, McNulty was a good man. He had demonstrated that this morning out in front of the courthouse when the sheriff's men had brought in the Dixieland prisoners. The deputies had forced their captives to stand on the front steps of the courthouse so the local paper could get their picture. The prisoners, reeking of chicken shit and covered with red paint, were hurting and near collapse but they were made to stand there on the granite steps like a graduating class while a crowd gathered.

Attracted by the noise, Winchester had come out of the courthouse just as Al Wirin pushed his way through the crowd and ran up the steps. The bespectacled little attorney had confronted the deputies, demanding that they release his clients.

McNulty, who had been meeting with his men in the courthouse basement, was there too. After a quick look around, McNulty had sprinted back to his men, armed them with shotguns and marched them out, positioning them on the sidewalk directly behind the crowd. Men deployed, McNulty bulled his way through the townspeople, shouting at the deputy in charge, "Sergeant! Stop this disgusting display!"

Surprised, the crowd parted, giving the captain a pathway as the sheriff's sergeant started down the steps belligerently. "You got no authority here."

Wirin started to say something, but McNulty waved him silent and turned his full attention on the sergeant. "Either you take those prisoners to the jail, clean them up and treat them humanely or I will order my men to take control! And sergeant, I'll throw you in jail if you resist."

Without waiting for a response, McNulty turned and shouted a command to his men. "Lock and load!"

There was the clack-clacking sound of the pump-action riot guns being readied for action. Turning back to the sergeant, his voice level but deadly, McNulty said, "If you don't instantly move those prisoners, we're taking over."

The sergeant backed up a step or two, hesitated, then gave in. "Get them prisoners out of here. Take 'em to jail."

Wirin, standing between the prisoners and the sergeant, butted in. "I demand these men be released, taken to the hospital and cleaned up, their wounds treated, the paint removed from their heads."

"They're going to jail!" the sergeant yelled.

"On what charges?"

"Inciting a riot. Assault on a police officer. Conspiracy to overthrow the government." The sergeant snapped out the words just as he had memorized them.

Wirin didn't back down. "Sergeant, you release these men, now, and I demand that—"

"Counselor!" McNulty interrupted the lawyer. "These are the steps of the courthouse, not the courtroom. You'll have to make your argument inside. Sergeant, take these men to jail. Clean them up and see that they get medical attention. Immediately!"

Wirin went rapidly down the steps, telling McNulty as he went by, "I'm holding you personally responsible for what happens to these men."

The crowd booed the lawyer and jostled him as he tried to make his way through. A fat woman spit in his face, screaming, "Dirty Jew!" And the crowd pressed in closer. Someone shouted, "Lynch the little Jew bastard." A hairy fist punched Wirin, nearly knocking him down.

McNulty waded back into the crowd, roughly pushing the people aside, shouting "Stand back! Get out of the way!" He grabbed Wirin's arm. "Come with me!" Quickly they had made their way to the patrolmen standing protectively at the ready.

Yes, McNulty was a good man, but the odds were too great, this thing was already out of control. Winchester could feel it in his bones. That afternoon he'd made one last stab at trying to get the farmers to accept outside mediation and, failing that, he had taken up a position in the courthouse, in the boardroom on the second floor where he could have a view of the park and hear what responses the local lawmen were making. Ramey didn't like having this intruder in the command post, but Winchester not only insisted, he commandeered one of the telephones.

The boardroom was quiet now, the phones were no longer ringing wildly; the two-way radio chatter had dropped off after the last of the strike caravans had disbanded for the day. Below him, Winchester watched the striking cotton pickers streaming into the park; they were in a noisy, belligerent mood, combat veterans who had been bloodied in the fight and discovered their enemy could be beaten. Defiantly, several picket captains rallied their people and staged an impromptu march on the jail, shouting encouragement and support for those who had been arrested. More strikers joined the procession encircling the jail, marching, singing, waving their placards and banners.

The bell in the clock tower atop the courthouse sounded once, its heavy gong echoing the half hour. Winchester checked his watch: five-thirty. Directly below he could see McNulty positioning half of his men on the side lawn between the granite courthouse and the park. From there they could keep an eye on the park and the jail, ready to move when ordered. Each patrolman had a truncheon at the ready and carried both a gas mask and a sidearm, but none of them had riot guns or tear-gas launchers. Those weapons were in the basement, where McNulty had positioned his reserves. From the basement side door they could be up and out of the building and into action within seconds.

Jake joined the stream of strikers marching arm-in-arm around the jail singing:

The farmer's havin' a terrible time, parley-vous,
The farmer's havin' a terrible time, parley-vous,
The farmer's havin' a terrible time
Keeping us off the picket line
Hinky dinky, parley-vous.

They circled the jail once and were starting around again when Jake spotted Clara and Homer over near the line of highway patrolmen on the lawn outside the courthouse. He broke free of the march and ran over to her. "Where ya been?"

"Jis' got here." Clara gave him a quick kiss, embarrassing him. "Looked for ya at El Adobe this mornin'."

"At El Adobe?" Clara was puzzled. "Pa said they was headed for Coco Oil and there was goin' to be a big fight. He made us stay in camp."

Homer butted in. "He got all mad when we said we wanted to come to the rally tonight."

"Why's he mad?"

"I don' know why he's so pissed off. But him an' Uncle Ott, they heard somethin' that had 'em all fussed an' they was talkin' 'bout pullin' out." Homer was excited. "They wasn't comin' to the rally so we hitched a ride in."

"Jake?" Clara reached for his hand, trying to lead him away. "Le's go some'eres, I gotta talk to ya."

Homer was looking at the line of highway patrolmen. "Who're them guys?"

"Motorcycle cops." Jake ignored Clara, still caught up in the excitement of the day.

"They look mean." Homer stared at the officers.

Clara whispered, "Come on," trying to get Jake to walk away with her.

"Clara, it's still light."

"That ain' what I want!" She was angry now, and hurt.

Halfway across the park, Susie came running toward them yelling, her red-gold hair flashing in the fading sunlight. "Jake! Jake! They're gone!"

"What?"

Susie was out of breath. "Parrots! They ain' there."

"What d'ya mean?"

"Mean they're gone! Come on, I'll show ya."

She was right, the cage was empty.

"Jeez," Jake whispered, "them deputies musta done it."

"Done what?" Homer asked.

"Got rid of 'em. Probably wrung their necks."

Clara was near tears. "They was so purty. Gawd, Jake, ya think they killed 'em all?"

"Musta."

Angry, Susie swore. "Sons a bitches!"

Puzzled, Homer wondered, "Why'd they do a thang like that?"

"You ask the dumbest questions!" Susie looked at Homer in furious disbelief. "Killed 'em 'cause they cussed them deputies out."

They stood forlornly before the empty cages for a few minutes, not saying much. Walking away, Susie kicked at a candy wrapper and asked Clara and Homer if they'd been out at El Adobe. When they shook their heads, she got excited again, telling them about Jake's wild dash through the barricades.

Astounded, Clara turned to Jake. "Ya coulda been killed!"

"Naw." Jake toed the ground. "Come on, let's find Pa and Lige, see what Junior's a-doin'."

A fire-orange sun was setting behind the granite courthouse, turning the sky red and casting deep blue shadows into the park. In the orange glow shinning through the upper windows of the courthouse Susie saw the silhouette of a man standing there, looking down at them. "Lookee, Jake, up there," she pointed. "Wonder who that fella is?"

"Don' know. Come on."

They found Junior near the bandstand huddled with several other organizers, making plans for tomorrow. C. J. was saying, "Word is more'n half of El Adobe crews walked off after we left. Looks like we got the whole harvest shut clean down. Boys, we got 'em on the run."

Lige and Ertie were nearby listening to a skinny hillbilly talking about the Dixieland fight. His name was Orley Simmons and a tire iron had cracked his skull. That, he said, was why his head was bandaged. Simmons explained, "We figgered they'd be a layin' for us down to Coco Oil, but nobody ever guessed that they'd bushwhack us thar in the gin yard, come at us with tar irons an' ax handles. Some of us had ourselves some clubs too, an' we busted some hay-ids, I'll tell ya."

"Any shootin'?"

"Nope. Weren't no shootin', but I tell ya somethin' boys, they had it in for Tommy Joad an' ol' Brad, seemed like they knowed 'em right off. An' the way they went at that big nigger, Thad Greene, why boys I'll tell ya, they meant to kill him, shorly did. Went after all them niggers, but they really had it in for ol' Thad. He was fightin' hard, picked one farmer up and smashed 'im down like a ragdoll, but they was all over him. Beat him near to death. Some of us tried to get back thar to he'p 'im, but that's when my lights got turned out. Never saw who hit me."

"How'd ya git away?"

"Shit, I don' rightly know. Fellas with me said I jumped up an' went to hollerin' an' fightin' again, but I don' recollect none of that. Next thing I knowed, we was out in some cotton patch a-hidin'."

Clara tugged at Jake's sleeve and with her eyes she again asked him to follow her out of the park.

He could see something was troubling her. "What'sa matter?"

"Cain' talk here." Clara nodded toward Susie and Homer.

"Okay." He followed her through the crowd and out of the park toward the nice houses and pretty yards, walking along under the sycamores, kicking at the leaves on the sidewalk.

After a while Clara stopped. Looking up at him, she said, "Pa's fixin' to pull out."

Jake put his arms around her. "That's what Homer said."

"Well"—she was defiant now—"I ain' goin' with 'em!"

"What're ya goin' ta do?" The question was out before he even thought about it.

"Honey"—she took a deep breath, then whispered—"I'm gonna have a baby."

The words were stunning, overwhelming.

"Ain'cha gonna say nothin'?"

"Ya shor?"

"Yes, I'm shor!" Clara flashed angrily, "Yor sorry, ain'cha?"

Jake shook his head no.

Her moods were fluctuating wildly. She grabbed for him, hugging him close, begging, "Jake, love me!"

Awkwardly he put his arms around her. "When?"

"What?" She looked up at him, hurt in her eyes.

"When ya gonna have it?"

Angry again, she pulled away. "Gawd, Jake. That all ya gotta say?"

Jake reached out for her tentatively, uncertain what to do. "I didn' mean nothin'."

She clutched him again. "Oh, Jake, we can git married. Live with yor folks."

"Yor shor? About the baby?"

Sobbing, she jerked free and started running back toward the park.

Jake ran after her. "Clara! Clara, don'." He caught her and pulled her close to him, no longer tentative. "Don' run away. I jus' don' know what to do!"

"Yor sorry, ain'cha?"

"No," he shouted, then his tone softened. "It's jus' a surprise. That's all." He held her now and felt her clinging to him, but his stomach was churning and he was frightened. What were they going to do with a baby? The idea was too new and he didn't know how to react. What was right? Marriage? No, not yet. He felt like a little boy and he wanted to run and hide someplace. Dammit, why'd she have to get pregnant?

They had been walking aimlessly along a side street and, without realizing, they were almost back to the park. Suddenly, coming around the corner, their way was blocked by a mob, a big one. Farmers. Townspeople. Lawmen. All ganged up along Sixth Street, flanking the park. The street Jake and Clara were on made a T intersection with Sixth, dead ahead, taking them right into the back side of the mob.

Jake froze. "Jeesus H. Christ!"

They were behind the mob, unseen. There were maybe two hundred men, maybe more, and it looked like they were getting ready to attack the strikers in the park. Each vigilante was wearing a white armband and carrying a club or a whip and all of them were strangely quiet, as if they were awaiting a signal and didn't want to attract any attention until then.

"Who are they?" Clara was frightened.

"Farmers, mostly. Ain' never seen 'em gathered up on this side of the park before."

Jake and Clara retreated, running back south a block, then east, paralleling Sixth Street, flanking the farmers' position until they reached Highway 99. There they turned north again toward the corner of the park.

"Gawd, look!" Clara stopped suddenly.

Another group of vigilantes had blocked one lane of the highway and were assembling on the east edge of the park. From the corner Jake could see both bunches and now he was certain there would be a third group over on north side, on the school lawn where the farmers usually gathered. Then there was that bunch of motorcycle cops covering the west side, by the courthouse. The park was surrounded!

"Run." Jake pulled Clara along behind as he dashed across the street and into the park, past the empty parrot cage and into the protective crowds of strikers who were rallied around the bandstand. Out of breath and frightened, Jake tugged on Clara's hand. "Come on." Pulling her along behind him, he pushed through the crowds, wanting to find his father and Susie, warn them and Junior that the park was surrounded.

Some union guy was up on the bandstand making a speech and the strikers were packed in solid around the bandstand, a dense throng so large it filled most of the park. People were everywhere. Clara clutched his hand fearfully, trying to keep up. The speaker was shouting now: "Them farmers an' their gun thugs don' wan' us to make one big union! They're against the CIO! Agains' the workin' man . . ."

The clock up in the courthouse tower tolled the hour, the mellow sound of the heavy bell ringing through the park: six o'clock. From three sides of the park a lusty cheer went up and the vigilantes charged in joyful anger, clubs and whips held high.

Only the thin line of highway patrolmen on the west side held fast.

The farmers' battle plan was simple; those who charged into

the park would trap the strikers between them, beating down those who resisted. Strikers who fled were trapped by a line of truncheon-wielding sheriff's deputies and city policemen who were waiting in the streets to capture those strikers flushed from the park. The lawmen carried extra handcuffs and short hanks of rope stuffed in their belts and they had two paddy wagons and a large stock truck standing by for prisoners.

The strikers were caught in the onslaught from three sides and had nowhere to go. Those on the outer edges of the rally retreated from the attackers only to be compressed into a crushing, swirling turbulence as hundreds of others backed into the center or tried to break out and get away.

"Stop! Stop!" the fellow at the microphone cried hysterically. "For Gawd's sake, stop!"

Women and children screamed. Strikers cursed and tried to fight back, but in that sucking whirlpool of violence there was no way to counterattack, no organized defense was possible. Each worker was caught up in his or her own eddy of pain and terror, battling wildly alone or trying to flee the rampage.

Some strikers had short sections of lead pipe or small clubs hidden under their overalls and they were swinging wildly at the attackers. Other strikers yanked off their belts and, giving the tails a turn or two around their fists, used the buckles as flails. A picket captain scrambled up on the bandstand and threw a dozen folding chairs to the strikers below who grabbed them up and started bashing them over the heads and backs of the charging farmers.

Captain McNulty heard the clock toll six and then the shouts of the charging vigilantes. He rushed up from the courthouse basement, shouting for his reserves to follow. "Grab the gas. Come on! Get your masks on!"

At a glance, McNulty saw the farmers charging in from all around the park and the crowds of strikers reeling in confusion. Yelling and pointing, he extended his line, flanking the entire west side of the park, and ordered the first rounds of tear gas fired. The launchers popped, lofting the canisters into the melee. As the first clouds of gas exploded, McNulty moved his line forward, advancing slowly, lobbing more gas canisters. With too few men to drive off the attackers or quell the riot, he had to depend on the choking, searing clouds of gas to drive everyone from the park, attacker and striker alike. His men were under orders not to take sides, all they could do was separate any combatants they came upon, physically if necessary, and force them all to leave.

Jake and Clara were only a short way from the bandstand when the attack started. At first there was only the noise rippling in from the where the fighting began, but then they felt eddies of pushing and shoving that quickly turned into crushing, swirling pandemonium. There, in the heart of the whirlpool's overpowering forces, Clara clung desperately to Jake as they were jostled and knocked about. Shocked and frightened, he didn't know what to do, recognized no one and couldn't find a way out. Panic clutched his throat as he heard the *pop-pop-pop* of the exploding tear-gas cans, mistaking the sound for gunfire. The first choking swirls of the gas seared his nostrils and they were quickly caught up in gagging clouds that burned their eyes. Something whacked him hard in the back. Stunned by the surprising impact, he fell. Clara screamed and grasped at him. He felt her grabbing hand, then she was gone and he was being kicked. Rolling over, he grabbed a booted foot, tripping a big man in overalls who had on a white armband. The wild-eyed farmer stumbled awkwardly and fell, losing his club.

Jake dove over the downed farmer, grabbing up the ax handle. Instantly he was on his feet, whirling around, swinging the club like a baseball bat just as the farmer struggled to his hands and knees. The blow thudded heavily against the man's butt, flattening him in a howl of pain. Terrified, backing and whirling, Jake swung at anything that came close to him, until his shoulders bumped into the solid framework of the bandstand.

Back against the stand, tears streaming from his eyes, he looked frantically about for Clara, shouting her name. But there was too much noise and confusion, his eyes were burning and he couldn't see very well. Dropping the club, he scrambled up onto the bandstand, coughing and gagging, hoping for a better view up there. Below him two strikers stood back to back swinging the broken chairs, bashing anyone they saw with a white armband. A terrified little girl, no more than ten or twelve, stumbled through the forest of legs, vomiting and crying.

Choking, Jake sagged to his knees, his eyes smarting so badly he couldn't see, yet he yelled again and again, "Clara! Clara!"

A hand reached up and tugged at him. "Boy! Ya best come down from there! Come on!" Whoever it was, he wanted to help, Jake sensed that as he crawled down. Nearly blind, he let himself be pushed under the bandstand. "Crawl in there and lay down, breathe through yor kerchief, boy!"

"Ain' got one." Bleary-eyed, he saw the shape of a man awkwardly crawling in under with him. One of man's arms was bent funny and dangled uselessly as he moved.

"Use your shirt then, wad it up over your face."

Jake struggled out of his shirt and, pressing it against his face, he started to crawl away, but the man grabbed him with his good arm. "Wait, boy, it ain' safe yet. Try to breathe the air down close to the grass, it's better."

Cheek pressed flat to the ground, eyes and nose burning, Jake gritted his teeth and looked over at the skinny, white-haired old man curled up beside him, clutching a blue bandanna to his face with his good hand. Coughing, he yelled, "What's wrong with yor arm?"

"Broke." Tears streamed down the old man's gaunt face and he gritted his teeth in pain.

Jake couldn't breathe, the irritating gas was choking off his airways. There was no escaping it. Coughing, he tried to pull away, afraid he was going to die, but the hawklike grip of the old man's good hand clamped tighter. "Stay down, boy! There's laws ever'where."

Panicked, Jake huddled there, eyes tight shut. All around them he could hear screams and yells and the sounds of clubs whacking and thumping. He had to get away.

A puff of wind cleared the gas away for an instant and the old man's grip loosened. "Easy, boy! Only a minute or two more, then we'll make a run for it. I got a truck up the street thar a ways."

The fellow was sitting up now, cradling his injured arm in his lap. Jake got a better look at him now. It was the rabbit man, the one who'd bought him the western. "Mister, ya hurt bad?"

The old man shook his head, but Jake could see he was in pain.

The air was clearer now and the old man crawled out, looking around. Most of the people were gone from the park and the fighting was off a ways, out in the streets. "Come on," the old man yelled. Cradling his broken arm, the fellow took off at a trot. "This way!"

Crawling out and running after him, Jake was surprised at how quickly the old-timer moved.

It was dark now and the streetlights were on, casting eerie shadow-patterns over the fleeing strikers as they fought past the cops waiting outside the park. When the first waves of strikers crashed into the lawmen it broke their line and a hundred club-wielding fights broke out. Strikers that got clubbed down were cuffed and shoved into the cattle truck or one of the paddy wagons.

The old man charged out of the park, clutching his broken arm to him as he ran, Jake following right behind. Then *wham!* Jake was knocked sprawling. He rolled and was up, looking around desperately. Where'd the old man go? That talon grip clamped his arm again. "Come on, boy!"

The fight was all around them. And there in the middle of it was a sight so ludicrous it froze Jake for an instant. A cop was standing with his arms around a lamppost, bare-assed, his pants and gun belt tangled down around his ankles. At first Jake thought the cop was taking a piss, but then he saw the lawman's arms embraced the lamppost and his hands were cuffed on the other side. Parked at the curb not two feet away from the bare-assed cop was a police paddy wagon, its rear doors open, prisoners gone. It was just a flashing scene in a world gone mad, glimpsed for only an instant as he fled past.

The old man was quickly across the street and down an alley, following a half dozen others who were fleeing ahead of them, dark shapes, flying shirttails, pounding feet. Bright lights turned head-on into the alley, blinding them all. They heard car doors banging and shouts:

"There's some!"

"Get them goddamn Okies!"

"Don't let 'em get away!"

The old man jumped back out of the light and tried to climb a fence, but with one arm he couldn't make it. "Gimme a boost, boy!"

Jake helped the old man over, surprised at how light he was, then scrambled over himself. They tore through someone's backyard, out the driveway and across the street, running through another yard. Behind him, Jake could hear shouts as they went over another back fence and down an alley, hearts pounding. Finally the old man stopped in a dark shadow, behind a garage, gasping for air. He slid down the wall and lay there, wheezing. Jake slumped down beside him. "Ya okay?"

The old man could only nod. In the distance they could hear sirens.

At the old man's insistence, they waited there in the alley for nearly an hour, not talking. After he'd caught his breath, Jake had tried to say something, but a dog barked, a little dog by the sound of it, right behind them. Jake heard voices and a door open, then close. They sat quietly, waiting. In the dark like that, Jake could barely make out the old man. As he watched, the old man carefully fingered his broken arm, exploring the extent of the damage. "Both bones's broke," he hissed between clenched teeth.

"How'd it git broke?" Jake whispered.

"Shhhh!"

When the old man considered it safe, they got up and set out to find his Model T Ford truck, the one with the tiny house built on the back. Getting their bearings, they kept to the dark shadows and hid from passing prowl cars. When they finally got to the truck, the old man handed Jake the key. "Boy, you gotta drive."

The old man had crawled in back and laid down on his bed. Jake got the ancient truck started and headed west. Once out of town, he drove slowly along the back roads. Tired and sore, his eyes still burning, Jake watched the mirror and kept an eye out for barricades, all the while worrying about Clara and Susie and Ertie. Had they gotten away? Chugging along through the black night, he thought again about what Clara had said. She was pregnant. He remembered the sound of her voice as he put his arms around her and she had whispered, "I'm gonna have a baby." He wanted to hold her close right now, wanted to be with her and he felt bad about the way he'd acted when she'd told him. But it had been such a surprise. He wondered what his mother would say when he told her and asked if Clara could live with them, at least until the baby came. The railroad house would be crowded, but next season he and Clara could get a truck like James Earl's and

Clara was a good worker, he'd bet on that. She would earn her keep. Just thinking of being with Clara made him feel better.

It was near midnight when he pulled into the strike-camp main gate. Late as it was, the camp was all lit up and a whole lot of people were astir. Cars were going in and out, there were bunches of men standing around in angry knots, talking. Some families were pulling up stakes and packing.

The guards at the gate had clubs now and as the Model T came up, they challenged Jake. "Hold up thar!"

Jake stopped, not sure what to say. "It's me, Jake Robertson."

"Whar's Mr. Ringsdorf?" The guard held a lantern up to get a better look at Jake.

"Who?"

"Feller that owns this truck?"

It was the first time Jake had heard the old man's name. "He's layin' down back thar," Jake thumbed toward the back of the truck. "His arm's broke an' don' feel so good."

The guard opened the door and held the light in to see Ringsdorf. The old man raised up, groggily.

"Best git 'im to the medical tent."

Jake nodded, then asked, "Did my pa an' them get back?"

"What's yor name?"

"Jake, Jake Robertson. My pa's Ertie Robertson an' he's with Lige Parsons."

"Don' know 'em, boy. If'n you don' find 'em, go to the camp boss's tent, they's a committee thar tryin' to keep track of who's here an' who ain'."

Jake nodded, asking, "Was there many hurt?"

"A bunch. Think maybe two fellas got killed, don' know for shor. Some folks was took to the hospital, that's certain."

Jake took the old man to the medical tent, left his truck there and hoofed it back to camp. Lige's truck was parked beside the tents and so was James Earl's pickup. The camp was all lit up and when Jake walked in, Susie jumped up, hugging her brother. "Gawd, Jake, we thought ya was dead, or 'rested."

Ertie and Lige both were slapping him on the back.

"Boy, where ya been?"

"Y'all right?"

"Yeah." Jake saw an angry welt across his father's bony forehead. "What happened?"

"Damn farmers was usin' fan belts." Ertie fingered the welt, asking, "How'd ya get out here?"

"Feller give me a ride."

Susie was excited. "Guess what Pa did, him and Lige? Gawd, Jake, it was funny."

"What?"

"This cop"—Susie laughed as she talked—"he had a bunch of strikers locked up in that wagon they haul prisoners in an' he was pushin' another feller in there, but the guy didn' wanna go, so the cop he was beatin' on 'im with a club when we come by. When Pa seen the cop beatin' on the guy, he grabbed the cop's club. Jus' come up behind him and jerked it away an' knocks the cop down. Lige jerks the door of the wagon open an' lets the rest of 'em out, had his pocketknife out and cut their hands loose. An' that ain' all. The cop, he's gettin' up when them fellers that was let loose, they jump 'im, take his gun away an' handcuff 'im to the lamppost, then one of 'em just jerked that cop's pants down. Gawd, Jake, ya oughta seen it."

"I did! I seen 'im," Jake laughed. He was looking around camp now and noticed Maybelle and the twins over by the fire alone. Sensing something was wrong, he asked, "Where's Junior?"

"In jail." Lige sounded tired and worried. "Yor pa, there, he seen 'im 'rested, 'long with some other guys."

"Had their hands tied behind their backs," Ertie added, "but it didn' look like they was hurt none."

The horror of it all pressed down on him and he thought of Clara. Was she back? "Pa, I gotta find Clara!" He took off for her camp, hurrying, angry with himself for not going there first. As he rounded the corner and looked down the street there were lights glowing in other camps but where the Tarpin camp had been it was dark. His heart pounded and despair flooded through him. The camp was vacant. Jake ran to the empty site, shouting, "Clara! Clara!"

She wasn't there. Stunned, he ran to the neighbors asking about her, but nobody seemed to know where the Tarpins had gone. They'd broken camp in a hurry and lit out. Was Clara with them? Had she made it back from the park?

The neighbor lady, seeing the pain in Jake's eyes, nodded. "Yes, the one they called Clara, she was with 'em. I know, 'cause she an' her brother rode back from the park with us. Soon's we pulled in I seen her folks was packed up an' I heard them yellin' at her to come on. She threw an awful fit. Screamin' an' hollerin'. Didn't wan' to leave atall, but her pap he smacked her hard upside the head, shoved her in the car an' they was gone.

"Boy"—the woman looked at Jake and touched his arm—"if it's any help, she didn't wan' to go."

19

"Oh Lord God, bless this brave band of men! They have fought hard today defending their homes and their loved ones against the Satanic forces of Communism. We ask Thy special blessing for those of our brothers who were injured this day and cannot be with us, heal their wounds and return them to the bosom of their families.

"Heavenly Father, we thank Thee for our successes thus far in this Holy Crusade. Now we bow before Thee once more, asking for Thy protection tomorrow morning in the final battle. Make swift our victory, help us drive out the forces of evil from our midst. We ask it in Jesus Christ's name. Amen!"

Three hundred voices responded: "Ah-men," and their assent reverberated through the Eagles Hall.

The preacher was a big, robust fellow from the First Presbyterian Church. He had an open, handsome face, lightly freckled, and a shock of graying red hair. Still dressed in rough work clothes and reeking of tear gas, his white armband snugly in place, he stepped back a little from the microphone and, extending his right hand high overhead, he blessed them. "In the name of the Father, Son and Holy Ghost, Ah-men!"

Wardlow took over. Chewing on his cigar, he growled the good news, "We whipped 'em tonight . . ."

Cheers and whistles interrupted him.

". . . and we'll whip 'em again in the morning."

There were more cheers and whistles.

"It's late and we're all tired, but let's go over it one more time. The way things stand, we've got nearly all of the agitators locked up, thanks to the highway patrol."

There were chuckles and smiles because that was now a common joke; McNulty's tear-gas attack had helped drive the Okies out of the park and into the cordon of waiting lawmen.

"But remember, the job's not finished. In the morning we've got to run them out of that camp. Judge Murphy's signed a warrant declaring the place is a public health threat, so when we go in it'll be all nice and legal."

Satisfaction rumbled through the hall.

"It isn't likely, but if the union tries to put pickets out in the morning, ignore them. The more of those bastards that leave the camp, the fewer we've got to deal with inside."

Red Barnes yelled, "What about women and kids?"

Wardlow nodded. "Word we got is that a lot of those Okie families are already pulling out. That's what we want. Tomorrow give them a chance to get out, if they don't leave, we burn them out. If they fight back, give 'em hell, all of them. Nits make lice."

A Legionnaire stood up. "Some of them Okies'll have guns."

"They're not likely to shoot down the law. Windy's men will go in first. And I don't want any one of you that isn't a sworn deputy to carry a firearm. Is that clear?" Wardlow waited for more questions. There were none. "Okay, we'll meet at Coco Oil's headquarters in the morning, eight o'clock sharp."

There were sounds of disapproval and shouts:

"Why so late?"

"Why clear out there?"

"Listen to me! We're starting late to give them plenty of time to get out of that camp before we arrive. I want to be at their main gate about midmorning. We're starting from Coco because we are going to use the company's crew trucks and go in together, rather than all of us trying to drive down that road in our own pickups and cars and getting all tangled up.

"Windy and his men will go in first with Doc Pebble and serve the warrant. The rest of us will back him up. Remember, the idea is to run them off, not trap them. So let them go. I don't expect much problem, not after the whipping we gave them tonight, but don't be easy on them if they resist. Okay, see you all in the morning."

Dead tired, Jake slept past sunup. It was nearly eight before the noisy stirrings of the strike camp filtered through his dulled senses; irritably he rolled over on the mattress, tangling in the blanket. Outside the tent he could hear Junior's little girls giggling and playing.

Maybelle was arguing with R'becky. "But they cain' keep 'im in jail for long, the union'll bail 'em all out."

"Daughter, this's the second time Junior's been locked up. Ain' no tellin' how long he'll be there, so we'll do whatever we gotta do."

Jake got up, yawning and stretching. He ducked out of the tent and, grabbing a cold biscuit from the table, mumbled his good mornings. "Where's Pa?"

"Him an' Lige wen' up to the camp boss's tent." R'becky shook her head. "Boy, ya better eat more'n that."

"Ain' hungry. Susie go with 'em?"

"Mmm-hmm." R'becky handed him a cup of coffee.

"Thanks." Jake gnawed on the biscuit and drank his coffee, then wandered back to where Clara's camp had been and poked around the debris, hoping for some sign, a note maybe. There was nothing but scattered trash. Clara and the baby were gone. Baby. Feeling empty and sad, Jake turned back and wandered the streets, drifting aimlessly along. All around him the camp was in chaos. Without leadership, the strikers' routine and discipline were gone; no strike caravans had rolled out the gate that morning, there was no sense of organization or purpose left, the people were anxious and confused. There was anger here too, but an anger vastly different from yesterday's wrath. Then the people had been noisy and full of piss and vinegar, eager to smack the farmers up alongside the head; now they were sullen. Some were loading up and pulling out. All over camp, men leaned against jalopies or squatted down on their hams, talking, talking, talking. Some argued that if it hadn't been for the tear gas they could have fought back, others said naw, there was no way they could whip that many lawmen and farmers, not without guns. The biggest problem was that, with C. J. and the other strike leaders behind bars or in the hospital, nobody knew what to do.

Up by the headquarters tent, Jake saw Lige standing head and shoulders above a large knot of strikers. He was arguing with Will Henry. Ertie and Susie stood close by, listening. Jake joined them.

Since Will Henry was camp boss, the balding, prune-faced little man was also the highest-ranking union official still free, except for the lawyer Wirin, of course. Flanked by several other workers, Will Henry was squinting up at Lige through wire-rimmed glasses. "Parsons, yor plumb wrong, them highway patrols was on the farmers' side! Used that gas to drive us out of the park so's them laws outside could jump us!"

"If that's so," Lige shot back, "why'd them farmers come a rushin' in on us an' get theirselves gassed?"

"Hell, it don' matter, one way or the other," Ertie butted in. "It all come out the same."

Somebody else agreed, "That's for shor!"

Will Henry snapped back, "Point is, we gotta git organized, git some kinda dee-fense set up."

"Dee-fense? Here?" Ertie couldn't believe what he'd heard. "You can't—"

Will Henry cut Ertie off. "If them farmers decides to hit us again, right here, we gotta have some dee-fense!" The little camp boss knew he had to take charge and at least hold out until help arrived. "Firs' thang we gotta do is find Mr. Wirin an' get the CIO to send us some help."

Lige pursed his lips and spit a stream of tobacco juice at an ant crawling in the dust.

"Goddammit, Will Henry." Ertie shook his head. "We can't fight here, not without gettin' all the women and kids caught up in it too."

"We kin put the womenfolks and the chil'un in back, out of the way, and then we make a stand, right up front." Will Henry was shaping the ideas as he talked. "Block off the road so's they can't come into camp."

Lige spit again. "Likely, they'd run right over us."

Will Henry had his chest thrown out stubbornly and was squinting up more wrinkles. "We outnumber them three to one. I say we make a stand."

"Shit!" Ertie's exasperation riled over. " 'Stead of standin' here with our thumbs up our butts, we oughta be hitting back at 'em right now, goddammit. Go after 'em. Burn their barns, blow up their gins. That's what those sons a bitches knows best. Fight 'em, goddammit. Fight 'em on their own damn ground like we done yesterday mornin'. We wait for 'em here, they'll kick our ass, certain."

There were shouts of agreement and Ertie's supporters were shifting around, lining up on his side. The reaction surprised him. Standing together was one thing, but the idea of leading the pack made him uncomfortable.

One cocky little string bean standing right next to Ertie's shoulder shouted, "I'm with you, by Gawd. An' I got jus' what we need to even thangs up." He hauled out a loaded Colt .45 Peacemaker and held it up.

"Put that thang away!" Will Henry shouted. "We ain' gonna shoot nobody. We're gonna stay right here till we kin talk with Mr. Wirin an' the CIO, see what they say."

There were mumbles of agreement.

"Will Henry's right."

"Them CIO fellers'll know what to do."

"Yeah, we gotta sit tight."

By the sound of it, most of the strikers seemed to be on Will Henry's side and that strengthened his resolve. Will Henry held up his hand to get their attention: "Spread the word, we're gonna have a camp meetin', settle this thang so's we can get organized." He checked his watch, then glanced up at the sun. "Meetin' starts in half hour."

Ertie turned and walked away, Lige beside him, Jake and Susie following along behind. The six-gun-packing string bean and a couple of other fellows who had sided with Ertie tagged along after them.

"Pa, whata we gonna do?" Jake asked, and Susie echoed the question, "Yeah, Pa, whata we gonna do?"

"I don' know. Was it up to me, we'd hit 'em again, like yesterday, not circle the wagons."

"Yor dang right," said the skinny little fellow with the big gun. Beside him, a square-set guy with a heavy German face and great cabbage ears agreed, "I don' thank that Will Henry fella's got any fight left in 'im."

Ertie looked back at them. "You fellas gonna speak up at the meetin'?"

They hesitated, mumbling a bit, nodding and shrugging, agreeing and not agreeing. Clearly they wanted to back somebody, not take the lead.

Damn! Ertie wished he had some tough hands like Smoky Day to back him up in this fight. Well, if they were going to turn this thing around they'd need a whole lot more support. "Can you fellas round up more fightin' men?"

That they could do, right enough, and they were gone.

Lige put a hand on Ertie's shoulder. "You an' them fellers is kinda hard on Will Henry, ain' ya?"

"Maybe, but I don' trust 'im. He's all talk."

"He's tryin'."

"Tryin' don' git it done, Lige."

Neither of them said anything more until they were back in camp, then Ertie asked his tall friend, "What're you gonna do?"

"I don' know. Yor probably right, we shoulda hit 'em again this mornin', not wait here. An' certain shor, I don' wan' my family around if them farmers come stormin' in here like they done at the park."

"We maybe oughta get Maybelle an' the kids out of here." Ertie pulled a pint from his hip pocket and took a slug. "R'becky could drive 'em over to Kakorian's an' they could all stay with Bessie an' them. Take Susie 'long too."

"Pa!" Susie was instantly protesting. "Pa! I'm a striker's much as Jake!"

"Gal." Ertie started to order his daughter to mind, but then just grinned. "Oh, hell. You can stay."

Lige was troubled by Ertie's suggestion. "I hate to ask favors of Kakorian, way he done."

"Hell, there ain' no favor ask of him. They'd be in my camp, an' welcome."

"Yeah, but it's his farm."

Ertie handed Lige the bottle. "Well, wha'cha gonna do?"

Lige was quiet for a minute, then let out a sigh. "Ertie, this here strike's busted." He looked at the bottle in his hand, then took a long swallow.

Ertie agreed, but added, "Let's see what happens at the meetin'. Dammit, Lige, we was strong there at El 'Dobe, real strong. Ya could feel the power in them people. They had 'em on the run and could do it again."

A large crowd was gathering on the baseball field, near the big cook tent. A flatbed trailer had been pulled up across the back-stop. Will Henry and his two boys were already standing up there with two picket captains who had escaped arrest. Spotting Ertie, Will Henry motioned for him. "Come on up here."

Ertie hung back, nervous now, but the little string bean and the German pushed him forward. They'd rounded up twenty-five or thirty supporters and Ertie was their spokesman. So, reluctantly, Ertie climbed up on the trailer and stood there awkwardly.

Shouting into a megaphone, Will Henry opened things up by saying that they'd gotten through to Wirin and the attorney was on his way, he'd be here tonight. Both the CIO and the longshore-men were rounding up some tough organizers and sending them down to help out. "Be here tomorrow, so all we gotta do is hang on till then!"

The morning sun was warm and the camp was dusty, despite the earlier rains. Sweat trickled across Will Henry's wrinkles. "Them farmers is likely to try an' shut the camp down, like they done before, but we ain't gonna let 'em. First thang, we gotta make shor the place is clean so that county health doctor won' find nothin' wrong."

Jake, standing with the other dissidents close down front, couldn't believe what he was hearing; keeping things clean wouldn't stop them farmers, not now. He wanted to shout Will Henry down, tell him he was crazy, but Ertie'd do that soon enough.

"We can't give them any excuse to come in here." Will Henry mopped his sweaty forehead with a red bandanna. "Then, if they try anythin', we can legally defend ourselves. If them farmers come at us, we gotta stop 'em out there!" He was pointing through the gate. "We'll stop 'em in the road before they can get into camp."

A rumble of agreement surged through the crowd. Will Henry listened, nodding, then held up the megaphone again. "Now there's some that don't agree with what we're plannin' an' Ertie Robertson here's talkin' for them."

The megaphone was handed to Ertie and he stood there, awk-ward and dumbstruck. Swallowing hard, he raised the megaphone and shouted, "Now I ain' no hand to make a speech! But I say we cain't jis' crowd up here like a bunch a dumb sheep an' wait for them wolves to come at us. We oughta be out there right now fightin' 'em on their own ground, like we done at El 'Dobe. Gotta hit them 'fore they hit us." He was speaking rapidly. "We was strong when we hit El 'Dobe. Real strong. Gotta do it again, gotta kick the hell out of them farmers, burn their damn barns down, make 'em hurt so bad they'll wanna quit. If we're out thar kickin' hell out of 'em, they ain' gonna be over here tryin' to burn us out."

Suddenly he was out of words and let the megaphone sag as he tried to think of something else to say, but the sight of all those faces looking up at him, waiting for his next words, was too intimidating. Shaking his head nervously, he backed away mumbling, "That's all I gotta say."

His small rooting section cheered and whistled and there were shouts of approval here and there through the the crowd, but Ertie hadn't sparked any fires. He pushed the megaphone at Will Henry and scrambled down off the trailer.

Will Henry shouted, "Like Ertie thar said, we're gonna hit 'em again, but first we got to git ourselves organized and get ready to defend this place . . ."

Ertie paid no attention to what was being said as he pushed out of the crowd now, limping determinedly back to camp, mad and embarrassed. He wasn't a speaker or a damn union leader. Why'd he get up there, anyway? Bunch of damn sheep, no way to make them fight.

Lige caught up with Ertie, saying, "Yor right, they ain' got no more fight in 'em. Let's shag ass out'n here, all of us. We kin pick up Bessie an' the rest 'em an' head south, go down around Arvin. I know a Slav down there, good farmer an' he treats his help decent."

Jake was hurrying right along behind Lige and couldn't believe what he'd heard. "You mean scab?"

"Boy"—Lige Parsons's voice was sad—"look 'round ya. There ain' no strike left."

"What about Junior?" Jake pleaded.

Lige stopped and looked down at Jake. "Junior's man growed an' he knows our ways. We been up an' down this road so many years he'll know where to catch up to us. We'll leave word which way we headed."

The decision was made. They'd pack up and head south. Back in camp Ertie got out the nickel-plated Remington .44-40, strapped on the gunbelt, checked the pistol's loads and defiantly shoved it back in the holster. It was an awesome sight, the old cartridge belt with a half dozen rounds pushed into the loops, the pistol's yellowed walnut grips and gleaming nickel-plated steel sparkling bright in the sun, the whole of it old, worn and deadly. Pistol on his hip and ready to fight if he had to, Ertie went about breaking camp. He might be leaving, but he wasn't running. Not by a damned sight.

R'becky and Maybelle didn't like the look of the gun, but said nothing as they packed up. For both families, packing was a routine that required little thought and, normally, they could break camp in a couple of hours, cleaning the tents out first, boxing and setting things in order. The tents were always the last to come down because they used the canvas to cover their loads. They worked quickly, without much conversation, until they heard the wail of sirens in the distance. Stopping, they turned and listened. The sirens were coming closer and that meant just one thing: farmers.

"Jake!" Ertie's hand dropped to the pistol. "Run up there an' see what's goin' on. Be quick an' get back here!"

By the time Jake reached the camp headquarters and could see the main gate, clouds of dust were swirling around a line of crew trucks that had stopped in the road just outside camp. The truck ladders were down and scores of lawmen and farmers were scrambling out and running, positioning themselves along the fences on either side of the camp gate. Some had clubs, a few had pistols and shotguns, here and there Jake could see men carrying wire cutters and big cans of kerosene.

Will Henry, backed by maybe fifty men, was blocking the entrance, confronting the sheriff and Titus Wardlow. More strikers were running into the breach carrying clubs, lengths of chains, anything they could get their hands on.

Dr. Pebble cowered next to the sheriff, clutching a sheet of paper. The sheriff had his hand on his pistol and sunlight glinted off his dark aviator's glasses. Wardlow, cigar clamped in his jaw, carried an ax handle and was backed up by a phalanx of shotgun-carrying deputies.

"This camp is closed! Everybody's got to get out, now!" Wardlow barked.

Will Henry stood firm. "This here's private property! No one can come in here without a warrant."

Wardlow roughly pushed Dr. Pebble forward. "Serve that goddamn warrant!"

Ranks of deputies edged forward, menacingly.

Will Henry had his hands up, chest high, as if he could ward off the advance. "Get back! We'll let the doctor inspect the camp, but nobody else. Get back!"

Will Henry's boys, Buford and Harlan, stood protectively on either side of their father, and the rest of the workers pulled in tight, ready to fight.

"We're not inspecting, we're closing this goddamn stinkhole down," Wardlow growled. "Windy!"

Just as Wardlow turned to the sheriff, a rock sailed through the air and a striker shouted, "Get outa here!" More strikers took up the yell, hurling rocks and clods at the lawmen.

Wardlow, club held high, shouted, "Burn 'em out!"

The lawmen charged and the tiny mob of strikers at the gate was quickly overwhelmed. Jake saw Will Henry go down, glasses knocked flying. His two boys were wrestled to the ground and disappeared in the dusty brawl. Simultaneously, the vigilantes that were flanked out along the fences cut through the wire and charged into the camp, yelling and clubbing down anyone in the way. Kerosene was sloshed over the nearest tents and they were set afire. Women and children screamed and fled. All around him, Jake saw frightened people throwing their belongings into the cars and trailers while frantic men tried to fight off the attackers. There had been no time to organize a defense but bands of strikers who'd fought together on the picket lines rushed the vigilantes and within minutes the whole strike camp was engulfed in turmoil.

Stunned by how quickly things had gone to hell, Jake ran for his own camp, pounding down the dirt street as fast as he could, yelling, "Pa! Pa! There's a whole goddamn army of farmers and laws out there!"

R'becky and the rest stopped packing as he came running into camp.

Breathless, he shouted, "Laws run right over Will Henry'n them at the gate an' now they're burnin' the camp out!" He pointed frantically back at the clouds of black smoke boiling up into the sky.

"Git them thangs loaded, get the tents down," Ertie hollered.

Jake jumped up into the bed of the pickup and began packing everything Ertie and Susie tossed up to him. The battle hadn't reached their street yet, but in the distance they heard screams and shouts, the slamming of car doors and the gunning of engines. From the pickup bed Jake saw plumes of smoke close by and, clambering up on top of the cab, he watched tents burning on the next street over. "Gawd, Pa. They're gettin' close."

Jake jumped back into the bed of the truck as Susie hurled up bedding and ran back to the tent. She came out with a box loaded with household goods, yelling, "This's the last one."

Ertie, standing just inside the tent, had unseated the ridge pole and was taking the supports out.

"Jake, look out," Susie screamed.

Jake whirled and saw two farmers rushing their camp. One, a big man in a leather jacket with a badge pinned on it, clutched a pistol in one hand and a kerosene can in the other, and headed straight for Lige. Charging right behind him was a snarling-mean bulldog of a man: Wardlow! Cigar clenched in his teeth, ax handle cocked back, he was going straight for Ertie in the tent doorway. Jesus God. Jake screamed, "Pa! Watch out!"

Wardlow rushed in swinging.

Ertie, caught in the sagging tent doorway with the ridgepole in one hand, reached for the holstered pistol, jerking it clear, but the hammer snagged in the tangle of canvas collapsing around him.

Seeing his father in trouble, Jake grabbed a shovel and leaped from the truck.

"Pa!" Susie screamed.

Wardlow's club smashed Ertie's skull, felling him before he could fire. The blow jarred the pistol from Ertie's hand just as Jake jammed the shovel in the farmer's back.

Knocked off balance by the cutting blow, Wardlow whirled and, seeing Jake, roared, "You little shit!" The club was winding up in a backswing, hatred overwhelming the farmer's pain.

Jake dropped the shovel and dove for the pistol his father had dropped, grabbed it up in two hands and rolled over. Up on one knee, he cocked the big weapon as Wardlow swung the club.

Jake fired. BOOM!

The heavy slug slammed into the farmer's belt buckle, blowing him over backward, blood and shreds of silver and raw meat flying. Shock stupefied Wardlow. Bewildered, his ugly face registering surprise, he landed flat on his back and his body convulsed, legs shuddering, arms jerking.

Jake whirled, cocking and firing at the farmer in the black coat. The man, stunned by the sound and sight of Wardlow being blown away, had forgotten his own pistol.

The big nickel-plate thundered, but the shot missed. The farmer's pistol was coming up now, aiming at Jake.

Raging, tears in his eyes, Jake stood up and fired a third shot. BOOM!

The slug tore into the man's chest, high up near the shoulder, spinning him around. He went down hard, then struggled to get up, but his left shoulder was shattered and bloody, his arm flopped uselessly. Whimpering, he frantically crawled away like a half-crushed crab.

Crazy with fear and hatred, Jake cocked the pistol again and aimed at the wounded man, ready to finish him off before he escaped, but out of the corner of his eye he saw somebody running toward him, pistol drawn. A deputy! Jake swung the pistol over, centering on the lawman's badge, squeezing the trigger. BOOM!

The snap shot shattered the lawman's right arm and the slug deflected down into his side, knocking him sprawling into a nearby tent. The deputy rolled to his feet, pots and pans flying as he fled. Jake fired another shot, missing.

The exploding sounds of the rapid shots and the acrid smell of gunpowder were overwhelming. Dazed, Jake stood there. Wardlow lay sprawled on his back, body quivering, deep red blood welling out of the ragged wound where his belt buckle had been.

Susie was beside her father. "Pa? Oh, Gawd, Pa."

Jake knelt by her, smoking pistol still in hand, tears streaming down his face. Fear and anxiety surged through him, flooding out the killing hatred. He dropped the gun, muttering, "Aw Gawd. Aw Gawd no." Gently, he lifted his father's shoulders and cradled him in his arms. Bloody mucus oozed out of Ertie's nose and ears, but he made no sound. He was breathing, but irregularly.

R'becky knelt beside them, gently touching Ertie's face.

Jake sobbed, "Oh, shit. Oh, shit."

Lige and the rest of the Parsons were close around, shocked

by the sudden, bloody violence. Then Lige, realizing the danger they were in, looked wildly about. They had to get moving, quickly. He yelled at Susie and Maybelle to throw everything in the truck. "Jake"—he lifted the boy's arm—"come on. Let R'becky tend to yor pa, we gotta git outa here 'fore them two fellas git help. Just throw the rest of that stuff in yor pickup. Come on now!"

Jake nodded. In the background they heard what sounded like other shots, off in the camp somewhere. Jake unbuckled the gunbelt from Ertie's waist and carefully slipped it out from under his father; he ejected the spent cartridges from the cylinder and quickly reloaded, shoved the pistol back in the holster and tossed the weapon on the front seat of the pickup.

Throwing the last of the gear into the truck, they lifted Ertie onto the bed that Susie had made in the pickup.

"Let's get the hell out of here!" Lige yelled.

"What about him?" R'becky pointed to Wardlow.

Lige shook his head. "Come on, woman, we gotta git outa here. Law'll be here in a minute."

"Which way ya goin'?" Jake asked, tears still rimming his eyes.

"Only way out's through the front."

"Thar's an ol' dirt road along the canal bank out back. We bust through the fence, could skin out that way," Jake said, pointing the way.

"Kin my truck make 'er?"

"She's rough, but we kin do 'er."

"Okay. You better lead." Lige turned to his wife. "Woman, maybe you'd best ride with Jake there, take the ax and chop the wire."

Susie scrambled up in back to take care of Ertie.

Horn honking, Jake nosed the pickup through the frantic people scrambling to escape. Halfway down the street the way was blocked by an ancient Hudson Super Six stalled crossways in the street. A frightened woman was bent over the front bumper, trying to crank-start the engine, but she wasn't strong enough to pull the crank. Jake and R'becky jumped out to help, got the Hudson running and eased it around so they could get by. From there it was only a short way to the fence. Chopping quickly through the wire, R'becky yelled and waved Jake on by. "Go ahead! I'll ride with them now!"

Jake floored the Model A, gunned up the steep ditch-bank and bounced along the rough dirt track, sloughing sideways in the soft sand, jerking the wheel back, trying to keep from getting stuck. In the back he could hear Susie yelling but he was afraid to stop. They had to get away, get Ertie to a doctor. Susie pounded on the cab and tried to yell through the door window, "Slow down!"

Jake couldn't hear what she said. He slowed and leaned out, yelling back, "What?"

"Slow down, ya'll kill Pa! Ain' nobody but Lige followin' us!"

They were maybe a half mile from the camp. Jake stopped and climbed up on the cab, looking back. She was right. As Lige pulled up, Jake jumped down and ran back to the Parsonses' truck. "Pa's hurt bad. We gotta get to a doctor."

Lige thought for a minute. "Head for Kakorian's place, it's our best chance. You go into town they'll arrest you shor."

"Think I killed Wardlow?"

"Likely. He was gut shot."

"Jake!" Susie yelled from the pickup. "Come on! Pa's hurtin' bad."

"Le's get 'im to the Kakorians. Then figger what's to be done," Lige repeated.

Jake nodded and ran back to the pickup. He drove along the top of the canal bank for nearly a mile before he found a lane leading down and out to the county road. Turning north and picking up speed, he drove frantically, his mind in a turmoil. He'd shot three men. Maybe killed Wardlow. He couldn't believe it. It wasn't true! Couldn't be! Then he remembered the shock on Wardlow's face when the slug hit him. God damn him, why couldn't he have just left them alone? Pa! Oh Gawd, don' die!

When Jake turned into the Kakorian farm he could see Ara and Navo and the other high school kids out in the field picking. Bessie and the rest of the family were at work down at the other end. Benjy, playing beside the field, heard the pickup, looked up and waved. Jake drove back into their old camp, parked and ran out into the field. "Ma! Ma! Pa's bad hurt!"

Bessie had watched them drive in. She slipped out of her cotton sack and hurried toward camp. "What happened, boy?" There was an angry, I-told-you-so edge in her voice.

"Ol' man Wardlow clubbed him up alongside the head. Gawd, Ma, it's awful."

Bessie hurried along after her son, the rest of the family following.

"Ma, I think I killed ol' man Wardlow!"

Bessie stopped dead. "What?"

"Shot him after he clubbed Pa, him an' another guy and I winged a deputy too." Jake was crying, sobbing out the story.

As the others crowded around, Bessie put her arms around Jake and hushed him, holding his head against her breast.

"What's he sayin'?" James Earl wanted to know.

"What's the matter?" Mary Ellen looked worried. "Where's Pa?"

"There's been trouble." Bessie shook Jake gently. "That's 'nuff, boy, let's look to yor pa."

R'becky and Lige had carried Ertie in and gently put him on the bed in the kitchen tent. R'becky tended to him while Lige went looking for Kakorian.

Bessie pushed into the tent. "All right, where's that ol' fool." One look at her husband and her anger disappeared. "Oh, my God." She dropped to her knees beside her husband. "Ertie? Ertie?"

The others tried to crowd into the tent. R'becky shooed them back out. "Go on, go on. We'll handle this."

"Ma, hadn't we oughta get a doctor or take 'im to the hospital?" Susie was pleading.

Lige found the farmer out in the barn. Kakorian, his hands black with grease, had a wheel off the tractor and was replacing the bearings. He was listening to the radio as he worked.

"Mr. Kakorian?"

The farmer didn't hear Lige because of the radio. ". . . Once again we interrupt this program to bring you up to date on reports that Communist agitators have shot down two prominent Jefferson County farmers and one lawman this morning . . ."

Lige yelled again, "Mr. Kakorian!"

". . . as they tried to serve a warrant closing down the CIO strike camp near Collins Corners. Seriously wounded were Titus Wardlow, president of . . ."

"Mr. Kakorian!"

The farmer looked up in surprise. "Yeah?"

"Gotta talk with ya. Ertie's bad hurt and we need some help."

"Lige! What are you doing here?" Kakorian wiped the grease from his hands with an old rag, ignoring the radio now.

"It's Ertie. He's bad hurt an' needs a doctor." Lige had the farmer by the elbow, guiding him out of the barn. "Can ya help us?"

"What happened?"

They were quickly across the barnyard and in the camp. The farmer looked in on Ertie, then came back out ashen-faced. "My God, what happened?"

"Gang a farmers and laws jumped the camp, burned it out. They come a-chargin' into where we'd pitched our tents an' there was a fight and Ertie got smashed up alongside the head."

"Let's get him in town to the hospital."

"We can't do that without them askin' a whole bunch a questions. Mr. Kakorian, they're throwin' ever' striker they catch in jail."

"Was he involved in that shooting?"

Lige hesitated, then asked lamely, "What shooting?"

"Titus Wardlow and Dusty Rhodes were shot down by the strikers, so was a deputy sheriff. It's been on the radio."

Lige didn't say anything.

Jake, standing behind Lige, asked, "How b-bad them farmers get hurt?"

"Didn't say. Just said that they'd been taken to the hospital." Kakorian turned and walked away, then came back, his face set. "You were in that camp, weren't you?"

"Shor." Lige nodded.

"How'd you all get away?"

"Lit out through the back, cut the fence and drove along the canal."

"Law after you?"

"Weren't no one followin' us." Lige didn't like the way Kakorian was questioning him. "Thangs was mighty stirred up and we heard shootin'. Folks was a-runnin' ever' which-a-way. Nobody knowed what was goin' on so we lit out."

Jake suddenly felt sick. His stomach heaving, he turned and ran for the outhouse, vomit spewing.

Kakorian shook his head, not really believing what he was hearing.

Lige went on, "So, ya see, we can't just drive up to the hospital. Can' we git a doctor out here?"

"Look, the two of you went off to the union. You could have stayed and worked. Now I'm not going to harbor somebody who's maybe wanted by the law."

"Ain' nobody said he's wanted by the law, Mr. Kakorian. Me and my family, we can skin right out of here and leave the Robertsons. It ain' our fight neither, but we ain' gonna do that. Them fellas came at me an' Ertie. All we was doin' was tryin' to get the hell out. Now you been a decent man, an' all we're askin' is some help to get Ertie a doctor."

"Lige, I don't want to add to your troubles, but I can't let you stay here and I won't be involved. I'm sorry, but I'll have to call the sheriff if you aren't out of here within the hour."

Lige started to say something, but the farmer held up his hand. "No, no. Don't say anything more, just go."

Frantic with worry, they decided the best thing was to head for Bull's Camp. He'd help them get Ertie to a hospital up in Fresno County. Quickly they loaded the trailer and sedan, tenderly put Ertie on a mattress in the back of the pickup and Susie climbed up in back with him. "Ma, kin I take care of 'im?"

Bessie hesitated, then nodded. "We'll be right behind ya."

James Earl started to get in the pickup, but Jake brushed past him and was quickly behind the wheel. James Earl snapped, "Get the hell out of there, that's my pickup."

"Like hell I will, I'm drivin' 'im. You wasn't there when we needed ya."

"Stop it, both of ya," Bessie stormed. "We ain' got time to argue. James Earl, you drive the car. Jake, you follow Lige."

They drove north, making good time, the truck, the pickup and the '32 Ford pulling a trailer. Twice they passed sheriff's cars going the other way, but the lawmen never gave them more than a quick glance. At Colby they pulled out onto Highway 99. From there it was only three miles to the river; once across, they would be safe in Fresno County.

Jake was feeling better now that they were on the road. In the mirror he could see Susie gently wiping the cool cloth on Ertie's misshapen head and he remembered how his father always said, "You can't kill a cowboy unless you cut off his head, and then you have to hide it from him." Cowboys were tough. They survived.

Tears streaming down his face, Jake wished he was a little boy again, that they were going to a rodeo. He could see his father climbing over the chute gate, the bronc standing there in the box, trembling, ears alert, as Ertie settled down in the saddle.

Buck rein measured and clamped in his right hand, his hat tugged down low, Ertie nodded to the cowboy on the gate. "All right, turn'm out!"

The big horse wheeled with the opening gate, rearing and jumping out, kicking up high behind. Ertie's boots were jammed into the stirrups, toes out, spurs digging into the horse's powerful shoulders. The horse was high in the air and coming down stiff-legged. The impact popped the spurs loose and Ertie's butt caught the piston-driving force as the horse exploded skyward, bucking horse and rider in perfect time. The memory was sharp, the details clear. Jake could see the big grin on his father's homely face and hear the crowds yelling and cheering as he spurred the wildly bucking horse.

Lige's truck suddenly slowed, then stopped in the middle of the highway. Jake's thoughts were jerked back to the present. Why'd they stop? He slowed and nosed the pickup out around Lige's truck, peering up the highway. What he saw chilled him: A long line of cars and, up on the approach to the bridge, police cars and barricades; a roadblock.

"Hang on!" Jake yelled the warning to his sister as he cramped the wheel hard to the right, shifted into reverse, backed out onto the shoulder, then shifted into low and turned hard left, tires spinning and throwing gravel. Coming out of the fast U-turn, tires squealing back onto the blacktop, he shifted quickly into second, then into high, picking up speed. Behind him in the mirror he could see the surprised lawmen running for their cars. One hand on the wheel, Jake tugged at the big pistol, shaking it free of the holster. He put the pistol close beside him, ready. In the mirror he could see two motorcycle cops were after him and in the back Susie was screaming, but he couldn't make out what she was saying. Far up ahead he could see the town of Colby and, as he raced closer, he spotted police cars pulled across the highway, blocking it. Shit! There were no crossroads, nowhere to turn. He let off the gas and started to brake just as one of the motorcycle cops pulled up beside him, gun drawn and pointed at his head.

Susie was screaming. Terrified, Jake raised his hands helplessly, indicating he was surrendering, then steered with one hand as he slowed to a stop. Both cops braked too, keeping just behind him, flanking him, their guns drawn.

Once stopped, they were off their motors, ordering Susie and Jake to get their hands up. Nearly paralyzed in fear, Jake kept his hands high, but out of the corner of his eye he could see the big nickel-plated pistol beside him. If he could just get ahold of it.

"Get out of the car, slowly. You in back, first."

As she climbed out Susie pleaded, "Please, our pa's in back, hurt bad. He cain' move."

Police cars and motorcycles were screeching in around them, braking to a stop; lawmen ran up, guns drawn. Susie was standing by the Model A, hands in the air. Jake sat rigid behind the wheel. Two deputies cautiously looked into the back of the pickup and one said, "Jeesus, his head's smashed."

The other deputy and a highway patrolman covered Jake and one of them shouted, "All right, you, the driver, get out!"

It was Sergeant Dobbs, who'd arrested Clara and Homer and come to Kakorian's looking for them. Jake looked in the mirror at his father lying there in the back and slowly started lowering his right hand toward the pistol.

"Freeze! Keep your hands in sight!" Dobbs screamed.

Jake froze.

"Your right hand! Reach out with your right hand and open the door from the outside! Keep your hands in sight!"

Jake thought of Pretty Boy Floyd shooting it out with the cops and Lancy Boyd who wouldn't be run off the high country range.

"Boy, move!" Dobbs cocked his pistol.

Terrified, Jake slowly twisted and reached out the window with his right hand, opened the door and climbed out. Dobbs and the patrolmen spun him around and bent him over the front fender, pulled his arms behind his back and handcuffed him. Hands patted him down, searching for weapons, then he was jerked upright and for the first time he saw a dozen lawmen and cars everywhere. The highway was jammed and curious motorists were out of their cars, staring. Roughly, Dobbs and the patrolman each grabbed one of his arms and propelled him toward a patrol car. Other cops were handcuffing Susie and she was loaded in the squad car beside him. The door slammed, locking them inside.

Twisting around, Jake saw one of the deputies reach into the pickup and pull out the nickel-plated pistol. The lawman yelled to a friend, "Goddamn! Look at this hawgleg, no damned wonder Wardlow an' them others had such big holes blowed through 'em."

People were crowding around the pickup now and a highway patrolman was pushing them away. "Get back! Get back in your cars!" The patrolman looked Ertie over and called to Dobbs, "Sergeant! Somebody ought to radio for an ambulance, this guy looks like he won't last long if he don' get to a hospital."

Dobbs only nodded and yelled to three of his men, "Arch, Ted, get this highway cleared. Tom, come with me, we gotta run those kids into jail."

Dobbs strode back to the patrol car, looked in at Susie and Jake, then climbed in and started the engine, yelling at the deputy, "Hurry up!"

"My pa!" Jake leaned forward. "Ain' ya gonna call an ambulance!"

The deputy shoved Jake hard. "Sit down, kid!"

Doors slammed and the car lurched backward. Jake struggled frantically to get free, yelling, "Pa's hurt, please get an ambulance!"

Siren wailing, Dobbs spun a U-turn and sped away.

Jake frantically twisted around and, tears blurring his eyes, he looked back at the jam-up of cars and crowd of gawkers, trying to see if anyone was helping Ertie. Was that his mother? He thought he saw her struggling past the cops, trying to get to his father, but he couldn't be sure. Beside him, Susie was doubled over sobbing, and he wanted to put his arm around her, but he couldn't. He was handcuffed. Aw Gawd! Rage overwhelmed him. Drawing his knees up, he kicked hard at the cage separating them from the deputies, kicking again and again, screaming, "Assholes! Motherfuckers!"

20

The jail was cramped and foul-smelling, a dull gray place of iron bars and stone walls. The muggy air reeked of stale cigarette smoke, urine and soured puke. Cockroaches scurried underfoot. Steel doors clanged and shouts echoed down the stairwells.

Still handcuffed, Jake and Susie were led in past the drunk tank to the booking room and Sergeant Dobbs held Jake as a matron led Susie off.

"Jake?" Susie struggled to pull away. "Help me."

But Jake was helpless. What was happening wasn't real. Hands pushed him hard up against the cage separating prisoners from the booking counter, the handcuffs were taken off and Sergeant Dobbs growled, "Book 'im on ADW, but hold 'im as a juvie until the DA decides how to charge him."

"Name?" the woman behind the cage demanded, pecking out the answer on an old typewriter. "Address?" She was a heavy woman, hostile and bored. "Occupation?"

Rubbing his wrists, Jake answered the questions.

Jerking the completed booking card out of the typewriter, she ordered Jake to empty his pockets. All he had was a frayed blue handkerchief, six cents and his union card. She dumped that in an envelope along with the jackknife that the deputies had taken from him. The booking was over.

"All right. Move it."

Jake was shoved through another barred door and into a room where he was strip-searched and given a loose-fitting pair of coveralls. Dobbs was gone now. A beefy jailor roughly manacled him again. "Okay, through that door an' up them stairs. Don' try anythin', I'm right behind ya."

Unlocking a solid steel door at the top of the stairs, the jailor pulled it open. "Inside."

There were the cells, two rows of barred cages, divided by a walkway. As he stepped into the cell block the putrid smells were overpowering and he gagged. The door clanged shut behind him and the guard gave him another little shove. "On down to the end."

This was hell. All around him were the iron bars and behind the bars, the cells and runways crowded full of men who had stopped what they were doing and stared at him. Most of the prisoners had peeled down the top half of their coveralls and tied the sleeves around their waists, like belts. Through the bars Jake could see their tattooed arms and sweaty torsos. Several crowded up to the bars, watching him pass.

"Jake?"

Startled, Jake caught a glimpse of Junior.

The guard poked him. "Shuddup and keep movin'."

At the far end of the cell block were four solid steel doors; each was painted forest green and had a small viewing slit at eye level. The guard unlocked one of these isolation cells, removed Jake's cuffs and ordered him into the dark steel cave. The door closed with a bang, the key turned in the lock and he heard the guard's shoes echoing back down the cell block.

Jake was alone. Abandoned in a nightmare. The only light in the cell came from a small barred window, high up. Layers of dust and grime coated the glass pane and it was shielded by a tightly woven wire mesh. Pale sunlight filtered through. Standing there, Jake still couldn't believe what was happening. As his eyes adjusted to the darkness he realized the tiny cell was no more than seven feet long and five wide, with barely enough room to slip past the iron bunks chained to the wall. At the far end a dirty white toilet jutted from under a washbowl and two metal shelves.

Suddenly, Jake was aware of someone else in the cell. There, on the upper bunk, a lumpy figure lay quietly, round head propped up on one arm, eyes staring at him.

The dark figure raised up. "Wha'cha in for?"

Jake was speechless.

The figure was sitting up now, feet swinging over the edge of the bunk. "Hey, I ask ya a question. Wha'd ya do?"

"Shot somebody." Jake doubled his fists, ready.

"Yeah? Who?" The voice was skeptical.

Jake didn't say anything, just looked at his cellmate, measuring him. A town kid, big and fat, maybe seventeen, pimpled, with liver lips and dark, stringy hair.

"Who'd ya shoot?"

"Ain' none of yor fuckin' business." Jake knew he had to fight if he was going to survive.

"Hey, you talk funny. You a goddamn Okie?"

Before Jake could respond there was a clanking noise on the toilet pipes, a signal. Distracted, the fat kid jumped down off the bunk, took a rag and stopped up the fresh water flow, then flushed the toilet and, after the water was gone, yelled, "Yeah?"

Throughout the jail, others had done the same thing, opening up the prisoners' intercom.

A hollow voice echoed through the pipes: "Jake? Jake Robertson?"

Jake stood there in wonder.

The fat kid turned to him. "That you?"

Jake nodded.

"He's here, whadda ya want?"

"Jake, this is Junior. Ya okay?"

Jake leaned over and yelled down, "Yeah!"

"Jake. Wardlow ain' 'xpected to live. Jailor tol' us. Deputy'n that other farmer'll make it though."

Wardlow dying? Jake couldn't think of anything to say.

"Jake, this is Aaron. Listen, we'll try to get word to Wirin. Don't talk to nobody till you hear from him. Okay?"

"Okay."

There was the sound of water flushing and the conversation was over.

"You shot three guys an' one was a cop. Shit! Put 'er there." The fat kid stuck out his hand. "My name's Fats, Fats Miller, from L.A. Got busted this time for stealin' a car. Ya been in before?"

"Naw." Jake shook the cold, soft hand.

"How old are ya, kid?"

Jake decided all the bad smells were coming from Fats. "Be sixteen next month."

"Jeesus Christ, an' ya've already shot three men. Goddamn! What'd ya use? A shotgun?"

"Six-shooter." The words were out before he remembered Aaron's warning.

"Christ, was they shootin' back?"

Jake stiffened. "I ain' talkin', goddammit."

"Hey." Fats retreated a step, hands up, joking. "That's okay by me, Okie."

"Don' call me that!"

"Jeez, you're touchy. I didn't mean nothin'." There was a hint of admiration in Fats's voice. "How's it sound? The Okie Kid, ya know, like Billy the Kid."

"Jus' don' call me Okie."

"Okay, Kid. Wanna smoke?" Fats unbuttoned his fly and reached into his coveralls, pulling out the sack of Bull Durham that hung down next to his balls.

Jake stared, unbelieving. "Wha'cha doin'?"

Fats laughed. "Keep your smokes on a string 'tached to a button down there so the screws can't see 'em." He rolled a cigarette, twisted the end, then pulled out a homemade cigarette lighter, a primitive little flint-and-steel kit that sparked a glowing coal in the tinder. When he got the cigarette puffing, he offered Jake a drag.

"Naw." Jake recoiled, shaking his head. "Naw, thanks."

For three days Jake saw no one but Fats and the jailor who brought them their food. Three days locked up in that stinking little cell not knowing if Ertie was alive or dead or what had happened to the rest of the family. Desperate for news, he signaled for Junior over the toilet intercom, but Aaron said Junior had been taken down to court and, no, Aaron hadn't heard anything about Ertie. Later, the word was out on the pipeline that the strike was broken, the workers were back in the fields picking cotton. Junior and the other strikers in jail were all being given thirty-day sentences, all but Aaron who still faced felony charges. The fucking strike had all been for nothin'. Shit!

Jake paced the two and a half steps from the toilet to the cell door and back. There was nothing else to do but pace or lay on the bunk and think. It was that, or listen to Fats. Fats talked a lot about the tough jails he'd been in and the time he'd done in reform schools. To hear him, he was a hard case. This time he had gotten a pistol somewhere and planned a robbery, but got caught before he could pull it off. "See, me 'n this cunt was out fuckin', parked out by the dump. Had a thirty-eight under the seat an' we was goin' to stick up some place, then blow this hick town, but a cop snuck up on us an' had a gun under my nose 'fore I knew what was comin' off. That'll wilt your dick, I'll tell ya.

"Anyways, since I had that gun under the seat, they been tryin' to pin a couple of other holdups on me," he bragged, describing in detail how the jailors had slugged him and beaten him with rubber hoses trying to get him to confess. "But I jus' spit in their fucking faces."

Ignoring Fats, Jake crawled into the bunk and curled up into a ball, making himself as small as possible. Hot tears burned his eyes and he choked back sobs, trying to muffle them in the scratchy wool blanket.

Midmorning on the fourth day, they heard footsteps thudding toward the cell, the keys rattled in the lock and the door swung open.

"Jake Robertson!"

Jake raised up. "Yeah?" He could see the jailor standing darkly in the doorway, holding chains and cuffs.

"Come on!"

Remembering how Fats had been beat up, Jake apprehensively swung his legs off the bed and stood in the back of the cell. "Wha'cha want?"

"Stick out your hands." The jailor stepped in and manacled Jake, then roughly pulled him out and slammed the cell door shut. "Hold still!"

He wrapped the chain around Jake's waist, securing his cuffs to it. "Now move."

Terrified, Jake hung back. "Where ya takin' me?"

"Downstairs, now move." The jailor yanked the chain.

At the bottom of the stairs Jake was steered partway down a back corridor, then yanked to a stop. "Okay, hold it right there." Opening a door, the jailor snarled, "Inside."

The room was tiny and filled with cigarette smoke. There at a small table sat Al Wirin, bespectacled and tired-looking. Jake's fear drained away and he tried to smile.

Looking at the chains and cuffs, Wirin scoffed, "Who's this, John Dillinger?"

"Security." The surly jailor unchained Jake, pushed him down in a chair, then backed out and locked the door.

"They must think you are a pretty tough character."

Jake nodded sheepishly. "Guess so."

"Son." Wirin glanced up at the door and saw the jailor's florid face in the small window; ignoring the intrusive glare, he turned back to Jake. "I've got some bad news. Your father died yesterday."

Those were the words, spoken gently but bluntly, "Your father died yesterday." And, before their stunning impact had fully registered, Wirin added, "They're saying that he came at Wardlow with a gun."

Jake jumped to his feet, screaming, "That's a goddamn lie! Wardlow was tryin' to kill Pa!" He stumbled back, knocking the chair over. "They all was comin' at us. Pa was takin' down the tent 'cause we was tryin' to get out of thar. Wardlow's lyin'! He's lyin'!"

Wirin was quickly up and took Jake gently by the shoulders. "Stop it!" Retrieving the chair, the lawyer seated Jake, explaining, "It's not Wardlow that's telling the story. He's still in the hospital, unconscious. The talk is coming from the other farmer and that deputy."

"They're liars! I shot 'em, shor, but not till after that son of a bitch smashed Pa in the head. Shit! Them other fellas had guns too an' they was comin' at us." Jake was half out of the chair again.

"I know." Wirin held Jake's arm, restraining him.

Jake slumped back down and stared at the lawyer, trying to understand what he'd been told. Pa dead. Gone. Jake collapsed in tears, head down on his arms, sobs convulsing through his body. Wirin sat silently for a few moments, then he put his hand on Jake's head. "Your mother said to tell you they are fine, that someone named Bull Skinner was helping them."

Jake looked up, wiping at the tears. "They at Bull's?"

Wirin shook his head. "They're camped out near Hyattville, above the bridge. She said you knew the spot."

Jake nodded.

"There is some good news. The judge has released your sister, Susan. She's out in my car."

"Can I see her? An' Ma?"

"No, not yet."

"Why?"

"They're not letting you have any visitors."

"But you're here."

"That's different. I'm your lawyer now, and we'd better talk about that for a moment. Jake, they're probably going to try you in superior court as an adult on charges of assault with a deadly weapon and attempted murder."

Jake was shaking his head in disbelief. "No. No."

"Those are just allegations," Wirin tried to reassure him. "To convict you they have to prove those charges to a jury, convince the jurors beyond a reasonable doubt that you wantonly shot down those men. Jake, they can't prove that because you were defending your home and your father. You acted in self-defense, it was the farmers who were attacking you. All we have to do is convince the jurors of that and you'll be acquitted." Wirin took out a notepad and pen. "Now, young man, I need to know everything that happened that day, every detail, so let's start from the beginning."

An hour later Wirin walked out of the jail feeling angry and depressed. Those damn farmers ought to be in jail, not that boy. Damn these counties and their vigilante justice.

"Al?" Roderick Munn fell in beside Wirin. "Got a minute?"

Wirin glanced up at the tall *New York Times* reporter. "What the hell do you want?"

"Christ, you're in a good mood."

Wirin grinned apologetically. "Sorry."

"You talk to the boy?"

"Yeah."

The reporter fixed a Camel in his ivory cigarette holder and lit it, a silver-haired lion on the hunt. "How are you going to fight this one?"

"Self-defense. No jury will convict that youngster once the facts are out." Wirin stopped and faced the reporter. He didn't like

Munn's arrogance, but the fellow was a good newsman and the exposure he could give this case was important. He had to feed the lion. "I got a call from McWilliams today. He said Senator LaFollette is interested in the case and the way the strike was broken up."

The raw hunk of information was snapped up. "How interested?"

"Call the senator and find out. The way Carey hears it, LaFollette's talking about holding full committee hearings in either Madera or Jeff City next month, December at the latest."

Munn and several other newsmen from big-city papers had rushed back to Jefferson County when the shooting story broke. They'd all filed stories that day and the next detailing the violent end of the strike, but with the cotton pickers back in the fields and the kid in jail, interest in the story had quickly waned in the metropolitan newsrooms. The other reporters had left. Munn stayed behind, sensing a bigger story here, and Wirin's tip confirmed his instincts. When the chairman of the U.S. Senate Education and Labor Committee was interested, a good story was bound to follow. LaFollette's investigators would subpoena everybody and all their records, there'd be investigations into the deaths of Cletus Sharp and Thad Greene and the shooting of Titus Wardlow, all on the public record. That kind of hearing, combined with the kid's trial, would give *Times* readers a close look at modern-day vigilantes. Munn had covered the LaFollette hearings on the Pinkertons in the Lake Erie Chemical Company troubles, and he'd written about the steel strikes in Johnstown, Pennsylvania, last year. In both of those cases, the committee staff had come up with solid information on union busting that made headlines. Add the dramatic impact of the kid's trial and this farm-labor stuff could be an even better story. He would focus on the boy caught up in a web of violence that killed his father, and on the mother. Her struggle to make a home out of an old railroad car was powerful stuff. There was enough here to put the story out on page one. Not bad, not bad at all, and who knows, the kid might even get off scot-free.

The shootings stunned Jefferson County. Anger quickly replaced the shock, and mobs of armed men roamed the back roads, burning out other squatters' camps. The strike was broken, its leaders were in jail or had fled the county. That was the good news the vigilantes carried to the wounded men lying in Jefferson City Memorial Hospital. Wardlow, still unconscious and in intensive care, could have no visitors, of course, but the other two heroes welcomed the attention. District Attorney Haggers personally came by, promising swift trials and stiff sentences. As for the kid, Haggers swore he would send that Jake Robertson to San Quentin for life.

Over in the hospital's surgery wing, the long hallway was empty and quiet. Only an occasional nurse hurried crisply about. A handsome blond woman sat erect on a bench, thumbing through a *Life* magazine, anxiously glancing up every now and then at a closed door across the hall. She was in her thirties, and wore an expensively tailored suit of soft tweed, brown in color, with a velveteen collar and matching pillbox hat. Beside her on the bench was a handbag of alligator skin and a neatly folded pair of gloves.

Across the way the door opened and an elderly doctor in a white coat came out. "Barbara?"

The woman rose, still holding the magazine.

"Sit down, sit down." The doctor's voice was gentle. "It will be a few minutes before you can go back in. The nurses are putting on fresh bandages."

"Is he any better?" Barbara Wardlow stood stoically, not a hair out of place. At first, the shock of what had happened had numbed her and she had even cried, but now she had control of herself. If Titus died, she wouldn't be destitute, no thanks to him. There was still enough income from the sale of the Braddock Land Company to keep the house, but little else could be saved. When Tom Barkham had come to her yesterday, quietly explaining that Titus had mortgaged El Adobe and everything else, including his life insurance, she realized for the first time what a big gamble her husband was taking.

"He's still unconscious"—the doctor, a brittle little man with a trim mustache, was nodding his head—"but his vital signs have stabilized. The bad news, I'm afraid, is that the X-rays show fragments of the bullet lodged in the spine and we think one of them has cut the spinal cord."

Despite herself, she sucked in a breath. "What does that mean?"

"Barbara, your husband is strong as a bull. We think he'll pull

402

through, but he'll be paralyzed from the waist down."

"Ohhhh," she gasped, hand over her mouth. That possibility had never occurred to her.

"Please, sit down," the doctor said, gently turning her. "Can I have an orderly get you some water?"

She sank to the bench. "No thank you."

"You can go in in a few minutes." The doctor bent over her, talking softly, "I've got to check another patient. Sure you're all right?"

Barbara Wardlow nodded and the doctor excused himself. As he walked away, she saw him pause near the nurses' station and speak briefly to two farmers, Red Barnes and Tiny Schmidtz, and to the fat little district attorney, Harlan Haggers. The doctor was introduced to a fourth man, a tall gentleman in an elegantly tailored silver-gray suit. The stranger shook hands with the doctor.

Barbara Wardlow opened the *Life* magazine lying in her lap, idly turning the pages. She paused briefly to look at a striking picture of an aviatrix, leather flying helmet in hand, standing under the nose of a powerful racer. The flier was a boyish beauty named Roxie Darling and the two-page picture spread had photos of the plane she had crashed during the 1938 Bendix cross-country race. The text highlighted Darling's comeback after the accident. In one picture her plane was only a few feet off the ground, banking wing-on-end in a tight turn around a pylon, a half plane-length ahead of another speeding racer. The caption read: NOSING OUT ROSCOE TURNER TO WIN THE BINDER TROPHY AT THE NATIONAL AIR RACES ON LABOR DAY. The story said Roxie Darling was racing full-time in open competition against men and her goal was to win the other three national trophies, the Bendix, the Thompson and the Greve, a feat no flier, male or female, had ever accomplished.

Barbara had heard of Jackie Cochran, but not Roxie Darling, and she wondered why any woman would want to race airplanes. It was so unladylike.

Across the hall, the door opened and Nurse Kelly called softly, "Mrs. Wardlow, you can come in now."

Down the hospital hallway the two farmers and the district attorney had the tall, well-dressed man surrounded and were arguing with him. The argument had started out softly enough, but the intense whispering escalated, drawing angry looks from the nursing supervisor. Finally, the nurse shushed them and the tall man in the silver-gray suit apologized quietly, sincerely. Turning to his companions, he suggested, "Let's talk outside."

"Sure," Tiny agreed.

"Damn right." Red Barnes headed for the door.

Out on the front lawn, Haggers and the farmers turned and faced the lawyer from Los Angeles. Haggers demanded, "Kincaid, what do you mean we shouldn't try the kid?"

Cyrus Kincaid explained again, "All I'm saying is that if you try that boy as an adult in open court, you'll be playing right into Wirin's hands."

"Shit! Are you suggestin' we turn the little bastard loose?" Tiny demanded.

Ignoring the big farmer, Haggers asked, "What're you getting at, Kincaid? We've got two witnesses who were wounded by the boy, we've got the gun. What more do we need to convict the little bastard?"

"Figure it out." Kincaid paused, then went on, "Wirin jumped at the chance to defend the boy. Why? Because he'll have you in open court, in front of the public and the press. He's going to put you growers and the association on trial . . ."

Haggers wasn't buying into the argument. "Judge Murphy won't let Wirin bring in all of that stuff."

"Face it, Murphy's not going to try this case," Kincaid argued. "Wirin can easily disqualify him by showing Murphy's warrant ordering the strike camp closed for health reasons was specious. He'll also try for a change of venue. Either way, you lose control of the case."

"Okay, okay," Haggers conceded the point. "So he gets the trial moved to Fresno or Visalia, we'll still be in front of a friendly judge."

"Maybe so, but you've handled enough criminal trials to know that any judge will have to give the defense some latitude and once Wirin attacks that warrant, he will be planting the idea in the jury's minds that it was the farmers who provoked the violence. He'll make it look like the kid was defending his father's life. Think about it.

"That's an attractive story for the press, and I don't mean the *Jefferson City Tribune*, or whatever it's called. And there's another problem. LaFollette's investigators are on their way out from Washington."

"What?" Haggers was skeptical. "How do you know that?"

"From a minority member." Kincaid was trying to restrain his irritation. "A public trial now would play right into the committee's hands. If LaFollette sees any advantage in holding hearings on the cotton strike, it will certainly lead to another effort by the New Dealers to bring agriculture into the National Labor Relations Act. If that happens, you can look forward to federally supervised union recognition elections, right here in Jefferson County."

Both Red Barnes and Tiny had been quiet, letting the lawyers argue, but now Red butted in, "So you say turn that little shit loose? Is that it, Mister Big City Lawyer? Well no sir! The little bastard needs to be hung—"

"Or locked up for life," Tiny snorted.

"Wait." Kincaid held up a hand. "I'm not saying turn him loose. Do that and the press'll make a hero out of him. Your best bet is to try him as a juvenile, in closed court, and quietly send him to reform school."

The idea was so simple Haggers nodded. "Good point."

"Like hell it is!" Tiny Schmidtz turned and walked away, Red Barnes following quickly behind.

Glancing at them, Kincaid asked, "They going to cause more trouble?"

"I don't think so, but you've got to remember Wardlow's a farmer. They really would like to lynch the little bastard. So would I, for that matter."

"Well," Kincaid asked, "will you do it?"

"Shit no!" The fat man looked up in surprise. "What do you think we are, barbarians!"

"No, no!" Kincaid chuckled, realizing his question had been misunderstood. "I didn't mean hang him, I meant will you try him as a juvenile?"

Haggers laughed, breaking the tension between them. "Yeah, I'll recommend it to Jervus."

"Jervus?"

"The county probation officer," Haggers explained. "Juveniles are his jurisdiction."

"Will he go along?"

"Well, with Jervus you never know. He's a cautious bastard, always covering his ass. If he thinks I'm trying to dump it on him, he might balk. On the other hand, getting a big case like this just might make him feel important."

"Well, if he doesn't take it, that kid might walk away free. Tell him that."

The Hyattville Cemetery was on a rise above Old River Slough. Shaded by large oaks, it offered a view of the town and the open fields. Bessie knelt by the grave, wishing they had money for a real stone. The marker was a small cement slab set in the ground with the words:

ERTIE ROBERTSON
1900–1939

She was wearing her Sunday-meeting dress and a simple little straw bonnet with a faded green sash. Hands clasped tightly in her lap, Bessie fought back tears as she thought of Ertie, remembering the young cowboy who'd come courting. He wasn't a pretty fella to look at, but he was sure a handsome sight on horseback. Oh how she'd wanted to ride with him in the parade, instead of Midge. Bessie smiled, recalling how awkward he'd been around her at first and how wildly he had ridden in the July Fourth Rodeo. That night, at the dance, she had known she loved him.

Suddenly, her keening heart could stand no more pain and she sobbed, quietly, her shoulders convulsing. Tears streamed down her weathered cheeks and, despite her struggle to repress the grief, a tiny squeal of anguish escaped, a piercing wail she couldn't contain.

Lige and Bull, who had brought her back to the cemetery to place the cement marker, stood uncomfortably by, not knowing quite what to do. Bessie remained there by the grave for a time, then sadly got up and, as Lige led her away, she looked back, saying, "He's resting now. Ain' mad no more."

Bull remained behind, leaning on his crutches looking out over the Hyattville Cemetery. "Well, ol' hoss, this ain' Texas, but it's purty here." From one of his pockets he took out a pint, swallowed a long drink and then set the half-full jar down on the grave marker. "So long, pard. Don' worry 'bout yor family, I'll watch out for 'em."

Bull had paid for the grave marker, quietly telling the mortuary man to add it to the fifty-dollar funeral that Bessie had ordered. Bull wanted to pay for the whole funeral, but Bessie wouldn't hear of it. Thanking him, she explained that Ertie had always insisted they pay their own way and she wouldn't change now. Bull knew the funeral cost had put a big hole in the family's savings, but he couldn't argue once she'd said no.

Lige drove Bessie back to camp and dropped her off. It was still early afternoon and the others were off in the fields, picking cotton, but she wanted to be alone. She told Lige to go on, she had a big laundry that needed doing. Bessie kindled a fire and put a tub of water on to heat, then broomed out the kitchen, scrubbed the table and stove, all the while worrying about Jake. Lawyer Wirin had said that at the trial they'd show that it was the farmers who broke the law and that Jake was only defending his daddy. And they'd have to convince the jury that Jake was a good boy. Well, that part she could do easy enough.

Waiting for the water to heat, she got out the tally book and worried through the numbers again, but no matter how she figured it, things looked bad. The hospital had made her dig up twenty-five dollars cash money before they'd take Ertie into the hospital. After the surgery to try and relieve the pressure on his brain, they'd put him in a recovery room but he'd never regained consciousness. He was in there two days before he died. Before they'd let her have the body, the hospital had demanded another twenty-five dollars, called it a partial payment. At the mortuary, the man said the cheapest pine box service was fifty dollars, without a grave marker. That was ten dollars extra. After the service, the funeral man had changed his mind and thrown in the marker, so now at least folks would know where Ertie was buried. But how was she goin' to pay off what they owed on the house? If she used any more of what she'd saved up, they couldn't make it through the winter, not with Billie Jo pregnant again and needing plenty of nourishment to keep her strong, so's she wouldn't lose another baby. No sir, even if it meant losing the house, they had to keep enough money put by to get through the winter. That was God's bitter truth.

Although Al Wirin had been in to see Jake before, when he returned to the jail Captain Ramey wouldn't let the lawyer past the front counter. No one was to see the prisoner. Wirin demanded to see the sheriff, who told him Jake Robertson was being tried in juvenile court.

Wirin, caught by surprise, stood there for a moment, then sighed. "Sheriff, at least let me tell him that I can no longer represent him. The boy deserves that much."

The sheriff shrugged, not seeing any harm in that, since Wirin had seen the boy before. "Okay, but just this once. You understand?"

Wirin was pacing the small room as Jake was brought in. As the jailor closed the door, Wirin tried to explain that he no longer represented Jake. "In adult proceedings we could represent you, but the juvenile court works differently because the judge sits *in parens patri*. That is lawyer talk meaning the judge is supposed to act as your parent or guardian.

"You see, when a judge sits in adult criminal court, he acts as a referee to make sure the lawyers play by the rules. But in a juvenile case, the doors are closed to the public and the judge isn't there to try you, instead he's supposed to be your friend and help you. The law requires him to act in your best interest."

Jake was confused. "I cain' have no lawyer 'tall?"

"That's correct. They'll let your mother attend the hearing, but no one else can be there except the judge and the probation officer."

Worried and near tears, Jake asked, "What're they gonna do to me?"

"Jake, I don't know, but don't give up hope. I may not be able to talk to you again, but whatever happens, I will be in touch with your mother. I'll let her know what rights you have and advise her as to what I think best. We're in uncharted waters here and I'm not certain what will happen, but understand this: I will not give up until you are free."

"You talk funny." Jake looked bewildered.

Wirin chuckled self-consciously, then looked at Jake intently. "I'm sorry. What I am saying is, they can put you on probation if they choose. That means they would let you go free, if you promise to mind your mother. They can also send you to the Whittier State School for Boys."

"They're gonna lock me up, ain' they?"

"That depends on the judge."

"For how long?"

"Jake, I don't know."

"It ain' fair. We was only tryin' t'get the hell away from there."

"Son, when you get before the judge, just tell the truth, maybe he'll listen."

Biting his lip, Jake nodded.

The talk with Wirin had been unreal. Jake had heard most of the words, but it was like the lawyer had been talking to someone else, in another language. It wasn't until he got back to his cell and was laying on the bunk that he realized that he might be locked up for a long time. Loneliness overwhelmed him and he thought of Clara, who was going to have a baby. His baby. He took a deep, shuddering breath and let it all out, slowly. Through the walls he could hear the sounds of the jail echoing dimly, the rattle of bars, heavy clanging doors, shouts and curses. "Fats?"

"Yeah."

"Ya been to Whittier?"

The bunk above him squeaked and the fat, pimpled face hung over the side. "Hey, they tryin' you as a juvenile?"

"That's what the lawyer said. Ya been there?"

"Yeah."

"What's it like?"

"Well, when ya first get there, they lock ya up in Receiving, that's where all the new fish go. It's a dorm on one side of this big building an' it ain't so bad, if ya keep your nose clean. On the other end of that building, down past the cage wire, that's Lost Privileges. It's for the fuckups, like me. They also got the strip cells there in Lost Privileges. That's solitary, man. They strip ya naked and throw ya in the hole. Ain' nothin' in them cells but a hole in the floor to shit in, nothin' else. No bed. No water. Ya get one old blanket, sleep on the cement floor an' it's bread and water twice a day."

Jake listened in horror.

"One thing, when you're in Receiving, don' let ol' Higgins get it in for ya."

"Who's Higgins?"

"The meanest fuckin' screw in there. Wears cowboy boots an' has this desk down at one end of the dorm, by the cage wire. Picks on young kids, late at night. Makes 'em crawl down under his desk when he's sittin' there, calls 'em dogs an' kicks 'em with them boots, won't let 'em out 'less they suck his cock."

Fats rolled over and swung down off the bunk, intent now on warning Jake. "Listen, kid, if they send you there, jus' don't smart off in front of that son of a bitch, but if Higgins tries to get ya under that desk, hit him. It'll get ya a beatin' and time in the hole, but he won' bother ya no more, at least not for a suck."

Jake shuddered and was quiet for a while.

"Hey, listen. Since you're a first-timer, maybe you'll get probation. They don't usually send first-timers to Whittier. Tell ya what, when that probation-department guy comes around to talk to you, give him the con, tell 'im how sorry ya are, that kind of bullshit. An' you gotta get your mother to cry a lot too, have her tell the judge how she'll see to it you don't fuck up no more. That usually goes over pretty good."

A man from the probation office did come by the jail and talk to Jake. His name was Mr. Berliner and he was a mousy little guy with thick spectacles. He asked a lot of questions and Jake tried to follow Fats's advice. Sure he wished the whole thing hadn't happened, but when he was asked if he was sorry for shooting Wardlow and those other two, he couldn't lie, not after what they'd done to his father. The little man didn't say anything else, he just closed his notebook and left.

Not long after breakfast on his eighth day in jail Jake heard the footsteps coming toward the cell. Keys rattled in the lock and the door opened.

"Jake Robertson?"

"What?"

"All right kid, come on out. You're goin' to court."

There were two jailors this time, one holding leg chains. The first jailor snapped on the cuffs, the second ran a chain around Jake's waist, then knelt and snapped on the leg shackles, looping the leg-chain up through the waist-chain, leaving just enough slack so Jake could walk up and down stairs.

As he moved past the cell blocks, Junior pressed close to the bars and reached his hand out. "Jake? Good luck!"

Outside, the day was bright blue and cold. Shivering in his thin coveralls, Jake looked around, glad to be out. The air was sweet in his nostrils, clean and faintly sharp with the smell of burning leaves. The big clock in the bell tower showed ten minutes to ten. The jailors let him stop, but only for a minute, then herded him up the back stairs and into the courthouse. They walked down a narrow hallway, coming out into a high-arching atrium ringed by second-floor galleries. Their steps echoed across the expanse of white marble tile. All around them the frosted glass panels in the office doors were etched with twining vines and swirls of birds in flight. Stark little signs hung over the doors: AUDITOR; TAX COL-LECTOR; CLERK.

A wide marble stairway with curving banisters of polished wood and filigreed wrought iron led up to the galleries. As Jake climbed the stairway, chains rattling, he looked up and there leaning over the railing were Susie, James Earl and Billie Jo. Benjy, his face pressed against the grillwork, looked down and yelled, "Jake! Jake!"

Jake stopped, his heart clutching. Just beyond his family he could see the Parsons standing silently, watching him. He looked for Clara, but she wasn't there.

The jailors coaxed him on. "Keep going, boy."

Benjy started down the stairs, but Susie grabbed his hand and held him back. They watched and waited as Jake climbed toward them. Atop the landing, Susie rushed up and threw her arms around him. "Oh Jake. Jake."

The jailors pulled her aside and pushed Jake on down the corridor. Benjy ran beside them, yelling, "Jake! Jake!" and the shouts echoed through the building.

Office doors opened and curious workers watched as he passed by and was turned through the double wooden doors opening into Judge Murphy's court.

The cavernous, wood-paneled chamber was nearly empty. Tall windows flooded the room with morning light, casting shadow patterns across rows of vacant public seats. A black-robed judge stepped through a small door behind the raised platform and climbed to his high bench. Below him, two men in business suits stood at a counsel table, smiling. "Good morning, your Honor."

The judge was an impressive man, big and sturdy, with broad shoulders and a thatch of snowy white hair. He had the square, rugged features and blue-steel eyes of a Western outdoorsman. When he saw Jake being led in, the judge's handsome face hardened.

Coming through the doors, Jake saw his mother standing in the first row, watching him intently.

Pushing past the jailors, she took ahold of her son. "Jake, honey. Ya all right?"

"Ma."

Bessie had her arms around him now, clutching him to her. "Boy, are ya all right?"

"Ma, get me outa here."

A bailiff came in a side door and handed up a file. The judge took it, nodding his thanks. Without opening the case document, he looked expectantly down at the two men at the counsel table. One was the county probation officer, a pasty-faced fat man who resembled a heap of soggy dumplings stuffed in a linen sack. His name was Gervais, a French name, although he pronounced it "Jer-vus." The slight, inconsequential man beside him was his assistant, Mr. Berliner.

"Mr. Jervus?" The judge seemed impatient. "Is the probation department ready?"

"Yes, your Honor."

"Bailiff!" The judge turned his attention to Jake now. "Bring the defendant forward."

The uniformed bailiff gave the judge a curt little nod and strode smartly through the low swinging gates that separated court functionaries from the public benches. "Ma'am?" He took Bessie's arm and gently disengaged her from Jake. "Ma'am, you can sit up there." He pointed to a second counsel table. "That's where your son'll be."

Bessie went to the table as directed. Satisfied, the bailiff whispered to the jailors, ordering them to unchain the prisoner. When the manacles and leg chains were off, he led Jake through the swinging gate and seated him by his mother, then returned to his own tiny desk near the door to the judge's private chambers.

"The Jefferson County Juvenile Court is now in session." Judge Murphy banged the gavel and glowered down at the probation officer. "Proceed, Mr. Jervus."

Gervais stood up, bobbing his jowly chin respectfully, proud that while he had never finished college, he knew the ways of the law as well as any attorney. "If it please the court, I have my assistant Arthur Berliner with me this morning to assist us in these proceedings."

"Very well."

"Your Honor, we have before us this morning a fifteen-year-old white male, one Jacob Elroy Robertson, from Sweetwater, Texas. He is charged with three counts of assault with intent to murder. Do you want me to read the complaint, your Honor?"

"That won't be necessary."

"As you wish. Your Honor, Mr. Berliner here personally has investigated this case and found that said juvenile did in fact wantonly shoot down these three men while they were lawfully evicting the occupants of an illegal, unsanitary farm labor camp, said camp constituting a threat to the public health." Gervais paused, then in an informal aside, pointed out, "I believe the warrant ordering the camp closed was issued by you, your Honor."

The judge was impatient. "Yes, yes, get on with it."

"As you wish." Gervais glanced at his case file and cleared his throat. "While this is the defendant's first offense, the intent clearly was murder, your Honor. Therefore we recommend that the defendant, Jacob Elroy Robertson, be sent to the Whittier State School for Boys and be confined there until his twenty-first birthday."

"Wait just a minute, there!" Surprised, the judge leaned forward. "Mr. Jervus, you aren't recommending that he be bound over to Superior Court for trial as an adult?"

"Sir, may we approach the bench?"

Judge Murphy nodded irritably, motioning Gervais and his assistant forward. "Well, what is it?"

Gervais stood on tiptoe, his hands clasping the high bench top as though he were chinning himself, whispering, "Your Honor, we would have to—"

The judge leaned over, his hand cupped to his ear. "What? What's that? Speak up, man."

Gervais cleared his throat and looked nervously over at Bessie and Jake, not wanting them to hear. "I was saying, the district attorney advises us that trying the defendant as an adult in open court would mean the boy would be defended by that Communist lawyer, Wirin. Your Honor, he would bring in the press and make a circus out of the trial, distort what happened. This way we don't have to—"

The judge was furious. "Why wasn't I advised of this?"

"I assumed the district attorney had told you, your Honor," Gervais whined.

"Well, he didn't," Murphy snapped. He didn't like surprises, but he could see the point. Well, at least this way he'd have control over the boy. "All right, proceed."

Gervais and his assistant returned to the counsel table. Speaking loudly, Gervais went on, "With your Honor's permission, we feel it is in the boy's best interest to send him to the Whittier State School for Boys."

"Very well. Boy, you have anything to say for yourself before I sentence you?"

Bessie stood up. "Judge, kin I say somethin'?"

Crossly, Judge Murphy looked at Gervais. "Who is that?"

"The boy's mother, your Honor."

The judge looked at Bessie. "What is it?"

"Judge, ain' there s'posed to be some kinda hearin'? Where ya talk to people, find out what happened?"

"This is the hearing, madam. Mr. Jervus there has told us what happened."

"But you ain' heard my boy's side of it, Judge," Bessie said, determined to defend her son. "Jake here's a good boy. He works harder'n most, kin pick better'n three hundred pounds of cotton a day, if the pickin's right good. What happened wasn't his fault." The words were coming rapidly now and Bessie was gaining confidence. "My daughter Susie, out thar in the hall, she can tell ya what happened, how the boy thar only picked up that gun after them farmers clubbed down his pa—"

The judge banged his gavel. "Madam, are you quite through?"

"No sir, I ain'. Thar's a whole family of others out there who seen what happened, the Parsons. They're out there in the hall too. They'll talk to ya . . ."

Astounded by this Okie woman's defiance, the judge sat there, gavel raised, listening.

". . . the Parsons will tell ya what happened. Them an' my husband an' Jake here was all tryin' to leave that there union camp an' come back to work when them farmer men come a-chargin' at 'em with clubs. It's them farmers that oughta be in court, them an' them lawmen that kilt that big nigger and shot down another union fella, a white man. Countin' my husband, that's three they killed."

Bessie saw the judge was listening. Hopefully, she drew in a deep breath and continued, "Now I ain' for no union, nor no strike neither. I tol' my husband so, an' he'd be alive today, if he hadn't been so bullheaded, but I gotta say this, yor Honor, folks cain' live on the wages them farmers pays. Folks is goin' hungry, the children gits sick and some of 'em dies—"

"Woman! That's enough!" Judge Murphy banged the gavel down hard.

Bessie flinched, but kept talking. "Judge, that there's a good boy, loved by his family . . ."

"Bailiff!"—the judge was on his feet, pointing the gavel at Bessie—"silence that woman!"

"This is 'Merica!" Bessie yelled back, "where folks is s'posed to be free. Ya can' treat us like slaves . . ."

The bailiff grabbed her arm. She shrugged him off, still shouting, "You're s'posed to give my boy a hearin', find out the truth!" She whirled toward Gervais, the bailiff clutching at her. "Lawyer Wirin said you was s'posed to help my boy. Ya ain' nothin' but a Judas goat!"

"Get her out of here!" Judge Murphy raged.

"Ma!" Jake was on his feet. Jailors rushed him, twisted his arms up behind his back and slammed him down hard across the table, handcuffing him.

Bessie struggled against the bailiff who was trying to pull her out through the doors. She shouted across the courtroom, "Boy! Don' give up!"

When the jailors let him up Jake looked back but his mother was gone. He wondered at her courage; she had stood there and defied the judge, unbending. Jake felt her loving strength and, in that instant, he knew that his mother had passed something precious to him; no matter what they did to him, they couldn't beat him down. Ever.

The judge banged his gavel again. "Boy, you got anything to say before I sentence you?"

Jake glared at the judge and spoke only two words, saying them quietly but with great force: "Fuck you!"

The words were a slap in the judge's face. On his feet now, Judge Murphy roared, "You miserable little bastard, you shot three good men. One of them will never walk again. You took away his legs and his manhood and you're going to pay for that!"

Jake stood there, defiantly.

"Jacob Elroy Robertson, I sentence you to the Whittier State School for Boys." The judge pointed the gavel at Jake menacingly, "And you'll stay there as long as they'll keep you. Take him away!"

Back in the cell, Fats asked, "What'd ya get?"

"Whittier." Jake collapsed on his bunk.

Fats was on his bunk. He raised up, nodding. "Well, ya did shoot a cop."

Jake didn't say anything.

"Listen." Fats wanted to be helpful now. "Once you're out of Receiving and into one of them cottages, it ain't so bad. Get yourself assigned to Lincoln or Washington. They got pool tables in the day rooms downstairs and lockers and showers and ya sleep upstairs, in this big dorm."

"Is there any school?"

"Yeah, they got things like readin' and math an' shops, just like in high school, but ya gotta have honor points to get in them. Can't be a fuckup." Fats climbed down and took a leak, flushed the toilet, all without stopping the conversation. "Mostly ya gotta work. They put ya out on the farm or cleaning up grounds. The best job is in BDR, get in there if ya can."

"What's that?"

"Boys' dining room. Wait tables, wash dishes, that sort of thing. That way ya eat plenty an' get more time off. And ya can do a little business: a grilled cheese sandwich goes for three smokes, ham'll get ya four. An' ya got more chance to get close to a free man, get stuff brought in to ya."

"Free man?"

"Delivery trucks, they're driven by free men. Slip one of 'em a five an' he'll bring ya a carton of Bull Durham."

"Shit, that only costs a dollar."

"Hell man, this ain't the outside. Gotta make it worth their while. Besides, with a whole carton ya can buy most anything ya need inside."

"How'd ya git the money?"

"My ol' lady used to send me a five-dollar bill ever' now an' then, rolled it up tight and poked it down in a can of Pepsodent Tooth Powder, down that little hole in the top. The screws, they never look there. She just mailed me the toothpowder along with soap an' candy."

Jake wasn't told when he'd be transferred and for the next two days he questioned Fats about Whittier, trying to learn as much as he could. Late in the afternoon of the second day the jailor opened their cell door. "Robertson! Got a visitor."

His mother was there, sitting at the pine table in the tiny, bare room. Bessie was quickly up, hugging him, then as they sat across the table from each other, she gripped her son's hands, whispering her concerns. "How are ya? They treatin' ya all right?"

"Uh-huh." Jake was surprised and overwhelmed. "Ma . . ." He looked at the jailor who stood in the doorway, watching. "Ma, any word from Mr. Wirin?"

"He's gonna find some way to git ya out, go to another court, a higher one. I tol' 'im how they never gave ya no hearin' an' he got mad, said what they done was against the Constitution, or some such. Said for ya not to worry, an' not to do nothin' foolish. He wanted to come see ya, but the judge, he won't let 'im in."

"How'd you git in?"

"Bull Skinner talked to the sheriff and the sheriff, he said that since they was takin' ya off to that Whittier place tomarra, I could see ya this afternoon." Bessie patted Jake's face gently, lovingly. "James Earl, Susie an' all the rest send their love. Said to tell ya the water system that you'n James Earl rigged up works first rate. We got a winter garden put in and—"

"Ma! Ya got the house?"

"That's right. We're all moved in."

"But how?"

"Honey, I sold the nickel-plated pistol to Bull Skinner for fifty dollars. He said that was the price that yor Pa put on it."

"How'd ya git it back to sell?"

"I never even seen it. Bull said the sheriff had the gun, so I signed a bill of sale, givin' Bull title to it."

Jake was surprised. "Was fifty enough to catch up what we owed on the house?"

"Nearly," Bessie nodded. "With what we'd put away, it was enough, but it left us awful short for gettin' through the winter, what with Billie Jo pregnant again and all, so I borrowed some from Bull. It was his idea. Loaned us enough to pay off Judge Rooster Barkham. All of it." Bessie was smiling now. "The judge didn' much like it when I marched in there an' plunked down the cash, but wasn't nothin' he could do but give us the deed." She paused, then added, "I wanted to sign them loan papers over to Bull, but he wouldn't hear of it. Said we could pay him when we got the money."

It took a bit for Jake to sort out all that he was hearing. "Did ya say Billie Jo's havin' a baby?"

"That's right, she an' James Earl's gonna have another child." She expected the news to make Jake happy. Instead, a sob shuddered through her son and he was biting his lip. "Boy, what's the matter?"

"Ma"—he clutched her hands—"Clara's gonna have a baby too."

"Oh, honey." Bessie was shocked. She hadn't even given that Tarpin girl a thought during all this trouble. "Where is she?"

"Don' know, Ma. She's gone. Her folks was in the strike camp, but after that big fracas in the park, they pulled out an' I ain' seen 'er since." Jake swallowed, hard. "I tol' Clara 'bout the house an' me an' her, we talked 'bout how she might come live with us. I kinda said it'd be okay, 'cause her own folks treats her awful bad." Tears rolled down Jake's freckled cheeks. "If she comes back, can she live with ya till I git out?"

"Why shor, an' welcome." Bessie took his face in her hands again, brushing away the tears. "Now ya stop cryin', boy. Don' never let 'em see they're gettin' to ya. We're strong people, takes a whole heap more'n they got to break our spirit. With God's help, we got us a house now, a place of our own an' no matter where we work, we'll come back to it whenever we can. Buried yor Pa there in the cemetery where he can rest easy. That's our home now, son, an' it's Clara's home too, if she wants."

Jake looked up, his face streaked with tears, and a faint smile touched his mouth.

"That's my boy. We'll write ya, an' come visit when we can. Hear tell thar's lots of oranges down 'round Whittier. Figger we can pick them oranges's good as the next folks, that ways, we kin come see ya right often when we're down that way. You can go to school thar, get a good education, learn a trade. Mr. Wirin, he says they got automobile repair shops, you was always handy that way."

Bessie looked directly at him now. "Boy, don' ever let them people change ya or get to ya. Be strong. You hear me? No matter what they do, be strong."

"Okay, Ma."

"Ain' nobody kin beat us down. Ya hear?"

"Yes, Ma."

The jailor standing in the door interrupted. "It's time, ma'am."

Jake stood up and his mother rose and hugged him to her, then quickly went out.

The rest of the family was waiting in the park and Bessie strode toward them as she left the jail. The smell of winter was in the air. A chill puff of wind swirled through the fallen leaves and blew a wisp of Bessie's blond hair free. She brushed it back and headed across the lawn, her back ramrod straight, her step determined. Benjy saw her and ran, arms outstretched, yelling, "Ma! Ma!"

Out at the curb Bull Skinner was leaning on his crutches beside the sheriff's car, talking with Windy Scott. When Bessie came out, the conversation stopped and both men watched as she walked by.

"She's a hell of a woman." Bull shook his head in admiration.

"Tougher'n granite." The sheriff nodded. "Say, did ya bring me some whiskey?"

"Got two jugs in the truck."

James Earl backed the sedan out and headed for home. Knowing that they wouldn't see Jake any more for a long while, nobody said much. As they passed through Hyattville and crossed over the bridge Bessie glanced down at the camps scattered there in the sandy willow bottoms, remembering, thankful they wouldn't be spending another winter in a tent. Then they were past the river bottom and driving along Old River Road. Bessie perked up as she thought about fixing supper in her own kitchen, on her own stove again.

Up ahead Susie spotted a young girl with taffy-colored hair walking along the road. Hearing the sound of the approaching car, the girl stepped off the road and turned, watching them pass by.

"Ma!" Susie jumped and twisted around, looking back at the girl. "It's Clara!"